BARRA'S ANGEL

Eileen Campbell was born in 1947 in Inverness, where she has lived all her life apart from a few years spent in Louisiana. She now works in the Highlands, alongside her husband in his security business, and is a committed member of the Scottish National Party. *Barra's Angel* is her second novel.

By the same author

The Company of Strangers

BARRA'S ANGEL

Eileen Campbell

(signature: Eileen Campbell)

FOURTH ESTATE • *London*

First published in Great Britain in 1999 by
Fourth Estate Limited
6 Salem Road
London W2 4BU

1 3 5 7 9 10 8 6 4 2

A catalogue record for this book is available from
the British Library.

ISBN 1–85702–977–1

Typeset in Palatino by
Avon Dataset Ltd, Bidford on Avon B50 4JH

Printed and bound in Great Britain by
Clays Ltd, St Ives plc, Bungay, Suffolk

This book is dedicated to the following:

My husband Robert, for more reasons than I can squeeze on this page. You have my love, my gratitude, and my admiration – always. (And I forgive you for buying the motorcycle on our anniversary!)

My daughter Laura. I don't know why I was awarded the special privilege of being your mother, but I'm more thankful each day that I was. The infinite pleasure of knowing you would be gift enough.

My son Andrew, who can tap-dance with the best of them – and who carries my heart on his wings.

Acknowledgements

Thanks once again to Caroline Upcher, who somehow manages to combine the skills of editor and author. Bringing this book to publication is testament to the first; the enormous success of her own novels testament to the second.

And again, heartfelt thanks to Jan Boxshall. I really cannot imagine completing a manuscript without the benefit of her insight and direction. The editing of this novel went way beyond the call of duty, and I am seriously, and happily, indebted to her.

Thanks to all at Fourth Estate for their continued belief in my work.

Thanks to the hard-working folks at Seol in Edinburgh, who really pushed the boat out on *The Company of Strangers*. Its success is due in no small part to their efforts. (A special mention to Laura Findlay, who deserves a dedication of her own.)

Thanks, as always to my family, who are as unstinting in their love as they are in their support. I am blessed.

Finally, thanks to my dear friend Shirley, who started it all with the gift of a pewter angel. It remains, along with our friendship, a most treasured possession.

CHAPTER 1

Rose glanced over her shoulder at the kitchen clock. Ten to four. Barra would be out of school soon, but when he'd arrive home was another matter. She sighed, and continued scrubbing the tatties. The velvety sound of Nat King Cole soothed her in her labours and she hummed along to her favourite, 'Nature Boy'. The song reminded her of her son each and every time she heard it, and she smiled. For wasn't it Barra himself in every line?

The smile dissolved, tugged downwards into a frown. If only Chalmers could see what she saw, could try to understand the boy – just a wee bit. Rose placed the tatties in the pan and dried her hands, tutting at her husband's scarf which hung carelessly on the back-door knob. Three times this week she had hung it on the hallstand, and three times Chalmers had taken it off; only to leave it dangling behind, having decided at the last minute that the April sunshine would last another day.

Rose reached for the scarf, holding it for a moment against her cheek. Her heart lurched, an uncomfortable habit that had begun just weeks ago.

Please God, let me be wrong. I couldn't stand it . . . Then fury, white-hot and suffocating, rose within her.

Well, Chalmers Maclean, if it's Sheena Mearns you want, you can bloody well have her! Rose wrapped the scarf around the doorknob, once, twice, three times, twisting it within an inch of its life.

She gave the stew more of a skelp than a stir, and walked back into the living room. The LP had come to an end and the needle whished irritatingly at its centre. Rose shook her head. Her husband was an electrician, for God's sake. You'd think he could get the damned thing to work properly!

She lifted the arm back on to its rest and switched off the radiogram. Throwing her small frame heavily into the chair, she snatched yesterday's newspaper from the basket by the fireplace. Her eyes scanned the headlines. Halfway through the 'swinging sixties' and the world's going to hell in a basket, thought Rose – what with Mods and Rockers, and free love all over the place!

The *Craigourie Courier* also contained a full-page report on the previous Tuesday's Budget, which had resulted in an increase in the price of a fag and a dram. And this from a Labour government!

Rose snorted. Who could you trust any more?

Unable to concentrate, she folded the paper and returned to the kitchen. Well, at least she'd have some company when Barra got home. The Easter holidays started today, and she'd be opening the house for the bedders next weekend. Wouldn't that be enough to keep her mind off things?

Rose gazed out at the ancient forest bordering her home, and knew that it wouldn't; for Barra would likely be spending every minute he could lost among the trees, giving her even more to worry about.

It was Rose's ever-present nightmare that Barra would be 'molested' (they were using that word more and more on the telly) while wandering in the woods which separated the Maclean household from the Whig at the other end. The Whigmaleerie was, in fact, the full name of the café but, as the building housed Drumdarg's only shop, bar and café under the one roof, the property had simply been referred to as the Whig for as long as anyone could remember.

The front was given over to the shop and the bar, with the back divided neatly between the café and the kitchen. Maisie Henderson owned all of it, and lived in the four rooms above with her bidie-in, Doug Findlay. It was no secret that Maisie and Doug 'lived in sin', but they were popular enough for folks to turn a blind eye to the fact. Besides, they had been together for ten years now, and everyone assumed they would marry some day.

Rose had been glad of Maisie's friendship when she first arrived in Drumdarg, and the pair had become even closer over the years. Rose had found an easy comfort in Maisie's company that she had never shared with anyone else. Yet even Maisie paid scant regard to Rose's complaints about the inordinate length of time Barra spent in the woods.

More than once, Barra had come upon some poor inebriated soul attempting to navigate the forest trail and had helped him back to the Whig, and the inevitability of yet another 'one for the road'.

'It's the boy's nature,' Maisie would insist. 'Y'might as well accept it.' And, despite Rose's most earnest entreaties, she could not encourage Barra to stay out of the forest. Chalmers, who had been known to stagger along the trail himself on occasion, could understand her anxiety even less than Maisie.

'I'd have given my right arm to live wi' the woods at my back when I was his age,' he would assure her; often, and in a voice that brooked no argument.

As soon as Chalmers had felt sure his electrical business could support it he had bought the house at Drumdarg; this despite Rose's concern over such a foreign idea as 'paying a mortgage'. Once installed, however, Rose had decided to make the best of it and, realising that the front room and the spare bedroom were destined to remain empty most of the time, set about contributing to the family coffers by planting a 'Bed and Breakfast' sign at the end of the road. A large carefully printed notice in the shop window of the Whig soon followed, and it wasn't long before the 'bedders' started arriving.

Rose quickly came to appreciate the small independence it brought her, but it didn't lessen her anxious concern for her son's well-being.

Barra had been seven years old when they moved from Craigourie to Drumdarg, and the woods were as comfortable to him as his own back garden. They *were* his back garden. As the seasons turned around him, Rose watched and worried as his childhood slipped seamlessly from him and adulthood began sweeping a gentle brush over the planes of his body; smoothing, preparing.

Yet Barra's eyes were childlike still, and the magic he found in every leaf, every flower, was captured and distilled, and fed to a heart not yet ready for a grown-up world.

Rose knew these things. Chalmers, of course, did not.

'You've ruined him!' had become his anthem, especially since the incident with Mama Iacobelli.

Barra had had a late start to his education, due to a sickly infancy which left him smaller and weaker than his contemporaries. Consequently, at the age of thirteen (almost fourteen, as he informed anyone who might care to ask), he was sharing his first year of secondary school with pupils a year younger than he. Among these pupils were the redoubtable Iacobelli twins – more usually referred to as the Yaks.

Once it became known that Barra had had to be pushed in the big pram until he was nearly three years old, the Yaks had all the reason they needed (if, indeed, any was needed) to pick on their new classmate. During Barra's first term at Craigourie

High School he had been beaten up twice in quick succession by the Iacobelli brothers.

Barra had taken his licks, refusing to fight back. First, and most importantly, he saw no reason for people to fight *ever*; and secondly, he knew it was a waste of time, when between them the Yaks outweighed him four to one.

After the second beating, Rose had urged Chalmers, whom she knew would have been better pleased if his son had put up at least a semblance of a fight, to call upon Mr Iacobelli Senior.

Mr Iacobelli was a small, mild-mannered man, whose entire conversation seemed to consist of '*Si*' and '*Prego*'. While his wife attended to the fish-frying side of the family business, Mr Iacobelli ran the ice-cream parlour. Fortunately for him, they were separated by an adjoining wall, for Mama Iacobelli was anything but mild-mannered. Her sons had inherited her imposing physique and belligerent attitude, and all three were inordinately proud of their ancient lineage.

As luck would have it, Chalmers had arrived just as Mr Iacobelli had taken the opportunity of a lull in his day's toil to nip across to the bookie's. Chalmers was therefore confronted by the formidable lady of the house, and had scarcely opened his mouth to complain about the twins' bullying when Mrs Iacobelli (dressed, as always, in readiness for a funeral) rolled up her black sleeves to reveal two massive, and very threatening, arms.

Chalmers was forced to step back out of the

doorway to avoid physical contact, and indeed felt fortunate to have had the chance to complain at all.

Retreating to the relative safety of his van, he was followed the length of the High Street by Mrs Iacobelli's voice – which was every bit as intimidating as her presence.

'Stay outta my shop, you hear me? My boys, they no doing bad to *no*-body. My boys, they look after their mama. Nobody pincha da sweetie in Mama's shop! My boys, they no allow it. My boys . . .'

And on and on she went.

Chalmers had been in a foul humour by the time he arrived back in Drumdarg. Even Socks, the family cat, and Chalmers' sworn enemy, deemed it politic to remain at a discreet distance.

'Barra!' Chalmers shouted.

'What is it? Chalmers, what is it?' Rose had tried to catch her husband's arm as he marched past her towards the staircase. Barra, who had earlier pleaded with his mother to leave well alone (it wasn't as though the Yaks had singled him out; they had already beaten up most of the other boys), appeared on the landing almost at once.

'Did you want me, Da?'

'Were you stealing sweeties from the Iacobellis?'

Barra came hurtling down the stairs. 'Course not! Course I didn't. I don't *steal*!'

Chalmers looked at his son and knew that he was telling the truth. The boy always told the truth. He didn't have the gumption to lie. Again his eyes surveyed the split lip and swollen nose, and Rose breathed a silent sigh of relief as Chalmers reached to ruffle Barra's auburn curls.

'Right, then. Well, that woman takes the biscuit, so she does. Stay away from those boys, son,' he warned. 'Let them take their Tally tempers out on someone else.'

Chalmers turned towards the kitchen. 'Cup o' tea, Rose,' he commanded.

A look passed from Barra to his mother. As so often, they had no need for words, and Rose smiled at him, her eyes sympathetic. They both knew it wouldn't be so easy to stay away from the Yaks. The boys were well known for picking on others at a moment's notice – and for no reason.

The twins, however, seemed to have lost interest in Barra, partly as a result of Barra's determination not to put up a fight, and partly because they deemed him too puny to bother with. Until, that was, Mr Macdougall inadvertently gave them a new excuse to make Barra's life hell.

The good teacher, in an effort to capture his pupils' flagging attention during an Ancient History lesson, rightly pointed out that Barra Maclean shared his middle name with the ill-starred Roman soldier, Mark Antony.

By the end of the period, the Yaks had worked out that the initials of Barra's name spelled B.A.M. From that day forward Barra was hailed as 'Y'wee poofy bampot' whenever he was in the near (or far) vicinity of the Yaks.

Barra had some idea of what 'poofy' meant. He certainly knew enough to recognise that, if indeed he *was* 'poofy', he shouldn't be interested in girls. But he was. Very interested. For in that spring of 1965 Barra had fallen in love, his young heart rendered helpless by a barefoot pop singer named Sandie Shaw; the only woman to have removed Rose to second place in the boy's affections.

Rose wouldn't have minded at all, if Chalmers didn't see fit to remind her of her demise every chance he got. 'Fair play to him. It's time he was cutting the apron strings.'

Rose gritted her teeth. How could Chalmers forget? Or was his mind so befuddled with thoughts of Sheena Mearns that he didn't *want* to remember. God, the long days and nights they had held on to each other – and to Barra – praying the child would make it, that he'd survive.

Well, dammit, didn't he just, though? And wouldn't she herself? Survive, aye. And she'd see Sheena Mearns in hell before she'd give her husband up *that* easily!

But as quickly as her resolve had hardened, it dwindled – and disappeared. For Rose had been abandoned once. And if her own mother hadn't wanted her, how could she possibly hope to keep this man she loved more than life itself?

The afternoon sunshine streamed into her kitchen, warm and bright, burnishing her hair, as vibrant and auburn as her son's. Rose Maclean lifted her face to it, and shivered.

9

'Wake UP, Maclean!'

Barra jumped. 'Sir?'

Mr Macdougall shook his head. All of his colleagues at Craigourie High School agreed that Barra was university material if he'd just put his mind to it. But that was the problem – Barra's mind was never where it should be. He would certainly have to be moved away from that window, Mr Macdougall decided, if there was to be any hope of steering him towards his O-level History.

Barra gnawed on his bottom lip for a moment. Then he smiled – a smile that would melt you if you didn't feel like giving him an occasional slap.

'Sorry, sir,' Barra apologised.

'Would you care to join the rest of us, Maclean?'

The bell sounded.

'Saved by the bell, sir.' Barra beamed.

'Indeed,' Mr Macdougall answered, too weary at four o'clock on the last Friday of term to argue further.

The teacher watched as his pupils, calmed as much by the warmth of the classroom as the knowledge that a fortnight of freedom awaited them, filed obediently out.

Barra, however, had leaped to life and rocketed through the door, throwing a cheery 'See you, sir', behind him.

The boy was just too exhausting altogether.

* * *

Barra headed for the bike sheds, relieved to see that the Yaks were nowhere in sight. Freewheeling down the brae and on to the High Street, he kept his eyes firmly ahead as he approached the Iacobellis' shop. Sure enough, the twins were lounging in the doorway, obviously having left school early – a not uncommon occurrence.

'Get back in yir pram, y'wee poofy bampot.'

'Aye, get back in yir pram.'

'Bampot! Bampot!' In unison.

People in the High Street clucked and tutted their way past the twins, some curious enough to stop and take a look at the 'bampot'. The traffic lights at the end of the High Street stubbornly refused to turn green and Barra, in an effort to get as far away as quickly as possible, dismounted and wheeled his bike across to the other side, barely missing an elderly woman pulling a shopping trolley behind her.

'Y'wee bugger,' the woman complained, leaning against a shop window to catch her breath.

'Sorry, missus,' he called back, swinging back on to his bike and heading for the bridge.

Barra said 'sorry' a lot.

Once across the bridge, Barra relaxed, and cycled slowly onwards to where the road rose steeply towards Drumdarg. Much of what had once been a thriving country estate had been swallowed into the suburbs of Craigourie, but over the crest of the hill Drumdarg House still marked the beginning of the old village.

Barra loved every inch of it. He was at home here, away from the noise and the traffic, his mind free to roam wherever he chose; the shifting patterns of the land, the big skies and open fields all grist to the mill of his imagination.

Within minutes he had put the Yaks and their abuse behind him, for stretching before him lay two whole weeks to spend as he chose. Mind, the Easter holidays weren't like the sprawling holidays of summer, but they were still great. Even though nothing much *seemed* to happen, Barra's days were full of them – the happenings.

Wild broom spread along the roadside and clung tenaciously to the rocky mountain reaches. Most of the shrubs were in full flower, but he inspected every bush until he found one with blossoms still held tight by the green pods. He stopped to listen, trying to isolate the little cracking sounds which signalled the birth of the golden flowers.

There! And there!

Barra grinned. 'Grand,' he said, and pushed onwards towards the crest of the hill.

Spring came late to Drumdarg, and this year March blizzards had almost obliterated any hope of it coming at all. But it did arrive, and it was everywhere, and all at once.

Where recently wild crocuses had carpeted the earth, new clumps of daffodils grew confidently in their place, and on the trees leaves burst from branches laid skeletal by winter. Snow still wrapped its crystalline blanket across the mountains' shoulders, but the air was warm, and softer than it had been for months.

Barra came to a stop as a flock of wild geese flew noisily above him, then wheeled in a perfect 'V' to settle on the greening earth. He watched them for long minutes before turning to make his own descent. As he swung back on to his bicycle he noticed a figure in front of the gatekeeper's cottage. Barra shook his head.

Poor Hattie. She'd been there every day this week, and she'd probably be there every day next week – at least until Easter had come and gone.

Barra had seen Kenneth More in quite a few pictures, and was bound to agree with everyone else in Drumdarg that the chances of the actor arriving at Easter to carry Hattie off into the sunset were slim, to say the least. Still, it hadn't stopped her from telling anyone who'd listen (and precious few did) that the great man was definitely coming to fetch her.

But as fanciful as Hattie's notion might be, it wasn't the reason for her nickname. She had been known as Mad Hatters for as long as Barra could remember, long before she had taken to waiting for Kenneth More.

Barra tried to recall when he'd first heard that Hattie had been taken to the jail for murdering her mother, but he couldn't – at least, not clearly. It had happened so long ago, and he supposed that the stories of the trial and how she'd been set free had been embellished over the years.

Barra couldn't help thinking that the folks in Drumdarg, and Craigourie too, if it came to that, loved nothing more than a wee bit of gossip.

Even so, he had yet to receive a satisfactory explanation for Hattie's mad – and quite uncharacteristic – behaviour all those years ago. It seemed to Barra that folks just naturally seemed to clam up any time he raised the subject. It was quite frustrating altogether, but then Barra had little time to dwell on life's frustrations.

Well, he'd stop and pass the time with Hattie anyway. Maybe it would take her mind off the waiting.

Barra pursed his lips in a soundless whistle. He had never been able to master the art, but it didn't bother him. In his head he could hear every note.

CHAPTER 2

Hattie was standing quietly in front of the large wooden gate which marked the entrance to Drumdarg House, just as she had done in the weeks before Easter for the past three years. Her eyes scanned the road in both directions, and Barra knew she had noted his approach long before he got there.

Barra was fond of Hattie, rushing to her defence whenever he heard someone remark that she 'wasn't the full shilling'. He didn't have to defend her too often, however, as Hattie Macaskill wasn't top of the list when it came to gossip. She was just part of the scenery.

He waved as he closed the distance between them and, tentatively, she waved back. Laying down his bicycle, Barra walked over and climbed on to the bottom spar of the gate.

'How are you the day?' he asked.

Hattie nodded. 'I'm OK,' she answered. 'I'll be leaving soon, when he comes to fetch me.'

'Aye, well . . .' Barra said. 'It's a lovely day for it.'

Hattie crossed her arms, waiting. She was a

small, rounded woman, and today was clothed as usual in a brown jumper and matching tweed skirt which looked as though they had withered on her. With her spiky hair and fierce features, it crossed Barra's mind that she resembled a malevolent hedgehog.

He was immediately ashamed of the thought, for he knew that her appearance masked a gentle heart and, when you got close up to her (which nearly everyone avoided), you could see that she had a nice smile – sort of shy; and that her eyes were a soft grey colour, like the velvet curtains Mam had in the front room.

Barra jumped from the gate and picked at a stray daffodil.

'Look at me,' he said.

'Och, Barra, don't be doing that.' Hattie looked uncomfortable, and shrugged a little farther away from him, her head bowed.

'C'mon, Hattie. Look at me. Lift yir head.'

She raised her neck free of its woollen collar and Barra tried to stick the flower behind her ear. It held for a moment, and then fell. Hattie caught it in her work-worn hands, cradling it as though it were the finest crystal.

'Aye, it's yirself that likes it.' Barra grinned.

'Away y'go,' Hattie murmured, but she, too, was smiling.

Barra jumped up, and reached for his bicycle. 'Yep! I'd better get going,' he said. 'Mam'll be at me for dawdling. Again!'

There was no need to say goodbye. Hattie wouldn't be going anywhere.

Barra looked up the driveway leading from the cottage to the big house. 'Where's Murd the day?' he asked.

As if in answer, a dog began barking and Murdo Macrae appeared from the back of the big house, Gallus running at his heels.

'Hi, Murd,' Barra shouted across the distance between them.

Murdo raised his walking stick in salute and bawled at the dog to stop barking, at which the little white Westie sat stock still and gave a melancholy howl.

'What a sense o' humour he's got,' Murdo called, bending to give Gallus a few fond strokes.

'He's great,' Barra agreed. 'How's Mrs Macrae?' he went on, as Murdo and Gallus neared.

'Fit to be tied, Barra. Fit to be tied.'

'How's that?'

'Och, we had word the young master's coming up, and . . .'

'But I thought she liked Mr Cunningham,' Barra interrupted.

'Aye. Aye, she does. Of course she does. But he's bringing herself with him.'

'Mrs Cunningham?' Barra was pleased. Marjorie Cunningham had visited the family home only once before, and he'd not had a chance to meet her. It would be a fine thing to have a new face around.

'The very same. And you know Helen,' Murdo

answered. 'She canna be doing wi' Sassenach ways.'

Barra grinned. There had been comments made about Mrs Cunningham's 'Sassenach ways' after her last visit. But then she *was* from London. You couldn't expect her *not* to have Sassenach ways. In fact, Barra was most interested in finding out just what 'Sassenach ways' were.

Murdo placed a hand on Hattie's shoulder, making her jump.

'Sorry, hen,' he said quietly. 'But I'm thinking he'll no be coming now. Not today.'

Hattie sighed, and lowered her head again. 'D'you no' think so, Murd?'

'No, hen, I don't.'

'But I finished my work early, and Mrs Macrae might no' be needing me now.'

'Och, I'm sure she can find a wee job t' keep you occupied. Go on up 'n' have a wordie wi' her. She'll no' be minding,' Murdo assured Hattie.

Barra and Murdo watched as Hattie trudged up the driveway, Gallus zig-zagging in front of her.

'She's a poor cratur, right enough,' Murdo said.

'But she's no' really bonkers,' Barra said. 'Y'canna' blame her for wanting to be whisked off by a film star.'

Murdo remained silent; silent and thoughtful.

Barra couldn't let the opportunity pass. Maybe Murdo could enlighten him.

'It's no' why they call her Mad Hatters, though, is it?' he enquired hopefully.

'No-o-o,' Murdo sighed.

'I mean, it was an awful thing that happened to her – to be accused o' murder. And her own mam at that.'

'Aye.' Murdo sighed again, heavier this time. 'It was awful, right enough.' Then he clamped his mouth shut, grimly jerking his beard upwards as he reflected on the trial. Few even remembered it now, but those who did recall that dreadful time shared Murdo's feelings, and were glad that Hattie had been allowed to walk free.

Murdo shook his head. It wasn't the kind o' tale you'd want to burden a young mind with – especially such a fertile mind as Barra's. God, wasn't it enough that they all had 'the waiting' to contend with now?

Barra's waiting, too, had come to its usual fruitless end. In the face of Murdo's silence, he was forced to swallow his disappointment, realising that he'd not be learning anything new this day.

He sniffed loudly, shaking Murdo from his reverie.

A firm command brought Gallus careening back towards his master. Murdo smiled his approval, then turned to confide in Barra. 'I canna' imagine where she got the idea that she'd be off at Easter wi' thon actor laddie, but . . . Well, y'just never know.'

'No, Murd, y'just never know,' Barra repeated, his voice as solemn as Murdo's own.

Murdo hid a smile. 'Are you off home, then?' he asked.

'Aye, I'd better,' Barra answered, cycling out on

to the road. 'See you later,' he called, some strenuous waving almost causing him to topple.

Murdo waved back. Smiling still, he bent to scratch the wee dog's ears. 'He's a fine lad, that,' he told Gallus. 'A fine lad.'

Gallus rolled on his back and waved his stubby paws in the air. It was his highest form of compliment.

Barra hadn't intended to stop at the Pascoes' house, but Jennifer was working in the flower-beds and her husband was sitting in a chair by the doorway, enjoying the day. It would have been rude to pass without a greeting.

'Yir flowers are bonny,' Barra remarked, cycling up to the fence and resting against it. 'Hi, Mr Pascoe,' he called.

'Aren't they?' Jennifer Pascoe replied, while her husband nodded a smile in Barra's direction. 'Would you like some lemonade?' she asked, straightening from her labours.

'No, thanks. I'd better get home.' Barra grimaced at having to refuse. He loved getting into the Pascoes' house. Everything was so modern and new-looking. He especially admired their green Mini, and had greatly enjoyed getting the occasional lift to Craigourie and back in it.

Of course, Mr Pascoe had been well enough to drive then.

'He's looking fine,' Barra said, quietly enough, he thought.

'And I'm feeling fine,' Jim Pascoe called out, making his wife smile.

'Sorry, Mr Pascoe.'

'You're an awful boy for "sorry",' Jim said. 'What've you got to be sorry about?'

'Nothing really, I suppose. It's a habit.'

'Aye, well, it's a bad habit, young feller-me-lad.' Jim leaned forward in an effort to look fierce, but the movement pained him and he groaned.

Jennifer was up like a shot and by his side. He held up a hand to let her know it had passed, and she took a deep breath and stroked his head.

'He's like an Easter chick,' Jennifer said, looking at Barra. 'Don't you think so, Barra?'

'Aye.' Barra grinned. 'It's good his hair's coming back though, isn't it?'

'Fluff.' Jim smiled. 'I wouldn't call it hair exactly.'

'It's what he wants for his birthday, Barra,' Jennifer said. 'A good crop of hair.'

'When is it, your birthday?' Barra asked.

'Easter Sunday this year. Eighteenth of April.'

'And how old will you be?'

'Were you always this nosy?' Jim asked, as though he didn't know.

'Aye. Always.'

'That's good then. I'll be twenty-five, in answer to your question. What next?'

'What next?'

'What next do you want to know?'

Barra grinned. 'That'll do,' he said, pushing off from the fence. 'See you.'

He hadn't gone far when he shouted back at them, 'You'll have some hair for Easter. What 'yis bet?'

Jim looked up at his wife, grudging the sadness he knew he would find in her eyes. 'I may have to refuse that wager.'

'No,' she answered, taking his hand. 'I won't let you.'

The road was clear all the way to the Whig. Barra was singing at the top of his voice – 'Always something there to remind me. Da-dah-da-dah-da' – when Olive Tolmie stuck her head out of the shop door to see who was making all the racket.

Had Drumdarg ever needed a town crier, Olive would surely have been first choice. There was little that passed in the village, or indeed in Craigourie itself that Olive wasn't aware of. Indeed, it was regularly said of her that what she didn't already know, she would soon find out.

'Och, it's you,' she muttered.

Barra placed his bike against the wall and followed her inside, hypnotised by the slap-slap of her sandals. Olive's feet overlapped the sandals in every direction.

'It's a grand day,' he remarked, lifting his eyes.

Olive didn't agree. 'I'm fair trachled wi' the heat,' she grumbled. 'My feet's like potted heid already. God knows what they'll be like by July.'

Barra hadn't eaten potted heid. He reminded himself never to try it.

'Are yis quiet the day?'

'Off an' on. Off an' on,' Olive replied, busying herself with polishing the counter. 'I'm in the wrong job, of course. Worst thing I could be doing, standing all day, with this feet. I'll be glad when Isla gets here.'

'Isla's coming back?' This was the best news Barra had heard all day.

'Aye. Maisie got a letter from her sister. Seems the wee trollop got caught wi' a boy again. Still, she's a good help round here.'

'Caught wi' a boy?'

'That's all I'm saying,' Olive stated, pausing in her endeavours to give Barra a knowing stare.

Barra was unsure what the stare was meant to convey. Certainly, there had been no mention of boys when Isla had arrived in Drumdarg last summer. She had told Barra that she simply wanted to stay with her Aunt Maisie for a while as she hadn't been getting along with her stepfather. Not that Isla had told Barra very much of anything. She was, after all, two and a half years older than he, and could therefore be considered a young woman.

'Less of the "young"!' Isla had reprimanded him when he'd sought to please her by mentioning the fact.

From that point on she had been scathingly dismissive of his presence, but it was to be expected from a woman of her years, and it didn't alter the fact that she was really, really beautiful.

Plus, she had an enormous chest. Barra couldn't

wait to see what she looked like now.

'When's she coming?'

'Well, Maisie says she left school at Christmas, and she doesn't seem able to hold down a job, so I think her mother'll have her on the bus as soon as Maisie gives her the OK.'

'She left school? And she wants to come *here*?'

'It's no' a matter of "wants",' Olive replied with another knowing stare. She was becoming more mysterious by the minute.

'Where is Maisie?' Barra asked, in the hope of getting some reliable information as to the date of Isla's arrival.

'Ben the back,' Olive replied, casting a sturdy thumb over her shoulder.

Barra ran outside and grabbed his bike, racing around the building. He pushed on the side entrance door to the café, but it was locked. He carried on around the back and entered through the kitchen door but, seeing no sign of Maisie, he rushed on into the café. Then he stopped dead in his tracks.

'Wow!' was all he could manage.

Maisie Henderson's bulk was contained in a flowing purple kaftan, patterned haphazardly with large yellow sunflowers. Her grey hair reached almost to her waist, and today was festooned with purple streamers woven along its length. Barra knew that, even though his mam and Maisie were the best of friends, Maisie was much, much older than Rose. Still, Maisie's laughing eyes and generous mouth gave her a youthful appearance which belied the grey hair.

It wasn't only her mouth that was generous, though. Maisie Henderson was the largest woman Barra had ever seen. At the moment she was tearing into a steaming bowl of soup and, by the looks of it, had demolished the best part of a sliced loaf and a half-pound of butter besides.

'Sit down, Barra,' Maisie instructed, pointing to the scarred wooden chair across from her. The café had seen better days, but then so had Maisie.

Barra kneeled on the chair. 'I like yir dress,' he said.

'This old thing?' Maisie laughed. She lifted an arm, and fanned out the huge batwing sleeve. 'It's my Lautrec look.'

Barra looked at the two posters on the far wall. Neither *La Modiste* nor the *Lady At Her Toilet* (which always slightly embarrassed him – even though the lady wasn't actually *at* her toilet) looked anything like Maisie Henderson.

'How d'you mean?' he asked.

'Toulouse, my cultural friend. Too loose.' She sighed. 'Except nothing's too loose on Maisie.' She buttered another slice of bread. 'I'm eating for two,' she said, and they both roared at the old joke. The 'two' Maisie referred to were herself and Doug. Doug wasn't much of an eater. He liked the drink, though.

Barra thought it must be a great thing to enjoy your work as much as those two – Doug at the bar, with all that drink around him, and Maisie in the café with . . . He'd nearly forgotten why he was there.

'Isla's coming back?' he asked.

'Aye. My sister Fiona wants her down here. Out of harm's way, so to speak.'

'What harm's she doing?' Barra asked.

'The same harm any buxom dame at that age should be doing,' Maisie answered, making Barra blush.

She noted the flush spread across his features and laughed again. 'You'll no' be letting her lead you astray now, will you?'

'Course not,' Barra replied, more sharply than he had intended.

Maisie leaned back. 'Begging your pardon!'

'Sorry, Maisie.'

'Och, Barra, I'm teasing you.' Maisie gnawed on her bread. 'Isla'll be here on the Sunday afternoon bus. You come in and have a blether. She'll be glad to see you.'

'I doubt it,' Barra answered, sounding unusually forlorn. 'She didn't take to me.'

Maisie leaned into him. 'Who couldn't take to you, Barra, y'bonny boy that you are?'

Barra cheered up. 'I'm off, then,' he said. 'Tell Doug I said hello.'

Maisie shrugged, and pointed above them. 'Always supposing he sleeps it off before you're back.'

'He will,' Barra assured her. 'He'll be opening up soon.'

'Another grand evening in front of us, then,' Maisie said, returning to her soup. 'I hope Isla will appreciate it, the sophistication of it all . . .'

Maisie was eight years older than her sister Fiona, and it had been shortly after Fiona's birth in 1923 that their father succumbed to the 'flu epidemic which had ravaged the British Isles. Their mother, a large, capable woman, had worked hard to keep the small grocery shop in Craigourie, and had quietly invested the profits over the years.

On the morning of Maisie's twenty-fifth birthday she rose to bring her mother breakfast in bed, just as she'd done every Sunday for as long as she could remember – and would never do again. Her mother lay cold as stone, having died in her sleep from a massive heart attack.

Maisie had taken charge, arranging the funeral, organising the shop, and interrupting each new heart-rending chore to stop and comfort Fiona. After her mother had been laid to rest, and Fiona had gone to bed, Maisie lay in her darkened room and waited for her heart to stop breaking.

She had never even guessed at the extent of the inheritance she and her sister had been left. That night she would gladly have thrown every last pound of it into the flickering coals if, for one day longer, she could have held her mother close.

The morning after the funeral Maisie rose, wash-ed and dressed, and opened the shop door on the second of nine o'clock. Over the next nine years she soldiered on single-handed, while Fiona took her less-than-impressive typing skills and set off across the Great Glen, moving from hotel to hotel in search of a happiness which seemed constantly to elude her.

In the summer of 1949, as the country recovered from the ravages of war, Fiona arrived back in Craigourie with her new husband – and a swollen belly. Duncan Gillespie had married Fiona in the mistaken belief that she had a substantial amount of her inheritance still waiting to be spent.

They had bought a small home in Fort William, under the glowering shadow of Ben Nevis, and Duncan looked cheerfully forward to giving up his back-breaking work in the hospital laundry for an altogether more carefree existence.

By the time his daughter Isla was a year old, Duncan had come to realise that he was having to work ever longer hours to provide for his wife and family. He strung his guitar across his back and walked out, whistling his way southwards.

Five years later, Maisie sold her parents' shop and bought the Whig, continuing to support her sister while Fiona, who had taken a part-time job in one of the hotels which stretched along the Fort William seafront, adamantly insisted that the monthly cheques she received from Maisie were temporary loans – just until she got on her feet again. When it became apparent that Fiona was unlikely ever to get on her feet, Maisie had purchased the house outright, providing a permanent home for her sister and her young niece. Fiona uttered not one syllable in protest.

Then, three years ago, she had once more returned, this time bringing with her Jack Strachan. Jack was the night porter at the hotel where Fiona worked – and her husband of two weeks.

Maisie detested him on sight and her heart went out to Isla, who had had to put up with her mother's endless stream of boyfriends over the years. She could tell from the hunched shoulders and sullen expression of her niece that Isla, too, felt less than happy at Fiona's choice.

Indeed, Maisie had no doubt that Isla's imminent return had more to do with Jack Strachan than even Fiona realised.

The rutted tarmac at the back of the Whig allowed parking space for five cars before ending at the woods which led further into the hills, and then down to Barra's home half a mile further on. He meandered along the trail, stopping here and there to explore this, examine that.

In a ditch long since carved by the rush of a stream escaping its lofty source, he spied the featherless frame of a dead nestling. He couldn't tell what it might have been, but the sadness of its short life washed over him as cold as the water which carried its body out to the distant loch.

A picture came to his mind – almost a year ago, the May holiday weekend, a day just like today, with the sun shining and the canopy of blue sky above. Jim Pascoe had called for him early that morning and they'd gone fishing together down by the banks of the river which flowed past the big house. Jim had landed a fat wee trout almost at once, and Barra had watched as Jim removed the hook from its mouth.

'Looks like we've made a good start on the supper.' Jim laughed. Then he noticed Barra's expression. 'What is it, son? We've done this many a time before . . .'

'Aye. It's just . . . It's just, well, d'you think he feels it?'

Jim had shaken his head. 'They're cold-blooded, Barra. You know that.'

'Aye . . .' Barra shrugged, 'but it's no' as if we're *needing* it for our supper.'

Jim held the trout for a moment, and then released it, skittering, back into the water. 'Well, that's put the tin lid on our fishing trip.' He sighed.

'Och, Mr Pascoe, I didn't mean . . . I didn't mean to spoil the day.'

Jim clambered up off the shingle and lay on the grassy bank. Crossing his long legs in front of him, he clasped his hands behind his head.

'You'd have to be the devil himself to spoil a day like this, Barra.' Then he had laughed. 'And there's not a single good reason why that wee trout can't enjoy it just as much as us.' Jim had sighed deeply. 'Aye,' he murmured, 'it's a bonny day like this that makes you feel you could live for ever.'

Barra shivered as he remembered, and looked quickly upwards towards the summit of the trail, seeking the comfort of the small clearing. This was his own place, his best place, an open circular mound where his world lay before him; the mountains cradling him in their midst, and the shining waters of the loch reflecting all that lay above them.

He squinted into the late afternoon sun. It looked as though someone had beaten him to it, though he couldn't imagine who. The bar was closed, and it wasn't a place that strangers would know about. Unless, of course, Mam had got some early bedders. She didn't usually take anyone in before Easter, but Dad *had* been talking about getting a new van.

Well, he'd soon find out. He set off purposefully towards the clearing, and the stranger standing in its midst.

The gate to Barra's back garden was open, awaiting his arrival. Through the kitchen window he could see his mother's head bent over the sink as she finished preparing the evening meal.

'Ma-am! Mam! MAA-AAM!'

'WHAT?' Rose was racing towards him, her worst fears taking form in her mind, her face contorted with worry.

She grabbed him. '*Barra!*'

'Mam . . .' so breathless he could scarcely talk. 'I just met . . . an *angel*!'

31

Rose dropped her hands. Turning back up the path, she trudged indoors.

'For the love o' God, Barra,' she mourned. 'What next?'

CHAPTER 3

Rose picked up her cup. Her tea was stone cold.

'Tell me again, what did he look like?'

Barra sighed, impatient to get to the rest.

'He has blond hair, curly, like Roger Daltrey's, only longer. And blue eyes. Very, very blue, like . . . I dunno, Mam, just very blue. He's taller than me, but that's 'cos he's older. He's fifteen. Well, he was . . . when he died. So he still is . . . fifteen.'

'And his name's Jamie?'

'Aye, that's his name all right. And he hasn't met God yet, 'cos he's just learning to be an angel. But . . .'

'Jamie what?'

The question silenced Barra.

'He doesn't have a last name.'

'Of course he does, Barra. Even if he is . . . well, he isn't, but even if he was, he would have had to have a last name.'

Barra cast his mind back to the scene, trying feverishly to remember exactly what he *had* seen. It had been so real. Very real. But now that his mother was giving him the third degree, he had to admit how far-fetched it sounded. He would have to try harder – to remember. So he could convince Mam.

Jamie hadn't given him a last name. Barra was sure of it. The stranger had reached out his hand as Barra approached and introduced himself.

'Hello, Barra. I'm Jamie.'

'Hello yirself. How y'doing?'

Jamie's hand was cool. Very cool, considering the warmth of the afternoon. But before Barra had time to absorb this fact, a sudden heat suffused him.

He snatched his hand free. 'Wow! What was that?'

Jamie had smiled. Just smiled. And the dazzle of it had lit the whole clearing.

Barra was transfixed. 'How d'you know me?' he managed at last.

Jamie beckoned him towards the old log and, obediently, Barra sat, all the while trying to take in every detail of this new acquaintance. Jamie was dressed in grey flannels and a white shirt – normal enough. But not even Mam's Surf could get a shirt that white, and Dad had never had a crease in his trousers as sharp as this one. God, you could slice yir hand open just touching it.

It seemed to Barra that Jamie hadn't said too much of anything – and yet . . . Well, he must have said quite a lot, really. He had told him that he was an angel. He definitely said that. He'd been in an accident, a car accident.

'He didn't say his last name, Mam. He was in an accident.'

'An accident to the head?' Rose asked, her voice edged with sarcasm.

'Aye. Actually it was. He went through the windscreen. His parents are OK. It was just him . . . y'know.'

Rose gasped, her eyes clouding.

'God,' she breathed. 'They're still about then? His parents? Could there be anything worse than that?'

'Y'see, Mam, he *is* an angel,' Barra said, excited anew. At last, Mam was beginning to understand. 'But listen, Mam. This is the best of it. He came here 'cos he needs me to *help* him!'

Jamie had been definite about that, too. Barra couldn't remember all of it. Not *every* word. You couldn't be expected to remember every word when you'd just met an angel. But Jamie had explained it. He *needed* Barra. There was work to be done in Drumdarg. Something pretty major, of course. It would have to be – for an angel to come here. To single him out – Barra Maclean. God, stuff like that didn't happen every day, not even in his comics. You could hardly imagine it!

'Imagine it, Mam. He came here for *me* to help *him*!'

Rose's scepticism returned in full measure. 'Aye, right. Here we all are – just waiting to be of service. And he was wearing grey flannels, this angel? And a white shirt?'

Barra gnawed on his lip. Who knew what angels were supposed to wear, anyway. Why couldn't they wear grey flannels?

'Well, at least he's no' a tink,' Rose mused.

He wasn't that. Whatever Jamie was, he was well brought-up. Barra shook the doubt from his mind. 'He knew my name, Mam. Without me telling him.'

Rose gazed at her son, her expression softer. 'He's in Drumdarg, son. Everyone knows yir name here.'

'But . . .' Barra gritted his teeth. Mam was right. It wasn't that big a place, Drumdarg. Not the kind of place an angel might choose. And Mam had been warning him about talking to strangers for *yonks* now.

But Jamie wasn't a stranger. It was as though they had always known each other. At least, Jamie had known *him*. And, after they'd talked (well, Jamie must have done most of the talking, because Barra couldn't remember saying anything. Nothing at all. And wasn't that the strangest thing?), Jamie had disappeared. He'd been there one minute . . . and then he was gone. Simple as that.

Barra had sat there, moments stretching before him, waiting . . . And then, the realisation dawned. Jamie wasn't coming back. Not then. But he *would* be back. He'd said they had work to do. He'd show up when he felt like it. Angels could do stuff like that. And Jamie was an angel. Simple as that.

'Anyway, I'll be seeing him again, Mam. And when he comes back he's going to tell me – what it is he wants me to do.'

'Don't you dare! Don't you *dare* do *anything* that

boy tells you, Barra. D'you hear me?'

'He's *not* a boy. He's not, Mam. Well, he is really, but he's an angel as well.'

Rose shook her head. 'He is *not* an angel,' she said, definitely. Definitely – dismissing the possibility.

'How do you *know*? I remember, Mam, I remember when I was wee, and you showed me that circle of flowers on the riverbank. You said it was the fairies that made it. You told me that. And I believed *you*! I believed about the fairies and Santa Claus – and everything, Mam! . . . Just 'cos you told me.'

Barra's voice tailed off, close to tears now. Even in the telling, he remembered. He remembered two Christmases – the two *after* he'd realised it was his father who put the presents at the end of his bed, his mother who lovingly filled his stocking. He'd believed for two years, knowing the truth, just because he'd *wanted* to.

Rose, too, struggled to keep her tears at bay. Nothing ever touched her more than this, this eternal need to protect her son. The sureness of knowing that sometime, somewhere along the way, she would find herself unable to shield Barra from the pain of growing – growing into a world fraught with betrayal. For the briefest of heartbeats, she wondered what it would be like . . . to be that sure.

'That was different, son. You were a child.' She swallowed. 'Yir still a child, Barra,' she murmured, lifting her gaze to his.

The boy's eyes were feverish, and Rose wondered for a minute if he was coming down with something.

The thought had scarcely entered her mind when she felt her shoulders slacken with relief. Of course. It had been such a sudden change in the weather, and wasn't it true that the bud of the leaf brought all manner of strange ills? She stood, reaching to touch Barra's brow.

'Gerroff!'

Shocked, Rose drew back her hand. 'Barra?'

Why couldn't Mam believe him? Why? She'd never doubted him before – not even when the Yaks had tried to blame him for stealing!

'Mam, there's nothing wrong with me. Honest to God, there's not. I'm *telling* you – there's an angel called Jamie in the woods. He knew my name and everything, and he can just disappear when he feels like it. *And* he's met famous people. Famous *dead* people. Look, Mam, look! He showed me this.'

Barra jumped from the chair and broke into a tap-dance. 'Al Jolson showed him how to dance, Mam. And *he* showed *me*.'

Rose grabbed him in the middle of a twirl and sat him back on the chair. She could see her knuckles white on his shoulders, but she didn't care.

'I don't know who this "angel" is, but he's definitely not right in the head – and if you go around telling people about him, they're going to think the same thing about you.'

Barra's face turned to stone, his eyes, as green as her own, luminous with defiance.

'I don't care what they think.'

Slowly, Rose drew her hands away. Giving them both time to recover, she lifted her cup and emptied her tea down the sink. As if she didn't have enough on her mind . . .

Turning, she folded her arms across her chest, and once more sought her son's gaze.

'Like I said, Barra, *everyone* knows yir name, and there are hundreds of trees up there he could have disappeared behind – you'd've only had to take yir eyes off him for a moment. And just because he could do a couple of tap steps doesn't mean he met Al Jolson.'

'Think what you like, Mam. I know he's an angel.' And Barra did know. It didn't matter *what* Mam thought. For the first time in his life, it didn't matter.

Silently, Rose counted to ten – and back. As patiently as she could, she began again. 'I'd have said he might be one o' the boys from the shows, but they're not due for another month yet. And they wouldn't be that well dressed.' She tried a smile. 'Honest, Barra, can you see an angel wearing a white shirt and grey flannels?'

'I can't help what he was wearing.' There was a new tone in Barra's voice, a tone which sounded dangerously close to insolence.

Rose felt her temper snap. Her heart had borne its share of emotions over the years, but anger had never been one of them. Until the party.

That night, the night of her fortieth, Rose had found anger. She didn't want it. If it was some sort of mad gift, she wished she could give it back. But it was here, it was here in her home, and in her heart. And even as she fought against it, she acknowledged it, welcomed it.

'I warned you, Barra. Warned you – and warned you.' Her voice was rising, strident even in her own ears. 'But you wouldn't listen. You're as thrawn as your father, and I wouldn't care if you *both* walked off into the bloody woods tomorrow – and *never* came out!'

Her fury found its target. Barra tucked his legs beneath him, seeming to gather the circumference of the table in his arms before bringing his head to rest in their cradle.

'You don't mean that, Mam.' His voice was muffled, and Rose knew that he was close to tears.

She pulled out the chair opposite and sat, her hand reaching to stroke her son's crown. Never, never before had she wounded him like that.

'Oh, Barra, I'm so sorry, son.' She swallowed, trying to get past the knot in her throat. 'It's not that I don't believe you . . .'

'But you don't.'

She sighed. 'Let's just keep it to ourselves for now,' she pleaded. 'The boy's probably staying around here somewhere. I'll ask Olive. She'll know, if anyone does. Please . . . Promise me you'll no' go round talking about angels until I can find out who this Jamie is.'

Barra sniffed.

'Please, son. Promise me, Barra.'

Barra raised his head, and shrugged wanly. 'OK. But you're wrong, Mam.'

'And, Barra, not a word to yir father. Not yet.'

'I wouldn't, anyway. *He* wouldn't believe me.' With that, he climbed from the chair and headed for the stairs.

Rose rubbed her forehead. She would give this Jamie a piece of her mind when she found him – *if* she found him. Barra's imagination had led her on more than one wild-goose chase before now, but then, how could she blame him? He'd had the childhood she had wanted for him, the childhood she had missed so badly herself. And if he was more naive, more . . . gentle than other boys his age, so what?

In her heart, Rose wanted to keep her son just the way he was, to prevent him from adopting the rough, tough, swaggering arrogance of his peers. And yet, as she reached to refill the kettle, she wondered if she'd been wrong to protect him so fiercely from the world. For wasn't it these same attributes which had first attracted her to Chalmers – that same 'manliness' (there was no other word for it) which attracted most women, and especially the Sheena Mearnses of this world?

Footsteps sounded on the path. Chalmers had been talking about building a garage ever since they'd moved here, but the old Morris van was still parked at the kerb. Rose usually heard its approach, but not tonight. Tonight she'd been distracted by angels, for God's sake!

' 'Lo,' Chalmers said, opening the back door and leaning on the handle while he cleaned off his workboots on the mat.

'Hello yourself,' Rose answered.

'What's wrong with *your* face?'

Rose knew her husband's day had gone little better than her own. No sense making things worse. 'Nothing, Chalmers. It's just . . . nothing.'

'Supper long?' Chalmers removed his newspaper from his pocket and hung his jacket on the knob of the kitchen door, frowning absent-mindedly at the state of his scarf.

Rose gritted her teeth. Just once, just once could he take the bother to hang it in the hall.

'I'm just boiling the tatties,' she answered, placing the pan on the ring. 'The stew's ready.'

'Pudding?'

'Apple crumble and custard.'

Content with the answer, Chalmers sat down and spread his paper. He glanced around as though missing something, and Rose slid a battered ashtray across to him. Chalmers nodded his thanks and reached in his shirt pocket.

'Hell's bells!' He threw a crumpled pack of Gold Leaf and a box of matches on the table.

'They'll be in the van,' Rose offered, knowing her husband's habit of mislaying his reading glasses – glasses which, at the ripe old age of forty-one, he detested having to wear at all.

Chalmers yanked open the back door, disturbing Socks the cat who had chosen the top step for a late afternoon nap. Socks, never pleased to see Chalmers under the best of circumstances, reacted by striking at his ankle with a hefty paw adorned by a ferocious set of claws.

Chalmers kicked out, yelling, but Socks was already at the end of the path, stopping to lick the offending paw as though wanting to be rid of the taste. He paused in his grooming and sat flicking his fat tail, all the while regarding Chalmers with utter contempt.

'I'll swing for that bastarding cat!' Chalmers promised as he stomped off back to the van.

Rose opened the press and grabbed the carpet sweeper, running it back and forth under the table where Chalmers' boots had left the last of their dusty deposit on the rug. Socks had decided to return to the house, and swung himself across the doorway, avoiding the sweeper with the same disdain he more usually reserved for Chalmers.

'Shoo, Socks! Shoo!' Rose whispered, hoping the cat would be out of sight before her husband returned. Socks ignored her, sashaying into the hallway and on upstairs to join his master.

Two years before, Barra had found the kitten sniffing about the rubbish bins at the back of the Whig and had brought him home. Rose, unhappy at having an animal in the house, had tried everything to find its owner. But nobody had wanted the stray and, after a week of placing futile ads in the local paper and the shop window, Rose had reluctantly agreed that the cat could stay.

'We'll call him Socrates,' Barra had insisted. 'You can see how wise he is.'

'Son, I'm not going to be standing on the door-step calling "Socrates" every time he needs fed. People'll think I'm a headcase!'

A compromise was finally reached, and the cat soon learned to answer to Socks. Chalmers, who had no initial objection to keeping the cat, became destined to endure the animal's unremitting anti-pathy, for no reason that he could fathom. At first aggrieved by the cat's attitude, he quickly – and painfully – became aware that Socks would employ any opportunity to sink his claws into Chalmers' flesh. It didn't take long at all before he came to detest the very sight of the animal.

Rose could hear Chalmers on his way back. She replaced the carpet sweeper in the press, sighing to herself. Lately it seemed that all her energies had been spent in keeping Barra and Socks as far away from her husband as possible.

And now she could add Sheena Mearns to the list!

Halfway through supper Chalmers' patience snapped.

'For God's sake, son, can you no' keep still at the table?' he blared, irritated beyond measure at Barra's restlessness.

Eating was a serious business for Chalmers.

44

Friday or not, he had a full day's work in front of him tomorrow and he'd eaten precious little all day today. Rose usually had his piece ready for him each morning before he left, but today he'd insisted he'd be done at the Wilsons' by lunch, and would have time to nip home for a bite to eat before setting off to examine the old croft at Dunfearn.

The new owners had telephoned from Surrey to ask for an estimate to rewire the croft, and Chalmers knew that they'd probably call a couple of the big boys in Craigourie to compare his quote. He was therefore anxious to get his price in early, in the hope of convincing them that the sooner he could get started, the sooner they could enjoy their holiday home.

It wasn't to be.

He had been held up at the Wilsons' by the painter, who'd been held up by the carpenter, who'd been held up by the plasterer. Around eleven o'clock, the painter, the carpenter and the plasterer agreed it would be best if they discussed a work-able timetable over a couple of pints.

Chalmers, fuming at this further delay, had thrown his pliers to the floor in disgust. All three seemed surprised, and somewhat disappointed, at this unwarranted show of bad temper.

'Yir being a wee bittie too anxious, if you ask me,' the painter informed him. 'Too anxious al-together,' agreed the carpenter. 'It'll all be here tomorrow,' the plasterer added, ambling off behind his comrades towards the nearest pub. They did, however, bring him back a can of McEwan's and a cold pie in recompense, at which point Chalmers had telephoned Rose to tell her he wouldn't be home for lunch after all.

It took the rest of the day to do what should have been accomplished in a couple of hours, and Chalmers still hadn't got to Dunfearn. Allowing for the half-hour drive there and back, it would be too close to dusk tonight to survey the croft. He'd just have to set off in the morning, before returning to the Wilsons' to finish up there.

If Barra would settle himself, he might, he just might, manage to avoid a night of indigestion.

'What's got you going now, Barra?' he asked rhetorically, hoping that, rather than having to contend with an answer, he might convey the extent of his displeasure at Barra's fidgeting. If Rose wasn't watching him the way she was – never looking at him, mind you, but watching him just the same – he'd tell the boy either to eat up or leave the table.

Well, things were strained enough lately. If she had any idea of the kind of day he'd had, maybe she'd spring to *his* defence for a change. But no! Barra – it was always Barra!

'I got some new stamps today. From Mauritius,' Barra answered.

Chalmers peered at him. Surely the addition of a few stamps to an already overflowing collection wouldn't cause this degree of agitation. He shook his head. He'd never understand his son. God knows he loved him. He truly did. But Barra wasn't in the real world at all half the time.

'Mauritius?'

'Aye, Da. They're gorgeous.'

'I'm sure,' Chalmers answered. 'Now if yir not going to eat your pudding, pass it here.'

'I am,' Barra replied. 'It's great. It's great, Mam,' he assured Rose. She smiled, glad to see that her son's natural enthusiasm had returned.

Chalmers continued eating. He didn't want to discuss stamp-collecting. He had never forgotten his own humiliation at Barra's innocent mirth when he'd asked where 'Par Avion' was. Well, he'd seen the blue stickers in the Post Office. It had been easy to mistake them for stamps.

To make matters worse, he had his own father to blame for Barra's hobby. Shawnie Maclean, a retired postman, had been instrumental in spawning Barra's interest in stamp-collecting. He and Barra could spend hour upon hour in rapturous attention to the flora, fauna and great peoples of a world yet to be explored – a world which Shawnie often talked of visiting, though he knew he never would.

He and his wife Ola lived in a small cottage on the shoreline of Kyle, a cottage too small to keep their only grandson out of sight – or mind – and the hours spent asleep at their home were hours Barra sorely grudged.

His first blink of daylight was inevitably accompanied by the roar of the ocean and the wheeling, screaming cry of the seabirds, his days filled with adventure and happenings, and his evenings brought gently to a close with fireside tales of myth and legend.

It was a magical place, and Chalmers could understand why Barra loved every minute spent there. What he could *not* understand was Barra's total lack of interest in football, or snooker, or any other pursuit more natural for a boy his age than stamp-collecting, for God's sake.

'The Cunninghams are coming up,' Barra ventured.

Chalmers straightened. 'Are they now?'

'Aye. Murdo says they are.'

'D'you know when?'

Barra shrugged. 'Next week, I think.'

'Find out, Rose,' Chalmers instructed. 'If I could get a word wi' Stewart, I think I could convince him to get the big house rewired. It's been needing it for years now.'

'What about Dunfearn?'

'Aye, well, I'm going there in the morning. But if I could get them both, it'd be the icing on the cake. The big house would be a job 'n' a half, and I'd have no bother getting my money from Stewart Cunningham. Might even take on an apprentice.'

'Oh, God, Chalmers, what would be the point of taking on an apprentice, when you'd just have to pay him off again?'

'Thanks for that vote of confidence, Rose,' Chalmers shot back. 'Can't you see I'm working every hour that's in it? Wouldn't you like me at home a bit more?'

'Aye. If it's home you'd want to be!'

A tense moment followed.

Barra rushed to fill the silence. 'Isla's coming back too,' he offered.

Rose shot him a grateful glance. Even Chalmers forced a smile.

'*That's* the reason for the excitement, then?'

'Course not,' Barra answered, grinning and blushing at the same time.

'Aye it is. That barefoot dame on the telly'll be taking a back seat now.'

'Och, Dad! It's Sandie Shaw. You know her name.'

Chalmers licked the last of the apple crumble from his spoon and sat back. His smile was genuine now. 'I know, son. Still, Isla Gillespie would put any o' thon pop stars to shame. She's a bonny lassie, right enough.'

Rose stood and began clearing the plates.

'I'm surprised you had the time to notice, what with all the work you've got on your plate. Finished?' The bowl was whisked from Chalmers' grasp, finished or not.

Chalmers glared at his wife's back. 'Thank you, yes.'

He lit a cigarette, hoping for the moment to pass. Rose busied herself filling the sink and stacking the dishes. Barra rose to help, pulling the dish-towel from under the sink, and knocking over the pedal-bin in the process.

'Leave it! Just leave it, Barra,' Rose said, bending to clear the mess.

'Sorry, Mam.'

'It's all right. I'll get this. D'you have homework?'

'It's the holidays, Mam!'

'So it is. Right then. Well, you can go through and watch the telly.'

'Can I go out?'

Rose stopped, her heart clattering. 'Where? Out where?'

'Just . . . out the back. I could sort my stamps. You can call me when *Ready, Steady, Go* comes on.'

'Just out the back, then. Where I can see you.'

Barra ran upstairs for his stamp collection.

Chalmers stubbed out his cigarette. Even with her back to him, Rose knew he was taking some kind of perverse pleasure from rattling the lopsided old ashtray against the table-top. 'He's a bit old to be watched every minute, Rose.'

Rose whirled. 'Really? You've forgotten what we went through with him, Chalmers? Or have you too many other things on your mind to remember he *needs* watching!'

She wanted an argument, a chance to get something, *anything* out in the open. But this particular argument was too well-worn to elicit much of a response in her husband.

'There's not a thing wrong with him, Rose. The operation cured the heart murmur; and he's been fine for years now. He's as healthy as the next one,

50

and he'd be a damn sight better off if you'd give him a bit o' slack once in a while.'

Rose closed the pedal-bin and turned back to the dishes. Angrily, she wiped the sudden tears from her eyes with the back of her sleeve. There had been a few sudden tears lately, and she hated them, felt betrayed and weakened by them.

'He's still so . . . impressionable,' she insisted, her voice little more than a whisper.

'He's got to grow up some time,' Chalmers said, his own voice gentle now. 'Let him be.'

Rose sniffed again, content to let it be. 'It's Dunfearn tomorrow then?'

'Aye. You'll be going to the town?'

Rose nodded, her back still to him. 'Mm-hmm. I'm changing my library books. D'you want anything?'

Chalmers busied himself lighting another cigarette, and Rose could hear him shuffling in his chair. What had she said now? For a second, no more, she puzzled over it. Then it hit her, and her mouth curled.

Rose borrowed her books from Boots in Craigourie, and Sheena worked at the No. 7 counter there. Had Chalmers reacted so quickly, knowing that? Or was her imagination becoming as overworked as her son's?

'No. There's nothing I want in the town,' Chalmers replied.

'You're needing shaving soap.'

'That, maybe.'

Barra reappeared, clutching a thick green album and the Cadbury's biscuit tin which contained his mounts and his newer acquisitions. 'D'you want to see my Mauritius stamps?' he asked, laying the tin on the table.

Chalmers rubbed his thumb across the lid of the old tin. 'Tell you what, why don't you come with me to Dunfearn in the morning? For the run.'

Barra glanced down. 'Well, I thought I'd . . . just be here tomorrow. Just . . . be about here.'

'Fine,' Chalmers said. He scraped his chair across the lino and marched into the living room, already reaching to turn on the television set.

As he switched the dial between channels, Barra looked up at his mother. 'Did I make Da mad?' he asked.

'No, Barra, you didn't make yir father mad. He's just in a bad mood,' Rose replied tightly, making sure Chalmers heard.

She heard Chalmers sigh heavily as he settled into his armchair. That was another thing! Chalmers had insisted on buying the black vinyl suite as soon as he'd seen it in Dawson's window, and had stubbornly refused to admit that it was nowhere near as comfortable as the moquette. Well, he'd bought it. Now he could put up with it.

Rose bit her lip, pained at her own mean-spiritedness. She couldn't deny how hard Chalmers worked to provide them all with a nice home, a home she was proud of. God, if she could just settle herself, get things back to normal.

Barra was hanging on the doorknob, unsure whether to go or stay.

'You'd be better off going with him tomorrow than hanging about the woods all day – waiting for some angel to appear,' she said, her voice low.

Barra held the back door open. He reached for her sleeve, drawing her closer. 'He'll be there, Mam,' he whispered back. 'He will.'

CHAPTER 4

Murdo Macrae had risen at five-thirty for as long as he could remember, and the first hour of the day had always been his own time; a time to ease himself into the needs of the day, and to enjoy a mug or two of strong tea and the first fill of his pipe. Even Gallus, without ever having being told, understood this.

Murdo had raised several dogs over the years, but none had had the quick high spirits of the Westie. And though Gallus was on the go from dawn to dusk, not even he disturbed this, the most precious hour of the day.

Right now the terrier was lying under the kitchen table, quivering with unease.

'D'you have to do that just now?' Murdo sighed.

Helen, in a candlewick dressing-gown, her hair plastered to her head under an ancient hairnet, was yanking the heart from a cabbage with a knife which might well have been the envy of her ancestors.

'I need to get the soup on,' she answered.

'It's ten past six in the morning, Helen.'

'I can read the time, thank you. Some of us *did* have an education, y'know.'

'Will this soup be ready for the breakfast, then? Or am I too ignorant in believing that it doesna' take six hours for a cabbage to cook?'

Whack!

Murdo needed to go to the bathroom. His bowels, like the rest of him, were used to a certain routine, a routine that did not include his wife's presence at this time of the day.

He rose.

'Where d'you think you're off to?'

'The bathroom, if you don't mind.'

'Open the window, then. And *don't* go mad wi' the toilet roll.'

The moment had passed. Murdo sat down, dejected.

'That'll be my piles back,' he murmured. The inference was clear. Helen would be responsible for the inevitable onset of this adversity.

'Don't go blaming yir piles on me! Blame herself if you want someone to blame. Stravaiging about the place giving *me* orders!'

'Wha . . . ?'

'Her wi' the Alice band!'

'Who?'

'Madam Cunningham to you and me. Thinks she's the lady o' the manor when she's here.' The cabbage was scooped into a large earthenware bowl to await further torture. 'Well,' Helen continued, waving the knife dangerously close to her husband's beard, 'I had enough of that last time round. She's no' even close to being a lady. Not like Alfie. Not a bit like Alfie!'

Murdo relit his pipe. It tasted sour, and there was no sign of another mug of tea. He had liked Alfreda Cunningham a lot, admired her even. But how on earth his wife could consider Alfreda a lady when the wild besom had met her end in a backstreet brawl in some dive in Marseilles (accompanied by a twenty-year-old waiter she had picked up in Monte Carlo, no less) was beyond him.

Alfreda Cunningham had been the only woman he'd ever known who had smoked Havana cigars, the bigger the better. And that was the way she had lived. Everything had had to be bigger and better, including presumably the young waiter. Murdo embarrassed himself with the thought, and reached down to calm his dog.

Well, Alfie was gone. Forty years old, and this big old empty house was all she had left behind her. This house – and her son, Stewart Cunningham, as different from his mother as night from day.

For a moment, Murdo cast his mind back to the years of half-terms and holidays when the bairn had walked by his side, hanging on Murdo's every word as the ways of the countryside were gently and carefully explained to him, learning to love and respect the cruelly beautiful land of his birth.

Stewart the boy had filled an empty, lonely

corner of Murdo's heart, but it had been Stewart the man who set off to gouge out a living in that foreign, heartless, concrete city – London. Murdo knew he had no right to the hurt he'd felt then, and he'd buried it a long time ago.

'They'll only be here for a couple of days, Helen. They'll be back down south for Easter.'

'He's going to sell this place out from under us, Murdo,' Helen warned, pulling off the hairnet to expose her still vibrant brown hair, hardly touched by the silver that had long since claimed Murdo's own.

He rose again, and gathered her in his beefy arms. 'No, he's no' going to be doing that,' he soothed. 'Dinna fash yirself wi' wild imaginings, Helen. We've a home here – as long as we want it. Stewart wouldna' do less.'

'There's something behind it, Murdo. I can feel it in my bones.'

'Bonny bones they are, too.' Murdo smiled, lifting his wife's chin. 'Educated bones.'

His teasing had the desired effect. Helen relaxed against him, a forlorn smile lifting the corners of her mouth. 'Yir an awful man,' she sighed, pulling gently away from him. 'But it's no' Stewart I'm worried about. It's her. She's got far more influence on him than us.'

'Hmm, maybe . . . At any rate, I'm no' going to stand still for a change o' residence at our age. OK now?'

Murdo reached for the kettle, and filled it under

the splashing of the old taps. 'If there *is* anything behind it, it wouldna' surprise me if he's going to sort out something wi' the fishing rights. That river's a wee goldmine, and there's many a one around here who's making a bob or two hiring out a stretch of it to the tourists.'

'Well, if that's the idea, he needna' think I'm getting tartanned up to put on a show for a bunch o' foreigners!' Helen's temper flared once more.

Murdo gave up on his tea. 'I'll be in the vegetable plot if you want me,' he murmured. Gallus had anticipated the move, and was already scraping at the back door.

Thank God for dumb animals, Murdo reflected, pulling on his wellies. A minute later, the pair set out together into the misty haze of the April morning.

'It's going to be a fine day,' Murdo informed Gallus, his natural good humour restored.

Gallus looked up at his master. 'I suppose you already knew that, though,' Murdo said, tickling the dog's rump with his walking stick.

Gallus barked. Of course he knew it.

Hattie finished making her bed, pulling the quilt over the blankets and smoothing its faded roses with the palms of her hands. She gathered the pitcher and glass from her bedside table, and carried it into the kitchen-cum-living room which made up the other half of the cottage. Only then did she walk back to the bedroom and switch off the light.

While Hattie had sat in the chilling dampness of her tiny prison cell, Alfreda had had the old scullery converted into a toilet, demolishing the outside shed which had served that purpose for so many years past. A new sink and stove took pride of place in a corner of the living room, but even they paled against the most precious gift of all.

Hattie had been welcomed home to the wonder of electricity. From that day onwards, she had never had to suffer the darkness again.

She ran her hand around the circumference of the metal fixture before flicking up the switch. 'God bless, Mrs Cunningham,' she said, as she did every morning – and every night.

A cheerful rat-a-tat brought Jennifer to the front door. She could see the pale blue reflection of Graham's Triumph through the glass panel at the end of the hall, and threw the door wide in welcome.

'You're early on the go.' She smiled, tucking a golden wisp of curl behind her ear.

Graham glanced at his watch. 'Ten's too early?' he asked, his kind features wary.

'No, of course not, Graham. You're welcome any time. Come on in, we're having breakfast.'

Jennifer led him into the kitchen, and motioned to a chair. 'Coffee?'

Graham nodded, bending to squeeze Jim's shoulder. He fought an instinctive shudder as he felt the sharpness of bone beneath his hand.

'How's it going, pardner?'

Jim stirred his porridge half-heartedly. 'It's going,' he answered. 'I'd be happier if I could get something decent to eat inside me, though.'

Jennifer poured a fresh coffee from the percolator, an acquisition which had brought them such delight in happier times.

'God, what're you complaining about?' Graham asked, rummaging in a battered briefcase. 'Wish I had someone to serve me a good bowl o' porridge once in a while.'

'Once in a while would be enough for *you*,' Jennifer chided, setting his coffee before him and sitting down. She smiled to take the sting from her words, and Graham's heart lurched at the desolation in her eyes.

'Well, no doubt there's a woman out there ready to make an honest man out o' me. I'll bide my time, though. No sense in rushing.' Graham resolved to keep his tone light. He could hardly bear it otherwise.

'Are we talking about the same man?' Jennifer smiled. Graham Kerr was the most *un*-typical accountant she had ever met. Rarely still for a moment, he had proved the perfect foil for Jim's steadfast, slower approach. Between them they had built a thriving, successful business, and now Graham was having to take the full brunt of its demands on his own wide shoulders.

'Indeed we *are* talking about the same man,' he answered, his eyes crinkling as a ready smile spread itself across his features. 'You'd be proud of me these days,' he assured Jim, patting his friend's hand. 'I'm at my desk for *hours* at a time! I've given up all this rushing about as though there's no tomorr . . .' His voice tailed off as he caught Jennifer's wide-eyed alarm at his thoughtless use of the expression.

'Bloody hell,' he muttered. 'I'm sorry, Jim. Jen . . .'

Jim shook his head. 'Away with you now,' he said. 'God, it's getting so no-one's comfortable saying ANYTHING around me any more.' He threw down his spoon. 'I'm sick of it!'

'Jim!' Jennifer reached for his hand, but he pulled roughly from her. She reached for her coffee mug, looking down and away from them both.

With difficulty Jim rose, tightening the cord on his dressing-gown. Graham held his breath as he watched his friend stumble towards the kitchen window. He knew better than to offer his help. Finally, leaning on the counter-top for support, Jim spoke again.

'It's a fine morning,' he said, his voice trembling with the effort of the movement.

'It is,' Graham agreed, forcing a cheerfulness back into his tone, a cheerfulness he no longer felt. He would never get used to this, never get used to seeing Jim wither in front of him; wither and die.

Last week, in a quiet hour while Jim slept, Jennifer had confided in him that she'd be glad when it was over. He had wanted to censure her

61

for her honesty, but in his heart of hearts he too had wished it over. And in that moment, he had died a little himself.

'And I've got just the news to make the morning even finer,' he breezed on, determined to try – for all of their sakes. He shot a smile of shared sympathy at Jennifer. She caught it and nodded slightly, grateful for the gesture.

'Well,' Jim said, reaching for his wife's arm, 'don't keep us waiting.'

Jennifer stood and helped her husband back into his chair, wrapping the blanket he had thrown from his shoulders around him. He tugged it away once more, and she sat, refusing to acknowledge this small rebellion.

Graham cleared a space on the white Formica top and pulled out a manila file. 'You know that Atkinsons have been scouting around the area? Well, yesterday their "man about town" dropped by the office, Jim. They've clients in London who've been buying up property all over the place. They're set on having a chain of bistros from Land's End to John O'Groats.'

'Bistros, no less!' Jennifer interjected, smiling at the thought.

'Don't laugh, Jen,' Graham said. 'If they've come this far north, they're not playing at it. Anyway, Jack Buchanan – that's the bloke from Atkinsons – was telling me that they're chock-a-block in the Glasgow office, and he was wondering if we'd like a crack at handling the account. He more or less let me know we could charge double our normal fees and, as long as we handled the first one right, they'd use us as their base in the Highlands. We could have accounts as far as Inverness. They're not intending to let the grass grow under their feet, that's for sure! What d'you think?'

Jim looked thoughtful. 'What property do they have in mind?'

'Wait, OK? Just wait a minute when I tell you – before you jump down my throat.'

Jim's eyes were wary, but he nodded.

'The Whig,' Graham breathed, turning sideways to face his partner, crossing his long legs in front of him.

'You've got to be joking,' Jim protested, his voice unsteady still. 'Maisie'll never sell the Whig. It's her life.'

Jennifer, too, was shaking her head at the idea. 'I can't see it, Graham,' she said. 'Not the Whig.'

'Well, dear friends and colleague,' Graham continued, smiling mischievously at them both, 'Mr Buchanan is one step ahead of us there. It seems he's had a word in Maisie's ear already, and she's definitely considering it. Definitely!' he added, wagging a finger in emphasis.

'We-ell . . .' Jim exhaled, slowly. 'That's a turn-up for the books.'

'A very lucrative turn-up,' Graham reminded him. 'And it's just the beginning. They're planning six more over the next eighteen months. They could become a major client, Jim, and Atkinsons would be happy to stay on the sidelines. No interference from them, as long as we're diligent.'

'No interference from me either,' Jim said, smiling ruefully.

'Come on, Jim,' Graham pleaded. 'Don't talk like that. There's always hope.' He wished desperately that it were so.

'There's no hope,' Jim said, very quietly, very definitely. 'I thought we were all agreed on that.' He paused briefly. 'Now, what d'you need from me?' he asked.

Graham shook his head, lost for words. 'Just . . . Just that you're happy with pursuing it. The account.'

Jim reached out, clasping Graham's arm with one hand and Jennifer's with the other. 'Look at me,' he demanded. Two sets of eyes met his own. 'All I want is for you to keep going, Graham. Keep rushing, and running, and busy, and alive! Don't get so bogged down with accounts you forget what it's like to be alive.'

Jim paused, gathering his breath. 'And take care of my Jenny . . .' he added, stroking her arm, his own eyes filled with an inestimable sadness.

Graham swallowed, hard. 'You know I will.'

Jim eased back from them both. 'Good.' He smiled, though it lasted but a second. 'What's the next step?'

Jennifer was trembling slightly. Graham knew it wasn't fear, for she'd long since faced her fear. Fatigue, then. At ten-thirty on a bright spring morning, he finally began to understand the depth of her fatigue. And, as he shuffled the unopened file back into his briefcase, he realised that he couldn't wait to get out of here, out into the sunshine, and away from them both.

Out, out, *out*!

'I'll . . . uh. I'll call in on Maisie, see what she has to say about it,' he stammered.

'Be careful,' Jim warned. 'She was talking about changing her accountant not so long ago; saying she wouldn't mind giving us a shot at doing her books. Don't go getting involved in a conflict of interests, Graham.'

Graham stood. His eyes creased with genuine mirth as he leaned towards his friend.

'A conflict of interests? In Drumdarg?'

They all laughed. It was too daft for words.

'We'll get the one o'clock bus from the Whig,' Rose said, avoiding her son's gaze.

'I don't know why I have to come to the town with you,' Barra grumbled. 'And if we see anyone from school, I'm walking off.'

'Don't give me a hard time, Barra. How d'you think I could concentrate on my messages, with you wandering about the woods looking for some headcase of a boy pretending to be an angel?'

'He *is* an angel,' Barra insisted.

'He is *not*!' Rose thumped her string bag with the two library books on the table, making Barra jump.

'Come on, son,' she said, her voice quieter. 'You've earned your pocket money. We could enjoy the afternoon together. I hardly get any time with you any more.'

'It's not that, Mam. Honest, it's not.' Barra's brow furrowed. 'It's just . . . it's cissy going up the town with yir mother.'

'You don't have to stay right beside me,' Rose wheedled. 'We can meet up after I've done the messages. Go to Bremner's, maybe.'

Not even the thought of Bremner's fresh cream cakes could interest Barra.

'I'd rather stay.'

Rose drew a deep breath. 'Barra, you've had all night to think about this, and all morning too. Surely you can see how ridiculous the whole thing is?'

'But that's just it, Mam,' Barra argued. 'The more I think about it, the . . . the realer it is! He *has* to be an angel. He just *has* to be.'

Barra pulled himself up on the draining-board, something he seldom did in Chalmers' presence, his legs swinging wildly with the thrill of his conviction.

'And he said we have things to take care of. Me and him, Mam. The pair of us!'

Rose grabbed his knees, halting Barra's movement. Never in her life had she been tempted to raise her hand to her son, but she really felt like clattering him now.

'People don't see angels, Barra, far less *talk* to them.'

'Catholics do. They see them all the time.'

'Catholics are . . . they're . . . they're brain-washed,' Rose said, exasperated beyond measure.

'The Yaks aren't brainwashed. *They* brainwash everyone else,' Barra answered, his eyes glowing with determination.

Rose glanced at her watch. 'We're going to miss the bus if you don't hurry.'

'Mam . . .'

'No, Barra. I'm sorry, but no.' Rose reached behind her son to pick up the old shaving mirror, and turned to retrieve her lipstick from her hand-bag. She painted on another coat of 'Pink Frost' and checked her eyeliner. No way Sheena Mearns was going to see her looking less than her best. Then she fished for a hairpin, pulling it through her fringe to separate each lacquered strand. Finally, Rose checked for spaces in her backcombing and, satisfied, turned to replace the mirror.

Barra hadn't moved.

Rose picked up her books and her handbag, and reached for the door handle. 'Go 'n' get yir blazer and comb yir hair.'

Barra slid to the floor and trundled through to the hall. He reappeared, shrugging into the jacket with one arm and using his free hand to press down his wiry curls.

Rose sighed again.

'Can I get a cream hornet at Bremner's then?' he asked, appearing quite broken-hearted at the prospect.

In spite of herself, Rose smiled. 'If you want. Now hurry *up*!'

They walked in companionable silence down the road and around the corner to the Whig. As they approached, Rose spoke again.

'Watch at the stop. Call me if you see the bus.'

'Don't say too much to Olive, Mam,' Barra implored. 'She's no' the type to believe in angels.'

Rose disappeared into the shop.

Barra raked the woods with his eyes, but there was little movement. Trees stirred here and there as birds flew among their branches, an almost soundless rustling in the warm, sweet stillness of the afternoon.

As he watched, Barra became aware of the swell of birdsong and he closed his eyes, lifting his face to the melody. The glory of it filled him, and he took a long, deep breath, inhaling the sound of it deep into his being.

He was standing like that as Rose stepped back out into the sunshine. She stopped in her tracks, and somewhere inside her a new fear took root. God, she thought, look at him there, his hair shining and that smile on him. If ever a boy was touched by the angels ... Please don't take him now, God. Don't take him from me now.

She shook her head violently. You're as daft as he is, Rose Maclean, she told herself. But her own heart had gone somewhere else for a little while, and she felt a sudden chill in the April air.

'Barra!'

He opened his eyes, smiling still.

'Olive says there's no strangers around that she knows of,' Rose informed him, as matter-of-factly as she knew how. She walked past him and gazed up the road. The bus took shape in a distant flurry of dust. 'But there's been a few stramashes at the snooker club in town, and she wouldn't be surprised if one o' that troublemaking crew had found his way out here.'

The bus pulled to a stop in front of them, and Barra held her elbow as she stepped up on the platform. They sat together on the long seat by the door. 'So you be careful, all right?' Rose finished. 'Just be careful.'

Barra appeared not to have heard her. He leaned forward. 'How's yir lambs getting along?' he enquired of the elderly gentleman sitting opposite them.

'They're grand, Barra,' the man answered. 'Getting as fat as pigs, they are.' A toothless cackle followed, and Barra crossed the aisle to sit by the man and discuss the progress of his flock.

Rose watched them, wondering anew. She had never seen the man before in her life.

CHAPTER 5

The afternoon proved uneventful. Rose had hung about the cosmetics department for a good ten minutes before going upstairs to the lending library, but wherever Sheena Mearns had disappeared to, she wasn't on her usual counter. Rose tried to broach the subject of her rival's whereabouts as Sandra Ledingham stamped her books, but was unable to find a suitably casual opening.

'It's Frank Yerby's latest.' Sandra smiled. 'We canna' keep them on the shelves. Course, he's a bit near the bone at times, but nothing compared to thon awful Harold Robbins.'

She winked, fully aware that Rose had borrowed *The Carpetbaggers* twice already, and was eagerly awaiting the release of the Oscar-winning film in Craigourie. Rose would have flushed had it been Miss Falconer behind the counter, but Sandra had been the one to suggest the book in the first place.

'I know what you mean,' Rose answered, and they giggled.

Sandra handed the books over to Rose, and stretched across the counter. 'He's usually at the

Natural History,' she remarked. 'He looks fed up.'

'He didn't want to come with me. You know how they are at that age.' Rose looked over to where Barra was inspecting the middle shelf of the Religion section. 'C'mon, son, we're ready,' she called. She'd be mortified if he brought up any of this latest nonsense in front of Sandra.

Barra started towards them, a look of enquiry on his face, and Rose locked eyes with him, silently forbidding him to even mention the word 'angel'.

'Were you looking for something partic'lar, Barra?' Sandra asked.

Barra broke his mother's gaze. 'I'm no' allowed to talk about it,' he answered.

'Never mind him,' Rose rushed on as Sandra opened her mouth to enquire exactly what it was Barra wasn't allowed to talk about. 'He just doesn't like being in the town on a Saturday afternoon.'

'Who does?' Sandra shrugged. 'If I hadn't taken so much from the club-book, I'd be taking a Saturday afternoon off myself once in a while. It'll be bloody August before it's all paid off. Just hope *I'm* no paid off before it.'

'Why?' Rose asked, shocked at the notion.

'Och, there's word they're going to be closing the lending libraries, Rose. No doubt we'll be one o' the first to get the chop.'

'Never!'

'Aye, well, Hazel's man's in for a job at Dounreay. If he gets it, I'm hoping they'll give me her counter downstairs. Fingers crossed,' she sighed.

'God, that's awful,' Rose said. 'What're they thinking about? Closing libraries like that!'

Sandra shrugged again. 'What can you do?' she asked. 'There's worse things than losing yir job.'

'Aye, there's much worse,' Rose agreed in sympathy, aware that Sandra was referring to Jim Pascoe's illness. Jim's wife, Jennifer, was Sandra's older sister, and the girls – though several years apart – had always seemed very close.

'I'm ashamed to say I haven't looked in on them at all this week,' Rose continued. 'It just gets to where you don't know what to say any more.'

'I know,' Sandra replied. 'There's nothing anyone can do now but wait.' She shook her head. 'It's hard, though.'

'I can imagine,' Rose agreed. 'They're so brave, both of them. I don't have any family of my own, but at least Jennifer has you 'n' your folks nearby. She'll need yis more than ever after . . .' It was impossible to say the words.

'The thing of it is,' Sandra said, a troubled frown creasing her youthful forehead, 'you'd think we'd be closer than ever just now. I mean, she *is* my sister. But . . . it's as though she doesn't want us near them, like we're not welcome. It's putting an awful strain on Mam.'

'It's probably just that she wants Jim to herself – while she has him,' Rose said gently. 'It's understandable.'

'I suppose so.' Sandra drew a deep breath, and

squared her shoulders. 'Enough o' that. Are yis off home now?'

'We're going to Bremner's first.' Rose smiled, nodding in Barra's direction. 'Cream hornets.'

Barra was leaning against the counter, a faraway look in his eyes.

'We're boring him to death.' Sandra laughed.

As Rose said her cheerios Barra made for the staircase, turning at the last minute to cast a cheery wave in Sandra's direction.

'Yis're all wrong,' he called back to her. 'I know someone who'll make him better. Jim'll be up 'n' running . . . aaaah!' he screamed, as Rose gave him a push that sent him flying. He missed the top two steps and scrambled to land upright on the third.

'Are you all right?' Rose asked, immediately horrified at the result of her action.

Barra blinked back at her, his expression a cross between surprise and terror.

'What did you do that for?' he asked in dismay.

Chalmers laid his paper on the floor by his chair, the pages in disarray. 'I'm off down for a pint,' he said.

'Can I come?' Barra asked.

'Are you into the drink now?' his father enquired, peering across the tops of his glasses.

'Och, Dad, I'd just like a bit o' fresh air.'

Chalmers glanced across at Rose, but she had another of her damn books in her hand, and refused to lift her head to look at him.

'I'm no' surprised,' Chalmers remarked. 'A fine day like this, and you haven't had a minute to yirsel to enjoy it. You'd've been better off coming wi' me to Dunfearn.'

'I would,' Barra agreed. 'You're right there, Da. I *definitely* would.' He was sitting on the orange carpet in front of the television, clapping the damn cat who'd stretched himself out to such an extent that Chalmers had had to cramp up his legs to avoid touching it.

As hard as he'd tried, Chalmers had found it impossible to concentrate on his paper, and trying to watch the telly and the cat at the same time was getting on his nerves.

What was Rose thinking about, keeping the boy cooped up like this? Barra was at his happiest out in the woods, enjoying the long spring evenings. Still, he had been relieved to learn that Barra had accompanied Rose into Craigourie. If his wife had intended any kind of confrontation with Sheena (Chalmers shivered at the thought), Barra's presence would have prevented her from making a scene. Not that Rose was the type for 'scenes', Chalmers consoled himself.

So what was going on? Rose was making a poor pretence of reading her book; she hadn't turned a page for ages. And what was all that at supper? Barra saying his mother had pushed him down the stairs in Boots, and Rose denying it, till the two of them got into an argument. That really *was* puzzling.

Half the time, Rose and Barra didn't even have to talk to each other, they were so attuned to what the other was thinking. Wasn't it himself that felt the outsider when those two got together? He could never remember them arguing like that. Never.

'Everything's going t'hell around here,' he said, thinking aloud.

'No argument from me,' Rose quipped.

Barra turned to look at them both.

'Are you going for a pint or not?' he asked.

'Aye,' Chalmers answered. 'Are you coming, Rose?'

'Nope.'

Chalmers glared at her. 'It's Saturday night. It'll do you good.'

'It certainly won't.' She finally looked up. 'Why would I want to sit wi' *your* cronies, listening to the lot o' yis rambling on about nothing, and getting crosswise with each other in no time flat?'

'Right then. Forget I asked!'

'Right then,' Rose repeated. 'And yir no' taking Barra with you. It's against the law.'

'I bloody well am!' Chalmers said, almost shouting. 'No-one bothers about that out here.' Socks stirred, fixing him with a malevolent golden stare.

'I'll get my shoes,' he said to Barra, his voice quieter.

As Chalmers headed for the stairs, Rose leaned forward in her chair. 'You're not to go through the woods, Barra. And sit with Maisie when you get there. I don't want you getting involved wi' that lot.'

Barra screwed up his face. 'Come with us, then, Mam. If we *all* went, and we walked through the woods together, you might get to meet Jamie. He'll be wondering where I am by now.'

'This is the worst day of my life,' Rose stated, slowly, and with conviction.

'It is not, Mam,' Barra reminded her. 'What about when yir grandad died?'

Rose gasped. 'I didn't mean . . . God, you're getting a quick tongue on you.'

Barra stared back at her. 'No, I'm not.'

'Aye, you *are*!' Rose insisted. She picked up her book, hoping to hide the hurt in her eyes.

Immediately Barra was beside her on the couch, his hand reaching to clutch her own. 'I'm sorry, Mam.'

'It's all right, Barra.' Rose nodded, squeezing his hand. She could barely trust herself to speak. Why on earth had he brought *that* up? She didn't need any more punishment right now, and she certainly didn't need reminding . . .

The evening darkened from the shadow of Rose's nightmare – a nightmare which had haunted her all of her life.

Martha Sinclair, a child herself, had given birth to Rose in a home for unmarried mothers, a home two hundred miles distant from Craigourie, a home where Rose should have been left, given up for the adoption that had been so carefully, so heart-breakingly planned.

It hadn't happened.

Martha, two months past her sixteenth birthday, had wrapped her baby daughter in a blanket and left the Salvation Army home in the dead of night, tramping the long road and the miles from Dundee back to Craigourie. A day and a half later, in the lambing snows of 1925, she'd knocked on her parents' door.

'I couldna' give her to strangers,' she'd said, pushing Rose into the arms of Bartholomew Sinclair, while his wife Joan stood weeping sound-lessly by his side. And with that, Martha turned, disappearing from all of their lives for ever.

Four years later Joan had passed on, leaving Rose in the only arms which had held her fast – 'Pops' Sinclair, otherwise known to the folks of Craigourie as Barra.

She remembered the day she had begun school, running home to pluck Joan's brown-edged image from the mantelpiece.

'Is this my ma?'

'No, Rose,' Barra had answered. 'She's yir gran. She died, slowly and with great pain.'

'Why, Grandad?'

'Because yir ma turned at the door, and was lost to us for ever.'

Rose hadn't understood. Throwing herself into her grandfather's lap, she'd cried. 'You'll no' turn at the door, Pops? You'll no' leave me?'

Barra had held her for as long as he could, but he too had had to leave. Months after the wedding, when he so proudly walked her down the aisle, Barra had slipped away.

And the first morning Rose had rushed to vomit into the cracked toilet-bowl, she knew she would have a son. And she knew he'd take his great-grandfather's name. Her heart had filled to overflowing when she told Chalmers her news, and he kissed her, and held her close in these new arms, the arms she had come to love so much.

'Barra it is,' he'd laughed, covering her with kisses. 'Barra it is.'

'Right, Barra. We're off.' Chalmers strode back into the living room.

Rose pulled herself from her reverie and glanced towards her husband.

'Sure you won't come, Mam?' Barra asked gently.

With a last squeeze of his hand, Rose released her son. She shook her head slowly. 'No. No, thanks.'

Chalmers had broken his stride only slightly. 'Yir welcome, y'know.'

'Am I?' Rose asked, her head back in her book.

Barra looked at his father. 'She should come.'

'For God's sake, don't *you* start,' he grumbled. 'C'mon, or the night'll be over before we get there.'

With a final look behind him, Barra ran to catch up with his father.

Chalmers was already around the path and on

to the road before he became aware of his son's presence at his side. There was no reason to go by the road. It would have been quicker and far more pleasant to cut through the woods. Chalmers was annoyed at himself for having given in.

'We said we'd take the road,' he told Barra, shoving his hands deep in his cardigan pockets. 'We're no' wise.'

'We're not,' Barra agreed solemnly. 'But we promised.'

'Well, we'll no' stay too long. There was no word about not coming *back* by the woods.'

Barra kicked at a stone. 'I can't remember,' he said, worried at the possibility of breaking a promise.

'I'd've taken note,' Chalmers assured him.

Barra caught up with the stone, and kicked it again with delight. 'Great.'

Chalmers smiled to himself. They were needing more time together, the two of them. Away from the womenfolk and all the problems they brought. God, wasn't it a fine thing to go for a pint on a Saturday night with yir boy at yir side.

'Aye, we'll be going back by the woods then,' he stated. Then he began whistling, a very tuneful rendition of 'Dark Lochnagar'. He clapped Barra on the back. 'Join in, son.'

Moments passed before he realised that Barra was silent still.

'I thought y'knew this one,' he said.

'I canna' whistle,' Barra answered cheerfully.

Chalmers came to a halt. 'Since when?'

'Since always.' Barra was unconcerned, skipping along ahead of him now.

Chalmers face darkened. 'It's time you learned.'

'I canna' learn, Da. I've tried.'

'Then yir no' trying hard enough!'

Barra turned, frowning. 'It doesn't mean anything. I just canna' whistle.'

Chalmers glared at him. 'You'll have a pint the night,' he commanded.

Barra grimaced. 'I don't want a pint.'

'You'll have one just the same.'

'I won't, Da. I don't like it.'

'What?'

'I've tried that, too. God, d'you no' remember? Last Hogmanay? I was sick as a dog.'

It was Chalmers' turn to grimace. How could he forget? It had been months before Rose stopped bringing it up, how he'd forced the brew on Barra and she'd nearly had to call the doctor as a result.

'I'll teach you to whistle, then.'

'You *can't*, Da,' Barra insisted, exasperated now. 'I'm good at spitting, though,' he added as an afterthought.

Chalmers raised an eyebrow. 'Are you now?'

'Aye,' Barra answered. 'Watch.'

Chalmers was impressed. 'No' bad. No' bad at all, son.'

Barra grinned. 'Doubt if you'll beat it,' he challenged.

'Huh, make way for the maestro,' Chalmers said,

pushing Barra aside, and making his point with great effect.

'I bet I could beat you,' Barra said, 'if I was taller.'

'Height's got nothing to do with it.'

'Aye, Da, it has. It's scientifically...'

The two argued and spat all the way to the Whig.

'Where's yir mam?' Maisie enquired, setting a knickerbocker glory in front of Barra, and having to squeeze her girth between his table and the wall to do so. The bar was full, but then it didn't take more than a dozen faces to give that impression. She was wearing another of her flowing kaftans, this one adorned with waves of cerise on a sea of inky blue.

'She didn't want to come,' Barra replied. 'Sorry, Maisie, but I don't know if Da would be wanting to pay for this,' he added, staring at the tall glass with longing.

'It's on me,' Maisie said. 'It's over from the afternoon teas, all two o' them. Imagine asking for scones when you could have the likes o' that? Besides, you'll be the only one here worth blethering to in another hour or so. *Bon appetit!*'

What should have been a delicate wave of her hand developed into a tortuous effort to extricate herself from behind Barra's chair.

'Where y'buying yir frocks?' enquired Eddie Bain, seated at the opposite table. His head lolled in circles as he tried to make sense of Maisie's kaftan. Already three sheets to the wind, he

81

appeared mesmerised by the pattern and was close to becoming violently ill.

Pulling herself free, Maisie sailed towards the bar.

'Abdul's,' she called over her shoulder.

Eddie scratched his head, trying to focus. 'The Paki in Craigourie? I thought his name was . . . something else.'

'No, darling,' Maisie trilled, pushing a glass up to the optics. 'Abdul, the tentmaker – in Jellalabad.' With that she guffawed with laughter, and the men at the bar, most of whom had no idea what she was talking about, joined in. Maisie's laughter was like that.

'A double Grouse, sir,' she said, placing the glass in front of Chalmers. 'Chaser?'

'Ta, Maisie,' Chalmers answered. 'McEwan's.'

'*Mais naturellement*,' she answered, pulling the pint as she spoke. 'Douglas?'

'In a minute,' he said, motioning to the tumbler in front of him. As happened most evenings, Doug Findlay had relinquished his duties to sit on the other side of the bar, drinking quietly and enjoying the craic with the customers. Though nine years younger than Maisie, the balding pate and thinning body deceived the most astute of their clientele, and it was a widely held belief that he was at least as old as, if not older than, his doting partner.

Maisie, aware that Doug was drinking himself into an early grave, did nothing to encourage his abstinence. He had come to her drunk, and she intended to keep him drunk. For Maisie was certain, beyond the most reasonable of doubts, that the harsh light of sobriety would illuminate each and every one of her failings. Only then would Doug realise that she was so much less then he deserved.

And that she could not bear. Not now, not ever.

CHAPTER 6

Sandy Robertson pushed open the back door of the Whig, standing aside to allow Olive to precede him. He had been courting Olive for nigh on six years, almost from the moment the first shovelful of dirt was scattered on his wife's cheap coffin.

'A tongue like a stinging nettle,' he'd been heard to mutter at the graveside.

It therefore surprised the inhabitants of Drumdarg that he had sought out Olive's companionship so soon after his wife's demise, for Olive Tolmie was not known for the sweetness of her tone, nor the warmth of her expression.

'A quiet life's no' for me' and 'Y'muddle on wi' what yir used to,' Sandy explained when pressed. In truth, he had always thought of Olive as a handsome woman, and had relished the secret smiles she had thrown his way over the years. Even more than the smiles, he had relished the shilling or two she'd knocked off his messages whenever Maisie's back was turned.

Sandy had never allowed his less-than-dear departed wife to take charge of the housekeeping.

Messages were getting far too dear to be careless with the money, and Sandy Robertson was nothing if not canny.

Olive had decided that Sandy's 'canniness' was in fact an inherent meanness almost as soon as she'd agreed to step out with him. It was her sole excuse, though never openly mentioned, for not marrying him.

Still, she looked forward to finishing her week's labour at five on a Saturday, and spending the better part of the weekend in his company.

The ritual two Harvey's Bristol Cream sherries at the Whig on a Saturday night, and Sunday afternoon bingo at the church hall in Craigourie, had become the highlight of the week. Sandy bought the sherries. Olive bought the bingo tickets.

She had quietly kept count, and felt somewhat embittered that he was a naturally lucky individual. At the last reckoning he was eighty-four pounds ahead, and had never once offered to share his winnings.

'Move over,' Olive demanded, as she pulled out a chair by Barra's side. He moved his chair a few inches to the right and Olive thumped herself down, placing her handbag on the floor and cradling it securely between swollen ankles.

'How's yir feet?' Barra asked.

'Och, it's worse they're getting,' Olive replied sorrowfully. 'It's a relief to be off them.'

Barra smiled. 'Aye,' he said. 'I'll bet it is.'

Olive squinted at him, trying to discern if there

had been any impudence in the remark, but Barra had returned to scraping the last of his knicker-bocker glory from the bottom of his glass.

Sandy placed Olive's sherry in front of her, and excused himself to discuss the gruesome result of the previous Tuesday's Budget with the men at the bar.

'Four shillings on a bottle of whisky,' he complained to Olive. 'I'm sorry I voted them in.' He was, of course, referring to the Labour Party, for whom he had almost certainly not voted. Sandy was a Tory to the backbone; a backbone which proved consistently too weak to supply him with the courage to lay claim to this aberration in the working-class confines of the Whig.

'Who cares who's in?' Olive muttered at Sandy's retreating back. 'If you've listened to the lies o' one politician, you've listened to them all.' She peered back at Barra. 'We'll be needing that glass again,' she reminded him.

Barra admitted defeat and laid the long spoon back in the glass. 'It was good,' he said.

'Who's been after you in the woods?' Olive asked, taking a genteel sip at her sherry.

'N . . . n . . . no-one,' Barra stammered. 'No-one's been after me.'

'Rose was saying there was,' Olive argued. 'She was in the shop this very afternoon. Said some boy had been after you in the woods. Some o' that lot from the town, if you ask me. If it was jist the one, it couldn't have been the Iacobellis. You'd have to split that pair apart wi' a hatchet. Besides, you *know* them! One o' their Mafioso, though. Cosy Nosters, or whatever they're calling themselves . . .' Olive had scarcely drawn breath.

'No! It wasn't. It was . . . just someone I met.'

'*Who* did y'meet? What kind o' boy? Was he a tink?'

'No, he was not. It was just a boy. Well, he wasn't an ordinary boy. He was . . . different.'

Olive leaned back, clasping her hands across her stomach.

'There was word – years ago, mind – that there was a ghost wandering up there. Some poor soul that'd lost her bairns in a fire.' She reached for her sherry again, and slanted it towards Barra in a warning gesture. 'Maybe it was one o' *her* bairns. There's a lot o' that in the Highlands, y'know.'

Barra looked at the sherry glass. There wasn't enough out of it for Olive to be drunk. Besides, she had never been known to get drunk, not Olive.

'A lot o' what?' he asked.

'Ghosts. Fairies. Things . . .'

Barra shook his head. 'What things?'

'Were you no' listening to a word I said?' Olive asked, remembering her sherry and taking another sip.

Barra scraped his chair closer to Olive again. 'D'you believe in angels?'

As soon as he'd said it, he bit his lip. Of all the people in the world to tell, he'd just shared his secret with Olive Tolmie!

'Certainly,' Olive replied, not even questioning the possibility.

Barra blew out his cheeks, his eyebrows almost disappearing into his auburn curls. 'Wow!'

'Why wouldn't I?' Olive asked, the familiar belligerent tone back in her voice.

'I just . . . I just didn't think . . .'

'Who is he, this angel? And what's he here for?'

'I don't know yet,' Barra confided. 'I just met him the once. But he said we had things to take care of, me and him.'

He let this sink in for a moment. 'Mam doesn't believe he's an angel. She wouldn't let me back in the woods all day.'

Olive gave an exaggerated shiver. 'Well, you canna' blame her. You've aye been a fey kind o' lad yirself, Barra. I wouldna' want to be yir mother.'

Barra looked hurt for a moment, before realising that he would absolutely hate it if Olive Tolmie *had* been his mother. Her own boys, all three of them, had got out of Drumdarg at the first opportunity.

Still, he thought, at least she's listening to what I'm telling her. At least she's *believing* me! A new respect for Olive began to form in his mind.

'So, you think he *is* an angel then?'

Olive snorted. 'How would I know?' She seemed to be losing interest, and was looking across to where Sandy was surreptitiously ordering another lager for himself.

She sighed. 'Yir poor mam, she's aye got something new to worry about.'

Barra looked disconsolate. 'She doesn't *have* to worry about it. How can I find out any more if she won't even let me talk about it?' Barra gnawed on his lip.

'Like I said, y'canna' blame her, Barra. There's them that'd be wanting to put you away, if they heard you.'

'Who?'

'Them. Y'know, folks who don't go in for that sort of thing.'

Barra nodded. The world was full of 'them'.

'Da would never believe it,' he added after a pause. 'You can be sure of that.'

'Aye, well, men are different.'

'How?'

'Ach, it's no use trying to explain it. You'll be a man yirself one day – just like the rest o' them.'

Barra was not so easily dismissed.

'If I thought Da *would* believe it, I'd tell him. Maybe then he could talk to Mam, stop her worrying about everything.'

'Well, he's no' going to believe anything he can't see wi' his own two eyes. Not Chalmers. And him 'n' yir mam don't seem to be talking too much at all these days.'

'Aye they are,' Barra answered, flying to his parents' defence. 'Course they are.'

Olive cast a sceptical glance at him. 'Glad to hear it.'

Barra looked more disconsolate than ever, and Olive took momentary pity on him.

'Who knows, son, maybe you'll meet up wi' yir pal on the way home. Then y'can tell yir da all about him.'

Barra grinned. 'Wouldn't that be grand?'

Olive nodded. 'And there's a way you can get him to prove he's an angel.'

Barra forgot he was kneeling on his chair and almost tipped himself into Olive's lap, so quickly did he dive towards her.

'How?' he asked, breathless with excitement.

'Get him to mend my bloody feet!'

'Dad . . .' Barra shook his father's elbow but Chalmers was leaning comfortably across the bar, discussing the shortcomings of the wiring at the big house with Murdo and ignoring his son's urgent appeal.

'Dad!'

'*What*, son?' Chalmers asked, frowning at the interruption.

'It'll be dark if we don't go now.'

Chalmers looked out of the narrow-paned windows at the encroaching twilight. It was nine-thirty, and there was a fair bit of drinking time left.

'What of it?'

'We'll need to go now, if we're going back by the woods.'

'We can find our way home in the dark,' Chalmers replied, puzzled. 'It wouldn't be the first time.'

'No, Dad,' Barra insisted. 'It'd be better if we had some light. In case . . . there's anything to see.'

'God,' Chalmers said, looking to Murdo for sympathy. 'Would that no' get on yir nerves?'

Murdo pointed his pipe at Chalmers. 'Yir lucky to have a lad o' yir own to walk you home on a Saturday night, Chalmers Maclean.'

Chalmers downed the last of his beer, and sighed. 'He can walk *you* home, then. I'm no' ready.' But he placed his glass carefully down on the counter, smiling as he said it. 'It's a helluva thing to have yir conscience at yir side.'

Murdo said nothing. Helen had reported that Chalmers' conscience seemed to have taken leave of absence lately. But then, women were aye looking to point a finger at a man – any man. Chalmers was a good sort, after all was said and done, and Murdo had no doubt he'd come to his senses in the fullness of time.

'You'll be in tomorrow?' Maisie enquired of Barra, clearing some glasses on the bar to make room for her arms as she leaned towards him. 'Isla'll be here in the afternoon.'

'Och, he'll be in all right.' Chalmers grinned, aware of the red flush creeping across his son's face. 'Try keeping him away.'

'Who would want to keep him away?' Doug smiled, his voice slow and gentled with the drink.

'See yis then.' Chalmers sighed again, holding on to Barra's shoulders. 'He'll no' sleep if he doesna' get a whiff o' the woods before his bed. It's worse than the opium.'

They left, Chalmers scuffing his way across the

tarmac and holding on to the dilapidated fencepost as he crossed into the woods. Barra was already ahead, turning to make sure his father was following.

'Come *on*! It's getting dark.'

'What's the hurry?' Chalmers called back, acknowledging to himself that he didn't relish returning to the stony rebuke in Rose's eyes. It didn't seem possible that only two weeks ago they had celebrated her fortieth birthday at the Whig. The night had been filled with laughter and music, and Rose had been all over him – at least until Sheena arrived.

Chalmers shook his head. How had it happened? He had never as much as thought about straying. Not once. But that night, under cover of the general celebrations, Sheena had pulled him up to dance, pushing herself against him at every turn, winding her body around him until his head was spinning. Dance followed dance, until he wanted nothing more than to pull that apology for a frock from her body and lose himself in the taste of her.

Then, and only then, had Chalmers pushed her from him. He walked her back to the table, depositing her firmly by her husband's side, and still she had looked up at him, her eyes promising, promising . . .

Staggering with drink and lust, he'd returned to Rose, avoiding the shocked hurt of her expression. Damn it all, she was no more shocked than he was himself, knowing that he'd let himself be drawn to that . . . that hoor!

Yet in the throes of his Sunday morning hangover it was Sheena's touch he remembered, Sheena's pulse that pounded in his temples and sent him shaking to drape his empty arms around the cold and righteous comfort of the toilet-bowl.

And his groin ached with the knowledge that what Sheena had promised, she was more than ready to deliver.

'Da-ad!'

'I'm coming, for Chris'sakes,' Chalmers bawled, tripping on a small pothole in the trail and running forward to avoid falling. The trip surprised him. He didn't think he'd had that much to drink.

Barra had raced back towards him. 'You OK?'

'I'm fine.'

'Don't be swearing then.'

'Who's to hear me?' Chalmers was thoroughly disgruntled.

'Just come *on*!' Barra entreated.

They were almost at the top of the incline, and through the branches of the trees above them the dusk stencilled awkward patterns at their feet. Barra had stayed by his father, forcing him forward with an urgency which seemed out of place in the susurrating hush of the gloaming.

As they reached the clearing at the crest of the trail, Chalmers moved forward to grab a moment's respite on the smoothened surface of the old log.

'God,' he gasped. 'I'm no' as fit as I once was.'

He watched as Barra stepped to the edge of the clearing, looking this way and that, seemingly unconscious of the dying sun whose lingering farewell trailed crimson fingers across the horizon, setting the big loch afire and highlighting the ancient gunmetal graph of the hills.

'He's no' here,' Barra said at last.

The sun's last flame burned in Chalmer's eyes. He closed them briefly, rubbing the blindness from them.

'Who's no' here?'

Barra came to sit by Chalmers, his head low. Not a word to yir father, Rose had warned. 'Nobody,' Barra whispered.

'Sactly,' Chalmers agreed. 'Nobody.'

Barra stood. 'C'mon home, Dad.'

Chalmers brandished an imaginary claymore. 'Home it is. Lead on, Macduff!'

Barra grinned. Dad was always saying things like that. Dad could be good fun when he tried – or when he'd had a drink or two.

Tomorrow. He'd find Jamie tomorrow! And he'd tell Dad.

Sometimes Mam got carried away with all her worrying.

Sunday brought total silence to the Maclean household, a silence which had infected the atmosphere from the night before, when Barra and Chalmers arrived home. If Rose had practised for a year – which she hadn't – her disapproval at her husband's tipsy state, and his proud confession that they'd returned via the woods, could not have been more obvious.

Barra wiped the last of his sausage and beans from the plate. 'Can I go out now?'

Silence.

Rose looked at Chalmers. Chalmers looked at Rose.

'If anyone's going to harm yir precious boy, it won't be at half past eight on a Sunday morning.'

Barra bit his lip. He hated when Dad said 'your precious boy' like that. As though he wasn't Dad's boy too. In a rare moment of silent defiance, he felt like telling them both he wasn't *anyone's* boy. He was grown up, nearly a man himself.

Barra never had learned how to keep silent, however.

'I'm not anyone's precious boy,' he stated.

'Yes you are!' Rose said, almost before he'd finished the sentence.

She hadn't understood!

Barra wondered, not for the first time, what was making his mam so . . . wrong-footed with everything lately. Pushing him downstairs when he wasn't looking, and being horrible to Dad. Of course Dad was being horrible to everyone.

Barra never understood how people could be nice and happy with the drink in them, and then be so horrible when it was coming out of them. He would never take to the drink himself. Not after last Hogmanay, when the beer Dad had given him made him so sick he thought he might die.

It had ruined the whole New Year, and Mam and Dad hadn't been right with each other for weeks. A bit like they were now. Except now was different. Now was worse.

And Barra felt that, in some way he couldn't understand, he was to blame for it all. Dad could just look at you sometimes and you knew, you *knew* it was your fault.

'Off you go,' Rose sighed, breaking his train of thought.

Barra left them then. As he reached the end of the path, he knew without looking that Rose's eyes were following him.

'Leave me alone, Mam,' he whispered.

Maisie looked up from the back door of the café, on her way out to the bins with the last of the Saturday night refuse.

Barra was almost at the bottom of the trail. He was calling somebody, but there was no-one else in sight.

'Jamie? Jamie!' She could hear him now.

Maisie set down the rubbish, waiting for Barra's companion to appear.

'Aw, God!' Barra swore. Almost immediately he cowered slightly, as though expecting to be split asunder by a bolt of lightning. Then he straightened, kicking a small rock ahead of him.

'I'm sorry,' he said. 'But I wish you wouldn't do that.' He cupped his hands to his mouth. 'I wish you wouldn't keep doing that,' he shouted.

Amused, and sure that Barra had not yet seen her, Maisie shouted back. 'I didn't realise it worried you! It's a dirty job, but someone's got to do it.'

CHAPTER 7

'I'm just lifting the breakfast,' Maisie informed Barra as he walked towards her. 'D'you want some? Or would you prefer to stay up there with yir thoughts?'

'I've had mine,' Barra answered. 'And they're no' just thoughts.'

'C'mon in anyway,' Maisie said, leading him into the kitchen. 'I'd enjoy the company.'

She pulled a plate down from the rack above the range and began shovelling the eggs from the griddle on to it, pushing them to the side to make room for the several rashers of bacon and two slices of fried bread which followed. Barra leaned against the door, knowing better than to interrupt Maisie when she was assembling her food. A couple of fried tomatoes and a hillock of mushrooms were daintily balanced on the side of the plate, and Maisie reached across the counter to set a steaming mug of coffee on the tray beside her meal.

'Follow! Follow!' she instructed, pushing through the swing door and on into the café. Maisie set the tray down on the nearest of the six tables, and took a moment to settle herself in her chair. Barra climbed into the one opposite, as he always did. You couldn't sit in the chair next to Maisie and be comfortable. It was better to give her some space – especially when she was eating.

Maisie reached across the waxed tablecloth for the brown sauce. Several dollops were thumped from the bottle, and a liberal sprinkling of salt and pepper dressed the whole thing to perfection.

She sat back in the enveloping folds of her ivory quilted dressing-gown and sighed with pleasure. Her hair was tied back in a cream-coloured hat that was supposed to look like a scarf. Mam had a blue one just like it. Mam looked nice when she wore hers. Maisie looked like the Michelin man.

Several mouthfuls later, Maisie looked up. 'You weren't really bothered with me taking out the rubbish, were you?'

'It wasn't you. I wasn't speaking to you.'

'Ah. Something in the woods, was it?'

'Kind of.'

Minutes passed. A final wipe round with the fried bread, and Maisie's plate was as clean as a whistle. 'I'll need another cup to wash it down,' she said, heading back towards the kitchen. 'Coke?'

Barra shook his head.

Maisie rested against the door for a moment, surveying Barra with a careful expression. 'We need to talk,' she said at last. 'Don't move. I'll no' be a minute.'

She wasn't.

'Now,' she said, leaning into Barra, her hands wrapped around a fresh mug of coffee. 'Did you leave that glorious smile back up in the woods? And if you did, why?'

Barra wet his finger and pressed it into the salt crystals ringing the space where Maisie's plate had sat.

'I've met someone . . . in the woods. I told Olive.'

'Then you might as well have put a notice in the window,' Maisie replied. 'Are you sorry?'

'No,' Barra said. 'She was amazingly . . .'

'Aye,' Maisie interrupted. 'That's Olive. Amazingly Olive!'

'He's an angel, Maisie. His name's Jamie.'

Maisie blew on her coffee, the force of her breath causing it to ripple almost to spilling. Then she put the mug down, and ran a purple-tipped finger around its rim.

'You told Olive . . . that?'

'Aye.'

Maisie sucked in her breath. Barra was sure she was going to burst out laughing any minute, but when she looked up her eyes were soft, and very pretty.

'How do you know he's an angel? This Jamie, how d'you know?'

'Well, I was sure, at first. Then I wasn't sure, not after Mam started explaining things.' Barra shook his head in frustration. 'No. I *was* sure. I was!'

'Then we can move on,' Maisie prompted.

'Well, then I met him again today, and he told

100

me straight I'd be the only one who could see him.'

Maisie sniffed. 'Ah. So I won't be getting an introduction?'

Barra shook his head. 'Sorry, Maisie. 'Fraid not. It makes it harder, though, when no-one else can see him.'

'Aye. And would I be wrong in believing that you had trouble seeing him yourself? When you were out there calling him?'

'Oh no. He'd disappeared by then,' Barra assured her. 'He can come and go when he likes. Y'canna' take yir eyes off him for a minute.' He looked thoughtful. 'It gets a bit annoying. That's what made me swear.'

'An annoying angel,' Maisie mused. 'Now there's something different for Drumdarg.'

'He can be quite sarcastic too.'

Maisie, who'd been resting her chins on her hand, covered her mouth with her fingers. 'Sarcastic?' she mumbled.

'He *can* be,' Barra confided. 'When I said he didn't look much like an angel, well, I meant . . . he looked real, well, anyway, he said "Who were you expecting? I'm afraid Gabriel's otherwise engaged." '

Maisie nodded, pressing her fingers even harder against her mouth.

'. . . And when I asked him to mend Olive's feet, he said he was an angel – not a chiropodist.'

Maisie thrust out her other arm towards Barra's chest, clearly intending to silence him. 'Give me a moment,' she said at last. After several deep breaths, she lowered her arm.

'What do your folks say?'

'Da doesn't know yet, and Mam . . . She's worried. She thinks there's someone after me, in the woods. You know what she's like.'

'She's a mother, Barra. Mothers are like that.'

'She kept me out of the woods all day yesterday. She made me go to the town. On a Saturday afternoon.'

Maisie let out a low whistle. 'That's out of order.'

'Then she pushed me down the stairs at Boots.'

Maisie gasped then, finally, and with great relief, roared with laughter. Barra joined in, even though it wasn't funny. At last Maisie wiped her eyes on her sleeve. 'Rose . . . pushing you down the stairs? What did you do, my bonny lad, to take that on yirself?'

'I don't know.' Barra shrugged, still wondering at it. 'I met Jamie on Friday, on my way home from school, and he said we had things to take care of, and Sandra was talking about Mr Pascoe, and Mam said not to mention angels, and I just said I knew someone who could make Mr Pascoe better. That's all that happened.'

He paused for breath. 'Then she pushed me down the stairs.'

Maisie's eyes cleared. 'This Jamie, did he say he'd make Jim better?'

'No. He hasn't mentioned anyone yet. He said we'd find out more as we went along. So today I told him about Olive's feet, but he got a bit . . .'

'I think Jim Pascoe would be higher up the list when it comes to needing an angel than Olive Tolmie's feet, don't you?'

'Aye,' Barra agreed. 'But I had to start somewhere.'

Maisie swallowed, her voice soft again. 'Barra, you do know that Jim's dying, don't you?' she said gently.

Barra licked the salt from his fingers. It had almost disappeared, but he could taste it just the same.

'That's what they say.'

'And you think this angel can save him?'

'I do.'

'Wouldn't that be great?' Maisie picked up her mug, apparently prepared to give it some thought.

'So what do *you* think?' Barra asked, impatient for Maisie's opinion.

'I don't know, Barra,' Maisie mused. 'But if you say an angel came to you – and I'm not saying he didn't, mind – it wouldn't surprise me a bit. Not a bit.'

'What wouldn't?' Doug shuffled through from the kitchen.

Maisie glanced towards Barra, silently asking his permission to share their conversation. Barra smiled back at her, his earlier dejection gone. Doug was a great listener altogether.

'Sit down, Doug. I'll get you some breakfast, and Barra can tell you all about it.'

'No breakfast, Maisie,' Doug said, pulling out a chair and coughing with the effort. As he lit a cigarette, Maisie made her way over to the ancient wooden server. Reaching inside the lower shelf, she pulled a bottle of Glenmorangie free from its hiding-place and poured a large measure into one of the glasses ranged along the top shelf. She set it down in front of Doug and, placing a loving hand on his arm, bent to whisper, loudly, in his ear.

'There's breakfast for you.'

Doug smiled painfully up at her, and coughed some more.

'So?' he sputtered, turning his attention to Barra.

Barra opened his mouth, and closed it again.

'I think I'd better get going.'

'Where now, Barra?' Maisie asked in surprise. As so often before, the boy's mercurial ways had caught her off-guard.

'I'm going to the Pascoes'. I'll be back later,' he called, already in the kitchen and racing for the back door.

Doug raised a questioning glance to Maisie.

'He says he met an angel,' she said, reaching for his hand and rubbing it against her cheek. 'He doesn't know I beat him to it.'

Doug Findlay had walked through her door ten years before, almost to the day. He'd heard she was looking for a handyman.

No, Maisie had replied, Murdo Macrae was good enough to offer his services when needed.

She didn't have enough business to pay for full-time help.

He didn't need a full-time job. Perhaps he could do an hour or so's work, just till the end of the week. Did she need someone in the bar?

Maisie looked at him. 'That would be a bit like putting a bairn in a sweetie shop, wouldn't it?' she asked gently. Doug nodded, and retired to an empty table. She sent a large whisky over to him 'on the house', and he'd drunk it quickly, sitting with the empty glass before him for the rest of the evening.

He spoke to no-one, and nobody spoke to him. Eventually he nodded off, huddled in despair and cloaked in a loneliness with which Maisie was all too familiar. Long after the last recalcitrant customer had been chased from the bar Doug had stayed, face down on the table, sound asleep.

He had, as it turned out, nowhere else to go.

Some months earlier, a day before his thirtieth birthday, Doug had returned from his milk round to find the house he had shared with his wife of nine years quite silent. Quite empty.

A cursory note of explanation was propped on the mantelpiece.

Barbara Findlay had packed herself, her belongings and their two boys into a newly purchased second-hand caravan, and set off for parts unknown. The owner of the caravan, and now apparently of Doug's family, was Freddie Johnstone.

Freddie was Doug's first cousin, his childhood

companion, his drinking partner and more-or-less constant visitor to his home. He was also single, full of life and laughter, and Doug's young sons adored him. Doug had trusted him implicitly. Never, not once, had he imagined that Freddie was preparing to steal his family from him.

Doug's marriage had foundered early on. Barbara had been just seventeen, and three months pregnant, when they'd sworn to love each other 'till death us do part'. A second son, born a scant year after the first, robbed her of the youth she felt she deserved. She had wanted to travel, she told him – often, and with bitterness. She'd wanted to see the world, not peer out at it over pails of nappies and lines of washing. She had wanted much, much more than a milkman's wage could provide. Freddie loved her, and was prepared to do whatever it might take to make her happy.

In the few seconds it took to read the letter, Doug's world fell painfully, irrevocably apart.

He had no idea where they had gone, had waited day after day to hear news of them. It came in the form of a postcard from Scarborough, and it robbed him of the last ounce of hope he had left.

Barbara would not be returning. He would be contacted by a solicitor in due time. He would *not* be contacted by Barbara, nor by his children. They belonged to Freddie now – all of them, and were apparently delighted with the arrangement.

Doug hit the bottle.

It didn't take long for his employers to determine

that the people of Craigourie deserved their daily pinta on a more-or-less regular basis, and within weeks he found himself unemployed. Barbara had thoughtfully emptied their tiny savings account and, as the drinking took over what was left of his life, he became not only unemployed – but unemployable.

There was no income to pay the rent. The council stepped in with an ultimatum. Three months to pay the rent arrears. Not a day longer.

It couldn't be done, of course.

On the day of the eviction, an hour before the bailiffs were due to arrive, Doug Findlay stumbled out into the daylight and locked the door behind him. He threw the keys down the nearest drain, and headed for the park. The bailiffs had had to break the door down, and the few sticks of furniture they found inside were auctioned off on the pavement. The proceeds came nowhere close to paying the rent arrears.

The bailiffs were unperturbed. They'd done their job.

Doug joined the ranks of the town's down-and-outs, depending on the auspices of the Salvation Army for food, shelter and the occasional bath. If the weather was kind enough, he sought out an empty park bench. There, he had nobody to answer to but himself; nobody to question his right to oblivion; nobody to intrude; and nobody to save him – however briefly – from his spiralling descent.

As days turned into weeks he began putting in

an appearance at the broo, realising that he would need some form of remuneration to keep up with his worsening habit. The wifie behind the counter had been kind enough, and not without standards of her own.

He agreed to sweep floors, wash windows, cut grass – anything which would give him the means to buy another bottle and, incidentally, further entitlement to the state's allowance.

That morning he had been tipped off that there might be some work in Drumdarg. The information had been wrong, but Doug was too heartsore, weak and weary to trudge back into town. He'd fallen asleep, hoping, as always, that he might never wake up.

Maisie had gently nudged him back to semi-consciousness, offering him the use of the spare room for the night. Perhaps, she would have to see, there might be something he could do the next day – enough to pay for a day's keep, nothing too heavy. He'd have his bed, his food, and a drink at the end of the day.

Doug had responded to her kindness, putting in a full day's work on nonsensical chores which Maisie dreamed up. He stayed a second night, and a third. And, as he sat in the bar each evening, gradually growing accustomed to the regulars, Maisie became aware that his gentleness, his understanding, was becoming more and more sought after. God knows, wasn't there an answering desperation in every heart?

She allowed him to pull a pint or two, noticing how much more comfortable the men were with a male host behind the bar. As though she were nurturing a child Maisie brought Doug slowly into the light, allowing him a dignity he could barely remember.

In the process, she fell hopelessly in love. Eventually, Doug moved out of the spare room – and into hers.

Maisie was much, much kinder to others than she was to herself. She truly believed that their roles had become reversed over the years, that she had come to depend on Doug far more than he depended upon her. She was also unarguably convinced that Doug's fondness for her would last only as long as he had a roof over his head, and that he found their 'arrangement' a mite too comfortable to risk upsetting.

Yet Maisie dreamed of so much more than fondness. She wanted to be loved, with the same deep and abiding love that she felt for Doug.

If Barra Maclean wasn't the fanciful boy that he was, Maisie would be on her knees right now, praying for a little celestial intervention of her own.

But then that was Barra.

And Doug was Doug.

And she was just Maisie.

CHAPTER 8

Jennifer Pascoe stared at the telephone. She did not want to do this. Finally, she lifted the receiver and began dialling.

One ring, only one. God, what it must be like to wait for that ring, Jennifer thought. She wanted to feel sorry for Violet Pascoe, but it wasn't in her.

'Hello, Violet. It's Jennifer.'

There was a second's silence, no more.

'Do we need to come?'

'I think so. Doctor MacAngus has just left. He said the fluid's building up in his lungs. 'Jim won't go into the hospital. He's . . . resting.'

A sharp intake of breath. 'How long?'

Jennifer gripped the back of the chair. It was a cheap copy of a Charles Rennie Mackintosh design, poorly displayed in the window of Craigourie's only 'antique' dealer. Jennifer had loved it instantly and Jim had brought it home to her, strapped to the top of the Mini, covered by a moth-eaten blanket which had cost him an extra ten-and-six.

'It looks like something from outer space,' she'd laughed, helping him to free the blanket he'd wrapped so carefully around it.

'It's yours,' he'd said, pulling her to him in the dark chill of the November evening.

As Jim carried it up the frost-encrusted path, he'd slipped and landed heavily on his back. But he'd held the chair aloft, safe from harm. For Jennifer it had started then. She'd never been convinced otherwise.

'Jennifer?' The cut-glass accent of Morningside cut into her thoughts.

'I'm sorry, Violet.' She swallowed. 'The doctor doesn't know. Days . . .'

'Can you arrange accommodation? It *is* Sunday.'

'You can stay here. You know that.'

'Better not, dear. Somewhere close, though.'

'Of course we'll stay with you.' The equally cultivated and deeply concerned voice of Donald Pascoe came across the line. Jennifer could hear Violet spluttering in the background.

'We'll be leaving here in about an hour, Jen. We should be there by supper-time. Don't cook. We'll eat on the road.'

'I'll look out for you, Donald,' Jennifer replied, grateful, as she had been throughout, for the quiet strength, the innate understanding, of her father-in-law.

'Is he expecting us?' Donald asked, knowing their sudden presence might alert his son.

Jennifer sighed, fighting the ever-present tears, tears which she'd learned so well to bury in the cold pit that had become her heart.

'Yes,' she answered. 'He's . . . prepared.'

'Hold on, Jen,' Donald said, his own voice breaking. 'We'll be there. Hold on.'

Empty and raw, Jennifer Pascoe slumped down at the small desk, gripping the seat of the damned chair. When this is over, I'll take a match to you, she promised. I'll burn you to hell and back.

But she knew she never would.

Breathing deeply, she tried to summon the energy to move. She raised her head slowly, her eyes reaching for the daylight which streamed into the white-walled room. Suddenly she clapped a hand to her mouth, stifling the scream which had risen in her throat.

Someone was watching her through the window.

As her battered system recovered from the shock, Jennifer marched towards the front door. Yanking it open, she railed at Barra. 'What on earth d'you think you're doing? You gave me an awful fright.'

'Sorry, Mrs Pascoe,' Barra said. 'I didn't mean to.' His face was so full of concern and apology that Jennifer stepped back, holding the door for him to enter.

'What were you thinking of?' she demanded, though more gently.

Barra scuffed himself across the threshold. 'I'm really sorry. I just thought I'd see . . . how yis were doing.'

Jennifer walked towards the turquoise velvet bucket chair and sat down, laying her head in her hands. 'Not good, Barra,' she said.

'I'm no' here to bother yis,' Barra explained, sitting on the yellow sofa.

'What then?'

'Well, I think you should know. I've met someone who can help Mr Pascoe.'

'Aawww, God,' Jennifer cried, her senses reeling. 'Don't come here breaking my heart, Barra. Please don't do that.'

'But I'm not,' Barra insisted, jumping up in his excitement. He came and knelt at her side. 'I met an angel, Mrs Pascoe. Honest to God, I did. He can sort Mr Pascoe if anyone can. I think that's why he's here. I'm *sure* of it.'

Jennifer glared at him, her eyes wild. 'Get out!'

'But . . .'

'Get out, Barra. And don't come back here talking of angels – ever again! There's no angels. There's no God – and there's no angels!'

Barra backed away. 'You're wrong. There's angels, all right. There is!'

Jennifer reached for something, anything.

Barra was gone.

He closed the little gate behind him and stood there, gazing towards the woods. This was much, much harder than he'd thought. If Jamie *was* an angel, he should be *here*! Here beside him, keeping him right, and . . . and not disappearing when he needed him most.

Barra rubbed his young forehead. He couldn't be imagining it. Could he? He just wanted everything to be normal again. Just . . . normal. Maybe he wanted it too much. It was getting complicated, and Barra's feelings had never been complicated.

Not until now.

He lifted his chin and sucked in the warm, clear air, but it wasn't enough. He couldn't taste it, or hear it, or feel it.

How could he feel normal with Mam and Dad not talking, and Mrs Pascoe mad at him, and Jamie coming and going like the Cheshire cat, and Isla arriving in the afternoon?

Isla!

Barra took off, heading back towards the Whig. Just as he turned the corner of the shop, it hit him. If anyone was going to doubt Jamie's existence, it would be Isla. She was just that sort of girl.

Barra slowed. He'd have to enlist Maisie's help. At least *she* hadn't dismissed it all – like Mrs Pascoe had. His brow furrowed at the memory.

How could she not believe in angels and God and things, when everyone was talking about how poor Mr Pascoe would be lucky to make the summer of it?

As he came level with the open door, he could hear Maisie's voice.

'It would be a new start for us, Doug. Away from all this.'

'What's wrong with "all this"?'

'Och, Doug. Y'know what I mean. It's all so . . . so small here. You can't turn sideways without someone taking note. At least I can't.' Barra heard Maisie laugh, but it wasn't her usual laugh. It sounded false.

Barra knew better than to eavesdrop. Knocking on the door, he inched inside.

'It's me. Barra.'

Maisie looked up. 'What's got into you?' she asked. Her voice sounded slightly irritated. It made Barra nervous. He'd been irritating everyone lately.

'Sorry. I just ran over to the Pascoes, but . . .' Even with the sun at his back, and the whole day in front of him, Barra felt more dejected than he could ever remember.

'Lord,' Maisie sighed. 'Yir like a cat on a hot tin roof, so y'are. Come in and sit a minute.'

Doug swung around and peered at him through a haze of cigarette smoke. The lilac cloud spread lazily across the sun-drenched room, distracting Barra momentarily.

'Maisie tells me you had a bit of an adventure in the woods?'

Barra walked across the room, and climbed back into the chair he had left such a short time ago.

'It's not an adventure, exactly,' he said. 'I mean, it's real enough, but . . . Jamie said it would be hard for people to grasp it, the idea of it.'

'Jamie?'

'He's a boy, an angel, actually. But I'm the only one who can see him.'

'An angel, is it?' Doug reached for his glass,

115

holding the smooth spirit in his mouth for a moment before swallowing.

'He is, Doug, and I'm getting pretty cheesed off already, trying to convince everyone,' Barra confided.

'I can't recall ever seeing you cheesed off,' Doug said, smiling across at him. 'Besides, why would you need to convince everyone? Isn't it enough that *you* believe in him?'

'That's what Jamie told me.' Barra nodded. 'The exact same thing.'

'Well then,' Maisie added, a note of finality in her voice. 'That's that.'

Barra guessed that she wanted him to leave but he wasn't ready to, not yet, for he truly did not know where to go next.

'Mrs Pascoe doesn't believe in him. She just about threw me out when I told her.'

Maisie and Doug exchanged glances.

'You told her you'd met an angel? When you were over there? Just now?' Maisie's voice was very quiet.

Doug regarded his glass, shaking his head slowly from side to side.

'Aye,' Barra answered, feeling more nervous by the minute. 'I thought she'd be happy.'

'And she wasn't,' Maisie stated.

'Not a bit.'

Maisie cleared her throat. 'Barra, d'you have any idea how frightened she is right now? Can y'no see that you were adding to her fear, talking about angels, and . . . all that goes with it?'

Barra frowned. He hadn't thought of it like that. Still . . .

'She doesn't believe in God, either.'

'I'm sure she does,' Maisie continued. 'But you can't blame her for feeling a bit deserted at the minute.'

Barra could feel her eyes on him. He looked up. 'But she's *not* deserted! How can she think she's deserted when she's not?'

Maisie closed her eyes. 'Best if you just leave it be for now, Barra.' If Maisie ever had a temper, it came close to showing itself right then.

'But I want her to know she's not deserted. If she'd let me explain, she'd get over that. She'd *know* . . .'

Doug blew a plume of smoke sideways, away from the intensity of Barra's stare. He turned back, his bloodshot eyes sad.

'She might never get over it, Barra, feeling deserted,' he murmured. 'And you mustn't be try-ing her. Not now.'

Maisie slapped her hands on the table. 'It's a grand day. We should be making the best of it.' Pushing herself away from the table, she looked at Barra. 'A strawberry Mivvi would be a good start.'

Barra smiled back. 'It would,' he agreed, his natural enthusiasm returning. 'I'll get them, if you like.'

Maisie shook her head. Holding herself side-ways so she could reach into her pocket, she pulled out a set of keys. Then she unlocked the adjoining door into the grocer's shop, and padded across to the freezer cabinet.

It would be mid-afternoon before the shop benefited from the bright sunshine and, as Maisie returned with her treasures, her vast form blocked what little light there was. Once back in the café, she relocked the door. She was already peeling the wrapper from one of the iced lollies as she approached.

'Thanks, Maisie,' Barra said, reaching for the other.

'*De nada*,' she said.

Doug watched them both for a moment, then rose to walk across to the server. As he poured another generous measure of the golden liquid into his glass, Maisie leaned towards Barra and whispered, 'He knows all about desertion, Barra. Please don't mention it again.'

Barra stared at Doug as he made his way back to the table.

'More secrets?' Doug asked, pulling his chair out to join them.

'No, sir,' Barra stated emphatically. 'None! I won't mention it.'

'Won't mention what?' Doug asked, puzzled.

'I won't mention . . .' Barra glanced at Maisie, the briefest nod indicating that he'd understood her instruction and would keep his promise. 'I . . . I won't be staying.'

With that, he was off again.

Doug shook his head. 'I couldn't put up with him sober.'

'I hope he tells Rose that he's been over by Jennifer's,' Maisie said. 'She needs to put a stop to it.'

'Aye, it's no' the time to be carrying wild tales to the poor lassie.'

'If only . . .' Maisie sighed.

'Aye,' Doug agreed. 'If only.'

CHAPTER 9

Barra left the trail, and wandered deeper into the woods. The wild ferns were already growing tall here and he startled a small roe deer, who sprang with surprise at his approach, darting off to the left and disappearing – just like Jamie had. Barra wanted to search for the fawn she had surely left nestling nearby but he knew he should leave, lest the mother became too afraid to return to her baby.

He turned back towards the trail, entranced by the dappled light which threw mosaics of sunshine across his path. As he reached the mound and clambered on to the old log, he was smiling again. The log was warm and smooth beneath him, and he let his hands play against its ancient surface.

Below him the loch glistened white hot. A soft wind rushed across the surface of a distant field, the grass swaying below it like the waves of an emerald ocean. Barra watched, and waited.

'Barra! Barra!'

He could hear Rose calling him and suddenly realised he was hungry. Well, not hungry really.

Peckish. Yes, that was the word. He set off towards the house.

'Were you calling me, Mam?'

'Are you OK?' Rose was standing at the back door, her hand shading her eyes from the sun.

'Course.' Socks appeared from around the shed, brushing his warm furry body against Barra's legs. He reached to stroke the cat. 'Is it dinner-time?'

Chalmers had set out one of the deckchairs on the back green and had dozed off in the sun, the *Sunday Post* spread across his lap. He stirred himself.

'Are we eating?' he enquired hopefully.

'I'll heat some soup,' Rose replied, 'And there's a bit of Murdo's salmon in the fridge. We can have sandwiches. I'll bring it out when it's ready.'

Chalmers looked vaguely disappointed, then removed his glasses which had fallen sideways across his face, and settled back for another nap.

'Well?' Rose prompted, as Barra followed her inside.

'I told you he'd be there.' He smiled, relieved to find his mother and father on speaking terms again.

Rose paused from opening the can of tomato soup, and laid the tin-opener on the sink. She turned to face her son.

'You're kidding me.'

'No, Mam, I'm not. He was there today. He didn't stay long. He was gone before I got to the Whig. He says I'm the only one who can see him – and Maisie believes it. I think Doug does too.'

'You were in the Whig?'

'Aye, and then I went to the Pascoes'. That didn't go so well.'

'What d'you mean?' Rose asked, a new note of alarm in her voice.

Barra lifted the tin-opener and swung himself up on the draining-board. 'Well, Mrs Pascoe doesn't believe in him, or God – or anything. She got a bit mad at me,' he confessed, spinning the butterfly of the tin-opener with his finger.

'Put that down!' Rose commanded.

Barra laid it down, and looked at her.

'You stay away from Jennifer with this nonsense, Barra. I'm warning you now.'

'It's *not* nonsense, Mam. It makes perfect sense. Why else would an angel be in Drumdarg, if it's not to help Mr Pascoe? Nobody else needs one – not here.'

Don't they now, Rose asked herself. 'What Jim and Jennifer *both* need is their privacy, Barra. You stay away, d'you hear?'

Barra looked fit to burst. 'It's really, really true, Mam. You've got to believe me. I wouldn't lie about it.'

'God,' Rose sighed, folding her arms across her chest. 'I don't know what to believe.'

'About what? And are we getting something to eat or not?' Chalmers appeared in the doorway and scanned the room, his eyes settling on the unopened can of soup.

'D'you want me to get that?' he offered, lifting the tin-opener.

122

'If you like,' Rose answered absent-mindedly. She opened the fridge, and began pulling out lettuce and tomatoes. She set them on the table and looked at them. 'The salmon,' she murmured, re-opening the fridge to reach for the Tupperware container.

Chalmers grimaced. Tupperware had recently been introduced to the village via Sally Walker who, not content with selling Avon cosmetics to every woman in the place, was now arranging 'parties' from here to Inverness.

He guessed that Rose had bought more than she'd intended to at the last get-together, and was now putting all sorts of things in the evil containers in an obvious attempt to justify her extravagance. Chalmers was utterly convinced that the plastic permeated the food in some way, destroying the natural goodness of it.

'Rubbish!' Rose had commented when he'd raised the point.

'What were you talking about, son?' Chalmers asked, returning to the tomato soup.

Rose straightened, flashing Barra a warning glance. She met the pleading in his look and closed her eyes briefly, indicating her permission. Perhaps it was better if Chalmers did know. He might have some idea how to handle it all.

Barra relaxed, aware that he had at last gained his mother's approval.

'There's a boy I met in the woods, Dad. His name's Jamie, and he's . . . he's . . .'

Somehow, it seemed harder to tell his father than he'd thought. He regretted not having told him last night. It would have been easier then, just the two of them, especially after Dad had had a few drams.

'Spit it out,' Chalmers said, peering over his glasses, which he'd rested on the end of his nose for fear of mislaying them again.

'He's an angel.'

Chalmers peered even harder at his son and then, unexpectedly, threw his head back and guffawed with laughter.

'A bloody angel, is it? Well, trust you, Barra. Trust you!' Chalmers' laughter degenerated into a coughing fit, as it inevitably did. 'Damn cigarettes,' he spluttered, fighting to regain his breath. 'I'll give them up as soon as they get to six bob a packet.'

Rose snorted. Cigarettes had gone up to five-and-five just the past week. Chalmers had been swearing to give them up since ever they'd reached three-and-eight.

Barra seemed unperturbed, but there was a hard glint in his eye. 'I didn't expect you to believe me.'

Chalmers looked at Rose.

'*You're* not believing this?' he demanded.

'He's convinced of it,' Rose said quietly.

'You don't *believe* it?'

Rose shrugged again.

'Well, this takes the biscuit! The Yaks must've given you one too many thumps in the head, son. That's all I can say.' Chalmers finished opening the soup and all but threw the tin-opener in the sink.

'And you're worse than he is,' he flung at Rose, before setting off back into the garden. Socks had curled up in the deckchair and was fast asleep. Chalmers didn't risk disturbing the cat and chance another ripping. He marched back inside, and threw himself down on the sofa.

'It's getting too hot out there,' he said, passing through the kitchen for the second time. Barra and Rose were just as he'd left them. It'd be teatime before he'd get his bloody dinner at this rate.

'Your girlfriend'll be here by now,' Chalmers remarked, looking at his watch. 'The bus would've got here half an hour ago.'

'She's not my girlfriend!'

'Well, maybe she'll keep yir mind off spooks and the like!'

Rose glared at him.

Chalmers sighed. He'd never get out of the dog-house at this rate. They'd managed to avoid the mention of angels all the way through the make-shift meal, even though Chalmers could see that Barra was dying to talk about it. He could thank Rose for that. She had managed to change the subject on each occasion, and Chalmers was reluctantly grateful to her.

He smiled at Barra. 'Och, I didn't mean it, son.'

Barra fed the last of his sandwich to the cat. Socks laid it down on the grass and began nibbling. The rustle of a bird's wings in the hedge distracted him, and he set off in stealthy pursuit.

'Don't let him chase the birds, Mam,' Barra urged.

Rose began gathering the soup mugs from the tartan rug she'd laid out on the grass. 'He's your cat. And anyway, it's his nature.'

Chalmers had regained possession of his deck-chair as soon as Socks had realised that food was on the go. He lifted his paper and settled back to read it.

'D'you need a hand?' he asked Rose, shielding his face.

'Huh!' she tutted, and headed for the kitchen.

'I should be cutting the grass,' Chalmers remarked to Barra, noticing the carpet of daisies spreading eagerly across the lawn. 'Still, it's not often I get a day off. I'll cut it later. Maybe get a pint in before I start.'

'I'll probably just go on down to the Whig now,' Barra said, in an obvious attempt to appear nonchalant.

Chalmers smiled to himself. 'See you later, then.'

'I'm off down to the Whig, Mam,' Barra called. Rose was already on her way back. She nodded, and sat down again on the rug. As she watched him disappear from view she lifted her head to Chalmers.

'What did you mean, I'm worse than him?'

'Och, Rose, I didn't mean anything.'

'Aye,' she said. 'You did.'

Chalmers blew out his lips. 'OK, maybe I did.' He frowned. 'I just don't think you should be encouraging him to be any . . . any stranger than he is.'

'He's not strange, Chalmers. How can you call yir own son strange?'

'I don't mean . . . I mean . . . God, Rose, he doesna' have any normal interests. He couldna' even tell you who Cassius Clay or Billy Bremner are.' The frown became a sneer 'Stamp collecting!'

'Lots of boys his age collect stamps, and just because he doesn't want to watch people pulverising each other in a boxing-ring or kicking a stupid ball . . .'

'OK! OK, Rose. Forget it. Forget I mentioned it.'

Rose stared up at him, her eyes glinting emerald with hurt and anger. 'I can't forget, Chalmers. I can't forget . . . anything.' She sniffed, and looked away.

Chalmers felt his heart twist within him. Looking at her, the sun on her hair, her shoulders hunched in pain, he remembered how they were – how they'd always been. And how much, how desperately, he loved her.

'Rosie . . .' He reached to touch her bare arm, melted at the feel of her flesh, warm, so warm. 'Rose . . .'

She didn't look up, but covered his hand with her own.

'I couldn't stand to see him hurt, Chalmers. I don't want to see anyone hurt.'

'You never did,' he murmured. 'And neither do I.' An answering squeeze of his hand encouraged

127

him onwards. 'He's conjured up a friend for himself. It's common enough. And we don't need to be letting that put us at odds . . .'

'But he's so *sure* of it. And he's nearly fourteen, Chalmers. You're always on about how he needs to grow up a bit. Don't you think that's a bit old to be making up imaginary friends?' Rose dropped her arm, and began picking wildly at the overgrown grass.

Chalmers retrieved his hand and shrugged, his jaw once more set. 'I don't think it's anything to worry about.'

'Well, I do! And I think we need to get to the bottom of it.'

Chalmers clenched his teeth.

'D'you think it's hormones?' Rose asked.

Chalmers didn't care what it was. 'What's "hormones"?' he was forced to ask. He had never heard the word.

'Y'know – when you're growing up, and yir body starts . . . making you want things.'

Unbidden, Sheena Mearns came to mind. He sat up.

'Who knows? It'll pass, Rose,' he said, setting off indoors. He reappeared at the back door with a can of lager in his hand. 'Want one?'

'Aye,' Rose answered, surprising him. He only had one left.

'There's just the one,' he called back, somewhat sheepishly.

'Why did y'ask then?'

'I can split it.'

'Don't bother yirself.'

Barra didn't even stop at the clearing. He was almost glad that Jamie didn't put in another appearance. It had all become too . . . difficult.

As he approached the Whig, he could see there were two cars in the car park. The café started to get busier when the days got longer; especially on weekends, when people didn't mind driving out into the country. It was a change from the winter months, when Maisie insisted she'd go bankrupt if it wasn't for the shop trade.

Nobody believed her, though. Maisie had pots of money.

Barra walked into the kitchen. Doug had just closed the bar for the afternoon, and was helping Maisie with the dishes. His sleeves were rolled up and he was wearing one of Maisie's pinnies, which he had wrapped twice round himself without any difficulty at all. He glanced over his shoulder.

'You're back,' he remarked. His alcohol levels had been sufficiently topped up for him not to be disturbed by Barra's reappearance.

'You've got customers?'

'We do.'

Maisie pushed sideways through the swing door, balancing an armful of plates, cups and saucers. She'd changed into a floor-length red pinafore, under which a red and white spotted blouse sent layers of ruffles cascading across her bosom. A scarlet ribbon held back a high ponytail which swung cheerfully at every move.

'Isla's upstairs getting sorted out.' Maisie smiled. 'She'll be down in a minute. We've three tables full.'

'That's grand.' Barra smiled back. 'It's no' even Easter yet.'

'The sun shines on the righteous.' Maisie laughed, removing a large tub of ice cream from the freezer. She set about scooping three servings into the green plastic shells and decorated each one with a triangular wafer. Reaching for a bottle of strawberry syrup, she drizzled it across the ice cream and, tilting her head back, poured some down her throat before recapping the bottle.

'Delish!' she remarked, smacking her lips. Then she placed the plates on a tray and Barra held the swing door open to allow her to return to her customers. He turned his head at the last minute, to avoid having his face crushed by her bosom.

The sound of feet on the wooden staircase caught Barra's attention. The stairs dissected the kitchen wall and ended on the bar side above the hatch to the cellar, where a second flight led downwards. Barra held his breath as Isla reached the last step, waiting for her to come into view.

As she walked into the kitchen, Barra's eyes opened wide in admiration. She'd grown taller, a bit, and she was wearing much more make-up than last year. Heavy black eyeliner hooded her eyes, and her mouth was frosted silver. Last year's titian curls had somehow been pulled poker-straight, falling from a centre parting to her shoulders. A heavy fringe brushed the thick black lashes, and her cheeks had developed mysterious hollows.

She was wearing a green dress which skimmed her figure and ended above her knees, accentuating long white-stockinged legs. Her chest was definitely bigger. Barra tried not to look at it, but he couldn't help it. It was enormous!

'What are you staring at, bratface?' Isla marched past him and into the café. 'I'll see if Maisie needs a hand,' she told Doug.

'She didn't mean it. Give her time,' Doug advised Barra.

'She's beautiful,' Barra breathed, having had no time to recover from Isla's chest – and barely noticing her rudeness. 'Ah, God, I hope Jamie gets to see her.'

Doug, slightly befuddled, had forgotten who Jamie was.

'Who?'

'My angel.'

'Who y'calling yir angel?' Doug grinned, preparing to wash the ice-cream scoop.

'I was jist telling you . . . earlier,' Barra replied, nonplussed at Doug's forgetfulness.

'What was that now?'

'JAMIE!' Barra shouted, at the end of his tether with it all.

'WHAT?' Doug whirled, holding the steel ice-cream scoop aloft ready to batter anyone in striking distance. He was trembling from head to foot.

'Jamie, Doug. My angel.'

Doug leaned heavily against the sink and dropped the scoop into the dwindling suds. He reached for his dram, and realised he didn't have one. Shaking his way towards the bar, he pushed a glass once, twice, three times against one of the optics then knocked back the whisky in a single swallow. A violent shiver shuddered through his narrow frame.

Turning, he walked back to the staircase and reached for the banister post. He fixed Barra with a stare. 'Tell Maisie I'm off for a lie-down,' he instructed. 'And, Barra . . .'

'What is it, Doug?'

'Please don't be here when I get up.'

CHAPTER 10

Marjorie Cunningham stood with her back to her husband, her arms wrapped tightly around herself in an obvious effort to deter his touch.

'I really do not believe you did this.'

'I thought you may have got used to the idea by now,' Stewart murmured.

'Used to it?' Marjorie turned from the tall window, reaching for the floor-length gold damask drapes as though needing their support. Staying her hand at the last moment, she slid her long fingers across their surface, smoothing an invisible crease. Her eyes met Stewart's only briefly. Then she resumed her stance, staring blindly across the mews to the distant dome of St Paul's. 'How could I possibly get used to it?'

'It's only a few days, Marjorie. I thought it might do you . . . do us both good.'

'And you have absolutely no conception of how much I detest the place?'

Stewart bridled. 'You never gave it a chance.'

Marjorie snorted, her thin nostrils flaring. 'How much of a chance did you expect me to give it?

Wasn't it enough that you had to bring me back from our honeymoon anointed from head to foot in calamine lotion?'

'It was a bad time for the midgies,' Stewart agreed. 'But it'll be cooler now.'

'Blizzards, I believe.'

Stewart sat forward on the chesterfield, leaning his elbows on his knees. 'The weather's fine now. Besides, there were blizzards here, too, Marjorie,' he reminded her. 'London's not exactly the south of France.'

'The south of France would be infinitely preferable.'

'Why don't you sit, darling? You shouldn't be on your feet.' Stewart's tone, though light, could not disguise his weariness.

Marjorie whirled to face him. 'Really! Your concern is touching. It doesn't prevent you, however, from forcing me on to a filthy, noisy, unimaginably dreadful train to travel hundreds of miles to visit an *unimaginably* dreadful place. And all of this during the night, when you know how much trouble I have sleeping!'

'It's a fine train, Marjorie. People make the journey every night of the week. And Drumdarg *is* my home. It's not a dreadful place. It's a quite wonderful place.'

Marjorie raised both her hands and clamped her Alice band even closer to her golden skull. 'How can you even think of it as home? Or have you forgotten that you chose to live here? Doesn't it

134

matter that you chose to live with *me*?'

'Of course. Of course it matters.' Stewart sighed heavily, weary to his very bones. 'We'll be back for Easter.' He tried to force a jocular note into his voice. 'I just want a wee look at the auld place.'

'I hate it when you use that Highland slang, Stewart, and we'd better be back for Easter.' With a last furious glance at her husband, Marjorie crossed the marbled floor and reached for the cut-glass doorknob. 'We will not miss Veronica's dinner party. We will *not* miss it, Stewart. I hope we're clear on that.'

Marjorie closed the door behind her.

'Bloody Veronica,' Stewart muttered. 'And bloody, *bloody* dinner parties!'

'The bed's aired now, Mrs Macrae.'

'Right, Hattie. Make it up wi' the white cotton sheets, and be sure to run the Hoover under it.'

'I hoovered already,' Hattie said. 'I told you – a wee while ago.'

'So you did. Och, I'm fair demented with it all.' Helen jabbed the pot roast with a lethal-looking fork. 'As sure as death, that Cunningham dame'll still find something to complain about.'

'But everything looks fine, Mrs Macrae. There's no' a thing she could find fault with.'

'That one could find fault wi' her own shadow,' Helen snapped.

'I'll make up the bed,' Hattie murmured. As she

shambled towards the wide hallway, Helen caught her arm.

'Thanks, hen. It's good of you to come in on yir day off. Murdo's meeting them off the sleeper on Tuesday morning, and I know it's a day or two away, but . . .' Helen sighed heavily. 'I just want to be sure that we're all prepared.'

Hattie raised a diffident smile. 'It's no' as if I'm doing anything else,' she answered.

Helen wiped her hands on her pinny and clapped Hattie softly on the back. 'On you go then. You're welcome to have yir dinner with us when you're through.'

Hattie beamed. 'Thanks, Mrs Macrae. I'd like that fine.'

Helen shook her head sadly at Hattie's retreating back. Poor Hattie. Believing some phantom Valentino was going to appear out of the blue and take her off to God knows what. It's a pity it's just a dream, Helen thought, for if anyone deserved looking after, it was Hattie Macaskill.

Still, she surmised, everyone needs their dreams, and as far as Helen was concerned it was Hattie's dream which kept her this side of madness, not the other way about as folks seemed to think.

She began filling the sink, dumping a potful of potatoes into the water, potatoes which Murdo had plucked from the ground that very day. She inspected them for a moment, already looking forward to the sweet taste of them drenched in good Scottish butter. 'You're a bonny lot,' she stated, her good humour returning. Switching on the wireless, she tutted as Tom Jones burst forth with 'It's Not Unusual'.

'That's enough of you, you vulgar trooshter,' she said, turning the dial until she found something more to her liking. On this occasion it was the Bachelors' version of 'Diane'.

Helen hummed along as she began scraping the tatties. That's more like it, she thought. Good clean-cut boys, they were; their mother would be proud of them. She heard a movement in the hallway and leaned backwards, expecting to see Hattie returning from her chores.

The light streaming through the open front door blinded her for a moment, and she called out, 'Are you finished upstairs already?'

A figure, smaller and thinner than Hattie's, came towards her. As he reached the kitchen door, Barra knocked on the doorframe. 'Hi, Mrs Macrae. It's me, Barra.'

'So it is,' Helen remarked. 'Well, come away in. There's an apple tart in the oven. It'll be ready by the time I finish the tatties. Was it the smell that brought you over?'

'No,' Barra replied, standing in the doorway. He sniffed the air, relishing the warm sugary aroma. 'But it smells great just the same.'

Helen cocked her head towards the big wooden table. 'Sit yirself down. I'll no' be long at the sink.'

Barra did as he was told.

'Is the tart for yir dinner?' he asked.

Helen smiled at him over her shoulder. 'No. It's to be enjoyed when it's ready. And there's aye a spare slice for a passing stranger.'

'I didn't get a chance to come in and see you the last couple o' days,' Barra apologised. 'There's been a lot happening.'

Helen finished with the potatoes and set them in a large pan of water. As she drained the sink and collected the scrapings, she turned towards Barra.

'Hand me one o' them newspapers,' she instructed, indicating the neat stack by the log basket. Barra brought one to her and Helen wrapped the scrapings in it, placing the parcel in a tall bin by the corner of the larder. 'Now,' she said, wiping her hands on her pinnie and pulling out a chair. 'What is it that's kept you from the door?'

Barra grimaced. 'You might no' believe it, Mrs Macrae,' he said hesitantly.

'At my age there's not much left that I don't believe, Barra,' Helen assured him.

Barra took a deep breath. 'Well, after I left here on Friday, after I spoke to Hattie, and after I saw Mr and Mrs Pascoe and went into the Whig, and . . .'

'Barra,' Helen interrupted him, 'The tart's coming out o' the oven in five minutes. D'you think you could tell me before then?'

He grinned. 'I was getting to it. Anyway. . . Anyway, I met an angel,' he finished, an earnest expression sweeping the smile from him.

Helen lifted an arm to the table, and rested her

cheek on it. 'I thought it was today the Gillespie girl was arriving,' she said, a mischievous gleam in her eye.

'No.' Barra shook his head. 'Not Isla. She *did* come today. Isla's great, but she's no' an angel. This was a real one.'

'Who are we talking about then?' Helen asked, the faintest note of impatience creeping into her voice.

'Jamie. He's a real angel. I met him in the woods, on Friday. I've met him since, of course, but he comes and goes a lot,' Barra finished ruefully.

Helen ran a hand across her brow and sighed again. 'I hope it's no' catching,' she remarked, rising to open the oven door.

'What?'

'First we've got poor Hattie seeing some actor in her dreams, and thinking he's coming to whisk her off into the great blue yonder, and now we've got yirself seeing angels in the woods. It's a wonder *I'm* no' wrong in the mind wi' the pair o' yis.'

'It's no' like Hattie's dream, Mrs Macrae. This is real!'

Helen removed the tart and placed it on the counter. 'Och well, don't go telling Hattie her dream's no' real, there's a good lad,' she warned him. 'Poor soul's got enough to contend with. Oh . . . there you are.'

Hattie stood meekly in the doorway. 'That's the room ready, Mrs Macrae. Hello, Barra.'

'Hi, Hattie.' Barra smiled back. 'How y'doing?'

Hattie looked down and away from him. 'Fine, thank you.'

Helen, unsure how much Hattie had heard, busied herself at the sink. 'I'll stick the kettle on,' she said briskly. 'We can all have a fly cup before Murdo gets in and demolishes that tart on us.'

'That's all right, Mrs Macrae. I'll come back up when the dinner's ready.'

'Nonsense. You'll have a wee cup o' tea right now. Won't she, Barra?'

'Aye.' Barra beamed. 'A strupach.'

Helen ruffled his hair. 'That's right, laddie. A strupach it is.'

Barra jumped up and held out a chair for Hattie. 'Your Highness,' he said, grinning.

Hattie sat down, her hands clasped tightly in her lap. 'Och, Barra. You're always tormenting me.'

'No I'm not,' he answered softly. 'I wouldn't do that, Hattie.'

The note of hurt in the boy's voice stabbed at Helen's heart. She felt the sudden prick of long-forgotten tears, and placed a gentle hand on Barra's shoulder.

'Yir as good as gold, Barra. So y'are,' she murmured.

God, what's got into you now, Helen silently reprimanded herself. It's that bloody wife o' Stewart's got you all through-other. Shaking her head in annoyance, she turned her attention back to the tart.

140

'You'll like the story he's brought us today, Hattie,' she said. 'Barra claims he's met an angel.'

Barra sighed. 'It's true. I did.'

Hattie's eyes flew at him, filled with the deepest dread. She threw her chair back and headed for the door.

'I'll . . . I'll come back later,' she cried, her voice full of panic. By the time she reached the front door, she was lumbering along with a frenzied gait, running to escape them both.

'What on earth . . . ?' Helen stood there, holding the tea caddy in one hand, a teaspoon in the other.

'What happened?' Barra implored. 'Did I scare her?'

'It seems you did,' Helen answered, laying the caddy down. 'Though I can't imagine . . .' Then she rapped the counter with the spoon. 'Of course. Angels!'

'What about them? What's wrong with her?' Barra's own voice sounded panic-stricken now.

'Her mother,' Helen answered. 'She'd be thinking that bitch came back to haunt her!'

'I'm sorry,' Barra said, looking abject. 'I didn't mean to frighten her.'

'I know, son. I know you didn't.'

Helen sounded distracted, but forgiving. Definitely forgiving. Barra seized this new opportunity. Avoiding her eyes he suggested, 'Course, her mother must've been a bi . . . besom – to get herself killed like that.'

Helen sat down, all thought of making the tea

gone. 'Well, it was a long time ago, and it's no' for us to be repeating old gossip.'

'It's not,' Barra agreed, eager to do just that. 'So were youse here? When they put her on trial?'

'No, laddie, it was before me and Murdo arrived. But they were right to let her off.'

'Aye. Imagine anyone believing Hattie could murder her own mother,' Barra snorted. 'She should never have had to go to the jail. Putting her through all that – just to let her off. It's ... sinful. It's sinful, really.'

Helen pursed her lips. 'Well, now, Barra, she wasn't acquitted exactly. The case was "Not Proven". It's a verdict they have in Scotland when the jury's no' sure if someone's guilty or ...'

'I know what it is,' Barra interrupted. 'But Hattie couldn't have done anything like that. She *couldn't*!'

'You don't know how badly her mother treated her, son,' Helen said softly. 'If she did do it, no-one round here held her at fault.'

The kettle whistled cheerfully. Helen rose. 'Anyway, it's ancient history. I think it's best left in the past where it belongs. Still,' she added, 'it might no' be a good idea to be talking to Hattie about angels and the like. You can see the effect it has on her.'

Barra nodded. It seemed no-one wanted to tell him what had really happened to Hattie – nor to hear about angels!

He turned to look out towards the gatekeeper's cottage. 'Maybe Jamie's here to help Hattie too.'

'Who's that now?'

'Jamie. My angel.'

Helen leaned against the stove and turned back to Barra.

'Y'know, son, everyone says you're yir mam's spittin' image, but there's a lot o' Chalmers in you.' She opened the oven door and removed the tart. 'Aye, you're a thrawn wee divil when you get something in yir head.'

Barra grinned, already tasting the tart. 'It's no' just in my head, Mrs Macrae.'

Helen looked askance.

'It's all in yir head, Barra. Keep it there,' she warned.

'Have you made a reservation?' Maisie asked, sweeping an arm around the empty café.

Graham looked thoughtful. 'I'm afraid not. But I don't mind waiting for a vacant table.'

Maisie roared with laughter. 'Grab a pew. I'm just getting ready to open the bar. Doug'll be down in a minute. In the meantime,' she said, 'I'll have our hostess take your order.'

Isla sauntered across from the server where she'd been twirling the sauce bottles so all their labels faced outwards, a bored expression on her face.

'You can have what's left of the pancakes and fancies. You're borderline for afternoon tea, though,' she stated. 'There's some fish, if you want that,' she added in a desultory fashion.

Graham raised his eyebrows. 'No "May I take your order, sir?" Or what about "Would you care to see the menu now?" Am I to be extended no interest at all in my culinary comfort?'

Isla stared off at a spot beyond Graham's shoulder, and sighed.

He caught Maisie's eye. She raised her eyebrows, conveying an expression of hopelessness. 'Isla's getting out of the kitchen this year. We'll be training her in the art, so to speak.'

Graham smiled. He'd been aware of the girl's crush on him when she was in Drumdarg the year before. It disappointed him only slightly that she'd obviously outgrown it.

'Actually, the fish sounds good. What is it?'

'Haddock. Haddock, peas and chips. D'you want it, then?'

'Served with your own fair hands, I hope?'

Isla headed for the kitchen. 'Don't get yir hopes up.'

Maisie stepped aside to allow Isla to pass. 'She'll do fine when she settles in again,' she confided, coming to sit by Graham. 'You might have a bit of a wait, though.'

'Has it been busy then?'

'Not specially. A few folks in all at once, and then it died a death. I don't know if the good weather brings them in, or keeps them away. Still, with Easter at the weekend we should see a bit of an improvement.'

'Has Rose any bookings yet?'

'Och, she doesn't bother with bookings. If she doesn't get passing trade, her cronies in Craigourie usually send some folks her way. Though they've no idea they'll be having young Barra to contend with when they get there,' Maisie added.

'He's certainly different from most boys his age,' Graham agreed. 'Still, he's a cracking lad. Always the same, you know? He never seems to let anything get him down.'

'Well, he scared the shite out of Doug today. I still haven't got to the bottom of it.'

'What happened?'

'Oh, Barra's convinced he met an angel in the woods. I think Doug was ready to go along with this latest nonsense, until Barra started shouting at him.'

Graham laughed. 'Barra? Shouting?'

'Well, of course no-one's believing him, and poor Rose must be demented with it all, but he's quite insistent. You know Doug gets a bit . . . vague sometimes, and I think Barra lost the head with him.' Maisie laughed. 'Poor Doug, the last thing he needs is some fairy story. He has to stretch his imagination quite enough, living with me.' She was smiling still, but there was a bitter-sweet sadness behind her words.

Graham drew a deep breath. 'Maybe the bar's not the best place for him, Maisie. Have you thought about that?'

She straightened, scrutinising Graham's face. 'If I thought there was even a *hint* of criticism there . . .'

'You know me better than that, Maisie.'

'Aye,' she warned. 'I hope so.'

'I just had a thought that you might have . . . more of a future . . . away from the Whig.'

'Hmmm. And I suppose Mr Buchanan of Atkinson & Co had nothing at all to do with this new-fangled thought of yours?'

Graham leaned back and shrugged. 'Caught red-handed.'

'That you are, Mr Kerr. That you are.'

The two surveyed each other for a moment. Maisie was the first to speak. 'I told him I'd think about it. No more.'

Graham sat forward again, cocking his head. 'I have to ask, Maisie. Why did you agree to think about it? What would you do without the Whig?'

It was Maisie's turn to shrug. 'Take a cruise. See the world. Spend some time with Doug.'

'But you spend all your time together now.'

'No we don't,' Maisie replied, the sadness more evident now, inverting the natural crescent of her mouth. 'We work. We eat – I eat. Doug drinks. Then we sleep – together, and alone.'

Graham guessed at Maisie's meaning, and looked away.

'So,' he said at last, 'you're looking to take a very long honeymoon?'

'You're far too clever for an accountant,' Maisie retorted. 'Anyway, it's just a thought. If I can keep Doug drunk enough for long enough, he just *might* marry me!'

'He'd be a fool not to,' said Graham, and the sincerity in his voice banished Maisie's melancholy.

'If Atkinsons don't have your nose to the grindstone for the next ten years, you're invited to the wedding. Bali, I thought. They like fat women there.'

Isla returned, a dish-towel shielding her hand from the heat of the plate she set before Graham.

'There y'are,' she said, thumping the plate down.

Graham looked up in surprise. 'Would it be too much bother to have some coffee with it? A slice of bread and butter wouldn't go wrong either.'

Maisie rose, chuckling. 'I'll get it, Isla. You can stay and keep Graham company for a minute.' Isla glanced at Graham, an expression of total indifference indicating her lack of enthusiasm at the prospect.

As Graham reached for the vinegar bottle, Isla rested one hip against the table and folded her arms across her formidable chest. 'Is that your Triumph out the back?'

'Aye. A Vitesse. What d'you think?'

Isla raised her eyebrows, fractionally more interested. 'Is it new?'

'No,' Graham answered, tucking into his supper. 'But it'll do just fine till I can afford a Jag.'

'Like your friend's?'

Graham frowned. 'What friend?'

'Jim Pascoe.'

Graham cut into the snow-white fish, and raised a portion of it to his mouth. 'Jim has a Mini, Isla. In

147

fact it's the same one he had last year when you were here.'

'Well, there's a Jag at his door now. I saw it when I went out for some air earlier.'

'When earlier?'

'About quarter to five. Just before you came in. They must be having visitors.'

Graham pushed his plate away and stood, just as Maisie reappeared with a plate of freshly buttered bread and a cup of coffee.

'How much do I owe you, Maisie?'

Maisie frowned. 'You don't like it?'

'Oh no. It's fine, really. Isla was just saying she'd seen a Jag over by Jim's house. I was going over there after . . .' Graham seemed totally distracted. 'It must be his parents, Maisie. Donald Pascoe drives a Jag.'

Maisie stopped, the awful realisation dawning on her, just as it had on Graham. 'Aw, God. Surely not so soon?'

Graham dug in his pocket. 'I was just there yesterday,' he muttered, his voice ragged with concern.

'Never mind that,' Maisie said, waving away the pound note. 'Just let them know we're here if there's anything . . . Anything at all.' She squeezed Graham's arm. 'Go through the kitchen,' she advised. 'It's quicker.'

CHAPTER 11

Graham rushed up the path, stopping briefly before reaching for the bell. Was it wise to call on them now? Perhaps Jim's parents had simply decided to drive up and spend a few days there? Perhaps there was nothing more sinister to it than a welcome visit before things got too bad? Before Jim . . .

'I heard the car,' Jennifer said, opening the door and smiling at him.

I over-reacted, Graham thought. She looks fine. She looks . . . fantastic.

There had to have been a day, an hour, a moment when he'd fallen in love with Jennifer Pascoe, but Graham was unable to recall it. He only knew that his heart and soul were filled with her. And, having acknowledged this forlorn truth, he determined to deal with it. He was an adult, after all, a fully grown, professional adult.

He could hide it, control it.

But the long, long nights held a terror Graham couldn't control. The nightmares were frequent and horrifying; the guilt and desire saturating the wee small hours with his sweat, stabbing him to the core of his being with the knowledge that he had reached the lowest, most despicable point of his life; a point where he was forced to admit that he was waiting – hopelessly, *hopefully* – for the death of his very best friend in the world.

Jim and he had been inseparable all through university. They'd laughed, drank, capered together; neither too busy to help the other – or to interrupt the long hours of study to down a jar or two at their favourite pub, tucked halfway along one of Edinburgh's ancient cobbled streets.

As soon as he'd graduated Graham had returned to Craigourie, apprenticing himself to one of the older firms on the High Street. The three flights of worn concrete stairs up to the offices proved no obstacle for his lithe frame, and he had often passed Jennifer on the way up as she arrived for work at the insurance company one floor below.

Yet Graham had hardly noticed her then, and it wasn't until Jim had paid his old friend a visit during a week's respite from his father's practice back in Edinburgh that he began to realise how much of a part Jennifer was to play in their lives.

Jim had fallen immediately, totally in love with her, and several months of long-distance wooing culminated in their engagement – by which time the friends had decided to set up their own partnership in Craigourie. And, although Graham was locally known and liked, it had been Jim who made the whole thing work. It was Jim who set up the office, Jim whose quiet charm eased clients from stunned competitors, Jim whose warmth, integrity and sound advice set them on the road to the kind of success Graham had only dreamed about.

And Jennifer was there through it all, the mention of her name enough to light up Jim's face with his love for her. Graham had delighted in his friend's happiness, warmly accepting Jennifer into their lives. They'd become a threesome and, as Graham had stood as best man at the wedding, he'd felt proud and privileged to be there, endorsing their union.

It had stayed that way for a long time. Jim and Jennifer had each other, and they both had Graham. They were still a threesome.

And then it changed. Why, or how, he didn't know. But in the changing, Graham had come to love Jennifer, and to loathe himself.

'Are you coming in?' Jennifer asked quietly, unaware of the dark passion she had ignited in him, her hair gleaming in the evening light, her mouth tilted in that heart-breaking smile.

I'm lost, Graham thought.

'You have company?' he asked.

'Aye. Jim's parents.'

'Is he . . . ? Is he . . . ?'

'He's slipping, Graham,' Jennifer murmured. 'I tried to phone. You weren't home.'

Graham stepped across the threshold and followed Jennifer into the living room. Donald Pascoe rose immediately, grasping Graham's hand warmly in his own. 'Good to see you, son,' he said.

'You too, Donald,' Graham answered. 'I'm sorry . . .'

Donald nodded, and sat, sliding his brandy glass across the tiled coffee table towards him. He wrapped his big hands around it as though he were afraid it would disintegrate before him.

'Violet.' Graham stepped towards her.

Violet Pascoe was sitting on the very edge of the bucket chair, her legs crossed neatly to one side. Immaculate as always in a black blouse and camel skirt, she lowered her sherry glass and reached to twirl the single strand of pearls at her throat.

'How are you, Graham?' she asked, the barest whisper of a smile cracking the powdered porcelain of her expression.

Jennifer had moved towards the kitchen. 'Will you have a dram with us?'

'Uhmm . . . A lager, if you have it.'

Jennifer met his eyes. 'Lager and lime. I can manage that.'

An almost imperceptible sniff from Violet reached Graham's ears.

'. . . Or coffee. A coffee would be fine.'

'Sit down, man. Sit down,' Donald said, patting the sofa beside him. Graham had hardly obeyed the command when Jennifer reappeared before him. She set a tall glass of lager on the coffee table, indicating with the subtlest of expressions that he was to drink it and, in so doing, remind Violet who was in charge here.

'Another brandy, Donald?'

'I don't think so,' Violet said, her voice strident in the hushed room.

Jennifer's eyes never left her father-in-law's.

'Donald?' she asked again.

'Thanks, Jen,' Donald Pascoe answered, draining his glass and proffering it for a refill.

Jennifer returned to the kitchen, ignoring Violet's tight-lipped disapproval.

There was an awkward silence. Graham reached for his lager, unable to broach the subject which had brought them all together. He tried to swallow quietly, but the noise seemed unbearably loud, and he set the glass back down.

'Wish I could say we're happy to be here,' Donald Pascoe said, reaching out to clasp Graham's thigh. 'He's been sleeping since we arrived. I haven't even seen him yet.'

'*We* haven't seen him yet,' Violet stated. 'It seems I'm to ask permission to see my own son.'

'Violet,' Donald warned. 'Jennifer knows better than any of us what's needed.'

Jennifer's eyes met Graham's as she stepped back into the room. He saw the quiet determination in them, and knew it must be masking the host of emotions she seemed to be eternally holding at bay. His admiration and love for her increased even as he watched her.

Finally she sat, glancing at her watch. For some reason, Graham became aware that the large black-framed clock which had hung above the desk had been taken down. There was the faintest imprint of its outline on the white wall. He tried to remember when he'd last seen it, but couldn't.

'I take it you'll continue in practice?' Violet asked, pulling him from his thoughts.

'Yes,' he answered uncomfortably. It was just like Violet to put him on the spot like this. She had never forgiven Jennifer and him for 'stealing' her son from the family business. Graham knew that if he'd answered no, she would accuse him of lying. But admitting it, admitting that he was soon to be on his own, seemed cruel – and unnecessary.

'Of course you must.' Donald came to his rescue. 'You've both worked so hard at it. Jim wouldn't want it any other way.'

As though on cue, a soft coughing reached their ears from across the hall. Jennifer and Violet both stood. 'I'll see if he's awake,' Jennifer said, prepared to stare Violet down.

Violet's mouth pursed, but at last she nodded slightly and Jennifer left them, softly closing the living-room door behind her.

Donald and Graham busied themselves with their drinks, quietly discussing the effects of the Budget, neither of them making a great stab at it. Violet remined silent.

Finally they heard footsteps making slow progress down the hall. Donald leaped to open the door, and for a long, heart-breaking moment he clasped his son to him, holding Jim as though he would never, never let him go.

Graham's heart clenched with pain and he

looked down, staring blindly at his misshapen reflection in the polished tile of the coffee table.

Jim eventually extricated himself from his father's embrace. 'I need what breath I've got, Dad,' he gasped, smiling weakly up at the big man.

As Donald and Jennifer held back, Jim slowly, painfully, walked towards his mother. Violet made no move towards him, but her eyes never left his face. As Jim came level with Graham he held out his left arm, a trembling wave of the fingers acknowledging his friend's presence. Only then did Violet rise.

'I wanted to come sooner,' she said, stroking her son's face, holding him at arm's length while she inspected him. 'But I'm here now. I'm here to look after you.'

'I'm well looked after, Mum. And you were here a couple of weeks ago.'

Graham was shocked at how much more of an effort it seemed for Jim to talk than the day before, his breathlessness increasing with each word. Violet led him to the sofa and Graham rose, pulling the coffee table aside to allow Jim to sit more comfortably.

Jennifer had disappeared back into the kitchen, returning with a glass of iced water. Soundlessly Jim took it from her, smiling up at his wife in gratitude. He drank from it slowly, then set it down.

'Am I to be watched every minute?' he asked, looking at each of them in turn. 'Thanks for coming,' he added, a wan smile lifting the corners of his cracked, dry lips.

'I'll make some coffee,' Violet offered, walking towards the kitchen with a proprietory air. Jennifer sighed.

'Sit. Sit,' Jim said, stopping Violet in her tracks. She turned to stare at him. 'Just . . . sit down, Mum.'

Violet did as she was asked, and another awkward silence ensued as everyone waited for Jim to regather his strength.

Donald remained standing by the window behind his son. He reached to lay his hand on Jim's shoulder, as though he needed to hold on to his son, rather than the other way round. 'So what's new in Drumdarg?' he asked, his tone unnaturally breezy.

'I just came from the Whig,' Graham said, glad of the chance to have something other than Jim's illness to concentrate upon. He turned to Jim. 'I had a word with Maisie. She *is* thinking of selling.'

Jim raised his eyebrows.

'Who would want to buy that old place?' Violet asked.

'It's a damn fine property,' said Donald, coming to sit on the arm of the sofa. 'A lot of potential there.'

'Hmmph. For what?' Violet asked. 'It hasn't had a coat of paint in years. The shop looks quite . . . dismal.'

'There's a company down south interested in it,' Graham said. 'They're looking to set up a chain of bistros, and they're using Atkinsons to negotiate the terms. We've been more or less promised the account.'

Donald let out a low whistle. 'Atkinsons! Well done, lad. Well done.' He clapped Graham on the back. 'Even here in the Highlands there's bound to be a shift in the market. It wouldn't take a dunce to see that the tourist industry could blossom, and a lot of the older properties are prime for the picking.'

'I never heard of such a thing.' Violet dismissed the idea. 'Who on earth would expect to find a bistro *here*? It's hardly the big city.'

'Craigourie's growing by the day,' Graham ventured. 'They opened a second Wimpy at Christmas, Violet. It won't be too long before Drumdarg becomes a suburb, and "bistro" is just a modern version of a café, after all. They could open the Whig right up, attract quite a crowd if it's done right.'

'I'd miss the shop,' Jennifer mused. 'And it wouldn't be the same, somehow. It wouldn't seem like being in the country any more. The Whig was part of the reason we built the house here. Wasn't it, Jim?'

Jim nodded. 'I think there's enough absentee landowners as it is. Still, things change . . .' he murmured. 'Life goes on.'

Jennifer's expression shifted. 'I suppose we have to accept it.'

'We don't have to accept anything of the sort,' Violet said.

'Yes. Yes, we do.' Jim nodded, his eyes back on his mother.

Violet reared, her expression fierce. Then, just as suddenly, she sunk back into the chair and turned to Jennifer. 'I'm afraid I'm rather hungry, dear. That awful journey always takes it out of me.'

Jennifer looked at Donald in surprise. 'I . . . I thought you'd be eating on the road,' she stammered.

'Violet was anxious to get here,' he answered, a note of apology in his voice.

'Well then, I'll start supper. There's not a lot in. I was going into the town tomorrow to stock up. But I have some mince in the fridge. I could make some . . . um, what? Spaghetti?'

'Oh, a sandwich would be fine. I'm not *that* hungry,' Violet said. Jennifer glanced at Donald again. She knew his hearty appetite of old. But he shook his head, and she realised that he, too, had little need of food when faced with the reality of his son's wasted body.

She smiled. 'That won't take long, then. And there's always plenty soup.'

'Soup.' Jim grimaced. 'The spaghetti sounded good.'

'I'll make that tomorrow, if you like,' Jennifer promised, knowing that Jim would be lucky to force down more than a forkful.

'Well, I'll be off. I ate already at the Whig,' Graham lied. 'And I know you'll be wanting the evening to yourselves.'

Nobody argued.

Jennifer rose to see him to the door and he turned on the step, looking back towards her.

'I'll come by tomorrow, see how he's doing.'

'The doctor's calling in again later,' Jennifer said, her voice low. 'He wanted to put him in the infirmary today, but Jim won't have it.'

'Did he say . . . ? How long?'

Jennifer bit her lip. 'Days,' she murmured, shaking her head. 'Doctor MacAngus warned me he could slip into a coma any time. I . . .' Jennifer shook her head. 'I'd almost prefer that. I can't stand to see him battling with the pain. The injections seem to be wearing off more quickly all the time.'

'Oh, Jen . . .'

She lifted her shoulders helplessly and, for the briefest moment, Graham caught the infinite pain behind her eyes.

'I don't know how we'd have managed without you, Graham. You've been so good to us both. But then, you know us better than anyone.'

Graham tried to smile. 'I've been about as much good as . . .'

Jennifer reached to hush the words, and a shock rushed through him as her finger brushed his mouth. 'Come by tomorrow when you can.' She smiled again. 'If you could keep Violet out of my hair for even an hour, I'd be eternally grateful!'

Graham nodded. 'See you, then.'

'See you.'

Graham climbed into the Triumph and looked back up the pathway. Jennifer raised a hand in a tiny wave, and closed the door.

Graham shivered, gripping the steering wheel in an effort to pull some of its warmth into his frozen veins. He could feel Jennifer's touch still, as though she had stamped it indelibly on his lips.

God forgive me, he prayed, turning the key in the ignition. What kind of miserable bastard am I?

'Where can I plug this in?' Isla asked, holding the brown cord of the Dansette record-player.

Maisie lifted the table-lamp and pulled out the bedside cabinet, revealing the socket behind. 'You'll have to do without this if you want to play your records,' she remarked, setting the small lamp on top of the dressing-table.

'I hardly need the light, the days are getting so long,' Isla answered.

A slightly worried expression creased Maisie's brow. 'Well, be sure to pull the curtains if you're undressing. That window looks right out over the road, and we want the customers *in*side, spending their money – not *out*side leering up at you.'

Isla looked faintly embarrassed. 'I hate it,' she said, looking down at her bust.

'Don't be daft,' Maisie retorted. 'Half the lassies your age would give their right arm to have your figure.'

'It's not fashionable,' Isla argued. 'You don't see

Mary Quant, or Jean Shrimpton, or . . . or Cathy MacGowan with big busts.'

'They can't help what they don't have,' Maisie said. 'And I can assure you that a big bust will never go out of fashion, not as long as there's one man left on the planet.'

'I hate men too,' Isla said, bending to plug in the Dansette.

Maisie sat on the bed. 'Not according to your mother,' she said softly.

Isla kneeled at her feet, sorting through her collection of forty-fives with rather more concentration than was needed.

'Well?' Maisie prompted. 'What's it all about?'

'I don't want to talk about it, Maisie.'

'Are you in trouble?'

'No, I'm not!' Isla answered, her voice surly.

'Then what's this about hating men? D'you have a steady boyfriend at home? Or *did* you have?'

Isla shook her head. 'I go out. But I haven't . . . you know.'

Maisie waited.

'I took a boy back to the house,' Isla continued, her voice low. 'We were just necking, well . . . petting a bit. But that was *all*! Anyway, Mum and Jack came home early from the pictures. They said they were going for a drink after, but I think *he* just said that to see if he could catch me.'

'He?'

'Jack. He's always on at Mum that I'm boy-daft – which I'm not!'

'You're still not getting on then?'

'I don't know why she married him. He's never liked me.'

'Perhaps he just worries about you – as any father would.'

'He doesn't worry about me, Maisie. He calls me a tart when Mam's not there. He says I look like Mandy Rice-Davies, except I'm not blonde. And she's a . . . she's a prostitute!'

Maisie frowned. 'How often does he talk to you like that?'

'All the time. And he . . . he looks at me.'

Maisie held her breath. 'How does he look at you?'

Isla glanced away. 'You know . . .'

'Have you told your mother any of this?'

Isla shook her head. 'She wouldn't believe me. She takes his side all the time. It's always me that's in the wrong. Never him.'

'You should tell her, Isla,' Maisie said. 'I'll talk to her, if you like.'

Isla sat up, grabbing Maisie's plump knees. 'Please don't, Maisie. It doesn't matter, as long as I'm here. Please don't say anything,' she begged.

Maisie held her niece's hands in her own. 'I won't then, if you don't want me to. And you know you're welcome to stay here as long as you like. But you'll have to go home sometime, Isla. You'll have to tell your mother the truth.'

Isla slumped again. 'I only just got here. Please

can I stay for a while? I'll . . . I'll think about it. I will.'

'OK,' Maisie agreed. 'You think on it.' She rose, and swished towards the door. 'But not tonight, darling girl. I think Doug can handle the bar for an hour or two yet, so I'll bring us up a wee something to eat and we can listen to that delicious Mick Jagger together.'

Isla laughed. 'You're absolutely the only grown-up I know who thinks Mick's delicious.'

'I could eat him for breakfast,' Maisie said, snapping her jaws together as she closed the door behind her. Isla's laughter followed her as she walked along the landing, but Maisie was no longer smiling.

She paused on the landing, listening to the sound of the Beatles emanating from Isla's room. 'I Feel Fine' came to an end as she made her way downstairs.

Well, Mr Strachan, I don't feel fine, Maisie thought. And I wish to God I knew what to do about it.

Maisie walked through the kitchen and entered the bar to find Doug twiddling the knob on the television set which took pride of place in the far corner. The screen flickered and wavered before settling on the image of a Ku Klux Klan member, who was screaming vitriolic abuse at an absent Martin Luther King.

Who ever heard of a *black* doctor? And who had given *him* the right to lead five thousand protesters in a civil rights march to Montgomery, Alabama? How had he *dared*? The interview concluded with the Klansman's threat that Dr King would soon follow his militant brother, Malcolm X, into the wilderness.

'How brave are the men in hoods,' Maisie remarked.

Doug glanced at her, as did the couple of men drinking quietly at the bar. None of them had ever heard such bitterness in Maisie's voice.

She swept them with a look, and returned to the kitchen.

CHAPTER 12

Chalmers had decided on an early night, and had given Rose the briefest peck on the cheek before retiring. Unable to settle, she'd pulled out the ironing-board and set to. By ten-thirty she was finished. Finished, exhausted, and still wide awake, the memory of the fracas at supper-time playing over and over in her head like an irritating tune she couldn't push from her mind.

She'd hardly taken the roast out of the oven when Barra raised the subject of Jamie. Rose had whirled on him, her nerves frayed beyond redemption.

'Shut UP!'

Barra had speared her with a look of such naked hurt that she'd wanted to hurl the roast to the floor and grab him to her. Even Chalmers had seemed shocked at her outburst.

'For God's sake, Rose. What's eating you now?'

'I'm sick to death of it all!'

'What all?'

'You. Him. The lot of yis!'

Chalmers and Barra exchanged a glance and

carried on eating, shovelling down their meal in record time. Barra had disappeared upstairs as soon as they'd finished and Chalmers had followed a scant hour later, leaving Rose alone with her thoughts, and the ironing, and her conscience.

When she could stand it no longer, she climbed the stairs. The noise of Chalmers' snoring drilled into her at every step, the possibility of a decent night's sleep becoming more remote with every footfall. She stopped at Barra's door and entered quietly. He lay facing her, his legs bent towards his chest, Socks curled in the hollow of his knees.

Rose bent to kiss her son, and the cat raised his head a fraction, nuzzling her fingers. 'I love you too,' Rose whispered, stroking Socks's ears. He purred contentedly at her touch and Rose reached once more towards Barra, tenderly pushing the auburn curls from his forehead. She gazed at him a moment longer and closed her eyes; that one moment of pure love filling her so completely that she thought her heart must break.

'I'm sorry, Barra,' she whispered.

He stirred, opening his eyes to squint up at her. Then he smiled drowsily, and went straight back to sleep. Rose kissed him once more, and left.

Frazzled and depressed, she climbed into bed, holding her breath to avoid signalling her presence to her sleeping husband. Chalmers had reached for her just the same, the weight of his arm pinning her to his side. She had automatically tried to pull away from him, to keep this new and detested distance between them.

Then, certain that Chalmers was asleep and would be none the wiser, Rose relinquished herself to the familiar comfort of his embrace.

She didn't know when she had drifted off, only that her sleep had been fitful, and plagued by sinister images. She had wakened once, bolting upright and searching for the solace of consciousness. Chalmers had rolled noisily from her, but the infested shadow of the nightmare pounded in her heart and her temples throbbed, labouring to rid her mind of the still-present terror.

She'd thrown back the quilt, anxious for the soothing coolness of the night air on her body; willing herself to abandon the dream to the new dawn lightening the sky beyond the bedroom window.

After a moment Rose lay back down, wrapping her body around Chalmers and inhaling the musky scent of him. And, between sleep and consciousness, she became aware that this, the oldest nightmare of all, was returning to claim her.

If she'd been so undeserving of a mother's love, how in the world could she hold on to a husband who was, before and after everything else, just a man?

The next morning Rose had risen, stiff and unrested, and glad that the night was behind her.

Barra arrived down for breakfast just as

Chalmers was leaving, and the two joked together as they did most mornings.

Only Rose seemed to have lost her sense of humour.

Finally Chalmers set off, leaving Rose and Barra together. 'I'm sorry I shouted at you last night,' Rose began, anxious to clear the air.

'I know, Mam. I heard you when you came into my room,' Barra answered. 'It's all right, anyway. I know I was getting on yir nerves. I got on a lot of people's nerves yesterday,' he added, not unduly worried. 'You wouldn't think folks would get so . . . *upset* by angels.'

'Everything seems to be upsetting me.' Rose sighed.

'Why?' Barra was truly interested.

'Och, it's nothing.' Rose reached for the Sqeezy. She summoned her energy, determined to keep her tone light. 'This angel's still on the go then, is he?'

'Hah! On the go's right, Mam. He's all over the place! I never know where he's going to turn up next.'

Jamie had been waiting for him in the woods yesterday as he'd set off for the Whig. But they'd barely greeted each other before the angel said he was needed elsewhere – and disappeared. No wonder Maisie had been curious.

And then, as he'd left the big house later in the day, Jamie suddenly appeared at his side again. Barra had just begun to tell him about poor Hattie's reaction when the angel had thrown himself forward in the most amazing cartwheel.

'Wow! Yir great at that.'

Jamie landed gracefully upright, his smile as dazzling as ever. 'Don't worry about Hattie, Barra.'

Barra had grinned back, relieved. 'Can you tell me what it is we're going to be doing, then?'

Jamie had shrugged. 'I'm working on it. It all takes time.'

That was the thing about angels. Everything they said set your mind off in different directions. It struck Barra then that maybe angels didn't have the same sense of time. You wouldn't really, if time was all you had. You wouldn't have to go to school, or turn up for meals. He wondered if angels ate. And how was it you stayed the same age? And what about baby angels? They'd be cherubs, of course, but would they ever grow up? And would they learn to speak? What about language? Did they have a language of their own in heaven? And would . . . ?

All of these thoughts had gone through his mind in a split second, but before he could ask Jamie about any of them, he'd realised that he was once more alone.

Barra caught his mother's arm. 'He's still around, Mam. That's what I wanted to tell you and Dad yesterday. But you lost the head with me, and I didn't get a chance.' Barra's tone was accusing.

Rose tried to smile. It became more of a grimace. 'I said I was sorry.'

'Och, it's OK.' Barra sighed. 'He hasn't told me

169

yet, what he's here for. But he will. And . . . y'canna help believing him – when he tells you things. I mean, I can't just *ignore* him, Mam.'

Rose did smile then. 'I suppose not.'

'And I'm still the only one who can see him,' Barra reminded her. 'It's an honour, don't you think?'

'I suppose. I just hope he doesn't turn up here,' she added, still smiling. 'I don't want him frightening the bedders.'

'I keep *telling* you no-one else can see him.' Barra grinned, delighted at this new approach. 'D'you think we'll get any foreigners this year?'

'I wouldn't mind getting some Italians again.'

'Yeuch!'

'The Iacobellis are a bit of an exception, son. That couple we had the year before last were first class.'

'I was hoping for Australians.'

The previous year a young Australian couple had arrived to spend two nights with the Macleans. They had been hitch-hiking around the world, and Barra had questioned them so thoroughly and constantly about their travels that they had crept off in the early morning hours, leaving a note of apology on the kitchen table, together with full payment. A second night of his incessant curiosity had apparently been more than they could stand.

Rose shook her head at the memory. 'The Australians were good souls, right enough,' she murmured, 'but I love having the Italians.'

'That's because you want to go to Venice.'

Rose turned, her hands dripping suds.

'How d'you know that?'

'Because I heard you and Maisie talking about it once. And Mr and Mrs Pascoe went there on their honeymoon, and your face was full of it when Mrs Pascoe was describing it. And Dad said it too. He said he'd like to take you.'

Rose frowned. 'I don't remember your father ever saying that.'

'Aye he did, Mam. Remember the night me and him went down to the Whig to pay Maisie for your party? Remember, Mam?'

'I wasn't there.'

'I *know*! But Maisie said to Dad that you'd always wanted to go to Venice, and he should have taken you there for yir birthday – instead of wasting . . . how did she say it?' Barra concentrated. '. . . Instead of wasting his money entertaining folks who weren't fit to lick yir boots.'

Barra scratched his head. 'Something like that . . . Anyway, Dad said he wished he *had* taken you to Venice. It was a good party, though, wasn't it, Mam?'

Rose nodded. So Maisie had noticed too.

Although she cringed inwardly at the thought, Rose was, at the same time, grateful for knowing it. Rose could think of nobody whose advice would be more welcome than Maisie's; nor would she be afraid to confide in her friend, secure in the knowledge that anything she might tell Maisie would go no further.

I'm sorry I didn't talk to her sooner, Rose

171

thought, deciding to call into the Whig as soon as she'd caught up with her housework. She became aware that Barra had asked her a question, and was waiting for an answer.

'What was that?'

'I was just asking you why we don't go to church?'

'We just don't, Barra. We don't have the time.'

'Yes we do.'

'No we *don't*! Dad's working most weekends, and I've got the bedders.'

'Only half the year, you do. Besides, the Yaks' shop's open *all* the time, and they're never out of the place. They're in the church more than they're at school.'

'Catholics are different.'

'How are they different?'

'They just are! God, Barra, can you no' just leave it be?'

'You're getting aggravated again.'

'I've just got a lot on my mind,' Rose protested.

'So have I!' Barra retorted indignantly. 'I've got an awful lot on my mind!'

'What else is new?' Rose sighed.

Barra reached for the back door. 'People are getting awful sarcastic round here.'

Rose stared at him. 'I'm not being sarcastic. You've *always* got a lot on yir mind.'

'Well, now I've got more!' Barra said, opening the door and setting off down the path.

'Be back for yir dinner,' Rose called after him.

Barra turned at the fence, lifting his chin to regard her with a look of pure determination. 'I might no' have the time. I've things to take care of,' he called back, and stamped off into the woods.

Rose watched until he was out of sight. Maybe he *is* growing up, she thought. He's never been that argumentative before.

'There's no' much doing on a Monday,' Maisie said, helping Isla to clear the breakfast dishes. 'Olive'll be in at nine. Maybe you could help her in the shop.'

Isla shrugged. 'Glad to.'

'Did you sleep well?'

'Aye. I always do – here.'

'Good then.' Maisie opened the back door. 'God love us, there he is,' she said.

'Who?'

'Barra.'

Isla grimaced. 'He was here yesterday.'

'He's here every day,' Maisie said. 'Two and three times a day.'

'How d'you put up with him?'

'Och, he's no bother. He's got a way with him.'

'Aye, just like the rest.'

Maisie turned at the bitterness in Isla's voice, her eyes questioning.

'He stared at me.'

'Of course. What did you expect?'

'I get tired of it.'

'Well, try being *my* size!' Maisie exclaimed, and the two of them giggled.

'Good morning,' Barra called from the car park, somewhat nervously, Maisie thought.

'Good morning yirself. Where y'off to?'

'I don't know. Depends.'

'On what?' Maisie asked.

'On Jamie.'

'Jamie?' Maisie enquired. 'Your *friend*?'

'Aye.' Barra stepped across the threshold and gazed directly at Isla, not at her chest, but right *at* her. 'He's an angel.'

Isla glanced at Maisie and snorted her disbelief. 'I heard.'

Barra continued to stare at her. 'You'll see. You'll all see.'

'See what?' Isla asked scornfully. 'That yir soft in the head, Barra Maclean?'

'I'm not,' Barra said. 'As a matter of fact, I'm thinking of trying for the university.'

'Hah! Are you taking a degree in havering?'

'I'm no' havering,' Barra replied, almost nonchalant. 'I'm telling the truth.'

The sound of a bicycle approaching caught his attention and he turned, missing the whirling of Isla's finger at her temple as she signalled his mental incompetence to Maisie.

'It's five to nine. There's no time to be blethering,' Olive admonished them all as she climbed awkwardly from her bike and entered the kitchen. She cast a single disapproving glance at Isla's bosom. 'Will you be giving me a hand?'

'Aye,' Isla answered. 'You'll be needing all the

help you can get wi' that queue at the door.'

Olive tutted and shook her head, reaching for the shop keys. Maisie handed them over, watching with amusement as Isla waddled behind Olive towards the shop, imitating Olive's scuffling progress as she went.

'You wouldn't think they'd get on together,' Barra mused.

'It never ceases to amaze me,' Maisie concurred. 'Diversity, Barra. It's a wonderful thing.'

'So it is,' Barra replied. 'I hope Isla gets to like me a bit better, though. I like her.'

Maisie lifted his chin. 'I'll put in a good word for you,' she promised. Then, holding his gaze, 'You wouldn't be going by the Pascoes', would you?'

'I might,' Barra answered hesitantly.

'Not a good idea, Barra. Jim's parents have arrived, and Jen's got enough on her plate right now.'

'Aye, but . . .' He looked down, away from her. 'I asked Jamie if Mr Pascoe could have hair for his birthday. I didn't think that was too much to ask, but Jamie said he couldn't promise anything.'

Maisie swallowed. 'Barra, I think we've all been very patient with you. But it really is time you got rid of this notion of yours.'

Barra's expression turned smug, surprising her. 'Jamie said that, too. He said it would get more and more difficult for people to believe me. I told him I didn't like Mam bawling at me and pushing me down the stairs, and getting thrown out of people's houses and everything, and you know what he said?' Barra paused for effect. 'He said I wasn't to take it personally.'

'I'd be taking it very personally, if I were you,' Maisie advised.

Barra shook his head, conviction in every movement. 'You might not believe me, Maisie, but it's all true, I haven't made it up, y'know.'

'I'm sure you believe it, Barra. But I have to say yir beginning to sound *un poco loco, mi amigo*.'

'What's that?'

Maisie headed towards the stove. 'Bonkers!'

Chalmers raked in the back of the van. He could have sworn he had at least one double socket left. Swearing with mounting frustration, he gave up the search and set off from the Wilsons', heading the van towards the town centre. His local supplier occupied premises at the opposite end to Boots. The thought that he might find a pretext to enter the chemist's shop tickled his mind for a moment, before he dismissed it with a mixture of guilt and annoyance.

He parked the van and got out. The Iacobelli boys were hanging about Woolworth's window, making eyes at the lassie behind the sweetie counter. The boys did little to lift Chalmers' black humour, but he was caught for a moment, marvelling at the oddity of nature which could produce two such identical human beings.

Primo, the older by seven minutes, must have

felt his stare, and turned to catch Chalmers' eye. He nudged his brother and the pair simultaneously raised a two-fingered salute. Chalmers stepped towards them but the two took off, darting across the empty High Street and into the haven of Mama's impregnable protection.

Chalmers cursed for the umpteenth time that morning, and glanced at his watch. The day was half over and he was no further forward. He entered the electrical shop, determined not to waste another minute.

He opened the back door of the van and was bending to place his purchases in their proper container when he felt a tap on the small of his back. Glancing over his shoulder, he straightened immediately, clattering his head on the doorframe.

'Shite!'

'Oh, Chalmers. Are you all right? I didn't mean to have such an effect on you!' The amusement in Sheena's dark eyes belied the concern in her voice.

'It's my own fault,' Chalmers mumbled, rubbing his temple.

'Poor Chalmers.' Sheena reached to brush her long fingers across the welt, but he moved back a fraction at the last moment, and her hand dropped to her side.

'I was just going over to Bremner's for a bite to eat.' Sheena smiled. 'Care to join me?'

'I havena' the time,' Chalmers replied. 'I've . . . I have to get back to the job.'

Sheena placed a hand on her hip, regarding him

carefully. 'Perhaps some other time, then?'

'I . . . I'm busy.' Chalmers set about closing up the van, trying to avoid looking at her, trying to avoid the open promise which danced in her eyes. Get going, he ordered himself. Get out of here. Away, away from her. He made for the driver's door.

'I'm mistaken then?'

Go, Chalmers. Just keep going. 'About what?'

Sheena stood on the edge of the pavement, swinging her handbag gently at her side. She reached to lift her collar, then ran a hand slowly across the V-necked opening of her blouse before letting her fingers slide inside and come to rest on the swell of her breast. Chalmers followed the movement, flushing as he finally looked away.

'I thought we had something going, Chalmers. Just a wee flirtation, anyway. Nothing to get so hot and bothered about. As a matter of fact, I'd been expecting to hear from you before now. I don't think I imagined what happened between us at the Whig.' She *was* amused at him, damn her!

'You were mistaken.'

Her eyes glinted for a second, then swept over him again, a long, velvet stroking that brought beads of sweat to his forehead.

'No strings.' Sheena smiled again, holding him in her stare. 'Just a wee flirtation. That's all.'

Chalmers sucked in his breath, the roaring of his blood deafening him. Still he kept silent, the metal door handle scalding in his grip.

'It's half-day Wednesday,' Sheena reminded him. 'It would be grand to take a drive somewhere . . . away from here. I'm off at one. If you happened to be around the back station, you'd probably catch me there about ten past. I like to watch all the comings and goings. So many people, off on adventures.'

Sheena turned the corner and swung her way down Corbett Street. She was one of the few women left in Craigourie who wore seamed stockings. Chalmers watched, hypnotised, for a moment before tearing his gaze from her and climbing into the van. He plucked a grubby rag from the dashboard and wiped his brow, wincing as he brushed the forgotten bruise.

He worked in the empty house until almost three o'clock before stopping to eat. As he opened the piece that Rose had so routinely, carefully, packed for him, his heart lurched. I can't do this, he told himself. I can't. In fact, he'd been telling himself just that every other hour for the past two weeks.

Well, here it was. Decision time. He had known it was coming. It had been a simple matter of which of them would be first to bring it up, put into words what had started that night.

But Chalmers was aware that he would never have known quite how to do it, what to say. He had to admit that Sheena was much more practised in the ways of these things than he was.

And with the admission came a new, and final,

realisation. He wanted no part of Sheena Mearns – nor her dangerous games.

Chalmers munched happily, his resolve returned in full measure. He was his own master, after all. He could more than resist the charms of Sheena Mearns. As he put the cap back on his flask, he looked at the calendar Mrs Wilson had hung on the kitchen wall. Wednesday would be the fourteenth, a full two days from now.

He had ample time to think about it . . . if he were to change his mind.

Not that he would.

CHAPTER 13

'What was there to talk about?' Maisie asked, dismissing the subject almost before Rose had raised it.

'C'mon, Maisie,' Rose said. 'She was all over him. I know I wasn't the only one who saw it.'

'That one's been all over every man who ever gave her a second glance,' Maisie jeered. 'God, Rose, Chalmers was half-cut. He'd never even have danced with her sober.'

'It was a bit more than dancing, Maisie. He couldn't look me in the eye when he sat down.'

'He couldn't look anyone in the eye.' Maisie laughed. Then, realising that Rose was in need of a great deal more than a flippant remark, she leaned forward across the table.

'Look, if it's made you that unhappy, we *will* talk about it. I'll get us something to eat.'

Rose shook her head. 'I'll be making the supper soon. I'm no' for anything, thanks.'

'Well, *I* am! And Doug's been slaving away at a hot stove the past hour. I had a taste for a nice pastry,' Maisie confided. 'He makes the lightest turnovers you've ever put in yir mouth.'

'I know,' Rose said. 'I've tasted them before now.'

'*Asseyez-vous*. Back in a jiff!'

Rose was already sitting, her fingers playing nervously across the scarred oak table-top as she waited for her friend's return. She surveyed the empty café, wondering for the umpteenth time why Maisie even bothered to keep it open.

Maisie returned, resplendent as ever. Today's apple-green creation was handsomely embroidered with hosts of golden butterflies. As she set the pastries and coffee down, she reached to pat Rose's hand.

'Now, there's nothing bad but could be worse. Tell all!'

Rose sipped at her coffee. 'There's nothing *to* tell. It's just that . . . He's thinking about her, Maisie. I *know* he is. And he wasn't so drunk that he didn't know what he was doing.'

'And what was he doing? She was wrapped round him like a bloody boa constrictor, Rose. You know Sheena Mearns. You *know* her! And so do half the men in Craigourie.'

'And you're telling me I've nothing to worry about?'

'Och, Rose. Chalmers is no' like the rest o' them. God, I've stood at that bar many a night and listened to their pathetic excuses. "Falling off the straight and narrow," Craig Dunbar called it. Well, he fell off the straight and narrow all right, and landed in the gutter when his wife threw him out on the street along with his dirty drawers and his cheesy socks!

'He wasn't so casual about it all then. He got exactly what he deserved. Unfortunately, *Mrs* Mearns has still to get hers! But Chalmers isn't the type to fall for that nonsense,' Maisie assured her friend. 'Whatever it is you think you know, surely you can see that you're his whole world, Rose?'

'I thought I was,' Rose said. 'But maybe I've taken him a bit for granted. Without realising it. And . . . well, he's always felt he took second place to Barra. You know, Maisie?'

'Every man in the world thinks he takes second place to his children. Most of them do, and that's as it should be. They want immortality, brag about it when they achieve it, and in the same breath curse the fact that they have to play second fiddle in their own orchestra.'

Rose smiled. 'I know what you mean.'

'Damn right,' Maisie continued. 'When a woman's expecting she can depend on her friends to help her build the nest. Bootees, shawls, cardigans . . . It's what we do, Rose. And then the baby's born, and what do the men do? Cigars and whisky and hangovers – just when you need them the most. They're a poor lot altogether.'

'We're off the subject.' Rose giggled, nibbling on the sweet pastry.

'Indeed we're not,' Maisie retorted. 'We're talking about men here. And the likes o' Sheena Mearns has never made it up the evolutionary ladder, Rose. She's as old as the hills, and as dangerous as the sun on a bit o' glass. I'd feel sorry for Raymond, if I didn't think he was such a jessie for putting up with it.'

'How *does* he put up with it?' Rose agreed. 'She has him whipped to hell and back.'

'I don't know,' Maisie said. 'He's got to be blind not to see it. But then, there's none so blind as those who cannot see. Still, the fact is she has to live with a cold and guilty heart, and *that* I wouldn't wish on my worst enemy.'

'If you're trying to make me feel sorry for her . . .'

'Not a bit. In fact, when I see her in here, cavorting about with some fool of a man who's left his wife at home ironing his shirts . . .'

Rose winced.

'. . . I've considered asking Mr Iacobelli if he doesna' have a distant cousin who'd take a fiver to crack her across the jaw – always supposing he'd get past the Pan-Stick.'

Rose laughed. 'I'd do it myself. For nothing!'

Maisie brushed some crumbs from her chin. '*You* don't have to. Yir own man's fallen across my bar before now, Rose Maclean, and the only name on his lips is yir own. I'd belt him myself if it was otherwise – and I wouldn't lie to you.'

'I know, Maisie. I can always depend on that.'

'Are you going to eat that?' Maisie asked, pointing at the half-eaten pastry Rose had left on her plate.

Rose shook her head. 'You have it.'

Maisie lifted it, smiling across at her friend. 'Share, and share alike. So, where's the other man in yir life? I haven't seen Barra since this morning.'

'God knows,' Rose replied. 'I haven't seen him either. He didn't come for his dinner. He's caught up wi' some ... I don't know, Maisie.' Rose frowned. 'He claims he's met an angel. He's another worry.'

'We've heard.' Maisie tried to keep her tone light. 'He's full of imagination, that boy. But I wouldn't let him get too carried away with this one, Rose. I'd be keeping him away from the Pascoes at any rate. At least until ...'

Rose swept a worried hand across her brow. 'God, don't tell me he's been back over there.'

Maisie lifted her shoulders. 'Maybe not,' she said. 'He's a darling boy, Rose, and wouldn't we all be better for meeting an angel. But ...' She reached for her friend's arm. '... he can be a wee bit irritating sometimes.'

'He means well,' Rose flared, her eyes sparking.

'I know that,' Maisie soothed. 'You know how much I love him, Rose. He's just like my own – if I had my own.'

Rose swallowed. 'I know, Maisie. I do, really.' She smiled wanly. 'I'll talk to him again, make sure he doesn't go bothering Jennifer just now.' Again, Rose sighed. 'I'm feeling guilty enough myself. I haven't even been over there myself for a few days. Now it looks like ... it looks like ...'

Maisie nodded. 'Aye,' she murmured. 'It doesn't

look good. And aren't we all feeling guilty? Sometimes I think we're born with it – guilt. It's like us women have it tattooed on our brains from the minute we're conceived.'

'Some of us,' Rose reminded her, her own mind back on Sheena Mearns.

'Enough!' Maisie said. 'Isla'll be joining the union if I don't go and give her a hand.' She patted Rose's arm again. 'Are you OK?'

'I think so.' Rose smiled. 'How is Isla?'

Maisie rolled her eyes. 'Stunning! If any of us can keep Barra's mind off angels, she can.'

'I don't think I'm ready for another worry,' Rose said ruefully. 'Angels might be easier to cope with.'

'Sometimes I think you *need* to have a worry, Rose Maclean,' Maisie admonished. 'It's all relative, y'know. None of us think of the poor soul with no legs when we're suffering wi' sore feet.'

The two women locked eyes.

'Olive!' they said in one voice, and roared with laughter.

'Where were you all day?' Rose asked.

'The big house, mostly,' Barra replied. 'I had my dinner there, and Murdo took me down the river banks wi' Gallus in the afternoon.'

'How's everyone?'

'Fine. Well, Mrs Macrae's a bit het up.'

'About what?'

'Mr Cunningham and his wife's arriving tomorrow. Mrs Macrae was bawling at Hattie, but then she got over it, and she apologised, and Hattie went home.'

'Poor Hattie,' Rose said. 'She's always there to take the brunt of it.'

'I had a word wi' Jamie on the way home. He told me yesterday not to worry about her – so I suppose I shouldn't. Besides, I think he's really here to get Mr Pascoe better. That would make sense, wouldn't it, Mam?'

Rose bit her lip. 'Did you go to the Pascoes' today?' she asked.

'No, Mam. Maisie asked me not to. Matter of fact, she's no' herself either. If Jamie hadn't asked me not to take things personally, I'd have been quite insulted . . .'

'Set the table for me, Barra.'

'D'you believe me yet?'

'Dad'll be home any minute. I haven't time to discuss it just now.'

Barra opened the cutlery drawer. 'I asked Jamie if Mr Pascoe could have hair for his birthday, but he didn't seem too sure. You'd think an angel could do that much, wouldn't you, Mam?'

'Barra. The plates.' Rose pointed to the cupboard.

Barra reached for the wooden knob on the cabinet and paused. 'Murdo thinks Jamie might not have got a clear instruction, about Mr Pascoe's hair. He says it's possible there's a bit o' confusion in heaven, what with so many folk milling about the place. It makes sense. I mean, there's far more people in heaven than there are here. I think I'll be a doctor.'

'That's grand, Barra. The table . . .'

Barra brought down three bowls, and reached for the dinner plates. 'Do *you* think Mr Pascoe'll get hair for his birthday?'

'What?'

'Mam! You're not paying attention. It's important, to pay attention.'

Rose wiped her hands on the dish-towel. 'I'm paying attention.'

'You're not. You've got that look on yir face again.'

'What look?'

'That one. Y'know, when yir worrying about things.'

'I'm *not* worrying about things.'

'Yes, y'are. And if it's something Dad did, yir making far too much of it.'

Rose gasped. 'Yir father hasn't done anything. Who says he's done anything?'

'No-one. Yir jist going on at him an awful lot, so you must *think* he's done something.'

'I don't,' Rose protested.

Barra looked straight into her eyes. 'He doesn't mean to be . . . I don't think he means it.'

'Be what?'

'Y'know, awkward.' Barra grinned then. 'He is, though, isn't he, Mam? Sometimes.'

And Rose found herself grinning back. 'Aye. Sometimes.' She reached for her son and hugged her to him. How could Barra drive her to distraction one minute, and bring her so much comfort the next?

'Mam!'

'I think you've been here before, Barra. And yir right enough. Yir dad hasn't done anything.'

'Grand!' Barra pulled himself free.

Socks sauntered through from the living room and stopped in the doorway, his tail waving ominously aloft, the fur rippling across his spine.

Rose winked at Barra. 'That's yir dad home now.'

Chalmers pushed open the back door, pausing to make sure Socks was out of the vicinity. The cat barely glanced in his direction before turning back towards the living room. Chalmers shook his head as he wiped his boots, then carefully crossed the threshold.

He pulled Rose to him, astounding her with the suddenness of his embrace. 'I missed you,' he growled into her neck.

Rose swatted him with the dish-towel, pulling away in pink-cheeked embarrassment.

'Go 'n' get washed,' she admonished.

Chalmers bent to remove his workboots, and punched Barra playfully on the arm as he headed for the bathroom.

Barra was still grinning as he turned his attention back to setting the table.

Stewart examined the small cabin, pulling open the cupboard door under the wash-basin. An enamel chamber-pot stared nonchalantly back at him.

Marjorie's eyebrows all but disappeared into her

hairline. 'How primitive!' she exclaimed, through lips drawn tight with distaste.

Quickly, Stewart closed the cupboard. 'It all looks comfortable enough – otherwise,' he suggested.

'I've heard the expression "hell on wheels",' Marjorie said. 'I did not expect to experience it!'

Stewart sat heavily on the lower bunk, grazing the back of his head on the rail above. He hardly felt it. 'Can't we *try* to enjoy this, Marjorie? It's only for a few days.'

Marjorie had pushed herself against the far wall, and even then there was scarcely an inch between them. She breathed in.

At that moment the train began moving, heaving its great body along the tracks on the first few yards of its long journey northwards. Marjorie stumbled slightly and Stewart threw out his arms to steady her, catching her around her narrow waist. Briefly, she leaned into him, seemingly glad of his support.

'Sit,' he said. 'Sit here beside me, Marjorie.'

It took less than a second for her to do so and, as she straightened her skirt, she could feel Stewart's arm move from her waist to her shoulder, pulling her even closer to him.

She resisted. 'Don't.'

'Why not?' he asked. Then, refusing to let her go, he turned her face towards him, stroking her cheek with infinite tenderness. 'We have to start sometime – somewhere, darling.'

Furious, she yanked herself from him. 'And you imagine it could be *here*? In this tiny compartment, with God knows who on the other side of these walls? If you can call them walls!'

Resolutely, Stewart reached for her once more. 'Not here, Marjorie. Of course not here. But maybe while we're away, once you see how lovely it can be up there . . .'

Marjoire stared at the wall. Her voice grew quiet. 'It may be . . . as you say, Stewart. The countryside, perhaps.' Then she turned back to him, her tone brittle. 'But the people! You know the housekeeper hates me, and as for that madwoman creeping about the place . . .'

'She's not mad, Marjorie. She saved my life.' Stewart's tone, too, had become brittle. 'She paid dearly for it, and I won't have you calling her mad.'

'Then we must agree to differ, Stewart.' Marjorie Cunningham stood. 'Would you get my gown, please?'

'It's early enough,' Stewart protested grimly. 'I thought we might have some supper in the dining-car.'

'If I'm to sleep at all on this monster, I'd prefer it to be sooner rather than later. I have no objection to you having a nightcap, if you wish.'

Stewart recognised the thinly veiled request for his departure. He had become no stranger to such requests.

'I'll leave you to get undressed then.'

'Thank you.' Marjoire smiled thinly. 'And Stewart . . .'

'Yes?'

'. . . Do try not to make too much noise when you return.'

'Of course.'

CHAPTER 14

Helen glanced at the clock. Murdo would be back from the station any minute. She put the kettle on to boil and checked the silver tray. You could see yir face in it, she assured herself. Nothing to worry about there.

Carefully, she placed the starched doily on the tray and arranged the Spode tea service on top. Three newly plucked tulips, butter yellow and wet with dew, were pushed into the matching china bud-vase, and a plate of freshly baked scones thick with home-made strawberry jam finished it off.

'Right, yir Ladyship,' Helen addressed the air, 'if that doesna' put a smile on yir Sassenach face, nothing will.'

The scrunching of wheels on the gravel signalled the return of the Rover and Helen raced across the hall, eager to welcome Stewart Cunningham home – albeit with the *un*welcome addition of 'herself'.

Murdo already had the boot open, lifting out two well-worn leather suitcases, while Stewart leaned into the back, extending a helping hand to his wife. As Marjorie stepped on to the gravel, Stewart turned. Seeing Helen in the doorway, he loped up the steps, reaching for her hand with both of his own.

'Welcome home, Mr Cunningham.' Helen smiled.

Stewart Cunningham looked down at her from his elevated height of six foot four, his face creased in a smile of pure pleasure. 'Oh, Helen, it's so good to see you. I haven't half missed you both.'

Gallus was howling in the back garden, furious at having been left tied to the kennel and anxious to get in the middle of all this excitement as soon as possible.

'What *is* that excruciating noise?'

'It's Gallus, Mrs Cunningham,' Murdo replied, closing the boot. 'I'll get him in a minute.'

Helen surveyed Marjorie Cunningham. She'd been secretly hoping that time and distance had exaggerated her dislike for the young woman.

It hadn't.

In fact, Helen noted that Marjorie Cunningham's long nose looked more pinched than ever, and her eyes, intractably hostile, seemed so pale as to appear almost colourless.

'I've a wee cup o' tea ready,' Helen said, tucking her chin into her neck in an effort to disguise her renewed animosity. 'Come in and get comfortable. I'll bring it through to the . . .'

'I need to rest,' Marjorie interrupted. She gave an exagerrated shiver. 'This country always seems so *cold*!'

'It's quite a beautiful morning, madam,' Helen

stated. 'I'm sure it's just that you're no' used to the pureness o' the air.'

Marjorie ignored the comment, sweeping up the steps and past Helen. Stewart moved briefly to follow her, but Marjorie extended an imperious hand behind her.

'By myself, Stewart, if you don't mind. I didn't sleep a wink on that dreadful journey.'

Murdo hobbled up the steps, setting the two pieces of luggage in the hall and placing a small holdall case on top. Marjorie paused, returning to grab the holdall before ascending the carved staircase.

'I'll bring the cases up,' Murdo puffed.

'Please don't bother,' Marjorie called back. 'Stewart can see to that later. I really do *not* wish to be disturbed.' She negotiated the landing and disappeared from view, her sharp footsteps muffled by the ancient Axminster.

Stewart cocked his head, a worried expression pulling his fair brows together. 'She's been a little under the weather,' he murmured.

That one will *always* be under the weather, Helen thought. There's no' a sunny bone in her body.

'Well, we'll soon put that right,' she replied. 'Some fresh Highland air and we'll have her good as new in no time.' Helen held Stewart's arm as they walked towards the kitchen. 'You're looking a bit peely-wally yirself if you don't mind me saying so,' she informed him.

Stewart smiled, and patted her hand. 'It's

deliberate, Helen. I was hoping you'd take pity on a poor weak soul, and insist on forcing some of that delightful cooking into me. A good pan of your Scotch broth would be just what the doctor ordered.'

Helen returned the smile, pleased at the compliment. She held open the drawing-room door and waited for Stewart to enter. 'I'll bring yir tea through.'

Stewart stared at her, an injured expression on his face.

'Och now, Helen Macrae, don't be relegating me to the parlour already. Am I no' good enough to sit in yir kitchen any more?'

Her kitchen!

In that instant, Helen's burdened heart relaxed, letting the warm flow of relief flood her veins. For she knew that this young man, who had spent so many hours of quiet contentment at the big wooden table in her kitchen, could never do anything to hurt them.

It wasn't in him, not Stewart.

'Och, it's glad I am to see you, Stewart. Welcome home, lad,' Helen breathed, her eyes misting.

'He should be in the hospital,' Violet insisted. 'I can't imagine why that doctor doesn't demand it.'

'He wants to die in his own home, Violet,' Donald said.

'*Stop that*! I won't listen to you. I won't.'

Donald reached across the back of the sofa and

pulled his wife tightly to him, ignoring the resistance he felt in the stubborn rigidity of her body. 'Yes, you will,' he said softly. 'I know how badly you want to believe otherwise, Violet, but you're not helping him like this. Jim's accepted it, and so has Jennifer. We have to do the same.'

'I can't, Donald. I can't take this. It's too hard.' Violet's mouth quivered briefly, but her eyes were as dry as the desert. Although Donald Pascoe had sobbed long and often since learning of his son's illness, he had yet to see the tiniest tear escape his wife's eyes.

Violet Pascoe detested weakness in any shape or form – and in herself most of all.

The sound of the front door opening and closing reached them, and Jennifer appeared in the living room. 'That's the nurse gone,' she said. 'You can go through and see him now.'

Violet rose immediately, but Donald remained seated.

'Is he fit to see us?' he asked.

Jennifer raised a shoulder. 'He's very weak.'

'Then we'll let him rest a while.' Donald reached to take Violet's hand. 'We can look in on him later.'

Violet whirled, tugging her hand free. 'You can stay here if you like. *I'm* going in to see him.'

Jennifer held the door open. As Violet came level with her, she reached to touch her mother-in-law's arm. 'He really is very weak, Violet. If you would just sit quietly . . . give the injection a chance to . . .'

Violet shrugged Jennifer's touch away, marching

towards the bedroom as though she had never heard the words.

'Come on, Jen.' Donald sighed, rising at last. 'I think we deserve a cuppa.' He ushered her towards the kitchen and held a chair for her to sit. 'You look washed out,' he said.

Jennifer nodded. She had never had to pretend in front of Donald Pascoe. Her hand sought his as he pulled out the adjoining chair, and she held on to him, relishing the comfort of a healthy human touch.

'Look, Jen, I know it's an extra strain on you, us being here. If you'd prefer, we can find somewhere in town.'

'Oh *no*! No, Donald. I couldn't think of it.'

'Please, Jen, listen now. I love my wife dearly, but I know she's not making any of this easier. The way she spoke to you yesterday... and poor Graham. He was just trying to keep things going, and she barely gave him the time of day. I'm surprised he stayed as long as he did.'

Donald gently pulled his hand from her grasp and rubbed it wearily across his forehead. 'All of our lives, I've been able to settle her down when she gets too... carried away with herself. But I'm getting nowhere with this, Jen. I don't know what to do any more.' His voice cracked. It was almost more than Jennifer could bear.

She shook her head. There was so little left in her now that she could hardly speak. Donald Pascoe was crumbling before her, and she couldn't help him. A tiny knot of fury formed in her throat.

Violet Pascoe was destroying the last hours any of them would ever spend with Jim. Jennifer doubted that she'd ever find it in her heart to forgive her.

The doorbell rang, making them both jump. Jennifer ran to answer it, afraid it may have disturbed her husband.

'Not now, Barra. I told you yesterday...'

'I know, OK? But I was just wondering if you needed any messages. Mam's always needing extra when she has the bedders. I thought, if there was anything you were needing, anything at all...'

'Thanks anyway, but Graham brought me a few things yesterday, and Sandra's coming out tomorrow afternoon with Mam and Dad. They can pick up what I need in the town.'

'But I've got my bike,' Barra interrupted, pointing to the fence against which his black Raleigh rested. 'I could be down to the Whig and back in no time.'

Jennifer looked thoughtful. 'I'm not sure if I have enough bread to last... And a few tatties...'

'Great. Gi'me yir list. It's no bother. None at all.'

Jennifer opened the door wider, a fragile smile signalling her surrender. 'Come on in, then.' She raised a finger to her lips. 'Quietly, though.'

'Hi, Mr Pascoe,' Barra said as Donald appeared in the living room. 'How's Mr Pascoe? The other one – yir son?'

Donald glanced at Jennifer. 'You're Barra?'

'Aye. D'you no' remember me?'

'Yes, I do,' Donald replied. 'I haven't seen you for a while. How are you?'

'I'm fine. I missed yis last time you were here. I like yir car.'

Donald moved closer, smiling too now. 'So do I, son. You know, when I was your age, I didn't even have a bike.'

'Och, don't tell me. Y'had to walk ten miles through the snow just to get to the school.' Barra grinned.

Donald's bluff good humour had returned. 'As a matter of fact . . . no, I didn't.'

Barra looked a little shame-faced. 'Sorry, Mr Pascoe. It's just everyone tells you that.'

'They do.' Donald's laugh boomed forth. 'I've heard it myself.'

'So, how's Mr Pascoe?'

Violet launched herself through the living-room door. 'What *is* going on? Jim's trying to rest!'

'Sorry, Mrs Pascoe,' Barra said fearfully, stepping backwards. 'I was just wondering . . . how he was?'

Violet shot a glance of pure malevolence at her husband. 'Is there anything to be laughing about?'

'For God's sake, Violet,' he answered. 'Are we so beyond it, we can't even have a laugh?'

'Who are *you*?' she demanded, pointing a well-manicured finger at Barra.

'Barra Maclean. I'm here to get the messages.'

Violet looked at Jennifer uncomprehendingly. 'The messages?'

'Barra's going to pick up a few things at the Whig for me,' Jennifer said, her voice quiet.

'How's yir son?' Barra persisted.

Violet's glare deepened into loathing. 'I . . . I . . . Does he have to be here?' she appealed to Jennifer.

Jennifer was closing the desk, her purse in her hand. 'You won't need a line, Barra,' she said, pointedly ignoring her mother-in-law. 'Just a loaf, a couple of pounds of tatties. And get half a dozen eggs if they're fresh.'

'Aye, they're fresh,' Barra replied. 'I met Dunc Macpherson on the road earlier. He was bringing a pannier o' them to Maisie. He's got some nice big duck eggs, too. He was saying he got a couple of double-yolkers last week.'

Violet shuddered.

Barra looked at her. She was the type who could frighten you with a look, *if* you hadn't had to withstand being beaten up by the Yaks. Maybe she just needed cheering up. 'D'you know what Pascoe means?' he asked.

'What?' Violet's eyes were crazed as she lowered herself into the bucket chair.

'I looked it up. It means Easter child,' Barra confided. 'Isn't that great, with Mr Pascoe having his birthday?'

Jennifer caught Barra by the arm and steered him to the door. 'Here, Barra,' she said, pulling out a pound note. 'Take your time. I'm no' in a hurry.'

Barra stood on the top step, a little surprised at how quickly the door had closed behind him.

Violet's voice could clearly be heard.

'He's asleep. The pain's gone, at least for now.'

Barra walked down the path and headed for the Whig, his mind busy with this latest piece of information.

Good then. Wasn't it Jamie at work after all?

Barra entered the shop. Isla was behind the counter while Olive, perched precariously on a set of steps, attempted to dust a high shelf which contained the iodine, Askit powders, Syrup of Figs, and other manner of cures. Barra stopped, horrified.

'What're you letting her do that for?' he demanded of Isla.

'What's it got to do wi' you?' she demanded in return.

'She shouldn't be up ladders!'

'You get up it then,' Isla retorted furiously.

'Is that you, Barra?' Olive asked, pausing briefly.

'Aye. C'mon down. You shouldn't be doing that at your age!'

Olive began her descent. 'Och, it's good of you to bother, Barra. It's a pity there's no' more like you.' She hurled the condemnation in Isla's direction.

Isla lifted both arms shoulder-high, throwing her palms wide in mock supplication. '*Mea culpa. Mea culpa.*'

Barra turned. 'I didn't know you were Catholic.'

She frowned. 'I'm not, stupid. Besides, she wouldn't *let* me.'

'Why not?' Barra asked, turning back to Olive.

'You canna' set a lassie to do a woman's work.'

Isla sighed and closed her eyes, her head moving in time to a silent melody.

Barra regarded her for a moment before catching on to the rhythm. 'Herman's Hermits,' he said.

Isla's eyes flew open. 'Which one?' she asked.

' "I'm Into Something Good".'

Isla looked impressed. Very impressed.

Barra grinned back at her.

Olive was busy shaking the bright yellow duster, releasing all the dust she'd collected back into the air. It distracted Barra briefly. Mam did that too sometimes. It had never made any sense to him.

'You let all the dust go,' he told Olive.

'You're weird,' Isla commented, resting a hand on her hip.

Barra hadn't expected that. His eyebrows fell.

'No, I'm not. I'm not weird.'

Isla closed her eyes again, the trace of a sneer on her glorious mouth.

'Aaagh!' Olive wailed, clasping a hand to her neck.

Immediately, Isla was at her side. Barra took two racing steps to the end of the counter, lifting the hatch and letting it clatter loudly behind him. 'What's wrong?'

'That's my neck out,' Olive groaned. 'Ah, God, it's sore.' Her head was rigid, carefully scanning the area above her right shoulder.

'Can you look at me?' Barra asked, pushing Isla

behind him and out of his way. Isla raised an automatic fist at his back but then retreated, folding her arms across her bosom. Her expression was clear. If anyone needed their neck twisting, it was Barra Maclean.

'How can I look at you with this neck?' Olive cried plaintively. She sat on the ladder, her ample behind squeezed between the second and third steps.

'But I'm needing messages,' Barra said, a slight note of panic in his voice. 'It's what I came for.'

'Isla can see t'you.' Olive rose gingerly and headed towards the café door. 'I'm off through to get Maisie to rub some o' that linament on me. It worked the last time I put my neck out.'

'She's upstairs wi' Doug,' Isla called out. 'You'd better give her a shout from the bottom o' the stairs.'

'I hope this is mended before the bingo,' Olive mourned. 'I'll no' be able to see my numbers if it's no' better by Sunday.' With that she disappeared through the adjoining door and into the café.

Barra returned to the front of the counter, happily prepared to let Isla 'see to him'. She was watching as Olive disappeared from view. 'It'll no' be "eyes down",' she remarked. 'It'll be like the army – "Eyes *rrright*!" '

Barra laughed. He couldn't help it. Wasn't it great to be laughing with Isla?

'You've lovely eyes yirself,' he said. He bit his lip as soon as he'd said it. He didn't even know where the words had come from.

Isla looked down, her hollowed cheeks with the mystery in them turning pink. Barra thought she had never looked lovelier.

'No-one's ever noticed my eyes before,' Isla said.

'I don't know why not,' Barra said, amazed. 'It's the first thing anyone would notice about you – after yir chest.'

'Get OUT!'

'Wh . . . ?'

Isla made for him.

Barra took off but she chased behind, catching up with him as he reached the door. A hefty shove landed him out on the pavement.

For the second time that morning, Barra turned to face a closed door. He shook himself, trying to come to terms with this latest indignity, and looked around.

He reached for his bicycle, knowing he'd have to go all the way to Craigourie for his messages. He didn't relish the thought. The Yaks would most definitely be hanging around the High Street.

After all, it was their holidays too.

As he headed towards town, a thought struck him. He wondered if Jamie was aware that Olive had hurt her neck, and if so, could he possibly mend it by Sunday. After all, it *would* make up for not mending her feet.

He would have to ask Jamie the next time he saw him.

CHAPTER 15

Hattie sat back on her heels and replaced the top on the tin of floor polish. She scanned the lino, looking for the smallest area she may have missed, but the hallway gleamed from one end to the other. The rugs had been laid over the clothes lines and beaten within an inch of their lives before being carefully rolled and set on the outside steps. Hattie gathered them, laying them back down in their usual positions.

Footsteps sounded on the stairs. Hattie looked up, and flattened herself against the wall as Marjorie Cunningham stepped past her, heading for the drawing room.

'I'll have some tea now,' she instructed.

Hattie nodded. She gathered her cloths and her polish, and hurried to the kitchen.

'Mrs Cunningham's wanting her tea,' she told Helen.

'Is she now?' Helen reached to fill the kettle. 'I don't suppose there was a "please" anywhere in that?'

Hattie shook her head. 'Will I set a cup for Mr Cunningham?'

'Och, don't bother, hen. He's off down to the river wi' Murdo. I doubt we'll see the pair o' them any time soon.' Helen glanced at Hattie. 'Take her tea into her when it's ready, and then you can go home. I'll straighten up upstairs.'

'I don't mind waiting.'

Helen smiled. 'You'll see yir precious Stewart before the day's over. Come back up about four, and you can help me wi' the dinner.'

Hattie coloured.

'D'you know what they're here for yet?' she asked.

Helen looked thoughtful. 'No' really.' She sighed. 'I'm hoping Murdo'll get to the bottom of it.'

'Maybe they just wanted a wee holiday,' Hattie offered.

Helen shook her head. 'I doubt that. Herself made it very clear last time around that she didn't care to be here at all. Of course, it *was* August, and the midgies know a good target when they see one,' she chuckled.

Hattie smiled her agreement.

'Besides,' Helen continued, 'they go all over the world on their holidays, y'know. Stewart was telling me they went on a cruise up the Nile not too long back.'

'The Nile?' Hattie enquired.

'It's in Egypt,' Helen explained. 'Where they have the Pyramids and that.'

'Gosh!'

Hattie lifted the tray. 'You'd think the midgies

would be worse there,' she added. Helen looked at her, wondering if there had been a trace of humour in the remark. But Hattie's face was as solemn as ever.

'Take her tea in now, that's a good lass,' Helen said.

She busied herself at the cooker, lifting the rings off the big Belling and placing them in the sink to soak. As she scrubbed at the surface, she recalled those first days at the big house, and wondered how it was possible that twenty-five years could have passed so quickly.

Alfie Cunningham was already a widow when Murdo and Helen arrived – though not quite as merry as she was later to become. Her husband, Alistair, had brought his young bride to the big house in 1936, and Stewart was born the following year. But Alistair had had little time to enjoy his baby son before the clarions of a distant war summoned him to the trenches of Europe.

He had fallen at the first battle, one of the earliest victims of 'the war to end all wars', and Alfie was left to raise her baby alone. Alone, that was, except for Margaret Macaskill, a full-time employee at the big house along with her daughter, Hattie. Alistair had never cared for live-in help, and the gate-keeper's cottage had become home to various servants over the years.

Murdo and Helen, too, had been in service all their married life, and it had been their good fortune that Alfie was in need of just such a couple when they had to move from their last position. The old bodach they had looked after until then had recently kicked the bucket, leaving them jobless *and* homeless – a common enough occurrence.

Well, it's an ill wind that blows nobody any good, Helen mused. If Margaret Macaskill hadn't died, they might never have had the opportunity to be here, to relish the comfort of Drumdarg House, and the quiet, contented living they had enjoyed ever since.

After Margaret's violent demise, Alfie insisted that Hattie was to remain in the cottage for the rest of her life, so Murdo and Helen had taken up residence in the rear quarters of Drumdarg House, delighted to take care of Alfie and her growing son.

Once the trial was over Hattie, too, had settled back in; learning to accept the gentle kindness of her new bosses – a kindness which had never permeated the thick stone walls of the cottage while her mother was alive. Every once in a while, though, a shadow would pass across Hattie's face, and Helen could only guess at the awful memories which beleaguered her.

As if on cue, Hattie returned to the kitchen.

'Are you sure you won't be needing me?' she asked.

Helen looked at her. 'You can do the upstairs if you want,' she relented, knowing how badly Hattie was looking forward to seeing Stewart again. 'They'll probably be back by the time you've finished.'

Hattie sighed with pleasure. 'Thanks, Mrs Macrae.' She cast her eyes downwards. 'Did Barra have anything to say yesterday? About . . .'

Helen laughed. 'Angels? No, hen, he was down at the river wi' Murdo most o' the time. Anyway, if it's an angel he met, it's a good one. Barra Maclean could never be prey to evil,' she assured Hattie, her voice soothing. 'So don't you worry, now. Don't you worry.'

Barra cycled into Craigourie, coming to a halt in front of William Low's, the first of the town's supermarkets. Laying his bike against the shop wall, he was relieved to note that the Iacobelli twins were nowhere in sight.

His relief was short-lived.

Having gathered his potatoes and eggs, he turned on to the bread aisle. Tomasso glared at him from halfway down the aisle, where Primo was busily stuffing a packet of mint Yo-Yos under his jumper.

Horrified, Barra glanced at the young woman beside Primo who had surely seen what had happened, but she wandered on down the aisle, unconcerned at the petty larceny.

Barra reached for a pan loaf, realising that the twins were unlikely to bother him for fear of drawing unwanted attention to themselves. He came level with them.

'Yis shouldn't be thieving,' he whispered.

'Piss off, bampot.'

Barra stood his ground. 'I hope yis get caught.'

Tomasso reached for Barra's arm, pinching it painfully. 'I *said* piss off!'

Barra pulled his arm free. 'See what you'll do on yirselves,' he warned. 'Yis'll *never* get to heaven!'

'*We* will. But you won't, bampot,' Tomasso hissed.

'Proddies *can't* get to heaven,' Primo finished.

'Says who?' Barra demanded. 'I'll get there before youse two, that's for sure!'

'Aye, right,' Primo sneered. 'In yir pram!'

'No,' Barra retorted. 'Not in my pram, smart-aleck. I've got a friend, and he's an angel. That's how *I'll* get to heaven!'

'Hoo-hoo!' Tomasso scoffed, in mock terror.

Primo was clasping his belly, the Yo-Yos pressed against him, as he pretended uproarious laughter at Barra's claim.

'Proddies don't even get to *see* angels!' he jeered, leaning further back into the assortment of biscuits.

At that, a trembling on the top shelf above the twins' heads caught Barra's attention. A dedicated (or just plain bored) assistant had over-stocked the shelf, and a teetering packet of oatcakes threatened to dislodge the whole display.

Seizing his opportunity, Barra held both his arms wide, fluttering them as though preparing for flight.

'Give them a sign, oh Lord,' he uttered, in his best church voice. 'Oh, Lord, strike the disbelievers.'

Half a dozen packets of oatcakes rained upon

the twins, quickly followed by the neighbouring Wagon Wheels.

The twins fell to their knees, crossing themselves furiously, before skidding off down the aisle together as fast as their legs could carry them – the packet of Yo-Yos abandoned on the floor among the others.

Barra began picking up the biscuits, giggling wildly to himself. 'Sorry, Jamie,' he gasped. 'I hope you won't be minding,' before collapsing again in mirth.

An irate shop-girl, not much older than he, appeared at his back. 'What d'you think yir doing wi' the biscuits?' she demanded.

Barra held out a pack towards her. 'I don't think there's too many broken,' he offered. 'I couldn't help it. They jist fell on the floor.'

'You could so help it. And you should bloody well have to pay for them,' the girl complained, placing them off to the side.

Barra didn't mind taking the blame.

He didn't mind at all.

Maisie pointed through the kitchen door. 'Look, Doug. Two rounds of sandwiches and a pot of tea. That's been *it* – all day! Don't you think we'd be better selling up? Think of it. We could be lying on the sands o' Hawaii right now.'

Doug eased the pancakes from the griddle and turned them expertly.

'Doing what?' he asked.

'Oh, I think I could give those hula dancers a run for their money,' Maisie said, setting her enormous hips into motion.

Doug laughed. 'You could.' His face grew solemn. 'Look, Maisie, it's your business. The decision to sell the Whig – or to keep it – has nothing to do with me. I just ... I'd miss it, that's all,' he said, returning to the pancakes.

'Wouldn't you like to see a bit o' the world, Doug?'

'My world's here, Maisie. It's the first place ... the only place, where I felt I've belonged.' He paused. 'And it's thanks to you. So, whatever you decide, I'll just have to go along with it.'

'But you wouldn't be happy?'

'I'd *miss* it, Maisie. God, can't you understand that?'

Maisie flinched.

'I'm sorry,' Doug said, the hurt in her eyes reflected in his own.

Maisie shook her head, smiling her forgiveness. '*De rien, mon amour. De rien.*'

She turned her back, pushing open the swing door. 'I'll see if I can wheedle our guests into paying for another pot o' tea. Save me a pancake.'

So Doug's world was here. Here at the Whig. And she was part of it – but *only* part of it. Well, Maisie, she told herself, why or earth would you think otherwise?

The elderly couple regretted they couldn't stay for more tea. Yes, the pancakes smelled delicious, but the pension didn't stretch that far.

They thanked their hostess and carefully counted out their shillings, cheered by the large woman's bonhomie. Perhaps it was the combination of age and frailty which prevented them from noticing the bleakness behind her genial farewell.

Barra knocked softly, wary of ringing the doorbell and having to face Violet Pascoe's wrath again.

'God, Barra,' Jennifer said, opening the door almost immediately. 'I said I wasn't in a hurry, but I didn't think you'd take *this* long!'

'Sorry, Mrs Pascoe. I went to Craigourie.'

'Why?'

'Och, Olive hurt her neck, and then Isla got mad at me, and . . .'

'Well, you're here now,' Jennifer interrupted. 'You'd better come in.'

Barra sidled up the hall, entering the living room behind Jennifer and scouting for any sign of her mother-in-law.

She led him to the kitchen, clearing the remnants of a meal from the table to make room for the groceries. Barra laid them on the Formica surface.

'They're no' Dunc's eggs,' he explained. 'But they're fresh enough.'

'I'm sure they are,' Jennifer said, reaching to put them away.

'Is Mr Pascoe feeling any better?'

Jennifer gazed at him. 'He's resting easier,' she

answered at last. 'His parents are sitting with him.'

Hesitantly, Barra began, 'I know you don't believe in . . . things, Mrs Pascoe, but . . .'

'Thanks for doing the messages, Barra,' Jennifer interrupted. 'I'll get the dishes washed up now if you don't mind.'

'Right then,' he murmured. 'I'll be off.'

Jennifer smiled briefly. 'Thanks again. You'll see yirself out?'

He nodded. 'Tell Mr Pascoe we're all asking for him. Mam said you're to call her if you need anything. She doesn't want to intrude.'

Jennifer nodded. 'She phoned earlier. She was wondering where you were.'

'She's always wondering that,' Barra said. 'She'd be frightened I'd be making a pest of myself.' He looked at the floor. 'I'm warned no' to be bothering you.'

Jennifer reached out and touched his shoulder. 'You're not a pest, Barra. I'm sorry if I've been short with you. It's just . . . a difficult time.'

'I know,' he answered. 'Maybe you should get out in yir garden for a while. Yir flowers are right bonny, and you'd probably feel better for spending a minute or two looking at them.'

Jennifer looked slightly surprised. 'The flowers . . . They must be needing a drink by now.'

'That's the stuff.' Barra grinned.

He set off down the path, looking skywards as he went. 'A drop rain mightn't go wrong,' he called out. 'The flowers are needing it.'

Jennifer heard him as she prepared to close the door. Pulling it wide, she stepped across the threshold, looking around to see who Barra had been speaking to. There was nobody there.

Puzzled, she glanced in his direction as he turned to close the gate behind him.

'See you, Mrs Pascoe.' He waved cheerfully.

Jennifer just nodded.

The lashing rain had conspired to keep everyone indoors; everyone but Danny Macfee, the only customer currently in the Whig. He drummed his fingers on the bar, keeping time to 'Baby Love' by the Supremes which beat down as relentlessly as the rain from the floor above.

'Looks like I'm here for the night,' he remarked.

'Thank God for small mercies,' Maisie muttered. She was playing Solitaire at one of the tables, while Doug tried in vain to get a picture on the TV screen.

The television was a better barometer of the weather than the heavy brass-trimmed wooden one which hung on the wall. Doug gave up on his labours, knowing there would be little hope of watching anything until the rain cleared.

He ambled back to the bar, refilling Danny's glass – and his own.

'Are you winning, Maisie?' Danny asked.

'Not yet,' she called back. 'But no doubt you'll still be here when I do.'

'Aye, well, if yis would close a bit earlier, I could get home t'my bed.'

Maisie turned. 'It must be a great discomfort to you, being joined to the bar at the elbow like that. Have you considered surgery?'

Danny shook his head dolefully in Doug's direction. 'She can be a right pain in the arse when she wants,' he remarked.

'Aye. But what an arse!' Doug smiled.

Maisie nodded her thanks, and returned to her game. Doug had intended the words as a compliment and she wondered why, after all these years, they had cut her so deftly and completely to the core.

CHAPTER 16

Barra was sorry he'd opened his mouth. Poor Mrs Pascoe had probably been busy watering her garden when the rain had started – *and* he'd had to stay in all night. Still, at least Mam and Dad were talking again.

'Is it Dunfearn tomorrow?' Rose asked.

'Aye,' Chalmers answered. 'I should be done at the Wilsons' by early afternoon, and it's myself that'll be glad to see the back of it. Still, the job at Dunfearn'll keep me going for a week or two,' he went on happily. 'I was lucky to get it. I just didn't think the owners would be that quick to decide.'

He rubbed his chin. 'I'll maybe stop on the way out and see if I can get a word wi' Stewart. Strike while the iron's hot.'

'Well, the Cunninghams aren't staying long,' Rose advised. 'Olive was saying they're going back on Friday night.'

Chalmers shrugged. 'Hardly worth their while coming. But he must miss the old place.'

'Not that much. Two visits in five years?'

'Och, I know, Rose. But he's got a hectic kind o'

life in the city, and you know *she* doesn't care to be up here, away from her English cronies.'

'Have you seen her yet, Mam?' Barra asked, anxious for a full description.

Rose shook her head. 'No. I don't think any of us'll be getting much of a look at her.'

'Why not?'

'Och, you know . . .'

'No, Mam. I wouldn't be asking if I knew.'

Chalmers peered over his glasses. 'I hope that wasn't a bit o' cheek in yir voice,' he warned.

Barra grinned at his mother, and she smiled back.

'A wee bit . . . maybe. Sorry, Mam.'

'OK,' Rose said, tucking her feet up under her. Barra moved further down the sofa, careful not to disturb Socks who had pride of place on the plump cushion between Rose and himself.

'Does she no' like mixing wi' us?' he asked.

Chalmers' expression became a trifle more fierce. 'Why wouldn't she? We're as good as she is. Better, in fact.'

'Why are we? Better, I mean.'

'Are you no' working at yir stamps tonight, son?' A faint note of impatience crept into Chalmers' voice.

Rose glanced at her husband. 'I'm sure Mrs Cunningham's all right in her own way,' she explained. 'But she set Helen's back up no end, treating her like a servant, and ordering her about her own house.'

'But it's no' Helen house,' Barra interrupted. 'It's Mr Cunningham's house, isn't it?'

'Aye, technically. But Murdo and Helen have had the run of it for so long that you canna' blame them for feeling like it's their own.'

'What happened to Hattie?'

'What?' Rose asked, trying to follow her son's mercurial train of thought.

Chalmers got up to switch the channel. 'Bloody rubbish they're putting on,' he muttered.

'I was thinking . . .' Rose said. 'If we do well wi' the bedders this year, we could maybe get a new set. They have them in cabinets now.'

Chalmers grunted. 'There's nothing wrong wi' the set. It's the putrid programmes they're showing.'

'What happened to Hattie?' Barra asked again, more insistently.

'Oh.' Rose remembered the question. 'Y'know fine, Barra.'

'I know I *know*,' he said, as impatient as his father now. 'I know she's supposed to have murdered her mother – which I don't believe. But I'd like to know the details.'

'What details?'

'All of them,' Barra insisted. He was fed up trying to get the story out of everyone – anyone! This time he wasn't going to let it rest until he got some answers.

'Youse were around then, you and Dad. You can remember the details, surely.'

'A lot o' bloody rubbish,' Chalmers muttered

again. 'Where could thon poor cratur hurt a soul?'

'What *happened*?'

'Christ, Barra, give it a rest.'

Rose shot another look at her husband, which he pretended not to notice. She turned to Barra.

'The whole thing got exaggerated over the years, but apparently Hattie's father had run off when she was a baby, and her mother had gone queer in the head . . .'

'Did nobody notice? That she was queer in the head?'

Rose shrugged. 'She was a good enough worker, and it was hard in them days to hold on to a job and raise a bairn too. It still is. Some things never change.'

'But they lived in the cottage. You'd think old Mrs Cunningham would have noticed.'

'She wasn't old then, Barra. In fact, she never got to be old at all.'

'She was a flighty bit o' stuff,' Chalmers interjected.

'There's worse than her!' Rose shot back. 'At least she was a widow. It's no' as if she was going behind her man's back.'

Chalmers picked up his paper, pushing his glasses further up his nose. Socks stretched and moved slightly, centring Chalmers in his line of vision. Chalmers glanced across. The bloody cat was smiling at him – an evil smile, if ever there was one. He turned to the sports pages and lifted the paper higher, covering his face as well as he could.

Barra folded his arms. 'Could someone *please* tell me exactly what happened?'

Rose frowned at him. 'You're getting awful argumentative.'

'I'm *not*! I would Just-Like-To-Know ...'

Rose shook her head. 'Well, anyway, it turns out Hattie's mother had been beating her black and blue for years, and keeping her locked up in the coal cupboard ...'

'Why?'

Rose, too, was beginning to lose patience now. 'I don't know, Barra. She was queer in the head.'

'OK,' Barra relented. 'Then what happened?'

'It seems Alfie Cunningham was off on one of her soirées, and Stewart started crying and wouldn't stop. He was just a baby, in his cot, and ...'

'When was this then?'

'God. When was it, Chalmers?' Rose asked.

'Hmm?'

Rose remained silent, knowing full well her husband had heard every word.

'Oh-h-hh! When was it now? Hattie was twenty-three at the time. I remember that. It was a year or two after the start o' the war ... forty, forty-one, thereabouts.'

'Right,' Rose said. 'Well, the story goes that Hattie's mother was holding a pillow over Stewart's face, and Hattie tried to save him and whacked the old bitch with a bed-warmer ...'

'Wow!'

'. . . But it seems her mother fell against a dresser, and they couldn't prove if it was the bed-warmer or the corner of the dresser that had killed her.'

'So that's how Hattie got off?'

'Aye,' Rose answered. 'And so she should have! Mind you, they tried to say that Hattie had done it from spite and made up the story just to cover herself. But Alfie Cunningham sat in that court right through the trial and insisted that Hattie was innocent. They said she had a lot to do wi' Hattie walking free.'

Barra was thoughtful. 'I don't think so, Mam. I mean, if Hattie got put on the stand, then everyone must have known what she was like. They'd have known she's not spiteful.'

Chalmers lowered his paper. 'It was "Not Proven", son. If they'd have been *that* sure, they would have acquitted her.'

'But you don't believe she could do that, Dad? You just said . . .'

'I know what I said. But the law's the law. "Not Proven" is how it came out.'

'Mam?'

'Of course she didn't do it for spite!' Rose retorted. 'And the law's not always right, either.'

'Well, that's a fine thing to be telling the boy!' Chalmers protested.

'Right is right,' Rose insisted. 'And wrong is wrong.'

Chalmers cracked his paper and returned to the football section.

Barra regarded his parents for a moment. 'Are yis not talking again?'

'Of course we're talking,' they said in unison.

Helen lay in the crook of her husband's arm, her head resting on his chest. She sniffed his pyjama jacket, wondering how the smell of his pipe could penetrate even that. They'll be washed first thing tomorrow, she decided, hoping that the rain would be off by then.

Murdo held her loosely, lulled by the warmth of her sturdy body, and the rhythmic buffeting of the rain on the window-panes.

'So he didn't give you any clue at all?' Helen asked – for about the tenth time that day.

'No, hen, he didna'. We talked of the fishing and the weather, and it was just like I told you. He's going to lease out stretches o' the river, and he's off into the town tomorrow to set it up wi' the factor.'

Helen sighed, worrying anew at the reason for the visit.

On his return with Murdo, Stewart had spent a scant few minutes in the kitchen. Murdo had set off outdoors again in pursuit of his interminable chores, and Helen was looking forward to enjoying some time alone with the young man. But as soon as she'd informed Stewart that his wife had retired once more upstairs, he had rushed to join her, casting a backwards glance in Helen's direction.

'We'll talk later, Helen. I promise.'

She had the distinct feeling that there was

something definite on Stewart's mind – something he was trying to say, and couldn't quite get round to. When she'd asked Murdo's opinion, he had assured her that it was just her imagination. Helen wasn't convinced.

There had been no evidence that Marjorie Cunningham was any happier about being in Drumdarg House than on her last visit. Helen had served the couple a lavish dinner but Marjorie had picked listlessly at her food and Stewart, despite enthusiastic praise for Helen's cooking, had eaten little more than his wife. The couple seemed to have nothing to say to each other, and Helen couldn't help but notice how forlorn Stewart looked.

'Why come here at all just to visit the factor?' Helen fretted. 'He could've sorted that out from London. Even if he felt he *had* to come, he could've left herself behind. There wouldn't be any reason for them both to be here.'

'As a matter of fact, it was me that brought up the fishing,' Murdo replied. 'I don't think it had entered his mind till then. I think he just got the inclination to see the old place again. No more to it than that.' He rescued his arm and turned on his side.

Helen turned also. As the pair lay back to back, she briefly rubbed his behind with her own. It was a habit started over thirty years before, and still it brought a smile to his lips.

'G'night, Helen,' he yawned contentedly.

'G'night yirself.'

'I love you, Helen Macrae.'

'Me too, Murdo Macrae,' she answered.

The last of the rituals over, Murdo settled into a heavy, dreamless sleep.

Helen did not.

Wednesday dawned bright and clear and Rose hummed happily as she set to cleaning the front room. Chalmers had held her close before setting off for work, and she had chided herself for ever having doubted him. God, there wasn't a man alive who could keep a clear head by the time Sheena Mearns had finished 'dancing' with him. Besides, it *had* been a party, and Maisie was right – Chalmers had had enough whisky in him to launch the *Queen Mary*.

'Mrs MacGillivray phoned this morning,' Rose informed Barra cheerfully. 'She's full up already. Looks like we'll have some bedders for the weekend.'

'Do I have to do the hoovering?' Barra asked fearfully.

Rose paused, smiling. 'Have you tidied yir room?'

'Sort of.'

'Sort of?'

'If I do it right, do I still have to hoover?'

'Oh, go on then.' Rose smiled. 'Do it right, and I'll do the hoovering. *Then* you can go out – but not before.' The sentence was wasted. Barra was already halfway up the stairs.

Rose lifted the lid on the stereogram, switching off the wireless and placing her favourite long-player on the spindle. As Nat King Cole's mellow voice filled the room, she began emptying the china cabinet, preparing to wash her collection of ornaments. Reaching for a small glass horse she paused, and a shadow fell across her face. Jennifer Pascoe had given it to her – a souvenir from her honeymoon in Venice.

Rose gazed at it for a moment, then placed it carefully on the carpet. She walked into the hall and dialled the Pascoes' number. Almost at once the phone was answered.

'Jen, it's Rose. I just wondered how Jim was doing.'

There was a second's silence. 'The doctor's here now, Rose. I . . . I'm afraid he's . . . Jim's . . .'

'What is it, Jen?' Rose asked softly. 'Is he worse?'

She could hear Jennifer swallow before answering, and held her breath.

'He's in a coma, Rose. It won't be long.'

Tears pricked at Rose's eyes. 'Oh, Jen. I'm so sorry to hear that.'

'Thanks,' Jennifer whispered. 'I need to go now, Rose.'

'Of course. Of course. If you need . . .'

'There's nothing. Thanks anyway.'

Rose replaced the receiver. Walking slowly back into the front room, she picked up the little horse and lowered herself to the carpet. Her mind was

227

numb, her ears deaf to the thundering on the staircase.

Barra hurtled into the room, and stopped dead. 'Are you all right, Mam?' he demanded.

She looked up at him, her eyes clouded. 'Aye. I'm fine, son. It's no' me.' Rose shook her head. 'I just spoke to Jennifer. Jim's in a coma.'

'What does that mean?' Barra knelt beside her. His eyes were a reflection of her own, deep with concern.

'It's the end, Barra,' Rose said gently. 'He won't last much longer.' The tears spilled from her eyes, and she wiped them angrily. 'It's just not fair!'

Barra grew pale. 'It *can't* be the end!' he exclaimed. 'I have to see Jamie, Mam. I have to go *now*!'

Rose slumped even further into the grey pile.

'Barra . . .'

'I have to go, Mam,' he insisted, rising and stepping backwards away from her. 'Will you be all right?' he added breathlessly.

She nodded and Barra turned, racing through the kitchen and down the path. Rose could hear his voice even from here.

'Ja-mie! Jay-meee!'

Rose got up and wandered to the back door, scouting the woods for any sign of Barra. He had disappeared from view, but still she could hear him. Socks was rubbing his fat body against her legs and Rose bent to lift him, burying her face in his silky fur.

If you're really out there, she prayed silently, do something now! Please, *please*, do something now!

Hattie seldom ventured into the woods. Mostly she was afraid of them, the big trees that could cast dark shadows even on the brightest of mornings. She had no idea why she was there now, aware only that she had wanted to get away, away from all the strange sensations swirling around the big house. Everything there had become so raucous; the air was screaming with all the tension, until her own voice, her own footsteps, sounded loud in her ears.

Even the cottage was full of it, infected with the noise, the terrible din of her memories.

Her shuffling steps had brought her well beyond her usual territory. She should get back, back down to the Whig, and then home. She shouldn't be here. She shouldn't be here at all.

Then she heard it – the wailing. Hattie clasped a hand to her mouth, gathering the remains of her courage, her eyes searching the small clearing above her. It was Barra! It was Barra doing all the wailing.

More curious than afraid now, Hattie pushed herself against the shrubbery. Why would poor Barra be sobbing like that? She should go to him.

But she stayed, unable to push herself forward. Moments passed, and still Barra sobbed. Hattie began trembling. Oh God, let him stop. Please let him stop.

But Barra didn't stop. His small body wrapped around the old log, he wailed on. Then, just as Hattie could bear it no longer, he sat up, jamming his fists into his eyes.

'I can't! I *can't* think! You said he'd have hair for his birthday. You promised!'

Once more Hattie's eyes searched the clearing, but there was nobody else there. She started forward, just as Barra began again.

'He can't die, Jamie. You said nothing ever dies. You *told* me that!' And then, quietly, the sobbing no more than a hiccup, 'You better not let me down, Jamie. Angels shouldn't be letting people down.'

Barra stood, and Hattie watched as he looked wildly around him.

Pale and confused, she set off, lumbering down the old trail faster than she'd ever moved in her life.

CHAPTER 17

Barra rubbed at his face for the umpteenth time, knowing that Jamie had left him again.

Anger flared behind his swollen eyes. What was the point of it all? Jamie smiling away and saying everything was as it should be. *Nothing* was as it should be! Barra knew it probably wasn't a wise thing to be mad at an angel, but surely Jamie knew how important it was for Mr Pascoe to get better.

And especially what was the point of putting Mr Pascoe in a coma? What exactly was a coma? Huh! Jamie hadn't even answered that one. Come to think of it, Jamie hadn't really answered anything. Not for the first time, a shiver of doubt swept through Barra. If he really had been singled out to help an angel, wouldn't he have some answers by now?

He lifted his head, momentarily distracted as he gazed through the overhanging branches to the sky above. God, it was big. Imagine, all that sky. No matter where you stood in the world – in Timbuktu, even – you'd be looking at the same sky.

Barra inhaled the pine-scented air, and wondered. Wasn't it natural enough for an angel to know more than he did? And wasn't it possible – in fact, wasn't it entirely likely – that Mr Pascoe might be needing a coma? Mam had said it herself often enough 'You don't sleep, Barra. You go into a coma.'

Well, Jamie had been somewhere higher than the sky, and *he* was sure things were as they should be. He'd laid his hand on the back of Barra's head just once, and told him. He'd said, 'Nothing ever dies, Barra.' You had to believe him. You just had to. Mr Pascoe would be taking a wee rest in his coma. Just resting.

And then he'd be fine.

Barra walked back towards home. Quietly, he retrieved his bicycle from the shed and skirted the house, heading towards the road. No sense in bothering Mam, she'd just get all worked up again. After all, if you couldn't trust an angel to sort things out, who could you trust?

Barra's spirits lifted considerably as he crested the hill above Drumdarg. The countryside smelled sweeter for the previous day's rain, and it seemed as though nature had dipped her brush in a newer, more brilliant palette before sweeping it over her canvas.

He free-wheeled down the hill towards Craigourie, waving at a passing car as he crossed the bridge into the town. Mr and Mrs Ledingham were on their way out to their daughter's house. He was sure Mrs Pascoe would be glad to see them.

It was a grand thing to have a family.

As the A40 passed, Barra caught a glimpse of Jennifer's sister, Sandra, in the back seat. She was crying, and Barra's heart plummeted once more. He wanted to shout after them not to be afraid, not to cry.

He wanted all this sadness to go away.

It was such a grand day.

Barra wandered up and down the High Street, but most of the shops had already closed. The traffic grew sparse as the town came to its weekly stand-still. Unable to shake off his despondency, Barra set off for the station. He loved the dirty, smoky smell of the trains and often enjoyed a blether with the guards. Sometimes he got invited into their hut for a cup of tea.

He realised he was quite hungry, and stopped at Bremner's. The bakery stayed open, even on half-day closing, and several of the tables in the tea-rooms at the back of the shop were already occupied. Barra bought two sausage rolls, devouring them in quick succession. He wished Maisie could get this much business, but then, he couldn't imagine starched white tablecloths on Maisie's tables.

Barra headed for the station. He could easily pass an hour or two there, and then he would head for home. He looked up at the cloudless sky.

It was a grand day, altogether.

Just not as grand as he'd been used to.

Chalmers parked behind the storage sheds, hoping their wooden bulk would conceal his presence. He had spent half the morning arguing back and forth with himself but, in the end, he knew he had to come.

He looked at his watch. Five past one. He'd give it until ten past, and then he was off. He was halfway hoping Sheena wouldn't come, would think better of it, and just leave the whole mess to die a natural death.

But still, he'd made up his mind and there was no turning back now.

At exactly eight minutes after the hour, Sheena slipped noiselessly into the passenger seat. Her perfume overwhelmed him and, instantly it seemed, she was in his arms and kissing him deeply, ferociously. Her hands slid across his back and painfully twisted the curled hair at the nape of his neck. He relished the pain, needed it.

Breaking the embrace, Chalmers pulled breathlessly from her.

'Let's get out of here,' Sheena said, her eyes even darker than he remembered.

'No.' Chalmers' voice was unsteady. He coughed, tried again. 'No, Sheena,' he said, more firmly this time.

'A bit late for cold feet,' Sheena mused. She stroked his bare arm, sending a shiver along his spine.

He pulled roughly away. 'It's not cold feet. I

don't know what madness made me even think I was up for this. That's why I came. To tell you . . . to get it quite clear. Nothing's going to happen here, Sheena. Nothing at all. Not ever.'

Her eyes sparked. 'I'd say it already had, wouldn't you?'

Chalmers shook his head. 'You took me by surprise.'

Her tone changed, became wheedling, seductive. 'Chalmers, ah, Chalmers. You're telling me you didn't enjoy it, the surprise?'

'I'm telling you I have a wife and a son, and they mean far, far more to me than *any* o' your surprises, Sheena. I'm sorry if I led you to believe otherwise. There's no doubt I'm in the wrong here. No doubt at all. I'll have to live with my conscience for ever having entertained the idea of this . . . nonsense. But that's the extent of it, Sheena. If anything more were to happen, anything at all . . . Well, that I couldn't live with. I hope yir understanding me. I hope we're quite clear on that.'

Chalmers engaged the clutch and began a three-point turn. He had already determined that it would be reckless in the extreme to drive out of town by the main road. 'I'll drop you at the end of Market Street.'

'Don't bother!' Sheena spat. 'I can walk home from here.'

'And that's another thing,' Chalmers said. 'Raymond's been a good friend over the years. I wouldn't want to be the one to hurt him.'

'Raymond's *my* problem, not yours, Chalmers Maclean. So don't worry there. I can take care of my own.'

'Me too,' Chalmers said. 'And that's exactly what I'm going to be doing from now on.'

'You bastard! You . . .'

Chalmers leaned across Sheena to open the passenger door, anxious to be rid of her. As he did so, he caught a movement from the corner of his eye, and looked up.

'Duck!' he commanded, pushing Sheena's shoulder downwards.

'Eh?' She was struggling against him, pushing his hand from her.

Panic-stricken, he caught hold of the dark crown of hair and pushed her head towards the floor. His hand sank several inches into the backcombed layers. Sheena was struggling harder now, but he kept her there, ignoring her spluttered protests.

'It's Barra!' he gasped. 'My son. He's here.'

'Where here?' Sheena's croaked, almost at the point of strangulation. 'Let me UP!'

'No. Stay down. He might see us.'

With an almighty burst of strength Sheena broke Chalmers' hold, jerking upwards like an irate jack-in-the-box.

'Get yir bloody hands off me!' she exploded.

Chalmers ignored her, fearfully watching Barra as he circled around the front of the shed, wheeling his bike this way and that.

'What the hell d'you think yir doing?' Sheena

was almost spitting with fury.

Chalmers couldn't answer. He thought he might be taking a heart attack. His throat had closed with fright and his heart pounded thunderously in his chest. As Barra advanced in their direction he grabbed Sheena again, this time by the scruff of the neck.

'Duck, for Chris'sakes! Duck!'

Her head once more between her knees, Sheena proceeded to slam her sharp-cornered plastic handbag into Chalmers' ribs.

'Cutitout!' he hissed. 'You'll scratch me.'

'I'll do more than scratch you! LET ME UP!'

Just as Chalmers saw his son's head crane in recognition, Bernie Sanderson whistled into view, stopping to talk to the boy. He lifted his guard's cap and smoothed his bald head, replacing the cap at a jaunty angle. Chalmers could see him pointing towards the small hut at the end of platform three and, to his relief, the two set off together, disappearing around the corner and out of sight.

Chalmers took several deep breaths. He was a big man and had punched his way out of more than one fight in his time, gaining a youthful, but nonetheless deserved, reputation for fearlessness. In all his life, Chalmers had never, never been more frightened than in those last few minutes.

He leaned back into his seat, releasing his hold on Sheena and washing his face with trembling hands.

Sheena's lipstick had smeared across her face,

and her hair looked like a rejected attempt at nestbuilding by a demented weaver bird. She was gasping for air, her face purple with effort and rage.

'What the *hell* did you think you were doing?'

'I'm sorry,' Chalmers muttered. 'I was worried Barra would have seen us together.'

'So what!'

Chalmers stared at her. 'So what?'

Sheena snorted derisively. 'I thought you were a man, Chalmers Maclean. You're just a hen-pecked nothing – like all the rest o' them!'

All the rest of them! Sheena was right. For that's exactly what he would have been. Just like all the rest – and not a man at all.

He leaned across and tugged on the door handle. The door opened, and he sat back. 'Get out,' he said.

Sheena didn't need a second invitation. She positively leaped from the old van. Stopping to lean back into it, she glared at him.

'Don't think I'm the only woman in Craigourie who's after a bit o' romance on the sly,' she snarled. 'Do you ever wonder what *your* wife's doing behind yir back?'

Chalmers didn't answer. He was looking at a face smeared with make-up and contorted by malice, a face he had imagined to be beautiful.

How could he have been so wrong?

Sheena slammed the door. Chalmers watched as the handle rattled loose and fell to the floor. He bent to pick it up and placed it on the dashboard, then started up the engine and nosed the van forward.

He knew Sheena had said what she did from spite but, for a moment, he wondered how he might feel if . . .

No, he thought, I couldn't stand it. Not my Rose.

As he cleared the town limits Chalmers wound down his window, inhaling the fresh air. Almost unconsciously, he began waving his left arm up and down across the empty passenger seat until he was happy that the last cloying whiff of perfume had been dispersed.

Driving homewards, the image of Barra on his bike came to him once more. There was something about it that gnawed at him, and then his mind cleared.

Innocence! How innocent Barra had looked.

A hot flush of shame swept through Chalmers, followed almost immediately by such a rush of love for his son that it almost destroyed him.

'I'll no' let you down again, son,' Chalmers whispered. 'Not as long as I live.'

'Are you no' going to eat at all?' Hattie enquired of Stewart.

He pushed his plate from him and smiled. 'I don't think I've quite got my Highland appetite back yet.'

Helen nodded at Hattie, and she picked up his plate, scraping it into a metal bowl of scraps which were destined to be greedily devoured by Gallus.

'Will it disturb Mrs Cunningham if I do the silver now?' she asked.

Stewart shook his head. 'I don't think so. She's reading, in the drawing room.'

'Just excuse yirself, and bring it all through to the dining table,' Helen instructed. 'You can lay it out there to clean it. Be sure to put a sheet down first. Don't get that polish on the wood.'

Hattie nodded, and left.

'She seems distracted,' Stewart remarked.

'She's no' been herself today, I'll grant you. But she'll be all the better for seeing you.' Helen smiled. 'She *is* doing better, though, but her poor mind's close to breaking sometimes. Did Murdo tell you about the waiting?'

Stewart shook his head, puzzled.

'Och, she's got some idea in her mind that that actor – what's his name – Kenneth More, came to her in the night and promised to come back and marry her. I know she's never been to the pictures in Craigourie – or anywhere, for that matter. Murdo 'n' me have talked about it, and the only thing we can come up wi' is that she overheard us talking about the war, and . . .'

'The war?'

'Well, not the war exactly. But they had that fillum out wi' Lord Lovat. Except it wasna' Lord Lovat, it was some American actor playing Lord Lovat, and you know, well, maybe Hattie got caught up wi' that story . . .'

Stewart shook his head as if to clear it. 'You've lost me, Helen.'

'Och, it's no more than we are oorselves.' Helen drew a deep breath, marshalling her thoughts. 'Y'see, there was that fillum out, *The Longest Night*, I think it was . . .'

'*The Longest Day*,' Stewart corrected.

'Aye, and the folks around here were talking about how brave Lord Lovat was, and wasn't it a shame that they got some Yankee to play him, and y'know Hattie. Y'know how she loved the stories yir mother would tell her about yir poor dad and all his heroism an' all . . .'

Stewart raised his eyebrows. He never once remembered his mother telling him such stories.

'Anyway,' Helen continued, 'Kenneth More was in that fillum, and no doubt someone brought his name up, and Hattie got herself all confused wi' the past and the fillum and everything . . .' Helen drew another long breath. 'That's about when she got this notion in her head.'

'When exactly was this?' Stewart asked.

'A couple o' years back. November, I think it was. There'd been quite a snowfall, and I'm sure it was before Christmas. Then she informed us that Kenneth More would be coming back for her at Easter, and she's waited at the gate for him for the few weeks o' spring since then. At any rate, it would've been after yir last visit.' There was a slight note of censure in Helen's voice, and Stewart responded immediately.

'Too long, Helen, I know. But I really have been awfully busy.'

Helen sighed. 'No matter. You're here now. As a matter of fact,' she said, gathering her courage, 'we've been wondering what prompted you to return.'

Stewart remained silent and Helen, afraid that she may have overstepped herself, rushed on with the first thing that crossed her mind. 'How did you get on at the factor's?' she asked.

'Very well,' Stewart replied. 'It's all in hand. You'll be seeing a few strange faces around the place before the year's out, I'm sure.'

'Och, I'll no' mind that,' Helen said. 'As long as they're bothering the salmon and not me.'

Another uncomfortable silence followed.

'Where's Murdo?' Stewart asked at last.

'In the vegetable plot. He'll be happy for yir company if you want a word wi' him.'

'No. Actually, Helen, I was hoping to have a quiet word with you – by yourself.'

Helen wiped her hands on her apron and sat down at the opposite end of the table. Her mouth had gone dry, and she suddenly became aware of the ticking of the wooden mantel-clock. It seemed very loud, and irritating.

Stewart glanced away, and then back. 'I think I mentioned that my wife has been . . . ill.'

Helen nodded. Her voice had deserted her completely.

'Actually, Helen, it's . . . it was . . . Marjorie suffered a miscarriage.'

Helen stared. What could this possibly have to do with her?

'I'm sorry to hear that.' She waited.

Stewart didn't get the chance to say anything further. Marjorie Cunningham had appeared in the doorway and was advancing at a great rate of knots, her soft velvet slippers soundless on the linoleum.

Stewart jumped as she crossed his line of vision. 'M . . . M . . . Marjorie . . .' he stammered.

'I'll thank you not to discuss my health with the hired help,' she fumed, her pale features flushed with anger.

Helen was immediately on her feet, her own face scarlet with indignation. Hired help indeed!

'Mrs Cunningham, I'd kindly remind you . . .'

'It is not your place to remind *me* of anything!' Marjorie snapped. 'Stewart, please join me in the drawing room. I'd like to talk to you – in private.'

Stewart glanced sheepishly in Helen's direction before following his wife out of the kitchen.

The bloody cheek of her! Helen seethed. Sitting once more, she twisted and untwisted her hands together, wishing, not for the first time, that she could tell Marjorie Cunningham to take her high-faluting English face and shove it up her arse!

After a few seconds' contemplation, during which Marjorie Cunningham's entire being was subjected to all manner of imaginary torment, Helen rose decisively and marched down the hall. The sound of muffled voices could be heard emanating from the drawing room, and it was clear that Stewart's conciliatory tone was having little effect on his wife's bad humour.

Helen threw open the dining-room door. *'Leave the bloody silver!'* she called to Hattie, and slammed the door shut again.

Hattie looked down at the array of cutlery, trays and assorted finery before her, all of which was covered in a layer of silver polish. She gnawed on her lip, her fingers twisting furiously at a strand of spiky hair.

Finally she backed out of the room on tiptoe, all the while staring at the table as though every piece of silver might suddenly fly at her and embed itself in her throat.

Her poor heart battered by the experiences of the past few hours, Hattie closed the door silently behind her. She had to lean on the banister for some minutes before her pulse returned to anything approaching normal.

Chalmers drove round the back of Drumdarg House, parking the van at the far gable end. Gallus came yipping at his heels and he stopped to pet him, chuckling as the wee dog threw himself high in the air, showing off as usual.

Letting the Westie lead, he approached the vegetable plot, calling out as he neared, 'Well, Murd, how goes it?'

Murdo straightened, nodding. 'You'll no' be going t'see Helen, I hope?'

Chalmers frowned. 'As a matter o' fact I was hoping for a word wi' Stewart.'

Murdo raised his hands to the heavens. 'Oh, for the love o' God, stay out o' there the day. Helen's on the warpath.'

Chalmers stifled a smile. 'What happened?'

Murdo shook his head. 'You dinna' want to know, Chalmers. It's herself that got Helen going. Mark my words, there'll be no peace till they're gone.'

'Well, I'm afraid I'll need to speak to Stewart before that, Murd. It's about the rewiring.'

Chalmers might just have well have said that the world was ending in the next few seconds. Murdo looked as though he was about to cry. He continued shaking his head, his face a mask of tragedy.

'No' the day. No' the day, Chalmers. Some other time.'

Chalmers sighed. 'If you say so,' he agreed reluctantly. 'I'll be off then.'

'Right, son.' Relief relaxed Murdo's features. 'Maybe tomorrow.'

Chalmers drove slowly away. As he cleared the house, he spotted Stewart Cunningham at the end of the driveway. Stewart's hands were pushed firmly into the pockets of his plus-fours, and his long stride was taking him closer to the main road at every step.

He turned as Chalmers came abreast and raised a hand in absent-minded salute. Chalmers reached over to open the passenger door, cursing as he remembered the broken handle. Pulling slightly ahead, he parked the van and stepped back towards Stewart.

'Oh, I didn't recognise you, Chalmers.' Stewart extended his hand in greeting. Chalmers shook it warmly, welcoming the young man back to Drumdarg. The usual pleasantries were exchanged and Chalmers seized the unexpected opportunity to offer Stewart a lift – to wherever he might be going.

'Thank you, Chalmers. I just . . . felt like walking. You don't mind?'

'No. Not at all. I was just hoping I might get a word in yir ear.'

'About what exactly?' Stewart seemed impatient to leave and was dodging around Chalmers' feet, looking somewhat trapped, and impatient to be free.

Chalmers planted himself firmly in front of his erstwhile neighbour. 'Well, I've been talking to Murdo about rewiring the big house, y'know, and . . .'

'Oh, that. Yes, of course. It's long overdue. Quite an overhaul though. I'm afraid. A bit much for one man.'

Chalmers shrugged off the remark. 'Och, I'm taking on an apprentice, Stewart. We'd handle it fine between us.'

Stewart Cunningham raised an eyebrow. Then he nodded briefly. 'Of course. Well, if you call into the factor's office, I'm sure . . .'

'Och, we wouldn't want to be bothering the factor now,' Chalmers said. 'If you'd be prepared to make a deal wi' me, man-to-man like, I'd be on it before you could sneeze.'

Stewart smiled thinly. 'That's exactly what the factor gets paid for, Chalmers. But if you're worried that he would cut you out of the equation, I can assure you that he will have my written instruction to award you the contract. Man-to-man.'

Chalmers grabbed the young man's hand, pumping it furiously. 'I'm much obliged, Stewart. And you'll get the best o' work from me. I can assure you of that.'

Stewart sidestepped neatly. 'Good. Well, I'll be on my way. I'm glad I've made *somebody* happy.'

CHAPTER 18

Frances Ledingham reached for a cigarette then, aware of Violet's pointed stare, replaced the packet in her handbag. She shot a glance at her husband, Bobby, indicating that smoking would not be tolerated in Violet's presence.

Bobby shifted uncomfortably on the couch, straining against the unwelcome strictures of a suit not commonly worn in the middle of a work week.

'Am I all right if I go outside for a smoke?' he asked.

'Of course, Bob. You too, Frances,' Donald urged.

Frances shook her head, though she was in desperate need.

Donald Pascoe rose. 'Come on, Bob, we'll take a turn in the garden. Leave the women to talk.'

Violet glared at him. 'This is hardly a social gathering, Donald.'

Donald placed an arm around Bobby's shoulder, steering him towards the hall. 'That's exactly what it is, Violet. It's all we have left at a time like this. Good friends – and family.'

'Please excuse me,' Violet said, as the men

stepped outside. 'I really think *one* of us should be with Jim. I'll relieve Jennifer.

'This is awful!' Sandra whispered to her mother as soon as Violet had left the room. 'We shouldn't have come.'

'I know,' Frances whispered back. 'But we're just as entitled to be here as them.' Her eyes swam with tears. 'Poor Jim. We didn't even get to say goodbye.'

Jennifer opened the door and stepped towards her mother. Her embrace was swift and perfunctory, as though all of her being was held in a vice so taut that she had not the will to break free of it.

'I'll help you put away the messages,' Frances said. It was automatic, and all she could think of.

As the three women walked into the kitchen Jennifer faltered slightly, and her mother rushed to her, helping her into a chair.

'Sit down, hen. I'll put the kettle on.'

Sandra, too, was at her sister's side, kneeling to chafe Jennifer's hand with her own. She had begun to cry again. 'Oh, Jen . . .'

Mindlessly, Jennifer stroked Sandra's hair. 'It happened so quickly,' she murmured. 'He went down so fast.'

'Why did you no' call us?' Frances asked. 'Could you no' have called us?'

Jennifer took a deep breath. 'Not now, Ma. I couldn't take another *ounce* of guilt.'

'That's not what I meant,' Frances replied, her own hurt apparent at Jennifer's words. 'I just thought we could maybe have helped you more . . . through all of it.'

Jennifer raised her eyes. 'You might never understand this, Ma, but I didn't want *anyone* to see him like this. I wanted everyone to remember him the way he was. And . . . I just wanted it to be . . . him and me . . . right to the end.'

Frances swallowed back the tears. 'I *do* understand, Jen. But we were only down the road. We could have had a wee bit more time with him, if only to let him know how much we loved him.'

Jennifer smiled wanly. 'He knew that, Ma. He always knew that. He was closer to you than . . .' The words hung in the air.

Frances glanced at Sandra and she dutifully rose, relinquishing her position at Jennifer's side. Frances took her daughter's hand.

'I can imagine what it's been like, having Violet here, but she's his mother, Jen. You canna' grudge her this.'

'I do,' Jennifer whispered. 'I grudge her every minute of it.'

The tears spilled from Frances's eyes. 'Jen, I pray to God you never have anything harder to bear than what yir' going through right now. But you don't know what it's like to be a mother . . .'

Jennifer tried to pull her hand free, but Frances held it fast. 'You don't know what it's like to be a mother,' she repeated, 'to have yir heart pushed and pulled – filled to overflowing one minute, and emptied dry the next. To lose yir only child, Jen . . .'

'She lost him a long time ago,' Jennifer said, her teeth clenched.

'No, Jen. He made his home here, and God knows he loved you. But she never lost him. She needs this time now, just like you do. And to tell you the truth, if it was you lying there, I don't know if I could stand it. I think I'd probably crawl in beside you and let the dark take me.' Frances sniffed back her tears. 'Violet's coping the best way she can,' she said, as firmly as her trembling voice would allow. Frances looked into her daughter's eyes, but there was nothing there. Nothing at all.

The back door opened and Donald stood aside, allowing Bobby and Graham Kerr to pass before him.

'Look who we found,' Donald said, making an attempt at a valiant, if false, cheer.

Jennifer looked up and her eyes latched on Graham's. 'I'm glad you're here,' she said.

Frances, too, looked up. She saw Graham's face, and the expression on it, and she shivered.

Barra ambled slowly back to Drumdarg, pushing his bicycle over the crest. His young brow was furrowed with concern. Should he tell Mam or not?

In his heart of hearts he knew it would be wrong, that he'd be giving her something else to worry about, and didn't she have enough of that? Yet . . . what was Dad playing at, sneaking off from his work with that strange-looking woman? Barra's thoughts returned to his mother's party. It should have been such a grand night. And it was – except for that.

He recalled the day Tommy MacGregor brought a dirty magazine into the class. They'd all looked at it – Barra included. And the woman with her knees stapled to the cover had looked just like her. Just like the woman in Dad's van. Just like the woman who'd put Mam all wrong at her own party.

Barra stopped, laying his bicycle at the roadside. He knelt down, pulling a boulder from an opening in the undergrowth.

'Someone put a rock in that burrow,' he muttered, rising to dust off his knees. Then he remembered what Murdo had told him.

'Sometimes you have to give nature a helping hand. Else the buggers'd be running *us* off!'

Reluctantly Barra knelt back down, replacing the rock.

'Bugger it,' he said. 'Bugger yis all!'

He climbed back on his bike, in no humour to be forgiving of the cyclist overtaking him on the right. The cyclist looked back over his shoulder and smiled, that same dazzling smile that lifted your heart.

Barra smiled back. 'Wait, Jamie! Wait for me,' he called.

Chalmers scarcely took time to park the van properly. He rushed down the path, flinging the back door open.

'Rose!' he shouted.

'I'm here.' She leaned against the living-room door, her eyes sweeping him from head to foot.

'I just got the OK on the big house.' Chalmers reached for her, swinging her round in his arms. 'I'm taking you to Venice.'

She pushed him from her, her eyes as cold as steel.

'You're saturated in perfume,' she said. 'And it's no' mine.'

Chalmers stood there, watching, as she walked away from him, his heart as hollow as a mountain cavern.

Rose stopped at the foot of the stairs, her hand clenching the banister post. Her body was perfectly, utterly still.

'So, Chalmers, whose is it?'

Barra laid his bicycle against the wall, and opened the back door.

'Why's Dad home so early?' he asked.

'He got finished at the Wilsons'.'

There was something wrong with Mam's voice. Barra leaned against the sink, watching as Rose stirred the cheese sauce.

'Are we having cauliflower?' Barra detested it, even with the sauce.

'We were,' Rose said, lifting the pan from the ring and scraping the sauce into the sink. 'It went lumpy.'

It was usually lumpy, but that had never prompted Rose to take such drastic action before. He reached for his mother's arm, encouraging her to look at him, but Rose resisted, making a great show of filling the pan with cold water.

'Mam? Mam, what's wrong?'

'Nothing.' Rose's voice broke.

'Ahh, Mam. Yir still upset about Mr Pascoe. Is that it?'

Rose didn't answer. 'It is, isn't it, Mam?' Barra persisted.

Chalmers rose from his armchair and entered the kitchen. 'Don't be upsetting yir mother, son,' he said, his voice gruff.

'It wasn't *my* fault!' Barra answered indignantly. 'She was crying before I . . .'

'It's nothing to do with you, Barra,' Rose said. 'I'm just feeling . . .' She leaned against the sink as though the very effort of holding herself upright was too much for her.

Barra stared at her. '*Is* it Mr Pascoe, Mam? Is it?'

'It's got nothing to do with Jim!' Rose exploded. Her voice caught again. 'Oh, God forgive me. I don't know what I'm saying.'

Chalmers just stood there, looking bereft and unhappy. Barra looked from one to the other. 'It's about that dame in Dad's van then, isn't it?'

Rose turned, her eyes drilling into him. 'What dame?' she whispered.

'Aye,' Chalmers repeated, striding across the floor to grab Barra by the shirt-front. 'What nonsense are you talking now, Barra? What nonsense is this now?' He lifted the boy clear off the floor, raising his hand as though to strike him.

In a split second Rose had blocked the motion, staying Chalmers' hand with her own.

'You touch him and I'm gone,' she seethed. '*We're* gone. Make no mistake, Chalmers.'

As deftly as he'd lifted his son, Chalmers dropped him, and Barra's knees buckled slightly as he landed.

'Go down to the Whig, Barra,' Rose instructed, her voice flatter than any of them had ever heard. 'Tell Maisie to give you yir supper, and wait there till I come for you.'

'If yis are wanting rid o' me I can go to the woods for a while. How long d'youse think you'll be?'

'Barra, just go to the Whig. Stay there till I come for you, and *don't* go anywhere else.'

'How long?'

'As long as it takes,' Rose said, her voice scarcely above a whisper.

'Well, don't be leaving me there all night,' Barra said.

'Mam says I'm to get my supper here,' Barra informed Maisie.

'*Certainement*,' Maisie said, ushering him into the kitchen. A silver blue kaftan patterned with white stars covered her massive frame, and her grey hair was plaited in a thick coil and wrapped around her head. Perched precariously at each temple was a white velvet bow. Barra thought she looked very glamorous.

'They're having a fight,' he said glumly.

'It's about time,' she answered. She looked at him thoughtfully. 'I'm surprised you noticed.'

'I couldn't help it,' he confided. 'They weren't right with each other when I got home. I think I made things worse.'

'How exactly?' Maisie seemed extremely interested.

'Well, Dad was home already. But I'd seen him earlier . . . with the wifie he was dancing with at Mam's party.'

Maisie coughed. 'Where was this?'

'In Craigourie. In Dad's van, behind the station. I told Mam.'

'Oh, Barra . . .' Maisie closed her eyes, then opened them. 'Could you not, just for once in yir life, mind yir own business?'

Barra seemed close to tears. 'But it *is* my business, Maisie. Except I didn't mean for Mam to start crying. D'you think she'll be all right?' Concern for his mother swam in his green eyes.

'She'll be fine,' Maisie said gently. 'They were needing to clear the air.'

'Is that what they've been fighting about, then?'

Maisie shrugged and said nothing. Barra shrugged back.

'I'm to stay here 'til she comes for me.'

'Maybe they'll both come for you. I hope so.'

'Me too.' Barra looked like an injured fawn, his long lashes sweeping his cheeks, which were drained of colour.

Maisie's heart lurched at the sight of him. 'Och,

well, maybe Isla can cheer you up. She's taking a bath. She'll be down in a minute,' she said, in an effort to take his mind off his worries. 'I've never seen a lassie take so many baths. It's her third this week.'

Barra coloured. The image of Isla in a bath took shape in his mind. Immediately he felt embarrassed and ashamed of the thought, and shook his head as though to discard the enticing vision.

Maisie smiled to herself, and pulled out a frying-pan.

Glad to change the subject, Barra asked, 'Have you seen Mrs Pascoe the day?'

'No, Barra,' Maisie answered sadly. 'I called, of course, but I think they all need to be left alone right now.'

'I think that's what got Mam going. I asked Jamie about it on the way home. He said I might have a hard time, understanding it all.'

'It wouldn't take an angel to work that one out,' Maisie replied. 'You're still in touch with celestial forces, then?'

Barra set his jaw. 'Don't make fun of me, Maisie.'

Maisie whirled, as easily as she could. 'Ach, Barra, I'm not. It's just all so "grim reaper", y'know.'

'But it's not, Maisie. I don't think it is.'

Maisie blew out her cheeks. The movement was almost imperceptible. 'Listen, *liebchen*, you're going to have to face this along with the rest of us. It's not going to be pleasant.'

'But we don't, Maisie. We don't have to. Thing

is, when I was coming back from Craigourie, I was feeling, well, unsettled. And . . .'

Maisie chuckled. 'Barra, it's about time you felt unsettled. You've been quite alarmingly unsettling to everybody else for your entire unsettling life.'

'Och, Maisie.' Barra grinned, protesting at the back-handed compliment. 'Anyway, next thing I knew Jamie was cycling along beside me.'

'No doubt he'll be entering the Tour de France next. I should think he'd have an unfair advantage.'

'Mai-*sie*!'

'OK!' Maisie threw her hands in the air, signalling her surrender. 'Continue, darling boy. I shall remain silent. Enthralled, but silent.'

Barra waited for a moment, until he was sure it was safe to speak. 'Well, like I said, we were cycling along. And I have to tell you, Maisie, Jamie enjoyed it. He misses his own bike.' Anticipating Maisie's rejoinder, he rushed on. 'And I asked him again about Mr Pascoe, and if I was right in believing that Jamie had come to Drumdarg to help Mr Pascoe.' Barra paused for much-needed oxygen.

'And?'

'Well, he never has answered that. Not exactly. But he said that everything was unfolding as it should. He's said that before.'

'Wind-chimes.'

'What?'

Maisie looked as sad as Barra had ever seen her. 'There's a prayer, motto, call it what you will, entitled "Desiderata". Seventeenth century, I believe. Have you heard of it, Barra?'

Barra shook his head.

'It's quite beautiful. There is a line – "You are a child of the universe, and no doubt the universe is unfolding as it should".' Maisie swallowed. 'Something like that. It's out there with flowers in yir hair, and give peace a chance . . . and wind-chimes.'

Maisie was making no sense at all. What's more, she had forgotten all about the frying-pan.

Barra frowned. 'I still think Mr Pascoe will be all right, Maisie. I mean, it makes sense, doesn't it?'

Maisie was saved from a reply.

Footsteps sounded on the stairs. Isla turned towards them, and Barra caught his breath. She had washed her hair and it was pushed back from her face, revealing perfect features devoid of the first lick of make-up. Her bare arms shone silkily with a dusting of talcum powder, and Barra could smell its hypnotic scent from clear across the room.

'Who invited *that* in?' Isla demanded.

'I'm here for my supper,' Barra informed her, trying to appear undaunted.

'Gawd!' Isla said in disgust.

Doug appeared at Isla's back. 'Can you make up some ham sandwiches, Maisie? There's a few in the bar watching that programme on Early Bird.'

'*Uno momento, mi amore*. The children need fed first,' Maisie trilled.

'*Children*!' Barra and Isla retorted in unison. Barra grinned and was rewarded by the barest flicker of an answering smile from Isla.

259

'I'd be wanting to try again,' he said.

'Try what?' Isla asked.

'To be nice t'you.' He waited for a response, but Isla looked guarded still. Desperately, Barra searched for something to say that would please her.

'You deserve it. You're so grown-up. I'm still trying to be that. To be grown-up.'

Isla snorted. 'You *are* weird!' she stated.

But something in her eyes had moved, shifted slightly, and Barra's heart leaped in hope.

CHAPTER 19

Rose carried her cup of tea into the living room. She could no more have drunk it than fly in the air, but it gave her something to hold on to – something warm and solid and real.

'Whatever happened, I want to know,' she began. Chalmers opened his mouth in protest but she rushed on. 'I want to know, Chalmers, and I want the truth.'

She waited as Chalmers struggled, praying harder than she had ever prayed in her life that he would lie, tell her something, *anything* but the truth.

Chalmers sat across from her, his mouth working to find the words. He pulled off his glasses, twisted them in his hands, and put them back. They provided little cover for the guilt and the pain which dulled his eyes.

'It was Sheena Mearns in your van, wasn't it?' She couldn't bear the waiting, every second stretching out like a silent scream before her.

'No. It was . . . It isn't . . . Nothing happened.'

The tears began again, and Rose fought to

control them. 'Chalmers, please . . . I have to know.'

'I kissed her. That was all, Rose. Honest to God, that was *all*!'

Rose felt something snap inside her. She *heard* it, as clear as the twang of an old guitar string.

'All?' she whispered.

'God, Rose, if there's anything I could do . . .'

And in an instant, Rose was a little girl again. You'll no' leave me, Grandad?

'I trusted you.'

'I'm sorry.' Chalmers was crying too now, heavy tears falling on to the backs of his hands, the hands she had loved, still loved.

'You knew I couldn't take this, Chalmers. You knew, and yet you did it anyway.' A distant rage was overtaking her. She tried to keep it at bay, but it was useless. It roared within her, rushing to explode.

'And no doubt it was planned? This kiss?'

'NO! I . . . Nothing happened, Rose. That's why I met her, to tell her that. I . . . I threw her out of the van, Rose,' Chalmers pleaded.

'The van,' Rose scoffed. 'Of course. It's not as if that hoor could take you home with her. I suppose "the van" was yir only option.'

'Would you let me tell you?'

The tears had stopped miraculously, held in a far place, safe for the moment. 'Please do.'

Chalmers took a deep breath, and another. 'You're right, Rose. It *was* planned, after a fashion. Not by me!'

'You just happened to be there.'

Chalmers ran a hand across his forehead. 'OK. All right . . . She was the one who suggested it. But I went there to tell her that I wasn't going to get involved wi' her. I promise you, Rose. I promise you that's why I went.'

'And you accidentally kissed her while you were telling her this.'

'She . . . I didn't expect her to . . . It was just a kiss.'

'And all of this in front of your son?'

'No. No, Rose. He didn't see anything. I don't think he saw . . .'

Afterwards, it seemed to Rose that she had moved in slow motion. She recalled every movement, every muscle stretching and pulling and pushing her across the infinite distance between them. And then Rose punched Chalmers full in the face, knocking his glasses to the floor.

Instinctively he swung back at her, lowering his fist at the last possible second. She had expected the blow, had moved forward to meet it, welcoming it and prepared to deliver several in return.

Instead, her wrist was caught and held fast in her husband's grip, and her eyes were caught too, and held just as fast as Chalmers begged her – *begged* her to forgive him. As quickly as it had happened, it was over, and she was in his arms.

They sobbed together; muffled promises, endless apologies, loving entreaties bridging the hurt and the pain. And then he was carrying her upstairs, and Rose Maclean pulled the sodden shirt from her husband's back and threw it to the floor.

Later, much later, Chalmers pulled her back into his arms. 'I'll make this up to you, Rose. I will,' he whispered, nuzzling her hair.

'I don't ever want to talk about it again,' she said. 'Not ever.' She was aware of the loosening in her husband's body, and briefly resented the fact that her words had cheered him, relieving him of a lifetime of atonement.

Though her own hurt still burned within her, Rose realised that she had faced the worst fear of all and would never have to face it again. Chalmers had resisted Sheena Mearns! And, kiss or no kiss, he was here, here with her – and he wasn't going away.

For that Rose was truly grateful. God, weren't you reading it in the papers every day? It was the sixties, after all. Free love, 'open' marriages, *wife-swapping*!

Rose sighed.

Chalmers, thinking it to be a reminder of his betrayal, leaned up on his elbow. 'I'm booking a holiday for us. In Venice. We'll go this summer, just the two of us.'

Rose raised her eyebrows. 'What about Barra?'

'He can stay with Mam and Dad. You know he loves it there. He'll be happy as the day's long.'

Rose looked up at her husband. She noticed with concern that his right eye was puffy, and already beginning to turn purple. How were they going to explain *that* to Barra?

'C'mon, Rose. We deserve some time together. Don't you think we could spend just a couple of weeks by ourselves?' Chalmers asked.

'What about the bedders? The summer's the best time . . .'

'I wanted to talk to you about that,' Chalmers continued. He kissed her forehead. 'Look, I know you don't mind the work, Rose, but our house isn't our own when there's folk staying.' He paused, kissed her again. 'You don't even want to . . . be with me when they're here.'

'I do!' Rose protested, lying.

'No you don't. You're full of excuses, and I know you've always got it in the back o' yir mind that they'll hear us.'

Rose swallowed. It was true. The idea of having to serve up breakfast to a couple of strangers who had been just a thin wall away the night before had always filled her with dread.

'So you don't want me doing the bedders now?'

'Maybe every other week. I could live wi' that. I'm going to be working harder than ever myself, by the looks of it.' He smiled.

God, what a relief that would be, Rose mused. Maybe she could get to enjoy the summer for a change, instead of up to her eyes in sheets and pillow-slips, and praying for dry days so she could have them all washed and back on the beds in time for the next lot.

'It's a thought,' she murmured.

Chalmers squirmed. 'I need the bathroom,'

he apologised. 'I'll be right back.'

Rose smiled, dropping her arm over the side of the bed. Her hand grazed the carpet, brushing against the crumpled shirt. The pain returned and she waited, hoping for it to disappear, but in her heart she knew that she could expect it to come and go at will for a long, long time. Sooner or later she would learn to master it.

She rose, picking the shirt from the floor. It crossed her mind that she might do well to wash it and hang it back in the wardrobe – as reminder to her husband. But she knew that if she were to do that, the pain would never leave her. It would be there for ever, like the damned shirt. Rose walked towards her dressing-table and opened her mani-cure set. With a tiny pair of nail scissors she began cutting it to shreds.

Chalmers made no comment when he returned, but their eyes met briefly in the mirror and, for the first time in her life, Rose recognised how it felt to have power. For the look on Chalmers face made it quite clear that he was relieved to see the shirt become victim of the scissors – and not himself.

Rose smiled to herself. It would be wonderful to visit Venice.

Less than an hour later, Jim Pascoe also rose – leaving his wife holding on to a body wasted by disease, and beyond repair. Jennifer sighed softly and laid her cheek against the recent warmth of his forehead, knowing he was gone.

Jim bent down from a great and glorious height and kissed the top of her head. How he loved her. How he would always love her.

'What d'you think happened to Chalmers' eye?' Doug asked.

Maisie removed the white velvet bows, placing them carefully in the top drawer of her dressing-table. She looked down at its contents. It was a young woman's drawer. A *thin* woman's drawer.

'Rose hit him,' she said.

Doug sat up, pulling the quilt around him. 'How d'you know?'

'She was needing to.'

Doug regarded her. 'Do you ever feel like hitting me?'

'Never,' she answered, reaching to draw the curtains.

'Maisie, leave them open,' Doug said. 'Let me look at you.'

'You don't have the time,' she replied. 'And I don't have the figure.'

'You're all the figure I'd ever want,' he murmured, but the words sounded automatic, without a trace of passion.

'Be careful of yir dreams, *mi amore*. They might come true.'

'Och, don't be handing me that old chestnut,' Doug said. 'You know I love every inch of you.'

Maisie sat on the end of the bed, struggling valiantly with her kaftan. 'Then you got yourself a bargain.' Her voice was muffled as she tore herself free from the cotton shroud.

She stood, sucking in her mighty midriff and hoping her knickers were still covering her dimpled behind. Pulling back the covers, she climbed into bed, detesting the sound of her body on the mattress, the groaning, shiff-shuffing noise of it.

'I was slim once,' she said. 'I could throw myself down on a sofa or bed and scarcely hear the rustle of fabric – or flesh.'

'Maisie,' Doug protested softly. 'What's got into you?'

'Every time I move it sounds like a fart, like the rush of air escaping. Haven't you noticed, Doug?'

'No. I have not,' Doug said firmly. 'And I'm not going to add to yir misery by agreeing with you.'

'Why do you stay?' she asked.

Doug sighed. 'Don't start on me, Maisie,' he said wearily. 'You've been all wrong since we heard about Jim.'

Maisie began to cry, very quietly. 'What will Jen do now? She loved him so much, Doug.'

'Jennifer's strong. She's had to be. And she's young enough to start over. Jim wouldn't want any less for her.'

'How can you be so . . . drunk? And still be so sober?'

'Maisie, I'm going to sleep now. You should do the same. I've a feeling tomorrow's going to be hard enough.'

Maisie turned towards him. 'Will you hold me, Doug?'

'For ever,' he sighed. 'You never give up on me, Maisie. I'm glad I'm not Jennifer tonight. I don't think I could cope without you.'

Maisie cried silently into the dark long after Doug had succumbed to sleep. The whole evening had had a surreal quality to it, as though it had happened to other people, in another place, another time. A thousand images played themselves out in her mind.

Chalmers and Rose arriving together, hand in hand, like a couple of teenagers. Barra's astonishment at his father's black eye, his questions halted in mid-stream by his mother, staunchly insisting that Chalmers had stotted his head off the living-room door. Chalmers' look of embarrassment as he'd caught Maisie's surreptitious 'thumbs-up' sign to Rose.

Olive being plied with a brandy and port by Sandy, hopeful that the ancient cure for an upset stomach might somehow also restore mobility to Olive's neck – in time for the Sunday bingo.

Isla laughing – laughing! – with Barra, as they exchanged tales of schoolday pranks.

And then, in the middle of it all, Roddy MacDonald arriving with the news that he had just seen the hearse pull up at the Pascoes' door.

Silently they had filed outside, standing together in the stillness of the April evening, waiting in hushed communion until the hearse had passed once more, bringing Jim Pascoe's body to Craigourie.

Unconsciously, Barra had leaned into his mother and she'd reached to pull him closer. His face had drained of all colour, his eyes were wide with shock. Chalmers had caught Rose's worried expression and gathered both of them to him, placing his free hand on Barra's trembling shoulder.

It was a sombre gathering which returned to the Whig.

Rose allowed her husband just time enough to down a whisky in remembrance of their friend before setting off for home. Barra had uttered not a word, sitting silently across from Rose. When they were ready to leave, Maisie had given Rose the briefest of hugs.

'He'll be all right,' she'd assured her friend. 'It's just the shock.'

But, lying here in the darkness, she felt such a sense of the boy's loss that her eyes filled again. 'Poor Barra,' she whispered into the night.

How she would have loved a son like Barra. Or a daughter like Isla . . .

Well, that was never to be. But was it so impossible that she might become Mrs Doug Findlay?

Was that really so much to ask for?

She fell asleep, praying for Barra, and Jennifer, and Jim – and herself.

CHAPTER 20

Graham arrived first, bringing Frances Ledingham with him.

'Yir dad and Sandra's coming by after work,' Frances explained, holding her daughter close. They stood like that for a moment. 'Can I go in and see him?'

'He's at the undertakers',' Jennifer replied. 'We agreed that he wasn't to be laid out in the house.' The words came out as though by rote. Jennifer knew she'd be repeating them several times in the hours to come.

Frances looked momentarily alarmed. 'I wondered . . . The curtains are open.'

Jennifer nodded. 'We agreed on that too, Ma.'

Frances could tell by the expression on Violet's face that denying the tradition of closing the curtains and blinds after a death was not something of which she approved. Nonetheless, it had apparently been her son's wish, and she seemed to have decided upon letting Jennifer have her way.

Nervously, Frances moved towards her. Violet stood to receive the mandatory embrace and

271

Frances pulled quickly away, uncomfortable with the stiff formality.

'Thank you, Frances. Good of you to come.'

A small rebellion forced itself upwards. Frances locked eyes with Violet Pascoe.

'I would go to the ends of the earth for Jen – or Jim.'

'Drumdarg? Hardly that!'

Frances took her place on the sofa, deflated and already calling to mind the words she should have said, could have said.

Graham followed, stiffly offering his condolences, no more comfortable in Violet's presence than she. Then he turned towards Jennifer, and Frances closed her eyes. How more naked could his love for her daughter be?

And how, how in God's name could Jennifer stand there, so beautiful, so . . . contained, at this, the worst time of her life? Frances had never felt a greater love for her daughter than in that one moment – nor had she ever felt so distant.

Graham kissed Jennifer chastely on the cheek and squeezed her arm, unable to tear his eyes from her.

'I can take you into Craigourie,' he offered. 'The arrangements . . .'

She smiled her gratitude. 'Donald drove me in first thing,' she said. 'He's over at the Whig. He thought we might run short on whisky. But everything's in hand. The undertakers have been very good.'

'Well, that's what they're paid for,' Graham said.

Frances swallowed, aware that Graham was probably wishing the ground would open up and swallow him. Violet Pascoe was looking at him as though he had two heads.

'Sorry,' he murmured, shaking his head. 'I'm so sorry, Violet.'

A stony stare acknowledged the apology.

'What can I do?' he asked helplessly, turning back to Jennifer. 'Is there anything you need?'

She began to demur, then stopped. 'Actually,' she said, moving towards the desk, 'you could maybe drop Jim's insurance policy into the office for me.'

'Of course.'

'I called in when we were in the town. I've signed everything, but I forgot to take the policy with me. I . . . I wasn't thinking. You'd never know I worked there.' She attempted a smile.

Graham took the policy from her. 'Will you be going back to work now?' he asked.

This time Violet actually gasped.

God, Frances thought, can't he say *anything* right?

Graham inspected the floor, and Frances's heart tightened with embarrassment for him.

'Yes,' Jennifer said firmly. 'I'm starting back on Tuesday. They're closed Monday, of course. Easter . . .' Her eyes filled, and she moved towards the kitchen. 'I'd better make a start on the sandwiches. We'll probably have a few folk calling in over the course o' the day.'

Violet and Frances rose simultaneously. Violet glanced at Jennifer's mother, and Frances quickly sat down again. Graham sat beside her, the two of them perched there like crows on a wall.

Frances realised that Jennifer would be just a floor below Graham when she returned to work. How would he handle it? He'd be seeing her every single day. Until now, all Jennifer had had in common with him was Jim – and the business, of course.

'I can't believe he's gone,' Graham whispered, and Frances reached to pat his arm.

'Me neither.'

'I'll never have a friend like him.'

'Nothing can destroy a friendship, Graham. Not if you truly cared about each other.'

Graham turned to face Frances. And in his eyes was the knowledge that Frances had detected his love for Jennifer. Somehow, somewhere, she had seen through him.

Frances did not have to hide any condemnation in her expression. There was none. The only thing on her mind was her daughter's happiness. And though she had loved her son-in-law deeply, and would miss him terribly, Frances was a pragmatic woman.

Again, she patted Graham's arm. 'Life goes on,' she said.

'Well, what do you think o' that?' Olive asked Sandy as they closed the gate behind them. 'No' a curtain closed, and Jim lying on an undertaker's slab, instead o' laid out in his own home. It's a queer kettle o' fish, altogether.' Olive was deeply offended by it all.

'It's the modern way o' doing things, I suppose,' Sandy replied.

Luckily, some tradition *had* been adhered to that afternoon. He'd had two free drams and a nice cup of tea. He'd barely swallowed the first dram when Donald Pascoe had risen, somewhat unsteadily, to refill his glass. It had been an extrememly generous measure for a city gent to pour – and a Lowlander at that.

'Poor Jennifer's looking fair done wi' it all,' Olive remarked. 'And as for that drum major of a mother-in-law . . .'

'D'you think you'll make the bingo on Sunday?' Sandy interrupted, as they walked back towards the Whig.

'If this neck ever gets better,' Olive retorted. 'It's hellish agony I'm in.'

'The linament's no' helping then?'

'Not a bit. I canna' even turn in the bed at night.'

'I'd soon rub it better if I was in there beside you.'

Olive tried to yank her neck in Sandy's direction, and nearly screamed in the process.

'Watch yir mouth!' she threatened. She glared at him a moment longer. 'You've had far too much to drink,' she said in disgust.

Sandy just smiled.

275

Maisie arrived in a bright orange floor-length creation, topped by a lemon crocheted poncho. She looked like a moving advert for Outspan. Wasting little time on condolences, she placed a wicker basket containing a loaf, a dozen softies, and two large tins of red salmon on the coffee table.

'Loaves and fishes, *mes amis*. Loaves and fishes.'

Jennifer smiled her first real smile of the day. 'Thanks, Maisie.'

'Doug'll be over when he closes the bar,' Maisie said, heading for the sofa. Graham and Donald rose immediately, an identical expression of alarm on their faces. Donald perched on the arm of the couch, weaving slightly to catch his balance.

'Howsh bisnesh?' he enquired.

'Hilarious,' Maisie replied. 'There is none.'

Some invisible string appeared to be pulling Violet heavenward. Had she been sitting any straighter, she would have been standing.

'I'd have thought we'd be getting a few more in, with Easter at the weekend,' Maisie continued. 'The town seems to be busy enough.'

'Have you given any more thought to . . . you know?' Graham asked.

Maisie nodded. 'We'll talk about it after the funeral,' she said. 'When is it, Jen?'

'Saturday. Eleven o'clock.'

'Good,' Maisie replied. 'The sooner the better.'

'Well!' Violet exclaimed. 'I've never come across such insensitive, primitive . . .'

'Vy-let!' Donald tried to focus on his wife.

'Don't "Violet" me!' she said. 'It's your son they're talking about!'

The atmosphere became even more charged.

'I apologise if I've offended you, Violet,' Maisie said.

'*Mrs* Pascoe. I hardly know you.'

Maisie inspected her golden fingernails. 'Well, I know you. And I knew Jim. I thought the world of him. And I knew him well enough to know that he wouldn't want this time of mourning to be . . . any longer than it has to be.'

Frances knocked back a large rum and cola.

'Mourning? *Mourning*? I've yet to see the first sign of mourning!' Violet flung the words at the company in general and fled from the room.

Donald rose to follow her, but lost his balance and collapsed into the bucket chair she had just vacated.

Jennifer was staring at the floor, her face as white as death itself.

'Well, Maisie, ten out of ten,' Maisie chided herself.

Jennifer looked up. 'Don't feel bad,' she said. 'I know exactly what you meant, and you're quite right. Jim would detest . . . would have detested all of this.'

She rose to clear the coffee table of the assorted cups and glasses, and glanced above Maisie's head.

Barra was coming up the path in full school uniform, a bunch of wild flowers held tightly in his hands, his hair plastered to his skull in an obvious attempt to control his curls. One, more disobedient than the rest, had escaped from his crown, looping upwards like a tiny halo.

Jennifer stared at him.

This is unbelievable, she thought, but she couldn't quite conceal a smile.

Jim, I could really do with a hand here. Stop laughing. I mean it.

She went to answer the door and, somewhere between the thought and the reality, Jennifer realised that Jim wouldn't be there for her – ever again.

'I was black-affronted,' Helen confided. 'She could have at least paid her respects.' Marjorie Cunningham was once again the topic of conversation. 'After all, it's no' as if they'll be here for the funeral.'

'Aye,' Murdo agreed. 'It wouldn't have taken too much out o' her just to call in. Of course, she never knew Jim.' He tapped his pipe on the saucer, but Helen was too dismayed by the prior day's occurrences to notice.

'At least Stewart was there,' Murdo reminded her.

'That's another thing,' Helen said. 'I know they'll be leaving tonight, but I'd have thought Stewart could manage one more day, at least stay for the service.'

'Well, it *is* the Easter weekend. I'm sure he was right that there wouldn't be any hope of him changing their tickets at this late date.'

'He could have tried,' Helen said.

Murdo nodded. It saddened him that he felt only relief that Stewart and Marjorie would be leaving that evening. The rapport he had once shared with the young man seemed to have evaporated, leaving a hollow silence in its place. The only time the two had come close to recapturing it had been on that first afternoon, down by the river.

Just two days had passed since then, but they'd been two of the longest days of Murdo's life.

He reached for his pipe, admitting to himself that he was sorely looking forward to regaining his morning solitude. Helen had been like a cat on a hot tin roof since the couple arrived – and for quite a few days before. He hoped their departure would bring a sense of order back into his life.

'Even poor Hattie managed a visit,' Helen continued, like Gallus with a bone he had no intention of surrendering. 'And you know how feared she is o' anything to do wi' death. She'll no' manage the funeral, I'm thinking.'

'Jennifer would make no difference over that,' Murdo said. 'She's a grand lassie.'

'Aye, she is that. Which is more than I can say for Violet Pascoe.'

'Och, Helen, the wifie must be feeling desolate. God, she didna' even know half the faces that were there yesterday. How could she do more?'

'She's a bloody snob! She hadn't a word for anyone until Stewart arrived, and then she was all over him, as though he was the only one worth the time of day.'

'Hmmm. Well, it doesna' change the fact that she just lost her boy. Maybe we should be a wee bit more understanding.'

'You mean *I* should be a bit more understanding?' Helen asked, her voice quieter now.

Murdo smiled. 'We all should.'

Helen sniffed, and lifted her cup. Preparing to drink her tea, she paused. 'Did you see the shiner on Chalmers?'

'Aye. He must have hit it at work.'

'Maybe. And maybe not.'

'What's in yir mind now, Helen?'

'Well, you didn't think it funny that Sheena Mearns didna' show for her work yesterday?'

'Away wi' you! Sandra was saying Miss Falconer in the library didna' show either. There's probably a bug on the go. You've just got it in for Sheena Mearns – ever since Rose's party.'

'Long before that!' Helen snapped. 'That dame's been a suggestive besom since ever I've known her. And it's all very well for you, Murdo Macrae, propping up the bar wi' yir cronies and leaving me at the table to witness thon carry-on! She was leading Chalmers on something awful, and he wasn't too disappointed, I can tell you.'

'That tongue'll get you in trouble one day,' Murdo warned.

Helen shrugged. 'Well, I'd love to know what *really* happened to Chalmers' eye. Still, Rose seems more like herself again.' She smiled. 'Though Barra seems quite desolate, poor thing.'

Murdo puffed on his pipe. 'To tell you the truth, I thought Jennifer looked quite relieved when Rose got up to go. Thon boy can be a bit of a handful, though the day would be poorer without him in it.'

'Och, it's a hard thing for a youngster to contend with. And I'm thinking he'll no' be so ready to believe in angels for a while – more's the pity. Still, wasn't it just like him to bring Jennifer flowers? What boy would think to do that?'

'Mmm! They're no' what you'd call flowers. They're weeds. They're all over the woods just now, and I just hope she doesna' take him at his word and put them in her borders,' Murdo mused. 'They'll be rampant in no time at all.'

Gallus was running in circles at the back door, chasing his tail. As soon as he was aware that he'd caught Murdo's attention, he stopped. Never taking his eyes from his master, he thumped the door twice with his behind.

Murdo rose. 'What a sense o' humour he's got,' he said lovingly.

'He'll get "sense o' humour" if he wakens herself,' Helen warned. 'Be off wi' the pair o' you.'

'Aye, aye, sir.' Murdo laughed, reaching for his wellies.

Isla wandered up the trail, glad to be out in the fresh, cool air of the morning. Unusually, Doug and Maisie weren't on the best of terms, and she'd decided to make herself scarce for a while. As she rounded the first curve she spied Barra ahead, down on all fours, rapt in attention at something outside her line of vision – something on the ground.

'What you looking at?'

'A beetle.'

'Did you see me coming?'

'Didn't have to. I heard you.'

'You're in a vile mood.'

'Go away.'

Isla moved closer, for the first time noticing the beetle. It was huge and glossy-black. She retreated again.

'Gyudders!'

The beetle became trapped in a rotting leaf. Struggling to get free, it flipped on to its back, legs waving wildly in the air. Barra picked up the leaf, using a corner gently to turn the beetle back on to its feet. It scuttled off, disappearing into the grass.

'He's not gyudders, he's marvellous,' Barra informed her. 'In relation to his size, he just travelled as far as a human being would crossing the Sahara. Except he did it in seconds.'

'God, aren't you the professor?'

Barra stood, dusting off his knees.

'What're you doing here anyway?'

'It's a free country!' Barra turned from her and began walking upwards, listlessly scuffing the earth with each step.

Isla hesitated, then moved forward to join him.

They walked in silence until they reached the clearing. Taking proprietory charge of the old log, Barra stretched himself along it, face down.

'What's wrong wi' you?' Isla's tone was puzzled. Barra glanced at her briefly before reaching to trace the lines on the end of the log with his index finger.

'It's ancient,' he murmured. 'I always lose count.'

Then, swinging his legs to the ground, he made room for Isla to sit.

She paused long enough to let him know that the decision had been her own, before carefully positioning herself as far from him as possible.

Barra hardly seemed to notice. He rested his elbows on his knees and dumped his head between them.

'People should get to be old,' he said. 'Not just trees 'n' things.'

'I hope she keeps the Mini,' Isla sighed.

'Course she will. Why wouldn't she?'

Isla shrugged, her bosom moving magnificently upwards.

Barra caught the motion from the corner of his eye, and felt himself grow hot. He squinted back down the trail, afraid that Isla might notice.

'You've been too long in the sun,' she remarked. 'Yir neck's red.'

'You think yir sophisticated,' Barra answered, glaring back at her. 'But you're not.'

Isla stood immediately. 'I'm off,' she retorted. 'No-one's got a civil tongue in their heads the day!'

She moved to pass him and Barra lifted a hand

as though to stop her. Then dropped it.

'I'm sorry,' he whispered. 'Y'can stay if you like.'

'I don't have to.'

'Then go. Everyone goes.'

Isla stopped, her eyes coming to rest on the crown of Barra's head. He had lovely hair.

'Yir angel couldn't help then?' she asked, her voice softer now.

Barra sniffed, shook his head. 'He's gone too.'

Slowly, Isla sat down again, closer this time.

'D'you think you imagined him?' She seemed interested.

'Dunno. He seemed real.' Barra sniffed again, louder this time, and for a moment his eyes filled. Isla looked away, uncomfortable, yet wanting somehow to console him.

Barra, too, turned his head, blinking back his tears. How could he possibly have imagined Jamie? He'd been so sure, so very sure that he existed, even though he'd never found out exactly why the angel had chosen *him*. And he'd truly believed that Mr Pascoe wouldn't die, would wake from his coma and start getting better again.

Well, if Jamie was some kind of stuntman, appearing and disappearing like that, he was pretty good at it. Barra's lip curled at the thought. He'd been made to feel daft, soft in the head, by some evil boy who should know better than to go around making a fool of people.

Isla's presence all but forgotten, Barra narrowed his eyes until they were almost closed, until the forest floor was no more than a shimmering verdant line. He hadn't imagined Jamie. He'd been real. He'd been *real*!

Perhaps, because Jamie was just learning to be an angel, he didn't *know* how to mend people. Maybe he'd got into trouble for making Barra believe in something that was never going to happen in the first place. Maybe he'd been called away as some kind of punishment.

Still, it would've been nice if he'd stayed around long enough to explain it all – or just to say good-bye.

Barra screwed his eyes completely shut, too late this time to prevent the escape of his tears. As surreptitiously as he could, he raised a finger to stroke them away.

Isla placed her hand on the log between them, inches from Barra's own, making a great show of studying the woods around them.

Barra looked at it for a long moment. Then, tentatively, he laid his own hand by hers.

For Isla, it was no stretch at all to cover it with her own.

CHAPTER 21

Stewart lifted the tray. 'I'll bring it up myself,' he offered.

Helen tried to hide her disdain. Imagine having breakfast at ten-thirty in the morning! Lord, the day was half over.

'There's no' enough there to keep body and soul together,' she remarked. 'A good plate o' porridge is what she's needing. You too,' she reminded Stewart, disappointed once again that coffee and toast had been all the breakfast he'd required.

Stewart laid the tray back down on the table. 'Helen . . .' he began.

'Aye?'

'I was wondering . . . before we leave, if you might be able to talk to Marjorie. About your experience, so to speak.'

'Experience?'

Stewart sat, the tray forgotten. He passed a hand across his forehead, his face flushed with embarrassment.

'I'm not sure how these things work, you know.'

'What things?' Helen was mystified.

'Women's things . . . Miscarriages.'

Helen walked towards the kitchen door, closing it firmly. If Marjorie Cunningham was to interrupt her again, she'd at least have to open the door.

Helen sat. 'Stewart, just because we've both suffered miscarriages doesn't mean we can *talk* about it. Surely you remember yir wife's reaction when you last broached the subject?'

'I know,' Stewart agreed. 'But she has nobody else to confide in, Helen. None of her friends have . . . suffered. And she won't talk to me.'

'How hard have you tried?'

Stewart shook his head. 'I *have* tried. But she pushes me away. I can hardly bear it.'

Helen's heart went out to him. 'You really do love her, don't you?'

'So very much,' he replied, his voice filled with anguish. 'She's a truly decent sort, Helen. You've just seen the worst of her, I'm afraid. You have no idea how much fun she is . . . was.'

Helen bit her lip. She could no more imagine Marjorie Cunningham having fun than she could imagine a man on the moon. It was unthinkable.

'Stewart, can you no' see that I'd be the last person on earth she would talk to about this?'

'No! I can't,' he said forlornly. 'It was my whole reason for booking this trip, Helen. I thought if anyone could talk to her, you could. You've been like a mother to me. I want Marjorie to feel the same way – and you about her.'

Helen looked away from him. If she lived to be a

hundred, she could never look upon Marjorie as a daughter.

'I'll do my best,' she murmured. 'But I doubt it'll be good enough.'

'Thank you.' Stewart raised his head to look at her. 'I knew I could depend on you.'

Helen smiled back at him. The years fell away, and he was once more just a little motherless boy, pouring his heart out at her kitchen table. She stood and walked towards him, ruffling his hair as he leaned into her, his arm around her waist, his head resting on her ample bosom.

A soft knock on the kitchen door made them both start.

Helen rushed to open it, gasping at the sight before her.

Hattie was standing there, arm-in-arm with a balding, middle-aged stranger.

'This is Kenneth More,' she said proudly.

Hattie stabbed at the fire, glad of the warmth it spread throughout the small room. She reached for the old fireguard and set it on the hearth. It was time to prepare for bed. Every light blazed, illuminating the windows and the blanket of snow which had fallen ceaselessly since early that morning.

She didn't register the sound of somebody tapping on the door, thinking it was just the cracking of the coals. Then it became more insistent and she moved towards the window, trying to peer into the darkness to determine the identity of this late visitor. The snow was thick, and the night dark.

Hattie pushed herself away from the window and crossed the short distance to the door. Holding her ear against the solid thickness of the wood she called out, 'Is that you, Mr Macrae?'

A stranger's voice came back to her. 'I'm Kenneth. Kenneth More. I'm stuck in the snow.'

Hattie unlocked the door, and opened it the tiniest fraction. A flurry of snowflakes swept into the room and she closed it back. 'I'm not allowed to let anyone in,' she said.

'Could you please tell me where the nearest phone is, then?'

Hattie opened the door wide. 'It's in here,' she answered, pointing to the sideboard.

The man stood huddled in the doorway, without even an overcoat to protect him from the storm. He gaped at her for a moment before setting a hesitant foot across the threshold.

'Is it all right? For me to come in?'

Hattie looked confused. 'I need to shut the door. The snow's making the floor wet.'

Kenneth entered the small room, backing against the wall to avoid getting close to this strange woman. 'Is there a garage close by?' he asked.

Hattie nodded. 'There's Mackay's in Craigourie.'

'Craigourie? I've just come from there. I was heading west.'

'There's no' one west of here. Not till you get past Dunfearn.'

The man looked exhausted, and thoroughly dejected.

'I'll try the one in Craigourie. I have to be on the road tonight.'

'It's closed,' Hattie said, removing the fireguard to allow the heat to permeate the room. 'D'you want to sit down?'

'I . . . No, thank you. Is there anyone here who could help me? I don't have a spade, and I'll need to dig the car out. It's about quarter of a mile back down the road.'

'Murdo'll have a spade.'

'Murdo? Your husband?'

'Oh, no,' Hattie replied, her face covered in embarrassment. 'Murdo lives in the big house.' She lifted her face to the stranger. 'You're shivering. You must be starved wi' the cold. It's not good for you.'

Kenneth inched closer to the fireplace. 'How can I get hold of this Murdo?'

Hattie shook her head, a worried expression on her face. 'He'll be in his bed by now. I wouldn't want to wake him.'

Kenneth looked close to tears. 'Is there *anyone* who can help me? I'm just hopeless when things like this happen. Mother was right. I'll never make it through life without her.'

Hattie stared at him. 'Sit yirself at the fire. I'll get you a cup o' cocoa.'

Kenneth sat, shivering still. Great pools of snow had melted at his feet, and Hattie brought a cloth from under the sink to mop up the mess. 'You'd

290

better take that jacket off. I'll put it over the fire-guard. It'll be dry in no time,' she said.

Like an obedient child, Kenneth removed the jacket, displaying a rather large belly covered by a sodden white shirt.

'You'd better give me yir shirt too,' Helen said.

'Oh no. I . . . I couldn't do that. It wouldn't be proper.'

'OK.'

Hattie put some milk on to heat. 'I was just going to have my own cocoa. There's Horlicks if you like that better.'

'Cocoa would be lovely,' Kenneth answered. 'It's what Mother used to make.'

'Two sugars?'

'How did you guess?'

'It's what I have myself. Why doesn't she make it any more?'

'Pardon?'

'Yir mother. Why doesn't she make cocoa any more?'

Kenneth looked seriously flustered. 'Well, she's . . . she died.'

'So did mine.'

'I'm sorry,' Kenneth murmured. 'I'm afraid I haven't quite got used to being on my own yet. Mother always took care of everything.'

'Mrs Cunningham looked after me,' Hattie said, pouring the hot milk over the cocoa. 'She gave me the lecktric.'

Kenneth appeared not to have heard. 'This is my

291

first real job since . . . since she died, and I don't think I'll be able to keep it much longer.'

'Why not?' Hattie handed Kenneth his cocoa, and sat down in the chair opposite.

Kenneth took a sip of the hot drink, his hands cradling the cup. Hattie watched as waves of steam rose from his wet shirt. The steam smelled moochy, and it crossed her mind that his shirt wasn't all that clean.

Kenneth sighed again, looking more crestfallen by the minute. 'I have six vacuum cleaners to sell by Monday, and I spent the whole day in Craigourie and only sold one.'

'Why?'

'It's just . . . selling. It's not what I'm cut out for. They're wonderful cleaners, they really are. They're a completely revolutionary design, with a full range of tools and attachments, and they represent the best investment the housewife can make for the smooth and efficient running of the modern home. Twenty-nine shillings is a small price to pay for such a miracle of engineering, don't you think?'

Hattie listened in awe. 'Twenty-nine shillings? For a Hoover? *That's* no' a small price. It's an awful lot o' money.'

'You're right,' Kenneth said. 'I can't do it. I just can't.'

He drank some more of the cocoa. 'Mother would understand. She wouldn't expect it of me, you see. She was always prepared to be disappointed.' He smiled wanly. 'She said she'd be disappointed if she *wasn't* disappointed, if you understand.'

Hattie shook her head, obviously not understanding. 'What happened to her?'

'She took a stroke. I had to nurse her for a very long time, but I thought . . . she gave me the impression . . . that there would be something left.'

'What?'

'Money. I . . . was led to believe there would be enough for my small needs.' Kenneth stared dolefully into the fire. 'There was nothing. Nothing at all. All that time, she was using the money she had to keep me with her, to keep us together, don't you see?'

'My mother kept us together, too. I wasn't allowed to leave her.'

'Oh, forgive me,' Kenneth apologised. 'Here I am prattling on . . . Is your bereavement recent?'

'Breevment?'

'Your mother, did she die recently?'

Hattie shook her head again. 'No,' she answered. 'It was a long time ago. I can't really remember . . .'

'I'm sorry, I'm distressing you. She must have been quite young.'

Hattie shrugged, and stared into her cup. 'They said I murdered her.'

What remained of Kenneth's cocoa shot up in the air and landed all over him.

'Yir clarted!' Hattie stated.

'Oh dear! Oh, dear, dear, dear.' Kenneth wiped at the offending stain, spreading it even further. He stooped to place his cup on the hearth, then reached for his jacket.

'I'll . . . I'll go now. Thank you. Thank you so much.'

Hattie looked up at him, her face miserable. 'I didn't murder her. It was an accident.'

Kenneth slumped back in the chair, his head low on his chest.

'You've been very kind to me. I'm sure it was . . . just as you say – a dreadful accident.' He raised his head. 'I should try to get help. I can't impose on you any longer, Miss . . . ?'

'Hattie. I'm Hattie.'

'I should go now, Hattie.'

'Yir shirt's an awful mess.'

'I don't care. I'm just about the end of my tether. Can you understand?'

'Course.'

'I loved my mother, Hattie. But she was very cruel.'

Hattie nodded.

'I can't imagine why I'm telling you this.'

'Sometimes, you just know about people,' Hattie offered, her grey eyes as soft as the falling snow.

Kenneth rubbed his eyes. 'I don't ever remember feeling so tired. I'm really awfully tired.'

Hattie took his hand. 'You can sleep in my bed. I'll wash out yir shirt.'

'I couldn't possibly,' Kenneth responded, but his protest was weak.

'Aye, you can. It's a nice bed.' She led him into

the narrow bedroom. 'Put yir shirt through the door. It'll be done by the time you wake.'

Kenneth reached for the light-switch, but Hattie covered it with her hand. 'No! You must leave the light on.'

'Why?' he asked.

Hattie moved closer, shielding the fixture with her body.

'I don't like the dark.'

Kenneth sighed, weary to his very bones. 'Did she keep you in the dark?'

'They asked me in the court. They were all dressed in wigs and cloaks, but I wasn't frightened any more. My mother always told me that the darkness was waiting for me. "It's waiting for you, Hattie Macaskill" she'd say – before she would put me in the cupboard. This one man kept asking me and asking me. Was I so bad that I had to be locked up in the dark? Did my mother have to do that just to keep me quiet?

'I told them the truth, Mr More. I told them, the dark's not quiet. It's very loud.'

Kenneth More reached out for her, clasping her hands in his own. 'My poor, dear lady.'

Hattie smiled. 'Och, I'm no' a lady. I'm just the cleaner.'

Kenneth did not relinquish his hold. 'You are indeed a lady. And it's been a kind star which led me to your door tonight.'

Hattie blushed. 'Just throw yir shirt through the door.'

Hours later, banking the fire for the last time that night, Hattie rose. She tiptoed into the bedroom and knelt by the bed, inspecting every visible inch of her stranger. He lay curled on his side, a wispy fringe of grey hair encircling his bald head. His face was plump and smooth, and slightly flushed.

Tentatively, Hattie stroked the hair into place. How handsome he was. She moved closer, feeling his breath on her face. Gently, gently she kissed him, awed at the softness of his lips on hers.

So this was how it felt. There had been no need to shut her in the darkness for fear of this. There was nothing here to be ashamed of. No terror burned in her. No demons reached to pull her into their infernal depths.

A rush of happiness spread through her, and again she kissed him.

Kenneth opened his eyes, immediately aware of her, his earlier tiredness and confusion gone. 'I've never kissed a woman before,' he whispered.

Hattie did not draw back. 'Me neither,' she said shyly. 'A man, I mean.'

'May I kiss you again?'

Hattie nodded.

Their lovemaking was awkward, the bed too narrow to contain them comfortably. Yet they were tender, and careful of the other, exploring together this new and cherished freedom, a freedom of which they had scarcely dreamed.

As the night sky cleared to reveal its star-sequinned mantle, Hattie Macaskill and Kenneth

More found each other. And in the finding came the knowledge that love was not reserved for a select few but was, indeed, available to all.

Together, they scurried hand-in-hand along the road, relieved to see that a thaw had already begun. Shrubbery dropped heavy parcels of snow at every step, and the prints of a nocturnal creature spread wetly outwards on the path before them.

Hattie pointed it out, glad that the creature's tracks had disappeared into the undergrowth.

'It's safe now,' she said.

Kenneth grabbed a handful of snow from atop a drystone dyke, and rubbed it across Hattie's face. She gurgled with delight, saturated with the powdery wetness – and the simple joy of it.

As they approached the stranded Morris Traveller, Kenneth laughed with relief. The bank of snow into which the car had slid had all but disappeared. He climbed in, praying the engine would turn.

It did.

'You're my lucky charm, Hattie,' he said.

She stood there, her hands pushed deep into the pockets of her worn tweed coat.

'You'll be coming back for me?'

Kenneth leaped from the car, holding her close and kissing her soundly.

'I will. I'll need some time, though . . . to get things sorted out. I want everything to be right when I come back, Hattie. But I *will* be back.'

'When?'

'By Easter.'

'You'll be back by Easter?'

Kenneth lifted her chin. 'As soon as I can. As soon as I'm in a position . . . to ask for your hand.'

Hattie took her hand from her pocket, inspecting it gravely.

'My hand?'

Kenneth frowned. 'In marriage.'

She reached to kiss him again. 'I knew that,' she laughed, and with a wave of a brown woollen mitt, she ran back towards the cottage.

Pulling off her coat, she rushed to warm her hands at the fire which still glowed cheerfully in the grate. She peered at the calendar above the mantelpiece. Kenneth would be back by Easter.

It wasn't that long to wait.

She had got confused. As time passed, she'd realised that. She'd misunderstood, had got it wrong somehow.

But she'd always believed he would come back. She'd always known that.

And here he was.

Helen stared at them both, stunned. Then she turned to stare at Stewart, but he just sat there, his fair eyebrows all but disappearing into his hairline.

Kenneth held out his hand. 'Mrs Macrae, it's my privilege to meet you at last.'

'You're not the actor!' Helen said, mindlessly returning the handshake. 'You're not Kenneth More.'

'Oh, madam, I am indeed. I'm just not *that* Kenneth More.' He turned a fond glance in Hattie's direction. 'What have you been telling them, my love?'

'My love!' Helen exclaimed. 'God help us.'

She retreated, reaching behind her for the support of the table. Finally she sat down, wiping her forehead with a corner of her apron.

'Would you mind explaining . . . ?'

'I must begin by apologising,' Kenneth said. He led Hattie forward, ushering her into the adjoining chair and stopping to shake hands with Stewart. 'It's taken rather longer than I had hoped to return to Drumdarg, though its distance from Arbroath was not the reason.'

Helen waved a hand. 'You'd better sit yirself down. I'll be wanting to know the whole story.'

Kenneth sat, reaching across the table to take Hattie's hand.

And then he began.

He had tried valiantly, but in vain, to sell his vacuum cleaners. There had followed a succession of 'inappropriate' positions, and he came to realise that he must first learn to take care of himself, before he could entertain the thought of providing for his wife.

Hattie's face was a picture. 'That's me,' she said.

He had delayed contacting Hattie, believing that she deserved so much more than he was able to offer. But each day he strove harder, in the hope that somebody, somewhere might offer him the opportunity which would allow him to return to her – financially secure and, most importantly, 'capable'.

As door after door closed before him, he had been smitten with a bout of depression which laid him low for 'rather a long time', and he had been forced to enter a nursing home – a wonderful place with landscaped gardens and the kindest, most caring staff who ever drew breath.

After his recovery, 'quite complete, may I add', he had made it clear that he would greatly enjoy tending the gardens – the one thing in his life at which he had always been, 'if I say so myself', rather good.

He had worked there for a trial period of six months, and the position was confirmed as permanent at the end of February. 'With the most wonderful serendipity' he had, that same week, been informed that he had finally made it to the top of the council's waiting list. He had received the keys to a small but beautifully appointed flat, and had moved from his lodgings at once.

He now felt that everything was suitably in order, and would appreciate it if Helen might indicate to whom he might address his request for Hattie's hand in marriage – Mr Cunningham or Mr Macrae?

Helen turned to Stewart. The two exchanged glances, and Stewart lifted his shoulders helplessly. Then Helen brought her eyes back to Hattie. The lassie was positively glowing.

'You already have her hand, I'm thinking,' Helen said. 'You're no' needing permission from anyone here.'

CHAPTER 22

Rose lifted her gin and bitter lemon. She didn't care to drink during the day, but this was definitely something to celebrate.

'And you're absolutely sure?' she asked Olive.

Olive tapped her nose, and winced with the effort. 'I have my sources.'

Maisie clapped her hands, then lifted her glass to chink it against Rose's. Even Olive managed to join in, holding her neck with one hand as she downed a second sherry with the other.

The adjoining door to the shop was flung open, and Isla appeared in the café.

'Is there any danger of getting a hand in the shop? Or are youse lot there for the day?'

'Darling girl,' Maisie called back, 'you won't be needing a hand in the shop till you have more than one customer at a time.'

'There's stock to be put away.'

'Then put it away.' Maisie peered over her whisky sour. Doug had given her the recipe. It was such a cosmopolitan drink. But then Doug was really such a cosmopolitan man.

'Yis better not be getting drunk,' Isla said.

'We's better not be staying sober.'

'Mai-sie!' Isla protested, stabbing her aunt with a look.

Maisie swirled her drink in its tall glass – with ice, no less. 'I'm joshing you, gal.' She turned to Rose. 'Isn't that how they say it? In the good ol' Yoo-nited States.'

Rose laughed, which seemed to enrage Isla even further.

'You should be seeing to yir son,' she remonstrated.

Immediately, Rose's expression changed. 'Barra? What is it, Isla? What happened?'

'What happened?' Isla gasped. 'What *happened*?' She continued to glare at Rose. 'Mr Pascoe just died, that's what happened! And Barra's angel's gone! And he *didn't* save Mr Pascoe. That's what happened!'

Rose's hand flew to her throat. 'Is he all right? Where is he?'

'Don't worry yirself,' Isla declared. 'He's in the woods, and he's a helluva sight better company than youse lot!' With that, she slammed the door noisily behind her.

Rose stood, shrugging off Maisie's arm. 'I'd better go,' she said, grasping her handbag.

'Sit, Rose,' Maisie urged. 'Leave him be.'

Rose shook her head. 'I can't, Maisie. He's been jist devastated wi' the whole thing. I'd better go 'n' find him.'

'Leave him *be*, Rose! He'll have to sort this out for himself. It's part of growing up, and he's sore in need of growing up.'

It was Rose's turn to glare at her friend. 'He'll grow up soon enough, Maisie. He needs me now.'

But Rose was held tight in Maisie's grasp. 'He does *not* need you now. What he needs is a friend, someone his own age, someone who's a mite more companionable than us old fogies. And if I haven't missed my guess, Isla's been far more use to him these past couple o' hours than you – or any of us – could be.'

Rose sat, but her eyes were worried still.

'She's right,' Olive stated. 'I'm no' saying I didn't believe him, mind, about this angel and everything. But it's time his mind was on the lassies, Rose. He'd be less inclined to be wanting "other" company, if you see what I'm getting at.'

Rose didn't answer, and Olive met Maisie's gaze across the table. Imperceptibly, she nodded in the direction of Rose's glass.

Maisie closed one eye, making a show of inspecting her own near-empty glass. 'Refills all round.'

'Oh no, Maisie. I've had enough. Really,' Rose protested.

Olive remained silent.

Maisie patted her hand. 'You've forgotten why we're here.' She smiled. Then she looked back at Olive.

'Tell us again, Olive,' she demanded. 'Then we'll have a wee top-up.'

Olive looked vaguely disappointed. 'It's hard to concentrate . . . with this neck.'

Maisie made a gargantuan effort. 'Lubrication necessary,' she prescribed, heading towards the bar.

Moments later she was back. Rose had another gin thrust in front of her – with lime, which she disliked. Olive had a vodka – with lime, which she found quite refreshing, and Maisie had God knows what.

'Aren't we all lucky to be here,' Maisie said. 'Whenever I get round to pondering the whys and the wherefores, I must admit I'm awed.'

'You were always that,' Olive said. 'You were always odd.'

'No.' Maisie frowned. 'Awed. I'm awed.'

Olive tried to nod. 'Swhat I said.'

Maisie stretched, knocking the Van Gogh print above her sideways.

Rose pointed. 'Yir picture . . .'

Maisie leaned back, reaching to straighten it and knocking it more lopsided than before. 'A madman, they called him. To be that mad . . .' She sighed.

Rose cast a worried frown in her direction, hoping Maisie wasn't about to descend into maudlin reverie. She turned her attention to Olive.

'OK. Tell us again, so I can get home to my bairn.'

'Right then,' Olive began, happy to be the centre of attention once more. 'Apparently, Raymond Mearns and Chrissie Falconer have been having a fling for quite some time . . .'

'Chrissie Falconer,' Maisie muttered. 'Who would have thought . . . ?'

'Aye,' Olive agreed. 'A quiet wee wifie like that. Anyway, she went over to visit her uncle in Spain last year, and that's when the plan was hatched.'

'All that time ago,' Rose said, tasting her gin and lime. It wasn't that bad after all. You could get used to it.

'So,' Olive continued, 'Uncle Ernie's ready to retire from his bar, or whatever they have in thon foreign places.' She smiled. 'I remember Ernie well. A fine-looking man in his day. Course he did a midnight flit, left a pile o' debt behind him.' Olive shook herself from her reminiscence. 'Still, he seems to have done well enough for himself out in the wilds. And here's Little Miss Librarian and her fancy-man waiting in the wings – all organised wi' *passports*, if you don't mind!'

Maisie chinked Rose's glass again, missing by a mile. 'Cheers!' she said.

'Cheers, Maisie. Cheers, Olive.' Rose grinned.

'Aye well.' Olive made a great show of twirling her empty glass. 'I'd drink yir health if . . .'

'*Refills!*'

'No, Maisie!' Rose held her glass tightly. 'I couldna' drink another drop.'

Maisie smiled indulgently, incapable of rising anyway.

Olive glanced pointedly at Maisie's whatever-it-was. 'Just say if you canna' manage that.'

Maisie slid the glass towards her. 'He'p 'self.'

Olive lifted it to her lips, swallowed, and grimaced. 'How can you drink that, Maisie?'

'Can't. That's how you got it.'

Olive drained the glass. 'Ugh! It's hellish.' She wiped her mouth, and paused for a moment. 'It took the sting from my neck just the same.'

Taking a deep breath, she resumed her story. 'Well, gang, Mr Mearns and Miss Falconer departed on Wednesday afternoon, and "Will Ye No Come Back Again" will *not* be requested on *Family Favourites* this weekend – no' by Sheena Mearns, anyway. No BFPO number there!'

'*Adios*, Ray-mundo,' Maisie howled.

'Sssh!' Rose laughed.

'Not a'tall,' Maisie retorted. 'Shout it from the rooftops! Sheena Mearns got beaten by a pair o' lisle stockings and the flattest feet since Dixon o' Dock Green!'

'Y'canna' help yir feet,' Olive reminded them. 'Chrissie Falconer's going to find it heavy going in thon tropical heat, and no mistake.'

'Where is it anyway?' Rose asked. 'What part of Spain?'

'Och,' Olive said, 'I never heard o' it. And I canna' imagine how they'll make a success o' a bar in a place wi' the daft name o' Bennydrome.'

'It's Benidorm,' Maisie corrected her. 'Sandra told me.'

Rose pointed a finger at Olive. '*That's* how you knew! Sandra told you. It's the talk o' Boots, more than likely.'

Olive looked annoyed. She prided herself in being first with the craic – any craic.

'Well, so what if it is? Yis dinna' know where Sheena Mearns took herself off to, when she found out.'

'Where?' Maisie and Rose asked together.

Olive studied her glass. 'I don't know. Yet,' she said, her eyes twinkling. 'But Sandra's getting her job on the make-up counter. Sheena Mearns won't be missed there, I can tell yis!'

Rose shook her head. 'When did you hear all this, Olive? Sandra hadn't got to Jen's when you left.'

Olive's face darkened. 'Och, she came by at closing. Donald had an awful head on him. He was needing an Askit.'

'And Violet was needing a slap,' Maisie added.

'Poor souls,' Rose murmured. 'It's no' like you, Maisie, to be hard on folks like that.'

Maisie's eyes became misty. 'I know. It's just that Jen's trying so hard . . . And to think we'll never see Jim again.'

The adjoining door opened again. 'Are yis *still* there?' Isla called.

She never did get an answer.

Marjorie paced relentlessly. 'Where *are* they?' she demanded. 'We have to be at the station by eight o'clock.'

'They'll no' be much longer.' Helen finished wrapping the sandwiches. 'There now. At least yis won't go hungry on the journey.'

'There's really no need,' Marjorie insisted. 'I won't be able to eat a bite until we arrive home. I really don't see the point of coming here at all. I'm no sooner recovering from the journey than we have to face it again. I can't imagine what Stewart was thinking about!'

Helen bristled but said nothing. Another hour at best, and she'd have the house to herself again.

Marjorie strode to the front door and gazed down the drive, her arms wrapped around herself as though it were the middle of winter.

'There's absolutely no sign of them!' she declared, returning to the kitchen. She sat, crossing her legs, one heel tapping impatiently on the linoleum.

'You have to understand, madam, that Murdo won't have the occasion to spend time with Stew . . . Mr Cunningham, for a while to come. And you know how men are, when it comes to the fishing.'

'Indeed I don't. My husband has no need of *fishing* companions in London!'

'Well, Mr Cunningham's a bit more than a companion to Murdo. He's more like a son . . .'

'Hmmph! Hardly that.'

Despite the rebuff, Helen continued. '. . . The son we never had.'

Marjorie stopped tapping. She lifted a hand to inspect her freshly manicured nails. 'I understand you have no family of your own?'

Helen held her breath. This might be her last chance, her only chance. And she *had* promised Stewart. She turned to look at Marjorie, but the woman steadfastly avoided her eyes. There was an interest there, though, Helen determined, even if Marjorie was doing her best to conceal it.

'No, we never did have. I had several miscarriages, and eventually time took care o' the rest.'

'Several?' Helen could see that Marjorie had had difficulty with the question.

'Five, all told. The first four were early enough. But we were hopeful of that last one.' Helen's voice became softer. 'A wee lassie, it was.'

At last the younger woman met her eyes. 'Five . . .' Marjorie drew a long, ragged breath. 'I don't think I could manage . . . five. I lost our second child a month ago.' She stared off into a place far beyond Drumdarg.

'It seems one is not supposed to grieve after a miscarriage, Mrs Macrae. One is supposed to get on with one's life, and try again. I don't think I want to . . . try again.' With great precision, Marjorie straightened the hem of her skirt. 'I can't bear it, you see – and it's such a disappointment for Stewart.'

'Well, madam, the men don't quite understand it, do they? I believe Murdo was at the end o' his tether with our own "disappointments". But I couldn't help him. I was grieving, just like you, and I hardly thought to notice that Murdo was suffering too. I'd been wrapped up in myself – and the loss – for so long.'

310

Helen paused. 'And then, he was late coming back to the house one night. He'd gone fishing that morning – a day much like today, it was. I remember I was quite furious with him. I thought, there he is – away enjoying himself, and here's me on my own, wi' nothing in the world to look forward to.

'And I was so tired. I never did get used to the tiredness,' Helen confessed. 'Anyway, the rage burned in me all day and, finally, I set out to find him. It was growing dark, and he didn't see me coming along the path. His head was in his hands, and his shoulders were shaking. At first I thought he was laughing, but as I came closer, I could see that he was crying.' Helen's eyes filled with the memory.

'Murdo's the old-fashioned sort, madam, as you've probably noticed. I'd never seen him cry before, and it hurt me – more than you can imagine. By the time I reached him, I was crying too. We just sat there holding on to each other, until long after dark, and in our own way we came to terms with all of it that night.

'You see,' Helen continued, 'it wasn't that he was missing the babies so much. Oh, he wanted them too – there was no question about that. But it was *me* he was really missing. Men get so used to us being there that when we shut them out – for whatever reason – well, then, they get . . . a wee bit lost.'

Marjorie reached as though to touch the older woman. Helen caught the movement, and might have responded. For a few brief moments, they had joined together in the ancient company of womanhood. But centuries of difference still conspired to keep them apart and, slowly, Marjorie's hand dropped back into her lap.

'Don't fret, lass,' Helen said then, her voice gentle. 'If you love each other enough, you'll come through. But do yir grieving together. It's less lonely that way.'

Marjorie swallowed. 'Thank you,' she whispered.

'Go home and enjoy yir Easter. And don't be afraid to share yir worries wi' God, Mrs Cunningham.' Helen smiled. 'He'll be up all night anyway.'

Marjorie returned the smile, and Helen caught a glimpse of the beauty hiding behind the pinched features.

'That's more like it,' she said, bustling towards the hall. 'And if I'm no' mistaken, that's our menfolk coming up the drive.'

Marjorie followed, stepping back as Gallus hurled himself into the house, skidding across the polished floor. Marjorie raised her arms in automatic protest, then bent to bestow a single nervous pat on the Westie's head.

Murdo and Stewart watched in amazement. 'I'm sorry we took so long . . .' Stewart began.

'We have plenty of time,' Marjorie smiled back.

Stewart's look of amazement deepened. Helen reached to take his waders from him, nodding imperceptibly as she did so. He passed her a look of such infinite gratitude that she couldn't help herself.

She clasped him in her sturdy arms, and gave him a hug.

CHAPTER 23

Clouds bruised the sky as Jennifer dressed. She stared out of the window, trying to determine whether or not she'd need a coat. It took her a long time to make a decision. It seemed important to get it right.

She walked through to the living room. Violet stared at her. 'Don't you think you'll need a coat? We'll be walking to the cemetery.'

Jennifer glanced around the room, her eyes coming to rest on the chair by the desk. 'It won't matter,' she said.

'Of course it matters!' Violet's voice was sharp. 'You'll be soaked if it starts raining.'

Jennifer turned to Donald. 'You'd better take your coat, Jen,' he murmured.

She returned to the bedroom, and opened her wardrobe. Her coat hung next to Jim's sports jacket. She lifted a sleeve of the smooth tweed and buried her face in it. Jim was still there. She could smell him. Reassured, she lifted her coat from the hanger and closed the door quickly, lest the lingering scent of her husband might escape.

Donald was holding the front door open, Violet already seated in the long black car at the roadside.

Charlie Maxwell, the undertaker, stood to attention as she walked down the path. He lifted his top hat in cheerful greeting.

'No' a bad day, Mrs Pascoe, if the rain'll stay off.'

She smiled. Charlie was not known for his tact. 'Let's hope it does,' Jennifer replied.

Charlie closed the door and ran round to the passenger side, nodding to the driver as he clambered in.

'Right then, off we go.'

Barra gazed up at the stained-glass window above the minister's head where a vast angel in golden cloth with widespread wings hovered over the congregation. The angel had captured Barra's attention far more completely than the monotonous tone of the minister.

He knew you weren't supposed to be angry in the church, but Barra did feel angry. He shouldn't be here at some horrible funeral, with people shuffling and sniffling and being miserable. At least the angel looked happy, like a real angel was supposed to look, not a bit like Jamie.

Briefly, Barra lowered his eyes to the coffin. He couldn't imagine Mr Pascoe lying inside it. He didn't want to try.

He looked around him, receiving a swift dig in the ribs from his mother. He winced.

'Ouch,' he complained.

'Be quiet,' his mother hissed back. 'And sit still.'

Barra gritted his teeth. The anger flared again, and his stomach growled noisily.

He shrugged at Chalmers, who had sat slightly forward to glare at him.

'It's just nerves,' Rose whispered to her husband. 'It's his first funeral.'

And my last! Barra thought. He'd often heard people say 'Och, it was a great funeral', or 'It was a grand send-off'. How could they find anything grand in all this?

He glanced across the aisle. Mrs Iacobelli, never known to miss a funeral – any funeral – had plonked herself down in the pew opposite. Her twin sons sat by her side, their heads lowered in apparent reverence.

Unaccustomed to the Protestant service, they had earlier stood when everyone else remained seated, but even that had failed to cheer Barra.

The service finally over, the pall-bearers stepped forward to lift Jim's coffin. As they moved slowly down the aisle, one of them caught the heel of the man in front. They were directly level with the Yaks, and the coffin listed slightly towards the twins. Simultaneously, the boys threw themselves sideways away from it, their eyes wide with horror.

Barra held his breath until the procession moved safely on. For a split second he'd had his first real image of Mr Pascoe in the coffin, rolling around trying to catch his balance, and this, combined with the frantic genuflecting of the Yaks, suddenly struck him as absurd.

As Rose urged him down the aisle ahead of her Barra surrendered to his amusement, giggling all the way to the heavy oak doors.

'Wait till I get you home,' Rose seethed as they crossed the threshold together.

'S . . . s . . . sorry, Mam,' Barra apologised, helpless with mirth.

Jennifer closed her eyes. Her only prayer that day had been that the minister would hurry up and be done with it. He had droned on for what had seemed like hours in the church. Now he was addressing those assembled at the graveside in the same sombre voice, showing little sign of bringing the ceremony to a close.

The sky had cleared and she felt the heat of the sun on her back, but inside she was as cold as stone. She briefly wondered if she'd ever feel warm again. Other thoughts swam around in her mind, none of them coherent nor in any particular order.

Several of Jim's friends and family had travelled up from Edinburgh for the funeral, its time set late enough in the day to allow for their arrival. She wondered how many would call back at the house, and if there would be enough food to go round.

The bedroom would be decorated immediately. She must remember to ask Sandy if he'd do the papering for her. Jim had liked the pattern. They had both agreed on it, gondoliers drifting across a background of palest blue. She wondered if she might need to change the curtains, too, and decided that she would. She would definitely change the curtains.

Jim, holding her hand as they stood on the Rialto Bridge, watching the water-buses come and go, and unable to eat his ice cream fast enough to prevent it from melting. She'd had to wipe the chocolate from his chin. He had laughed.

Struggling up the path with the damned chair. 'Did you hurt yir back?' she had asked. He had laughed then too. 'I'm lying here half-dead. What do you think?' Then standing, laughing still. 'But you'll be pleased to know your chair's not hurt. Your chair's just fine.'

'You'll need to see about it.' How long after the fall had it been? She couldn't remember.

She felt Violet move beside her, shifting her weight. 'My mother married beneath herself,' Jim had said. 'Unfortunately, so did my father.' They had laughed together at that. When had the laughing stopped? She couldn't remember that either.

'I'll make an appointment with the doctor. I promise,' he'd said. And he had, and he'd gone alone. She should have been with him. She should have guessed, long before he'd had to tell her.

A split second.

'Six months, maybe less,' he'd said.

In a split second, her life had changed. She'd never seen it coming, had had no chance to prepare.

One minute her life was normal – and then it changed. And everything changed with it. Now it would never be normal again. She had left a different person behind, on the other side of that split second.

'Why didn't you tell me? Damn you! *Damn* you, Jim.' She had been furious, yelling at him through her tears.

'I'm damned, right enough,' he'd said. That was when the laughing had stopped. She remembered now.

They had held on to each other and wept together.

'Merry Christmas.' The diamond solitaire in the black velvet box. 'Will you marry me?' She had wept then too, happy tears. Tears were tears. How could they feel so different?

The slow ride down the Grand Canal and out into the bay. Docking at Murano, Jim's quick flash of jealousy as the handsome Italian youth helped her from the boat, holding on to her hand much longer than was necessary.

Jim's rapturous attention to the glass-blowers' art. She had been watching him while they stood together in the Fornace Gritti, careless of the talented trio before them, eyes only for her husband. She'd even loved the sound of the words – practising them long before the wedding. 'This is my husband, Jim.'

And endless practice of her new signature – Mrs Jennifer Pascoe – revelling in the look of it.

On to Burano, strolling through the tiny island, stopping to watch the centuries-old art of lace-making. Jim had been patient, sitting by the quay while she wandered from stall to stall comparing prices. She had come up behind him, leaning to kiss the nape of his neck, now golden brown from the Venetian sun. How tanned and healthy and *young* he'd been then.

Venice had been full of it. Glass. There had been glass everywhere; mirrors, tables, chandeliers. Everything glittered. So much glass.

She imagined lifting a large rock and hurling it through time and distance, shattering all of it. How satisfying that would be. Where would you find such a rock?

'I hate that chair.'

'It wasn't the chair, Jen. It was there long before that. Please don't hate the chair.'

'I don't,' she'd cried. 'I love it.'

And, 'Why don't you ever get angry? How can you just accept it?'

'I want to go quietly, Jen, not kicking and scream-ing, and holding back.'

'I *want* you to hold back. I don't want to be the only one with this anger inside me,' she'd sobbed.

'Anger fools you into believing you're strong,' he'd said. 'But when it passes it leaves you weaker than before. I can't afford anger.'

'Can we afford it?' She was gazing at the Mini in the garage showroom.

'You love it, don't you?'

She'd nodded.

'Then we can afford it. You know how I feel. If you want something badly enough . . .'

'. . . you'll find a way to make it happen,' she'd finished, hugging him with delight.

It wasn't true, though.

Jim had been wrong about that.

She felt her mother slip an arm around her, and leaned gratefully into the embrace. Would the minister *ever* finish?

She wiped her face, surprised at how wet it was. She hadn't been aware that she was crying. She drew her hand across her chest, drying it on her dress before covering her mother's hand with her own. Holding on.

How different Frances was to Violet. 'I never felt close to her,' Jim had said. 'Never felt she had the time for me. That's why I love Frances so much. She's more of a mother to me than my own ever was.'

'We're not good enough for her.'

'No, Jen. You're altogether *too* good for her. I love you so much.'

And as he slipped quietly from her, 'I loved you once – and for all time. Never forget that.'

There was the rock! In the mound of newly excavated dirt by the grave. The perfect rock. If she could just get to it, she could hurl it into space. And it would never stop spinning, never come to rest, until it had shattered all the glass in the world.

* * *

It had been Doug's idea to bring them back to the Whig. Jennifer's home was packed to capacity with the folks from Edinburgh. Her neighbours in Drumdarg, however, had waited only long enough to drink the customary toast to the dear departed, before agreeing that they'd be better off out of Jennifer's way.

After all, they'd be here for her tomorrow, and every day after – God willing.

The Whig was cheerful and comfortable, a refuge from the past few harrowing hours. Chalmers had joined Maisie behind the bar, while Rose kept company with Helen at one of the tables. Murdo was propped against the bar, regaling Sandy with tales of the bonny salmon which had escaped from Stewart's line the day before. Isla, meanwhile, was in the kitchen with Doug, being initiated in the art of making the perfect bacon and egg piece.

Only Olive was missing, the tension of the funeral firing her neck with ever more painful strictures. Sandy had seen her home from the Pascoes' before returning to the Whig for what had all the makings of a fine end to the day.

'Well,' he sighed happily, getting ready to down yet another free pint. 'Here's to the one that got away.' He smacked the foam from his lips. 'Y'canna' beat a good funeral.'

Murdo sucked on his pipe. 'I heard Jennifer asking you to paper her bedroom. I wouldna' have thought she'd have something like that on her mind the day.'

'Well, I'm a dab hand at the papering, right enough,' Sandy replied proudly. 'But, my God, it seemed a bit out o' place.'

'It seemed perfectly right,' Maisie stated, removing the long black chiffon scarf from her throat. It was getting quite warm. 'If it was me, I'd be wanting to fumigate the place, get rid o' all that . . . illness.'

Helen bit her lip. 'Och now, Maisie, that's a wee bittie strong. Lord, she'd just planted poor Jim not an hour before.'

'She planted a corpse,' Maisie said, unperturbed. 'Jim's in her heart, where he belongs. And the smell o' fresh paint's sorely needed in that room. Besides, Jim helped her choose the wallpaper. She can lie in her bed and look at it, and remember happier times, instead o' feeling like she's sleeping in a morgue herself.'

She peeled off her long black evening gloves, admiring them as she did so. Unfortunately, they weren't very practical. Violet Pascoe had made a point of staring at them. Now how could anyone find a pair of gloves so offensive?

At least Barra had liked them. 'Where's Barra?' she thought to ask. 'I haven't seen him since we left Jen's.'

'He's in the woods, Maisie,' Rose replied. 'I hope he's having a good long think about his behaviour the day. Imagine giggling like that in front o' everyone.'

Chalmers winked at Maisie, his earlier

annoyance at his son mellowed by the company – and the drink. 'He'll be having a word wi' his angel, no doubt.'

'Cut it out, Chalmers,' Rose said sharply. 'He's not the first one round here to feel betrayed.'

There was a second's silence in the bar. Nobody had heard Rose Maclean use that tone of voice to her husband before. Chalmers looked most surprised of all.

Helen broke the silence, her gaze fastened on Chalmers' by now purple eye. She lifted her glass.

'I couldn't help smiling myself, Rose. He was in such a fit, so he was.'

Rose frowned. 'It looked bad, him carrying on like that. I don't know what got into him.'

As if pushed on to the stage by an unseen hand, Barra appeared, his hand filled with two thick slices of bread from which emanated the enticing aroma of fried bacon. All eyes turned towards him.

'I'm starving,' he said defensively. 'Doug's bringing yir pieces through in a minute.'

He climbed on to the chair between his mother and Helen, licking his arm where some egg yolk had trickled downwards.

'Isla's getting good at the cooking,' he informed them. 'She's got the bacon just right.' He chewed happily for a moment, then turned to Helen. 'I wish I'd seen Hattie before she left.'

Helen waited while he munched on the last morsel of his sandwich. 'She'll be back in a couple o' weeks to say a proper cheerio to everyone. They were anxious to get back down the road, so Murdo offered to clear the cottage for her.'

'What's he like?'

Helen raised her eyebrows. 'Kenneth?'

'Aye,' Barra said.

Rose and the others were also paying attention as Helen considered her reply.

'He seems nice enough. Of course, the whole thing was a bit o' a shock to us, y'understand. But I think he'll be good to her.' Helen knitted her brows together. 'He'll have myself to answer to if not.'

Barra nodded. 'I hope he will. I thought Jamie . . . Well, anyway, I'm glad he came back for her.'

Helen smiled. 'Barra, this . . . meeting o' theirs took place ages ago – long before yir angel put in an appearance.'

It was Barra's turn to frown. 'I know. I just thought . . .' He shrugged. 'Och, who knows what I was thinking?'

'It's a hard thing to deal with, Barra,' Helen said, quietly enough not to be overheard. 'But dinna' lose hope, son. It's all we have at the end o' the day.'

'I don't think Mrs Pascoe has hope,' he answered, his voice as low as hers.

Rose strained forward, trying to catch his words over the general din.

'Aye, son,' Helen agreed. 'By the looks o' her today, I'm thinking it'll be a long time before that lassie'll know happiness again.'

Barra nodded, his expression still solemn. 'I

don't mind . . . if Jamie wasn't an angel. He was still right about a lot of things. I jist wish Mrs Pascoe could've believed in him, jist for a wee while. 'Til she feels better, anyway.'

Rose's heart caught. 'She'll come to it all in her own time, Barra. I'm glad you'll no' be bothering her wi' that nonsense any more.'

'It wasn't nonsense, Mam. Whatever it was, it wasn't nonsense.'

And Rose wondered if she'd ever be able to stop worrying about him. He seemed determined to be . . . to be . . . Barra.

'The big house'll seem a bit empty now,' Sandy remarked. 'What wi' Hattie gone, and the Cunninghams back down south.'

'That reminds me, Murdo,' Chalmers said. 'I'll be over tomorrow to do a proper survey. I'm hoping to get started on the rewiring in a couple o' weeks.' He glanced over at Helen. 'You'll be glad to have seen the back o' Stewart's wife, then?' he called across.

'Och, the lassie's no' as bad as I thought,' Helen replied. 'We came to a kind of agreement before she left. As a matter o' fact, we might be seeing a bit more o' them from now on. Stewart's talking about coming north for the grouse in August.'

'I still never got to meet her,' Barra said. 'Is she very Sassenach?'

'Oh aye,' Helen nodded. 'Very.'

'What is it exactly?'

'What?'

'Sassenach. I mean, I *know* it's being English. But, what *is* it?'

Helen shrugged. 'Well, that's what it is, Barra. Just being English.'

'Is that no' enough?' Sandy asked. 'I couldna' stand it myself – being English.'

'Why not?' Barra looked puzzled.

'Och, they're just . . . no' like us. They're different.'

'Well, they would be,' Barra stated in frustration. 'They're from a different country.'

'Y'can say that again.' Sandy lifted his glass.

'*Vive la difference!*' Maisie called out, and they all drank to it.

Isla appeared with a tray of steaming sandwiches, passing them around the small group. Barra reached for one, and she smacked his hand. 'You had one already.'

He looked hurt. 'Doug said there's plenty for everyone.'

'Go on then,' she said, proffering the tray. 'I'll take it as a compliment to my cooking.'

'I wouldn't go that far,' Barra teased. Rose looked at him in amazement.

He caught the look and blushed, but he was well pleased with himself just the same.

CHAPTER 24

Graham was the last to leave. He looked at his watch, and stood. 'It's getting late. I'd better be off.'

Jennifer took his cup. 'You're all right to drive?'

He smiled. 'I just had the one.' He peered into the empty cup. 'I'll probably be up half the night with all the coffee I drank, though.'

Jennifer nodded. 'Me too.'

He gave her a worried look. 'I hope you get some rest, Jen. You look all in.'

'I'll try,' she said, her voice little more than a whisper.

'I'll look in on you in the morning. What time are you leaving?' Graham asked, turning towards Donald.

Donald looked up at him from the sofa, bleary-eyed and exhausted. 'I'd like to be on the road by ten. Don't feel you have to come by that early, though. If I don't see you before we leave, I'll be back up in a week or so – to help you straighten things out.'

Violet had been clearing the mantelpiece of glasses. She paused. 'I'm sure Graham's quite capable of running the office without your help, Donald. After all, it's *his* business now.'

Graham sighed heavily. 'No, Violet, it's not. Jim's share of the business will belong to Jennifer now. It's up to her if she wants the partnership dissolved.'

Jennifer started. It had never occurred to her.

'But I couldn't . . . I mean, I couldn't take Jim's place. I have my own job to go back to. I'm not an accountant.'

'You don't have to be,' Graham said gently. 'You could still keep an interest in the business. Anyway, we can talk about it some other time.'

He turned again to Donald. 'Your help *would* be invaluable, Donald. There are several accounts Jim's been working on. I'd be happy for you to take a look at them.' His voice cracked, and he glanced away.

Violet had set the glasses back down, her eyes glittering as they swept over Graham. She folded her arms.

'Well, everything should be hunky-dory for you now, Graham. You'll have Jim's business *and* his wife – all to yourself.'

'Violet!' Jennifer looked shocked. 'That's an awful thing to say.'

'Christ, Violet,' Donald exploded. 'Can't you ever think before you open your mouth.'

Graham stepped towards the hall. 'I think it's better if I leave now. It's been a terrible day for everyone.'

'Graham?' Jennifer grabbed at his sleeve. 'Graham! Tell her she's wrong.'

'I'm sorry, Jen,' Graham muttered. 'I haven't the heart for an argument.'

She followed him to the front door. 'How can you let her off with something like that?' she demanded, her voice low. 'It was such a . . . an evil thing to say.'

He opened the door and turned back to look at her. Once, twice, he tried to speak. Then, helplessly, he closed his mouth, and walked away from her.

Slowly, Jennifer closed the door behind him. She knew what Graham had tried to tell her, had seen the pain in his eyes, the torture that he was enduring.

Please let me be wrong, she prayed silently. She couldn't deal with it now. Maybe not ever. She wanted it to disappear. She wanted everything to disappear. She especially, more than anything in the world, wanted Violet Pascoe to disappear.

Donald was still on the sofa, but Violet had left the room. The sound of running water reached Jennifer's ears.

'She's doing the dishes,' Donald murmured. He was crying again, as he had been, on and off, all day long. 'Poor Graham,' he sniffed. 'He didn't deserve that. Maybe when things get back to . . . when things settle down, she'll get round to apologising.'

'I doubt it, Donald,' Jennifer answered, her father-in-law's despair bringing an answering tear to her own eyes. 'I can't ever remember her apologising for anything.'

Donald nodded. 'If she would only cry,' he said. 'She hasn't cried, you see.'

After the funeral, several of the mourners had remarked on Violet's lack of emotion. Some had put it down to courage, others to shock. Only one had had the temerity to suggest that it might stem from callousness.

'She's a cold fish, so she is,' Frances had whispered to her daughter.

Jennifer had silently agreed.

'Go on to bed, Donald,' Jennifer urged. 'I'll finish tidying up.'

He didn't protest. Standing, he embraced her and kissed her good night, then stumbled blindly down the hall towards the spare room.

Jennifer gathered the last of her flagging energy, and headed for the kitchen.

'I can manage this, if you want to go to bed,' Violet offered. She had finished stacking the crockery and glasses on the counter-top.

'No. *I'll* do it,' Jennifer replied, stepping towards the sink. 'You go on through. It won't take long.'

'I wouldn't dream of it.' Violet nudged Jennifer firmly out of the way.

Swallowing, Jennifer surrendered her position at the sink, reaching instead for a clean dish-towel.

The two women worked in silence for a time.

'It went quite well, don't you think?' Violet asked at last.

'I don't think we have to worry about how "well" it went,' Jennifer answered. 'It wasn't a wedding, Violet.'

'I'm perfectly well aware of that. He was *my* son, after all.'

'I know.'

Violet glanced sideways at her. 'I daresay you'll feel better when we leave.'

Jennifer shook her head, her eyes swimming with new tears. She tried to concentrate on drying the saucer, but the pattern blurred. 'I don't know . . . if I'll ever feel better.'

'Well, that's just the typical selfishness of youth. You'll have a whole new life for yourself in no time.'

Jennifer clenched her fist, imagining the feel of the rock in her hands.

'As for me . . .' Violet sighed, drawing a deep breath. 'I will never . . .' She lifted a crystal brandy glass, inspecting its pattern . . . '*never* get over it.'

Violet Pascoe raised the glass higher, before bringing it down to smash against the sink with all her might. Then she slid slowly towards the floor, a high keening sound escaping from her as she curled into a ball at Jennifer's feet.

Jennifer stood stock-still, suspended in time and space. For a moment she waited, expecting Donald to appear, to rescue her from this last, terrible assault on her senses.

But he didn't come. Nobody was going to come.

She knelt, reaching tremulously for her mother-in-law. 'Violet. Please . . . Violet . . .'

The keening stopped, to be replaced by racking sobs. Jennifer pushed an obstructing chair aside and tenderly lifted Violet into her arms, holding her close, allowing the woman's bitter heartache to pour from her – until it had drenched them both completely.

Finally, Violet pulled away, reaching for a chair. Settling clumsily into it, she watched as Jennifer poured them both a hefty measure of brandy.

'I suppose it's obvious – that I blamed Graham,' Violet began, patting her eyes with the sodden dish-towel.

Jennifer sipped on her drink, relishing the burning sensation on her throat. It was almost painful. But it was warm. Very warm. She held her glass tightly, relieved that her hands had stopped trembling.

'I don't understand,' she said softly. 'How was any of it Graham's fault?'

Violet took a swallow of her brandy. No ladylike sipping for her. She had weakened, after all. Well, it couldn't be helped.

'Graham took Jim from me,' she said.

Jennifer shook her head. 'How, Violet? How?'

'Oh, you don't know the half of it, Jennifer.' She drained the glass and lifted the bottle, pouring herself another. 'We weren't always well-off, you know. We had to struggle, just like everyone else. In those days a mother didn't go out to work. You stayed home. You looked after the home, the family.

'Neither of us had well-to-do parents. We were married just before the war, and Jim came along the following year. We lived in a tenement at the top of Dalry Road, and Donald was making a pittance at one of the firms up by the Law Courts. He was little more than a message-boy then, running errands, making tea.' She smiled bitterly. 'But at least I had them both. Jim was just a baby, of course, but we were . . . very happy.

'Donald was studying every chance he got, and there was never enough money. I can remember, once, looking in the fruit shop, wishing I had the money to buy a pound of plums. I can see them yet. They were big, fat, purple plums.'

She wiped her mouth with the back of her hand. 'They were the happiest days of my life. As a matter of fact, I often thought that I might have made a decent accountant myself, you know. So many nights we sat together, Donald studying, me asking him question after question – especially when the exams approached. I knew almost as much as he did then.

'And through it all, Jim would be lying sound asleep in his cot beside the fire. He was such a good baby.' She shrugged. 'We only had the one room, and a shared bathroom on the landing below. Primitive in the extreme . . . but there you are.

'Well, as you might have guessed, Donald passed all the exams with flying colours. He changed companies, did better and better. And we moved, of course.

'Jim was in school by then, bright as a button, just like his father. Donald seemed to be working longer hours, but I didn't mind. Jim was always rushing about the place and the house was full. He had so many friends, and there was always noise. "Fun and laughter", I used to tell Donald. "The house was full of fun and laughter today".'

She looked down at her glass, surprised to find it empty. Again she reached for the bottle, but Jennifer stayed her hand. 'Violet, I don't think . . .'

Violet shrugged it away. 'Oh no. That was *my* problem, don't you see? I didn't think.'

She poured another generous measure. 'Donald came to me. We discussed it for quite some time. He felt confident he could set up in practice for himself. He had even found the perfect assistant. She was working for one of the partners, but she didn't like his old-fashioned ways. Would much prefer to work for Donald. Her husband thought it was a good idea.'

Violet stared into her glass, then stretched backwards to gaze at the ceiling for a long moment. 'Her *husband* thought it was a good idea . . . I mean . . . you don't think . . . Do you?'

Jennifer took the bottle, refilling her own glass. She was wide awake, and calmer than she'd felt all day.

'Well,' Violet continued, 'Donald had his way. We went back to eating beans on toast for supper. Not for long, though. He did manage to make a success of it all quite quickly, considering.

'And his assistant . . . Do you know, I can't even recall her name now. Can you imagine? Anyway, his assistant seemed to have a peculiarly forbearing husband. Between he and I, we managed to . . . encourage this success. As a matter of fact, it took me close to three years to find out the truth.'

Violet grimaced. 'I was quite unsophisticated, believe it or not. Even then, I found out by accident. Jim was spending the night at one of his friend's houses and I thought I'd surprise Donald at the office, take him out to dinner, just the two of us. He *had* been working such long hours.

'I caught them together. Just . . . walked in on them. They hadn't even bothered to lock the door.'

'Oh, Violet . . .' Jennifer could only imagine the pain this proud woman had suffered. 'I had no idea.'

'And neither did too many others, I'm happy to say.' Violet's bitterness was more apparent now. 'I said I couldn't live like that, that I'd just take Jim and go. I didn't even want his money.' She pushed her glass aside, disgusted with the brandy – and the memory.

'It wasn't to be. Donald informed me that it would have a . . . how did he put it? A detrimental effect on his integrity. That's what it was all about then, Jennifer. An accountant, especially such a successful accountant, was supposed to have integrity; high moral standards.' Violet's mouth curled in a sneer. 'It's different now, of course. They seem to be getting away with murder . . . But that's another story.

'At the end of it all, I was the one presented with an ultimatum. If I left, if I dared to make any of it public, Donald had the clout – and the money – to keep Jim from me. That way, it would be assumed that it was I in the wrong. After all, what mother would relinquish her child?

'I'd have nothing. Nobody. I'd never worked, would scarcely have known where to begin. Ergo – no money. Half the house, perhaps, but what good was that? He was – *is* – a highly respected business-man. It would have been very easy to cut me out completely.'

Violet appeared to have regretted her earlier decision, and pulled her glass back to her. 'There were several more "assistants" over the years. The funny thing was, Donald insisted that they were unimportant, that he loved only me. Don't you think that's hilarious?'

Jennifer shook her head. 'No,' she said. 'No, I don't.'

'Neither did I,' Violet confided. 'I couldn't accept that. It wasn't the kind of love I wanted, Jennifer. It wasn't the kind of love I believed in. And I never, never got used to it. I screamed and cried and battled my way through. And I knew that, sooner or later, I would have to walk away from it all, before it destroyed me completely.

'So, you see, I . . . I had to protect Jim. It was always possible that I might be seeing him for the last time, that today might be the day that I'd leave, close the door on it once and for all. And as often as

I dreamed about it, I knew that the only way I *could* leave would be knowing that Jim wouldn't break his heart pining for me. He was still so young . . .' Violet's eyes clouded again then, roughly, she pushed a hand through her sculpted hairdo. 'I learned to be cold, Jennifer. I had to – for Jim's sake.'

'But you stayed?'

Violet nodded. 'The years passed. I became better at putting a face on it and, whenever I weakened, whenever I decided that I really couldn't take any more, I would look at Jim – and know I could never leave him.

'He grew up, went on to university, and my "job" – if that's what you want to call it – was almost complete. I was ready, then, to pack my bags. I'd even managed to save a little without Donald's knowledge when he upped and had a heart scare. Nothing serious, as it turned out, just enough to frighten him, settle him down.'

Violet sighed. 'And so my husband finally came home.'

Jennifer yawned. She was tired, after all.

'I'm sorry,' she said.

Violet waved the apology away, stifling a yawn of her own. 'I shouldn't keep you up . . .'

'No, please . . . I still don't understand what Graham had to do with all of this.'

'Don't you see? I was finally free to *love* my son again. Donald was home. He needed me. If Jim hadn't met Graham, he'd never have come to

Craigourie. He'd have stayed in Edinburgh, working with his father, and somehow... somehow, I might have had the chance to catch up on all the love I'd denied him, all the love I'd had to hide from him.'

'And he wouldn't have married me,' Jennifer finished.

'Oh, I blamed you too. I don't deny it. The first Christmas Jim ever spent away from home was to come here, to ask you to marry him. You can't imagine how that hurt me, Jennifer. Donald and I sat across from each other at that table, and I prayed – I *prayed* – you'd refuse.'

'But I didn't.'

'No. No, you didn't.'

'Violet, I want you to know... It's important that you know how much we loved each other,' Jennifer said.

'I do know,' Violet said. 'And I'm grateful that he found that. That he knew what it felt like to love somebody, the way I had once loved his father.

'To be honest, there's so much water under the bridge now that I'm not sure if we can ever be friends.' Violet raised her eyes to Jennifer's. 'But I'd like to think it's possible.'

'It's possible.' Jennifer smiled. 'Who knows?'

'And I owe Graham an apology.'

'Yes. You do.'

'He *does* love you, though. I'm not wrong about that.'

Jennifer didn't answer. She would take it one

339

day at a time. They'd agreed on that. One day at a time, Jim had said. She closed her eyes. Jim . . . how I need you now.

'I'll write to Graham,' Violet said. 'I think that would be best. Everything's just too raw right now – for me to go crawling to him.'

'You've never been one to crawl,' Jennifer reminded her.

'Oh yes, I've crawled. You weren't listening.'

Jennifer reached for Violet's hand, and held it. She had done that earlier today. She tried to recall it. It had been at the cemetery. Except it had been her mother's hand she'd touched then.

Violet looked down, entwining Jennifer's hand in her own. She swallowed. 'Did he ever say . . . that he missed me?'

Jennifer hesitated. She could tell the truth – or she could lie.

'He never stopped missing you.'

Doug wiped the last of the tables. 'Are you about ready for bed?'

'I am,' Maisie replied. 'I'm thoroughly exhausted.'

Doug ran the cloth over the bar one last time. 'How can you think about giving this up, Maisie?'

'God, Doug, it's a bit late for that, don't you think?'

'Where would they all have gone today, if we didn't have the Whig?'

'Somewhere else?' Maisie suggested.

'Where else?' Doug demanded. 'It's important

340

that we're here. Can't you see that?'

'It's not as if we made a profit, Doug,' Maisie replied quietly.

'It's not all profit, Maisie.'

'It's not at *all* profit, Doug! We're not a charity, y'know.'

'But we *are* important. The Whig's important. Even I get to be important, Maisie.'

'Of course you're important, my darling.' Maisie smiled, opening her arms to him.

He sidled past her, avoiding her completely. She heard his footsteps on the stairs and closed her eyes, her arms dropping to her sides. She looked around the bar before switching off the lights.

'I didn't hear you say *I'm* important, Doug,' Maisie whispered into the darkness. 'I definitely didn't hear you say that.'

Rose sat on the end of her son's bed. 'You look ready for sleep,' she remarked.

Barra yawned. 'I am tired, Mam,' he agreed. He swung his upper body over the side of the bed and peered underneath. Two amber slits of light stared back at him.

'Can you get Socks to come out o' there?'

Rose frowned. 'I don't know what's wrong wi' him. He's been queer all day.'

Barra gave up trying to encourage the cat forward. 'Jamie once said that cats are aye halfway between this world and the next. They're very ancient. Maybe they know more than we do.'

Rose smoothed the quilt back into place. 'I thought we were through talking about angels,' she sighed.

Barra appeared not to have heard. 'He said love conquers all things – even death.'

'Don't you think this Jamie was maybe here just long enough to help you accept things?' Rose asked gently.

Barra looked pensive. 'I still thought . . . Y'know, Mam, with it being Good Friday yesterday, maybe he'd come back. Maybe . . . even today, after Mr Pascoe's funeral, I thought . . .'

'You really are as thrawn as yir father, Barra.'

'It's not being thrawn, Mam. I really believed in him. It's hard to think Mr Pascoe's dead.' Barra's lip trembled, and he clamped his mouth shut.

Rose reached to cup Barra's face in her hands. Her throat hurt, and her own eyes stung. 'I know, son.'

Barra took a deep breath. 'Well, I'm glad you and Dad are speaking again,' he said, trusting himself to speak again.

'Me too,' Rose agreed. 'You have no idea, Barra, just *how* glad.'

'And yis'll be all right now?'

'We will. We'll be fine. Don't be worrying about yir dad and me.'

Barra grinned then. 'Imagine you telling *me* not to worry, Mam.'

Rose smiled back. 'Imagine!'

'Thing is, I didn't think I'd *have* to worry – about

anything. I thought Jamie would take care of it all.'

'I know. I know that's what you were thinking. But there's some things we can't change, son. We just have to accept them. Like I said, maybe that's what yir angel was there for. To help you through.'

Barra's eyes flew at her. 'But he *didn't*, Mam. He didn't help me. He made me *hope*!'

Rose swallowed hard, trying to get past the ache in her throat. 'We all have to hope, Barra. But sometimes . . . sometimes, well, there's just no hope.'

Barra yawned. 'He seemed so real,' he whispered.

Rose folded the quilt under his chin. 'Everything'll look brighter in the morning, Barra. Get some sleep now.'

As she crossed the room, she caught a movement, and turned to see Socks spread himself across Barra's chest. The boy reached to stroke him sleepily.

'You see,' Rose said, 'he was just waiting for me to get out of his way.'

'Murdo says animals have the second sight,' Barra answered.

'Well, I don't know about that, but they make good companions, Barra.'

Barra chewed on his lip. 'Real ones, you mean.'

Rose shrugged. 'You're *my* angel,' she whispered. 'I love you.'

'Love you too, Mam.' Barra settled into his

pillow. 'I'm sorry about laughing at the church,' he added.

Rose turned, her hand on the light-switch. 'You're forgiven.'

'And I'm sorry you didn't get any bedders for Easter.'

'I'm not,' Rose answered. 'Go to sleep.' She plunged the room into darkness. 'And stop saying you're sorry!'

CHAPTER 25

Doug wiped his brow. 'It's going to be hot.'

'Aye,' Maisie agreed. She opened the back door and returned to sit by his side, laying two freshly poured mugs of coffee on the table.

'You're no' eating?' Doug asked.

'I will.'

Doug stood, heading for the server, but Maisie reached for his arm.

'Sit down, Doug. I don't want you drinking 'til we decide what we're going to do.'

'About what?' Doug asked. He stared at Maisie, confronting only silence. 'All right,' he said at last. 'What are *you* going to do?'

'It's a joint decision, *mi amore*,' Maisie said softly.

'How can it possibly be that?'

'What d'you mean?'

'Maisie, it's your property, it's your money, and that makes it *your* decision.'

'I want the best for both of us, Doug.'

'And you think trailing a broken-down alcoholic around the world would be a good idea?'

'You're not that, Doug. I've never said . . .'

Doug stubbed out his cigarette. 'No. You've never said it. But you're obviously ready for a change. And I can't help wondering how long it'll be before I'm out of the picture altogether.'

'Oh, Doug. How could you think . . . ? That's the very last thing on my mind.'

'Is it, Maisie?' His voice was as gentle as ever, but his eyes were hard. Harder than she'd ever seen them.

'Doug,' she pleaded, 'the only reason, the *only* reason I thought about selling was so we could spend more time together. You and me.'

'Hah! And how could we possibly spend more time together, Maisie? God, we *live* in the place. We work together.'

'I know that. But it's not . . . Doug, I don't want to be just part of the furniture. I want to be more than that.'

Doug sighed again. 'We're getting nowhere. If anyone's part of the furniture, it's me. God, Maisie, who else would have me?'

'I don't want anyone else to have you, Doug.' Maisie made a forlorn attempt at humour.

'Well, you don't have to lose sleep over that!'

'You're right,' Maisie said. 'We're getting nowhere.'

A tense silence ensued. Doug lit another cigarette, while Maisie sipped on her coffee.

'Doug . . . ?'

'What?' His voice was flat.

'Why are you so intent on wanting to stay here?'

'It's my home.'

'It's been my home too. That doesn't mean we can't make a home together somewhere else.'

'No, Maisie. You don't understand. It's where I belong.'

'But . . .'

Doug pulled his chair closer. 'Look, Maisie. All I have in the world is here. I have nothing else, nobody else. Without this, I *am* nothing.'

'You could survive without the Whig, Doug. We both could.'

'It's not just the Whig, dammit!'

Maisie flinched, and Doug lowered his head. 'It's you, Maisie.'

'Me?'

'Don't you know how much I love you? I couldn't stand to be . . . deserted by you.'

'I'd never desert you. Never!'

'Aye, you would – eventually. Anything, everything I have to give you is right here, Maisie. Without that, what use would I be to you? I'd be just another bit luggage hanging off yir arm. And everywhere we'd go, there would be other men after you – trying to impress you wi' their looks, or their money.'

Maisie blinked. Then she threw back her head, and bellowed with laughter. Doug stared at her, horrified.

'What's so bloody funny?'

Maisie scraped her chair back and descended on him, lifting him to his feet and whirling him in a manic polka.

347

'I love you. I love you. I love you,' she sang, her voice scattering the starlings from the eaves.

Finally, she dropped him.

Doug reached dizzily for his chair. He was out of breath and gasping, his skin grey and beaded with sweat. Maisie thought he had never looked more handsome.

'I love you, too,' he said, struggling for air.

Maisie swayed above him, planting kiss after kiss on his balding pate. 'I thought you didn't. I thought you didn't love me – at all – any more.'

Shakily, Doug reached for another cigarette. 'God, Maisie. How could you ever think that? I was just so afraid of losing you.'

Maisie threw herself into her chair, righting it neatly as it threatened to collapse under the sudden weight. She grabbed Doug's hands, knocking the end of his cigarette loose and burning them both with the sparks. Some hurried slapping brought the threat of fire under control, but Maisie's ivory satin housecoat would never be the same.

She cared not a jot.

'I was afraid of losing *you*, Doug. I was so afraid.'

Doug shook his head. 'Why would you be afraid of that?'

'Because I really, truly love you. And I don't ever want to be alone again.'

Doug smiled, his breathing returning to normal. 'Oh, what a tangled web we weave . . .'

'Not to deceive, Doug.' Maisie smiled. 'I would never deceive you.'

'Nor I you.'

Isla's footsteps sounded on the staircase. They waited as she approached, exchanging conspiratorial smiles like children caught passing notes in the classroom.

'What's all the skirling?' Isla demanded. 'It's Sunday morning.'

Maisie beckoned her forward. 'I've decided not to sell the Whig.'

Isla blanched. 'You were going to sell?'

'I thought about it. For all the wrong reasons, it seems.'

'But what about me?'

'You?' Maisie asked, mystified.

'I'm not going back,' Isla announced. 'You can't make me go back.'

'Oh, Isla . . . Of course you don't have to go back. Not yet, anyway. We'll sort something out.'

'I'm *not* going back!'

'All right, sweet girl,' Maisie soothed. 'You can stay. But the coffers aren't too full at the minute.'

'I don't care.'

Doug looked pained. 'We *will* have to think of something.' He turned to Maisie. 'Maybe we should advertise.'

'What's to advertise, Doug? Another run-down tea-room somewhere in the Highlands? The place is littered wi' them, most of them a sight more attractive than the Whig.' She met Isla's terrified stare. 'Don't worry, Isla. Whatever happens, you're welcome to stay. As long as you want – and that's a promise.'

Isla drew a long, deep breath. 'Thanks, Maisie.' She turned gratefully to Doug. 'Thanks, Doug.'

He patted her hand. 'Just what I need. Now I have *two* women to answer to.'

A single tear slid down Isla's cheek, and Maisie reached to brush it gently away.

'Well, now that we've got all that settled,' she said, 'there's just one question left.' She took Doug's hand in her own. 'Will you marry me?'

Doug smiled, a long, slow smile. 'I thought you'd never ask.'

'Blech!' Isla pretended to vomit. 'Youse two give me the boke.'

'I'm glad you came,' Violet said.

Graham nodded. 'I couldn't let it go,' he said. 'Not for me . . . it doesn't matter for me. But Jennifer . . . I won't see her hurt.'

Violet stood at the window, watching as Jennifer talked with her husband while he swung their cases into the boot of the Jaguar. She had thought there might have been some difference in Jennifer's attitude to her father-in-law.

There had been none. They were as they'd always been, her husband displaying his masculinity even now, the masculinity she had detested, and yet still admired.

And that, Violet thought, was the story of her life. Nobody had ever truly known how much she loved him, how very badly he had hurt her.

'To tell you the truth, Graham, there isn't any of us who can stand in somebody else's shoes for a minute – far less an hour, or a year. We respond only to what we can see, what we can touch, what we can feel.'

'I'm not out to take any part of Jim . . . for my own.'

Violet turned. 'It's his birthday today. Did you know that?'

Graham closed his eyes. 'Yes. Yes, I did.'

Violet's eyes were still on Jennifer 'She doesn't believe. It seems such a waste for him to be buried here.'

'She wouldn't have minded if you'd wanted to bring his body home.'

'Home? This was his home, Graham. This god-forsaken place, in the back of beyond. This was his home.' Violet reached briefly to touch his shoulder. 'Take care of his grave for me.'

'I will. And don't worry. Jennifer will too.'

She lifted her coat, carefully folding it across her arm. 'We'll be back from time to time. I hope you'll forgive an old woman her bitterness.'

Graham stood, awkwardly reaching for her. 'I have myself to forgive first. You're not even in the queue.'

She held him briefly, her eyes full. 'Oh yes. I'm in the queue, Graham.'

Violet Pascoe squared her shoulders and walked towards the waiting car. Halfway down the path, she stopped.

'Look after Jennifer, too,' she called back, her voice carrying to Graham, and to Donald – and to Jennifer. 'She deserves it.'

'Will you let me help you, at least?'

'There is no help for this, Graham.'

'Then will you believe that I didn't plan it? That I didn't want it?'

Jennifer sighed. 'Graham, you're our friend. You've always been that. I just can't . . . Right now, I just can't cope with anything more.'

'I'm sorry.' His tone was abject, his voice low.

Jennifer forced cheer into her voice. 'Look, it's Jim's birthday. It's all I want for today. Just to have that.'

'Would you rather be alone?'

'But I'm not.' Her voice was soft enough to tear the heart from him. 'I have Jim.'

He made a final, solitary voyage down the hall.

'You'll call if you need anything?'

'I will,' she promised. She kissed him lightly. 'Thank you for caring.'

He climbed into the Triumph, and set off for Craigourie. Passing the Whig, he spun into a turn and reversed, pulling into the gravel car park. It was Easter Sunday. He could have one dram with Doug. The man had faced desperation. He would understand.

Maisie was alone in the bar. Doug had gone back upstairs, intent on a bath and a change into his better clothes, for there would be celebrating at the Whig later in the day.

'And she knows you love her?' Maisie asked.

'I believe she does.'

'Then wait.'

'What?'

'Wait a while,' Maisie advised. 'We all enjoy having a man around. But we can usually only deal wi' one at a time. Unless, of course, you happen to be Sheena Mearns.'

Graham smiled ruefully. He had not been totally immune to Sheena's charms himself, but he had been too fond of Raymond to allow himself to get involved.

'I suppose that, somewhere along the way, Raymond decided what's good for the goose . . .' he suggested.

'. . . is good for the gander,' Maisie roared. 'And I'd be willing to bet there's more than one man in Craigourie who's enjoying his Sunday breakfast all the better for knowing that Mrs Mearns has taken herself off to parts unknown!'

'I'm sure you're right,' Graham agreed. 'But I have to confess, I hope Raymond's made the right decision. I hope he's happy.'

'Och, he'll be happy, right enough. After all, as I hear tell, he was great friends with Chrissie Falconer for years.' Maisie's voice became gentle. 'Friendship's the very best part of love, Graham. Remember that – while you're waiting.'

Graham nodded thoughtfully. 'I would always

be Jen's friend. If need be, I'd settle for that.'

'Never settle, darling.' Doug reappeared in the café as she spoke, and she stretched her hand outwards, clasping him to her as he approached. 'Go after what you want. I did.'

Doug chuckled softly, accepting Graham's congratulations warmly.

'So,' Graham enquired, 'when's the honeymoon? Is it a Mediterranean cruise for you both?'

Maisie shook her head. 'No, Graham. As a matter of fact, *we* have a proposition to put to *you*.'

Graham raised his eyebrows, giving them his full attention.

'It was Isla who came up with it,' Maisie explained. 'When she'd got over the shock that I'd been thinking of selling the old place, she suggested that we open our own bistro.'

'We-ell,' Graham breathed. 'Why not?'

'I've taken care of my money over the years,' Maisie continued. 'I'd thought of it as a nest-egg, some security for my . . .' She smiled indulgently at Doug. 'For *our* old age. But then, the more carried away Isla got wi' the idea, the more I could see it working.'

Doug was nodding fervently in the background, anxious to interrupt. Maisie deferred to him, clutching his hand even tighter in her own.

'Y'see, Graham,' Doug said, 'we could knock out the wall between the bar and the café, open the whole place up. We could be promoting the local produce a bit more in the shop too. There's no end o' specialities we could offer. We could have the food and the drink on one side, and some craftwork on the other. That was another of Isla's ideas,' he confessed.

'But she's right enough, Graham,' he went on. 'Sally Laing does marvellous things wi' her pottery. Then there's Mrs Cameron up by Dunfearn – she makes the bonniest jumpers you ever saw. Arrans, Fair Isle, Shetland, there's no' a pattern she canna' do. And her sister Ellen, well, she's always made that silver jewellery. It's selling like hot cakes in the shops on Princes Street, so why not right here, where it's made?'

Graham felt carried along by this new, and unexpected, enthusiasm. 'I can see how that might work.'

Doug nodded. 'Here's one for you now, Graham. If they put tables and chairs on the pavement in Edinburgh, they'd call it a café. What would they call it in Craigourie?'

Graham shook his head.

'An eviction!' Doug and Maisie roared at the joke, and it crossed Graham's mind that the very word 'eviction' had been banned from any conversation in the Whig for as long as he could remember. He joined in the laughter.

Maisie hardly waited for their mirth to subside before rushing on. 'We'd need to do a wee brochure, a few posters maybe. But we could look into that. Maybe get some pointers from the Tourist Office. And then we could refurbish the café, make it more continental-looking. It wouldn't take that much. And the bar . . .'

'Och, we could get one o' those young blokes from a hotel in the town,' Doug interrupted. 'Someone wi' a bit o' go in him, maybe even a knowledge o' one or two wines we could serve. I'll be too busy myself wi' the food an' all,' he added. 'I was thinking I might take one o' thon cordon bleu courses. I fancy learning a new dish or two.'

'Aye,' Graham agreed. 'You've always had a knack for the cooking.'

'I'll have to lay off the drink, o' course. I'll be needing a good clear head to keep everything running smooth. And Maisie would make the perfect hostess. Don't you think, Graham?' Doug's earnest belief in Maisie's prowess brought a blush to her cheeks.

'Absolutely!' Graham was grinning with delight. 'So where do I fit in?'

'I'm not sure how much money all this is going to take, Graham,' Maisie said. 'I'll need to be handing the books over to someone who knows what they're doing. And if we need to borrow, I want the best possible advice. Would you consider it?'

'It would be a privilege,' Graham said. 'I'd be thrilled to take it on. Have you thought what you might call it?'

Maisie and Doug exchanged a look of surprise.

'The Whig,' Maisie answered. 'What else?'

'I was thinking,' said Chalmers, 'what would it hurt

to take a few hours off on such a fine day? We could go for a picnic.'

'A picnic? I haven't anything in for a picnic.' Rose was surprised but pleased at the suggestion.

'You don't need anything special, Mam,' Barra put in. 'We can just have sandwiches and things.'

'Well,' Rose said. 'Yes . . . That would be lovely.'

'Grand.' Chalmers rubbed his hands together. 'I'll have a wee read o' the paper in the garden. Let me know when you're ready.'

Rose nodded, smiling to herself. Some things never changed.

'How about if I boil some eggs? You could paint them when they're ready, Barra.'

'Och, I'm a bit old for that, Mam. I don't mind giving you a hand, though.'

Rose held her chest, pretending heart failure, and Barra grinned at last. 'Come off it, Mam. I *do* help, sometimes.'

'Course you do. But it won't take me long to get organised. Don't you want to go to the woods?'

'They'll be there tomorrow.'

Rose raised her eyebrows. 'God, if that's no' a first!'

She opened the fridge, then closed it again, turning back to him. 'Barra . . .'

'What?'

'Yir dad and I were thinking o' taking a holiday.'

'Aye?'

'Abroad.'

'Wow! Where?'

'Venice. Yir dad asked me to go to Venice.'

'Oh, great. I've a stamp wi' St Mark's Square on it. When are we going?'

Rose caught her breath. 'Son, would you mind if it was just us? Just me and yir dad?'

Barra stared at her. 'Am I not going?'

'Well, of course, if you wanted to . . .'

'So, if youse two go, where would I be?' Barra looked quite dejected, and Rose's heart dropped. How could she have thought of leaving him behind?

'We thought you might want to go to Gran and Grandad's in Kyle for a couple of weeks. Sometime in August . . . we thought.'

'Oh, *grr-reat*!'

'You wouldn't mind?'

'Ma-am! Mind? I haven't seen Grandad in yonks!' he said, his face alight.

Rose laughed with relief. 'It's all right then? If we book it?'

'Oh, aye.' Barra's expression changed, became solemn. 'But you'll have passports and things to get sorted out. You don't want to be wasting time, Mam.'

'No, Barra. We won't. We won't waste any more time.' Rose reached for the fridge again. 'Take out the bread. At least I can get *one* man in the house to make himself useful.'

'Och well, if it's all the same, maybe I'll sit wi' Dad a while. There's a lot about Venice I could be telling him.'

Rose bit her lip.

'You do that, son,' she murmured – into the empty air.

CHAPTER 26

Olive rose to answer the door, grumbling to herself with every step. Her neck was wrapped in a length of red flannel, the traditional cure for all manner of aches and pains.

'Pheugh!' Sandy said, stepping backwards. 'That's some strong linament you've got there, Olive.'

'Come in, and stop yir moaning,' she griped. 'It's no' your neck that's sore.'

Sandy stepped jauntily across the threshold, loosening his tie as he did so. 'I came wi' some good news.'

'It's me that's needing good news,' Olive said, motioning him towards a chair. 'And sit straight. I'm no' wanting yir hair-oil all over my anti-macassars.'

He took off his suit jacket, and Olive moved automatically to hang it on the hall-stand.

'What's yir news?' she asked, returning to settle gingerly into her armchair. 'Don't tell me. Mary Rankin won the snowball again.'

'No.' Sandy grinned. 'I did.'

'You? *You* won the snowball?' Olive tutted in disgust. 'The one day I wasna' there. You probably got the ticket I'd have bought myself.'

'It doesn't matter whose ticket it was,' Sandy informed her jubilantly. 'The fact is, we're sixty-eight pounds richer!'

'*We*? Don't tell me I'm finally going to get a sniff at yir money, Sandy Robertson.'

'Och, Olive. I've been saving it up. I didna' want to say anything 'til I had enough, but I've enough now. I've more than enough.'

'Enough for what?' Olive's tone was guarded, her expression wary.

'There was a hundred and forty pounds left owing on the house. Now I know that might no' be a lot to some folks, but it's a lot to me.'

'Aye, isn't it?' Olive sneered. 'It would be a bloody fortune to you.'

Sandy dismissed the slur. 'Anyway, wi' today's winnings added to what I'd put aside from the rest, I can pay the house off.'

'Bully for you.'

Sandy dived forward, landing on one knee in front of her. 'So I'm asking you to marry me, Olive, and take me for yir own.'

Olive glared down at him. 'Get up out o' there, and don't be depressing me.'

Sandy appeared nonplussed. 'I didna' think I was *that* mistaken.'

Holding her neck, Olive stared at him. 'You're no' serious? Y'canna' be serious.'

'Why not? If Mad Hatters can do it, no' to mention Doug and Maisie, what's to stop us? I'm no' getting any younger, y'know.'

Olive's hand dropped. 'You *are* serious!'

Sandy nodded.

'What about my own house?'

'Yir aye moaning about the rent the Forestry charges you. You could give it up easily enough.'

'And you'd support me?'

'I don't get careless wi' offers when it comes to money, Olive. You know that.'

Olive drew a deep breath. 'I could think about it.'

'Grand,' Sandy said, trying to rise. His knee gave out, and Olive reached to help him. As he struggled to his feet, she realised that something in her neck had clicked into place. In any event, the pain had gone.

She began to unwind the red flannel. 'I think I could manage a sherry.' She nodded towards the sideboard.

'Get yir coat on. We'll away down to the Whig and join in the revelries. I'll *buy* you a sherry.'

Olive sighed happily. 'You must have taken a turn.'

'Give us a kiss,' Sandy prompted.

'I'll do no such thing,' Olive retorted. Then she swept a glance in his direction. A stranger might have taken it as flirtatious, which was something Olive Tolmie had never been in her life.

'No' till we're married,' Olive said archly.

* * *

Maisie moved among her guests with the aplomb of a New York socialite. She was swathed from head to foot in shades of purple, her hair loosely woven with white plastic daisies, her feet encased in embroidered slippers which had recently had pride of place in the Oxfam window.

Chalmers had started a kitty, before remembering that he'd left his wallet at home. Rose, digging in her handbag, informed Helen that she might never see Venice at this rate.

'Och, but it's a grand thing to have something to celebrate,' Helen said.

'It is,' Rose agreed. 'Who'd have thought we'd be at a funeral one day and a betrothal the next?'

'Indeed,' Murdo said, keeping a watchful eye on Gallus who was wandering from table to table with a pitiful expression on his face, an empty bowl clenched firmly in his mouth.

'If that dog gets any more to drink, he'll be legless.' Murdo shook his head. 'He's way ahead o' me already.'

'You didna' have any bedders yet?' Helen enquired of Rose, reaching to pull the bowl from the Westie's mouth. He refused to give it up, and she sat back.

'No. I think I might go a bit easier this year,' Rose replied. 'Chalmers thinks it would be a good idea for us to have the house . . . more to ourselves.' Rose coloured and glanced towards the bar, away from Helen.

Helen smiled. 'I'm right glad to hear it.'

The shrill of a telephone sounded through the wall, and Maisie asked the company's indulgence while she stepped through to the café to answer it.

'The *Tatler*, I'm sure,' she gaily informed them.

Moments later she was back, beckoning Isla to join her.

Isla, who had taken it upon herself to refill the little glass dishes of nuts and raisins, paused from her chores.

'Me?' she mouthed.

Maisie waved even more vigorously, dislodging a daisy, which fell from her hair and disappeared into the mass of her bosom.

'What?' Isla demanded, closing the bar door behind her. 'What is it?'

'Sit!'

'Stop it, Maisie,' Isla said, her voice concerned. 'You're scaring me.'

'Oh, darling girl, do not be afraid. I am about to impart the best, the most exciting, news of the day – except, of course, for my own.' She flourished her arms in a mock curtsey and came to stand behind her niece, her hands pushing Isla firmly into the chair.

'Guess who just called?'

'Who?' Isla's voice was sullen again.

Maisie swung herself round to face the girl, lifting Isla's chin towards her.

'Your mother just called. My dear sister Fiona. Soon-to-be-divorced Fiona!'

'What're you talking about?'

'It seems your less-than-beloved stepfather got his jotters. A search of the cubby-hole he called his office turned up quite a few items of underwear. Guests' underwear. *Female* guests' underwear.'

'I knew it. I *knew* it!'

'Thou wert not mistaken,' Maisie continued. 'Your mother, shocked and upset, but apparently not all that surprised, decided to take a look round the house.' Maisie's voice grew very quiet. 'Isla,' she said gently, 'he had some of your knickers in his tallboy.'

Isla stared at Maisie for a long moment. Then she shivered, her eyes as dark as coals.

'The creepy bastard!'

Maisie rubbed Isla's hand with her own. 'The creepy bastard was sent packing!' she said, her own eyes gleaming now. 'And my dear sister, your mother, will be here next week. She has to work over Easter, it's a busy time at the hotel. But she's taking the bus first thing Wednesday morning. She'll be here by lunch.

'Oh, and I forgot to add,' Maisie's smile spread even wider. 'She said to tell you she loves you.'

Isla looked disconcerted, then she shrugged. 'So here we go again.'

'Isla?'

'Och, Maisie, I'm glad. Really, I am. But she'll no' be long without a man. I want to stay here, work with you and Doug.' She shrugged again. 'Mam'll manage better without me and, to tell you the truth, I'll manage better without her.'

Maisie frowned. 'You have so much to offer, Isla. Why would you want to be hiding yirself away here?'

'I don't think I would be.' Isla was indignant at the suggestion. 'We have a business to get going. You'll need decent staff.'

Maisie shook her head sadly. 'I'm afraid . . .'

'What?' There was real panic in Isla's voice now.

'I'm afraid that we would be wanting a bit more than decent. We'd be wanting the best.'

'Ohhh!'

'So, you'll take the job then?'

Isla threw her arms around Maisie's neck, and held on for a very long time.

'Hi, Mrs Pascoe.'

'Barra! You scared me.'

'Sorry. I did wave. I didn't think you'd seen me, though.'

Jennifer trailed a hand across a sapling. 'I felt like a walk. It's been a long day.'

'You've no' been into the Whig?'

'Not yet,' Jennifer said. 'I didn't feel up to it.'

'Aye,' Barra answered, walking back up the forest path with her. 'I can understand that you wouldn't.' He smiled at her. 'We had a great picnic the day.'

Jennifer stopped to breathe in the evening air. 'That's nice. So, what are you doing here? By the sounds of it, there's a grand party going on down there.'

'Och, they'll be there for a while yet,' he said. He turned to her, resting a hand lightly on her arm. 'You know they haven't forgotten? About Mr Pascoe, I mean?'

Jennifer sighed. 'They say life goes on, Barra. It certainly seems to – in Drumdarg.'

'But they're no' meaning to be . . . disrespectful.'

'I know that,' Jennifer said, moving forward quickly. 'But you can't blame me for not feeling up to a party just yet.'

Barra caught up with her. 'Of course not.'

She stopped, turning to him once more.

'Barra. Would you mind? I'd really like to be alone right now.'

'Sometimes it's better to have company, someone to talk to.'

'Please don't,' Jennifer interrupted. 'I know you mean well, but . . .'

'Mrs Pascoe, I'm sorry for all the bother,' Barra interrupted, his voice earnest. 'I was jist hoping . . .'

Jennifer had stopped again, but now she was holding his gaze, her eyes almost feverish.

'Barra, this Jamie, what did he look like?'

'He was quite tall,' Barra began, his voice hesitant. 'And he had wide blue eyes, and long curly hair.'

'What colour?'

'Blond. He had blond hair. And he had this great smile, Mrs Pascoe.' He rushed on, anxious to tell her now. 'It was jist brilliant when he smiled. You couldn't notice anything else . . .'

Jennifer held out a hand to stop him. Then she rubbed her eyes. 'I . . . I had a dream. At least . . . I fell asleep, after everyone left. And I . . .' She moved forward, and then stopped, as though she didn't know in which direction to go.

'And what, Mrs Pascoe? Did you dream about him? Did you dream about Jamie?' Barra kept his voice low, as though aware that the first hint of excitement in his voice would startle her into leaving.

'I'm not sure. It wasn't like a dream. There was this boy beside me. We were walking together . . . like you and me, just now. It seemed like we were here – here in the woods . . .'

Jennifer looked up towards the clearing, and Barra's eyes followed. For a second he almost expected to see Jamie there, but the clearing was empty.

Jennifer gulped in the warm air, as though she were having trouble breathing. '. . . Then I turned to look at him properly – and he changed.' Her voice was scarcely more than a whisper and Barra leaned further towards her, trying to catch the words. 'It was Jim. It was Jim, Barra.' She looked at him again and, though her eyes swam with tears, they were clear. Clear, and shining bright.

'He looked so happy, Barra, and he held out his hand and touched me. So lightly, and yet . . . I woke then, and there was this warmth all over me. It was right through me.' Still, Jennifer held his gaze. 'It was Jim. And, Barra . . . ?'

'What?' he whispered.

'. . . He had the most beautiful crop of hair.' She collapsed against him, sobbing.

For the first time in his young life, Barra held a woman in his arms. He too felt his throat catch, and had to struggle to get the words out.

But they came out, just the same.

'I knew he'd have hair for his birthday.'

'Sit yerself there,' Barra instructed. 'Mam'll see to you.'

Jennifer surrendered, smiling at Helen and Rose as she took her place at the table.

The two women reached for her, each holding a hand in silent support. They were there. They always would be. It was that simple.

'What'll you have, hen?' Murdo enquired kindly.

'Nothing, thanks,' Jennifer replied.

'Och, you'll have to have a wee dram. It's Easter.'

'A wee one,' she said.

Graham brought the tray of drinks to the table, distributing them carefully. 'If I have to keep up wi' them, it's only fair you should,' he whispered in her ear.

Jennifer raised her glass, and looked up.

'Happy birthday, Jim,' he mouthed.

Jennifer smiled and nodded, unable to speak.

She lifted her glass.

Happy birthday, my darling.

Isla was leaning across the bar, making a point of ignoring him.

'Are you enjoying yirself?' he asked.

'Not particularly.'

Andy Blackwell was squeezing the life out of an accordion in the far corner, while his brother whipped out an accompaniment on the fiddle.

'It would be better if they could play a decent tune,' Barra remarked.

'That two's for the chop when we open the bistro,' Isla remarked, somewhat unkindly. The brothers were the pride of Drumdarg.

'What's a bistro?' Barra asked.

'God, yir ignorant.'

Barra grinned. 'D'you like Sandie Shaw?'

'She's OK. I prefer Dusty Springfield. I wish I knew where she gets her mascara.'

'You don't need mascara.'

Isla finally turned her attention to him. 'If you say anything . . .'

'You've got beautiful eyes. They're the mirror o' yir soul.'

'They're what?'

'God, yir ignorant.' Barra laughed.

'They'll all be mirack in an hour,' Isla stated, careworn and weary. 'Would you want to listen to my records?'

'Great! We could get a dance.'

'Dance? With *you*?' Isla sneered. 'I hope yir better than that.' She nodded at Sandy and Olive, who were engaged in a waltz of sorts. Olive's feet had apparently found a life of their own.

'Och, I'm way ahead o' them' Barra replied. 'Watch this.'

He broke into a few tap steps.

'Where d'you learn that?' Isla asked, making a decent show of hiding her admiration.

Barra grinned. 'From a friend.'

'I'm impressed,' Isla said, though her tone left room for doubt.

'What about it then? D'you want to dance?'

'Get going! Yir far too young for me, Barra Maclean.'

Barra's face fell and he bowed his head, unable to hide his chagrin.

'But we don't have to be dancing partners. We could still be friends . . .' Isla took pity on him.

'Aye,' Barra agreed, a great deal happier. It was a start. 'I'd like to listen to yir records, anyway.'

'I have to leave the door open,' Isla warned. 'Maisie's rules.'

Barra coloured. 'Rules is rules.'

'C'mon then.' Isla stepped towards the door but Barra raced ahead, holding it open while she passed through.

Isla turned. 'A gentleman!' she exclaimed. 'Yir a gift from the gods, Barra Maclean.'

Barra pulled himself to his full height, unconsciously reaching to flatten his curls as he closed the door behind him.

Rose had watched the whole exchange. Something tickled her mind, refusing to make itself known. Then she remembered.

It was her favourite song, Nat King Cole's 'Nature Boy', with its story of that strange enchanted boy.

Well, her own 'enchanted boy' had just followed Isla up the stairs!

She frowned – a mother's frown. Then she too straightened her shoulders, glancing towards her husband.

Chalmers was smiling back at her. He raised his glass in silent salute, and she returned the gesture.

No sense worrying about it, Rose Maclean, she told herself. No sense at all.

THE COMPANY OF STRANGERS
Eileen Campbell

A heart-warming story about eleven-year-old
Ellie who, following her mother's nervous
breakdown, is sent to the small Highland
village of Inchbrae to stay with the
grandmother she has never met.

£6.99   1 85702 767 1

PUPPIES ARE FOR LIFE   Linda Phillips

Susanna can't wait to retire, give up her
boring job and move into a more manageable
home. But this is nineties Britain. Her children
are struggling with unemployment and broken
marriages and Susanna finds herself torn
between her duty to them and her duty
towards herself.

£5.99   1 85702 605 5

MEADOWLAND   Alison Giles

A compelling first novel about a young
woman called Charissa and her attempt to
cope with the emotional legacy of her father's
death: two widows, his mistress and his wife.

£5.99   1 85702 609 8

HOW TO ORDER

**All Fourth Estate books are available from your local bookshop, or can
be ordered direct (FREE UK p&p) from:**

**Fourth Estate, Book Service By Post, PO Box 29,
Douglas, I-O-M, IM99 1BQ**   *Credit cards accepted.*
**Tel: 01624 836000   Fax: 01624 670923
Internet: http://www.bookpost.co.uk   e-mail: bookshop@enterprise.net**

*All prices are correct at time of going to press, but may be subject to change.
Please state when ordering if you do **not** wish to receive further information
about Fourth Estate titles.*